THE WARRIOR RETURNS

ALLAN COLE

A Del Rey® Book
Ballantine Books • New York

A Del Rey® Book
Published by Ballantine Books

Copyright © 1996 by Allan Cole

All rights reserved under International and Pan-American
Copyright Conventions. Published in the United States
by Ballantine Books, a division of Random House,
Inc., New York, and simultaneously in Canada by
Random House of Canada Limited, Toronto.

Library of Congress Cataloging-in-Publication Data

Cole, Allan.
The warrior returns / by Allan Cole. — 1st ed.
p.   cm.
"A Del Rey book."
ISBN 0-345-39459-3
1. Witchcraft—Fiction. I. Title.
PS3553.04485W36   1996
813'.54—dc20   95-45473
CIP

Manufactured in the United States of America

First Edition: April 1996

10   9   8   7   6   5   4   3   2   1

To all those
who know why
Janos laughed.
And to Kathryn
who suggested the Rali stories.

BOOK ONE

THE
LYRE
BIRD

THE CITADEL OF ICE

> My sword is a pen
> My ink the blood of men
> My paper the hearts of my foes.
> My words are your fate
> If you stray past the gate
> And my book is the sum of your woes.

You know me as Rali Emilie Antero. In my first life I was a warrior. In my second a wizard. And then I slept for fifty years until my lady Maranonia came to awaken me from my lover's arms.

Though she is a goddess whom I revere above all others, I did not awaken easily.

My tomb was ice. The castle that held that tomb was ice, and it crouched in a realm of frigid stone washed by frozen seas. But in my dreams I dwelt in a land of eternal summer where my lover Salimar was queen. We lived in a crystal palace with jetting fountains and gardens of roses, pink and red and yellow. It was a life of laughing days and sweet sighing nights and I was loath to leave it.

But the goddess said leave I must.

I was angry. "This was my reward, O Lady," I said, "for all the suffering I've endured in your service."

Maranonia smiled, and that smile lit the vast chamber with its brightness. My ship gleamed silver, my chests of jewels gave off a rainbow glow, and my weapons racks were sharp, glittering steel. I rubbed my good eye, disturbed by all that light. Beside me Salimar stirred in her down coverlets and whispered my name.

My left arm throbbed and I groaned from the ghost pain. The pain made me angrier still. I'd sacrificed an eye and a hand for my goddess and my people. A golden eyepatch covered the right socket, and a small scar cut that same cheek. I had a magical golden hand in place of the living one, which I'd lost in the mines of Koronos.

Although it worked much better than the one I was born with, it was a hurtful reminder of all I'd suffered to earn this sleep.

I dared to turn my back on the goddess, snuggling close to Salimar. I was determined to drift away to our land of summer dreams. There, I was whole. There, I was fresh. There, I was free of all trials. There, my only concern was the daily gift I'd choose for my lover. Would it be a bouquet of wild meadow flowers to grace her hair? Perhaps a songbird to enchant us that evening before we freed it to bless our embrace.

Maranonia's voice rang through: "Rise up, Rali," she commanded. "Your sisters have need of you."

The Guard in peril? I bolted up.

I hid my alarm with a snarl: "Tell them to seek another."

"There is no other," the goddess answered.

"I've done enough," I said. "Let me rest."

But I swung my bare legs over the lip of the coffin of clear blue ice that held our bed.

Behind me I heard a sob. It was Salimar, weeping in her sleep.

Maranonia was tall, her peaked helmet nearly touching the vault's distant roof, black tresses tumbling to her shoulders. In one hand she held the torch of truth. In the other her spear of justice. Her boots were gold, her tunic shone white under her light mail. Her eyes glowed like an armorer's hearth. The air crackled with her power. But I did not fear her.

I have defied the gods before.

The goddess sighed, her breath filling the chamber with the scent of violets. Then she laughed, and it was the sound of distant bells tolling the news of war. "Why do I put up with you, Rali?"

I touched the eyepatch with my false hand. "I could ask you the same question, my lady," I said. "I've honored you all my life. I've permitted my body to be mutilated in your service."

I turned, gesturing at the restless form of Salimar. Silver teardrops fell from her closed eyes. Her lashes were dark fans against smooth olive cheeks. The coverlet came away, exposing her sweet breasts to the chill.

I covered her tenderly, saying, "Why can't you let us be?"

"Your sisters will die," the goddess answered.

My reply was an accusation. "Death is no stranger to the women of the Maranon Guard, my lady. How many souls have I delivered to you myself? Thousands? Tens of thousands? When will you be satisfied?"

Maranonia ignored this. "Orissa is in danger, Rali."

I shrugged. "So get my brother. Amalric never seems to weary of his civic duty."

We both knew my harsh words were lies. There was no one—even Salimar—whom I adored more than Amalric. Our mother died when he was very young, and I'd heaped all my love on that redheaded child. That thought made my lips curl into a wry smile. No matter his age, no matter his accomplishments, Amalric would always be a child to me.

"Your brother is dead," the goddess answered.

Her reminder gashed open a wound I'd thought long healed.

In a vision I'd seen my brother and Janela Greycloak take their own lives. Although their death pact had been joyous, its purpose to gain another life in a world of splendors beyond, my heart still bled for him.

I tried to hide my pain from the goddess.

"Get another Antero, then," I said. "There's plenty to choose from. I come from a family of breeders."

Except for myself, I thought. I like children well enough. As long as they are the children of others. My own maternal stirrings are meager.

But I was standing by the tomb now, naked and shivering in that vast chamber of ice.

"All the Anteros are dead," Maranonia said. "Save you . . . and one other."

I stumbled back from that bleak news. What catastrophe could have overtaken my family?

The goddess gestured and I was suddenly warm. I glanced down and saw that I was dressed in the cloak and tunic and leggings of the Maranon Guard. My captain's badge was pinned to my shoulder. I felt earrings dangling from my lobes. I didn't have to investigate to know what baubles my goddess had chosen. There would be a miniature of Maranonia's golden torch in one ear, her spear in the other.

I sighed. "Show me," I said.

The goddess gestured again.

A cloud of purple smoke swirled up, then parted like a curtain. I was peering into a chamber. A child cowered in a bed. Two armed women in the uniform of the Guard were posted on either side.

They were gray-haired women—soldiers well past their prime.

I could hear shouts and the clash of weapons nearby.

The child had Amalric's red hair. It was long and framed a delicate face with porcelain skin and eyes the color of sun-kissed seas.

"She is your murdered nephew's child," Maranonia said, voice gentle. "They've named her Emilie—for your mother."

I shivered, this time not from the cold.

There was a crash of magical thunder and the child cried out, holding up a small trembling hand as if to ward off a blow. Instinctively I took a step forward to confront whatever it was that threatened her.

Smoke swirled and the image vanished.

Questions flooded my mind. Who would harm such a child? And why?

The goddess, as if reading my thoughts, said: "Emilie carries the seeds of great power, Rali. Power even greater than your own.

"With *her* rests all of the hopes of Orissa. If she is slain, all that you and your brother sacrificed so much for will be lost. Perhaps forever. For where will I find another Antero when you and she are gone?"

"Who has done this thing?" I asked.

As I waited for the answer, my eyes flickered over the weapons rack, picking over the tools of my old warrior's trade.

"You know her," the goddess said, "as the Lyre Bird."

The shock was like the collision of two mailed giants. "Novari? But I killed her!"

The goddess ignored this. "When next the snow falls in Orissa," she said, "the child Emilie will reach the first level of her powers. Our enemies are determined to prevent this."

I was aghast. "I have one year?" I said. "That's all?"

Then I babbled, testing my goddess's patience, no doubt, for it was obvious my decision had been made. "Why, it might take that long just to reach home!"

"Nevertheless," Maranonia said, "that is all the time I'm permitted to give you."

"Who sets these limits?" I bellowed. "What fool commands the heavens these days? Show me his holy face so I can spit in it!"

But my wrath hammered on emptiness. The goddess was gone.

I conjured stores and loaded my ship. She was a fleet-footed little thing, single-masted and easy for one person to manage in any seas. The sails were silver, like the body of the ship itself. I called her my *Ilumna*.

I chose my weapons carefully, wrapped them in oilcloth, cast a spell to further protect them from rust, and locked them in a trunk in the cramped cabin that did double duty as my quarters and a sail locker.

When I was done, I approached the ice tomb. It was clear, like blue-tinted glass. Salimar looked small in the vast down bed that had contained us both only a short time before. Her auburn hair was spread out on the pillow and I ached to tangle my fingers in it. We'd twine our legs and arms and I'd be cast into that dream world again where we'd play forever and a day. A frown marred her beautiful face, and I kissed the wrinkles to smooth them away. She said my name and opened her long slender arms.

But I couldn't stay.

I whispered a promise I wasn't certain I could keep. Then I kissed her again and closed the curved ice lid to lock her away from all harm.

I mounted the deck of my ship, grasped the tiller and cast the spell.

Lightning crashed and thunder drummed, drowning out my final whispered farewell.

Then I was sailing on seas of ice, the wind at my back and hate in my view.

I never dreamed I'd write another journal. The first—a history disguised as an adventure—gave me much difficulty. I'm not a scholar like my brother, so I used a scribe to pretty up my barracks manners. It must've worked, for the bookstall merchants sang my praises for many a day, all to the merry tune of rattling coin boxes.

This time I've dispensed with scribes. They are a prickly, shortsighted breed who drive me mad with their romantic ravings. The first fellow is long dead, and I have no intention of breaking another into my ways. Besides, I like to think I might have improved after more than fifty years. My words may not be pearls, but they aren't rodent droppings, either.

Be forewarned: this book is not for the gentle-hearted. And if you are offended by my same-sex inclinations, turn away now. Love is as much a part of this tale as its warnings.

You would be advised, however, to appoint someone in your household to read these words and inform the rest of the warnings they contain.

For I speak for Maranonia, and the goddess commands that all listen. Ignore her—and me—at your peril.

I sailed for many a day on the Southern Sea but made scant forward progress. I dodged squalls, bumped through great ice fields, and once sailed for half a week maneuvering around an iceberg the size of a large island. It was pink, striated with blue, and when I dropped chips of its ice into my wine cup, they bubbled and frothed and made a delicious brew.

Although I had far to go—five thousand leagues or more—it was good that I was delayed those first days. It was still summer at the bottom of the world, where all seasons are the opposite of Orissa. There are only two seasons, actually, winter and summer. And those are contained in one interminably long day. For six cycles of the moon the sun never rises and it is always night, with unimaginably fierce storms that roar down from the mountains and gouge the rocks and ice into nightmare shapes. The cold is so bitter that few creatures could survive. And those who make their homes there are the hardiest and most stubborn on earth.

The other six moon cycles are day, and the sun never sets during that time. The storms are less frequent, although they still pack winds that could drive a loose spike through heavy armor. The cold is also easier to bear. When you spit, it still freezes before it reaches the snow, but it doesn't explode with a loud retort like molten beads of iron falling into a smithy's tempering pot.

I used the first days of my journey home to shake off the effects of my long sleep. I'd been a woman nearing her fourth decade of life when I entered that tomb with Salimar. In the outside world, fifty years had passed. In Salimar's kingdom five decades is equal to five months, so I was still several years shy of forty summers when I emerged.

My body was stiff, my actions hesitant, and for some time I lost my grip too easily when hauling on the ropes to shift the sails. I also worried that my soldier's skills might be rusty as well, and I dared not wait for an unknown enemy's sudden appearance to test them.

Whenever I could, I'd follow a dolphin pack to a large flat iceberg, where schools of succulent fish gathered to tempt them. I'd clamber onto the 'berg with a sack of my heaviest battle gear. I'd don the gear and trot back and forth and around and around until I was gasping like an old sea lioness in heat. When I could take no more, I'd strip naked, rub my body with snow, and dance about like a madwoman. I must've made a wondrous entertainment for all those seals and penguins who gathered to see the pink-fleshed thing that hooted and hollered with every jounce of her flab.

It was well worth it. Each day in my mirror I saw muscle swell. My skin glowed with health and I kept it plucked smooth, treating myself to frequent massages with warm sweet oil that I coaxed into the pores. I'd let my hair grow long to please Salimar, who said she loved to stroke the waves it made on my pillow and called them her golden fields of delight. Long hair may be good for a lover, but an enemy has reason to praise it as well. It gives him something substantial to grip when he slits your throat. So I used a bowl to razor my hair short enough to fit under a helmet. I suppose it made me look boyish, although no one had ever been fool enough to mistake my figure as such. And with my pirate's eyepatch, scarred cheek, and golden hand, not many would have the nerve to test my mettle if I wandered into a tavern in a man's tunic and cloak.

When I got my sea legs back and could more easily weave about the pitching deck, ducking swinging booms and leaping over coiled rope to do my work, I tackled the next part of my self-training.

Out came my weapons—sword and bow and dagger and axe.

My friend Polillo had been the great mistress of the axe. She'd been big, although with the form of a maid, if you can imagine a seven-foot beauty who could lift a castle's keystone with ease. I'd seen her charge a line of shields, burst them apart with her axe, and then pulp the men in their armor.

By the gods, I thought, if I had Polillo with me, the job would be much easier. But she's dead.

It had taken a mighty wizard to take down Polillo—the last Archon of Lycanth.

I mourned her as I honed my axe and set up a target—a spare hatch cover about the size of a man. My first throw went wide, chipping the rail and nearly going over the side. I tied a long leather thong to the handle, looping the other about my wrist so I wouldn't lose the axe if I missed again. My second throw hit the hatch, but the axe had tumbled too much and struck the wood with its butt instead of the blade.

I considered the many errors I'd made in only two attempts. I thought about Polillo and how she'd trained our green troops in the art of axe throwing.

"What do I have to do to get your attention?" she'd snarl at an errant recruit. "Get your tit out of your ear and listen. See yon target?" The frightened recruit would nod. "How far is it?" The recruit's bobbing head would now swerve side to side.

"Are you telling me you've been tossing that damned thing all day and you don't know how far you're throwing it?" There'd be a shamed nod of yes. "Well, step it off, then." The recruit would pace the distance then trot back to tell Polillo the result. "Twenty paces, you say? Very good. Now, watch closely."

Polillo would haul back, talking as she moved. "Think of your throwing arm as a bar of iron. Completely straight. Don't bend your elbow. And for Te-Date's sake, do not—I repeat, do not bend your wrist. Now the leg. The one on the same side as your throwing arm. Think of it as the extension of your arm—that iron-bar arm.

"Next, when you throw, take a step forward with your opposite foot. Not quite a full pace. Keep the whole side of your body stiff. Don't use just the strength of your arm and shoulder. Your throw will be as weak as a lad who tends the tavern piss pots. Use all the power of your body as you come forward . . . and let go . . . like this!"

And she'd let the axe go. It would turn once in a long slow tumble, then thunk into the target dead on—burying its head so deep that only Polillo could draw it out.

"You saw how many turns it made?" she'd ask. The recruit would nod, yes, and hold up a single finger.

"That's right, once. So properly thrown, this particular axe will turn once in twenty paces. If it's forty, it'll turn twice. Ten, half a turn. Thirty, a turn and a half. Got it?" Much eager nodding would commence, for now that the recruit had learned the secret, she'd be anxious to test it. If she followed Polillo's direction, she'd rarely fail again.

I remembered Polillo's barked instructions as I made my third try. How far? Ten paces. Half a turn, then. Iron-bar arm. Welded to the leg. No elbow bending. No wrist bending. Step forward with the opposite foot. Throw.

The axe bit deeply into the hatch.

An axe has never been my weapon of choice, and it should only be thrown as a last resort. But it can come in handy when pressed by large numbers, and there are few things that can tone you up faster than repeatedly hurling it, switching hands frequently to give all parts of the body a heavy working.

My left hand, the false one, is very strong. So I have to be careful that the right gets full attention; although it can never be the equal, for not only is my sinister hand metal, but it's enchanted metal, formed from a substance I stole from Novari. I call it my etherhand.

It can withstand intense heat and cold. It has a grip that can crush stone. More remarkably, with my mind I can command it to behave exactly as a living hand would behave, flexing the fingers, rotating the thumb—anything but cracking the knuckles.

My etherhand is a wondrous thing indeed. But I missed its warm, weaker sister. She'd been a good hand to me, and ghostly nerves ached to have her back.

I practiced until the misses were minimal. It took getting used to, because with only one eye it's sometimes difficult to judge distance accurately. This infirmity is lessened because the golden eyepatch I wear is made of the same material as my hand. With it I can see into the Otherworlds at will and with no spell-casting. I call it my ethereye.

Next came sword practice.

With my strength growing daily, I had to concentrate on being nimble. The sword has always been my favorite, and I do not boast when I say I've never met a man or woman who could best me with the blade. Naturally,

such a person does exist somewhere. That is the nature of all human abilities. No matter how good you are, there's always someone who is your equal, or better. In my tavern-brawling youth I used to dream of meeting that person so I could really test my talent. Which only goes to prove that you don't have to be a man whose bravado is commanded by his balls to consider such folly.

While I continued to grunt and strain with the physical, it was most important that I didn't forget my Otherworldly self. So I got out my wizard's chest and unpacked the scrolls and unguents and powders and other Evocator's devices.

I conjured up small things first—a glass bead, a fiery scrap of parchment, a drop of perfume so powerful it filled the cabin with its odor, a large beetle with wings of green and black who made a song as sweet as a bird's as it flew around looking for a way out. Then I turned the beetle into a glittering-jeweled scarab necklace for Salimar that would make music and scent.

I came to the Evocator's craft late in my life and with much reluctance. Dire circumstances and a blind master wizard forced me to overcome that reluctance. I eventually realized my abilities were a gift from my mother. And that it is from her side of the family that some Anteros inherited the talent for sorcery. I'd used it to destroy the Archons of Lycanth and end that ancient threat to Orissa.

Amalric was not magically blessed—or cursed, depending how you looked at it—but his presence seemed to act as a magnifier when he was in the company of the two Greycloaks, first Janos and then Janela. With Janos he found the Far Kingdoms, at that time the greatest feat in our people's history. With Janela he'd topped even that accomplishment by traveling to the Kingdoms of the Night and joining with the Old Ones to defeat the demon king, Ba'land, who'd plunged humankind into a thousand years of darkness and ignorance. As a parting gift to all, he helped Janela Greycloak discover the principle that unifies all physical forces with the magical.

He'd made his final, most difficult expedition as an old man. The dangers he'd faced awakened me enough to see his troubles in a vision. It was the only time in my fifty years of blissful sleep that I'd been so disturbed. At first I'd seen no means to help him. Then I'd cast a spell that made Amalric grow younger as he traveled until he had the strength and stamina of a man in his prime. My brother never realized I was the cause of this, but he questioned the effect so little that I sometimes wonder if deep inside he knew.

I'd thought when he'd found his peace and I had returned to mine that all would be the best it could be in the world we'd both abandoned. What should have commenced was an age of great challenge and enlightenment.

As I trained myself to face whatever task lay ahead, I hammered my skull for some hint of what could have gone wrong.

Then I remembered Amalric's parting words. As he'd written them in his journal, his thoughts had been so powerful that they'd echoed across the vast distances separating us. I'd heard them in my ice chamber as clear as if he'd been sitting next to me speaking aloud:

"... I have made a pact with King Solaris. All the knowledge Janela gained will be shared with Orissa. A company of wizards will depart soon and I beg you to make them welcome in Orissa. They bring truth that two Greycloaks stole from the gods. If that truth is freely and generously bestowed to all, then we will at last be free of our masters who so jealously guarded it. There will be nothing you will fear to dare. But if it is kept locked away in a miser's treasure house, there will come the fated day when all will curse the ones who slew Ba'land, and call his lashes a father's stern kindness."

My brother's warning had been quite clear. But had it been ignored? Was this the source of the troubles now threatening Orissa? Was this why my sisters of the Guard were in grave peril? The reason all the Anteros had been slain save my little niece Emilie?

Maranonia hadn't said. I felt my ire stir anew when I thought of the goddess. Why couldn't she have been plain? Why had she kept all a mystery, other than telling me my task in the vaguest of terms?

I polished my casting bones with angry vigor. The gods are such a maddening lot, I thought. They sit in their heavenly palaces, posing and deposing, judging this, punishing that, bidding and forbidding all the live long day. And it's up to us poor mortals to dash about trying to make sense of it all.

Well, she'd been plain about three things at least:

I had one year to set things straight.

Failure would result in a great disaster.

And the Lyre Bird was behind it all.

Novari—the beautiful and powerful succubus who'd nearly destroyed me once. I'd lost an eye and a hand in that war.

If Novari was my foe, I'd need more wits and tricks than even the last Archon of Lycanth had required.

I went back to my self-training, doubling all my efforts. The key to Novari, I thought, must lie in all the events that led to our first meeting.

I cast my mind back ...

Remembering.

CHAPTER TWO

AMALRIC

There are few alive who knew my brother. He's a man remembered mostly in books. Some of the treasures from his travels are displayed in our museums, and his likeness can be seen in portraits, busts, and statues that gather bird droppings in the parks. He has no tomb—no grand sepulchre—to mark an Orissan of such renown, for his ashes had been mixed with Janela Greycloak's and, following the wishes of both, sprinkled on the waters of the river he loved that flows past our city to the sea.

I doubt his name is spoken much by the average man or woman, many of whom are the children and the grandchildren of the slaves he set free. Oh, you'll hear it now and then in phrases that've fallen into the language. "Lucky as Amalric Antero," is one. And if you say, "You have my Amalric on that," it means a gilt-edged assurance or IOU. Most people probably don't even know the origin of such sayings. One of my favorite sarcasms is, "Thinks he knows more'n Amalric Antero." My brother would've seen double irony in that phrase. Amalric, more than any I've known, enjoyed irony.

He'd put his eyes on more places and things than any other. He'd faced and overcome the greatest of obstacles and dangers. He'd experienced much sadness in his life, including betrayal by his greatest friend and, late in his years, by his only living child. But he'd also known love and known it deeply.

Amalric used to say that Janos Greycloak was the wisest man he'd ever met because the learned Greycloak knew how ignorant he really was. This was doubly true of my brother, who in the end knew more than even Janos.

So I'm sister to a legend. Amalric Antero, the greatest adventurer and discoverer, merchant prince—and some say even scholar—in our history.

To me he'll always be the boy with fiery hair and skin so fair it showed his every emotion. He was a mischief as a child, a wastrel as a youth, and I think the kindest person I ever met.

As a boy he'd do small favors for scullery servants and young lords alike, but in such a way that the other person would never know a favor had been done and chalk it up to good fortune. When he grew older, overcoming all the temptations of wealthy sloth, he ventured all for friendship. He was betrayed by Janos Greycloak in an act so sinister that in my view Janos' name should be a curse to describe traitorous friendships. Yet my brother was Greycloak's greatest defender. He strove his whole later life to understand Janos' action, and in the end forgave him, concluding that the good outweighed the evil.

Despite the several years that separated us, Amalric and I were the closest of friends and confidants. As a child he thought of me as a hero, and I must say when I was a raw recruit it made me feel good to see the pride shine in his young eyes. I'd be on leave after weeks of drill sergeants blistering my ears with curses at my clumsiness, and he'd come shyly to my rooms to beg me to show him a new sword trick.

He never thought it strange that his sister was a soldier. He found my taste for women rather than men the natural order of things. In fact he used it to his advantage during his wild seed-scattering youth by questioning me closely about the ways of women, figuring I'd be doubly wise in those matters.

He understood instinctively that women in Orissa had only four roles they were allowed: daughter, mother, wife, or whore. A few, like myself, were permitted a fifth role as a member of the all-woman Maranon Guard that had defended the city for many generations, forswearing men for the honor. For most of us that was no sacrifice at all.

In later years Amalric opened a sixth door to me. When I'd returned from my adventures in the Western Sea, I realized my profession as a soldier had to end. I'd seen too much flowing blood and been the cause of much of it. Besides, along with my newly discovered abilities as a wizard came the wanderlust that is the curse of the Antero family. Familiar horizons quickly bored me. I yearned for the scented mysteries of fresh winds on virgin seas, the cast of the sun setting on distant mountains no man or woman had crossed before.

Amalric won me an appointment as the first woman Evocator to lead an expedition. It wasn't the favor that impressed me so much as that he'd thought of it at all. I hadn't known myself what I'd wanted . . . what it was that troubled me. As an aside, I'll note it's no credit to the all-male leadership of Orissa that I'm still the only woman who has ever held that post.

What I remember most about Amalric is his smile. By the gods, my brother had a smile! It was so broad and white in that beardless face of his, his features flushing nearly as red as his hair at the pleasure of seeing me.

The last time I saw that smile was fifty years ago.

I sailed into Orissa with four ships loaded to the rails with rich cargo. I had every reason to be pleased with myself. The trading expedition had been my most successful yet. I now had four such voyages under my belt, three as fleet Evocator and this last as chief trader, as well.

This meant not only had I been in charge of the sorcery used to protect our sailors and ships and goods, but I'd been in command of all things dealing with commerce. Naturally, as is the custom of Orissan merchant expeditions, sailing and soldiery were dealt with by the captains and fighting masters. Since the sole purpose of such voyages is profit, however, my word held sway in almost all circumstances. It goes without saying that as an Antero sailing with a fleet flying our family flag, my word had been taken very seriously indeed. I'd also had a lucky streak, and my holds were swelling with all sorts of rare goods—colorful carpets and healing herbs, perfumes and raw gems, precious metals and great bundles of buttery leather, and wondrous furs.

All this was to my credit, and I knew Amalric would be pleased that everyone in Orissa could see how correct he'd been to break all precedent to win me this berth. The point would be doubly hammered home because I was returning during the festival that ends the Harvest Month. Wine, sin, high spirits, and money would be flowing freely as the whole city celebrated. As any merchant will tell you, this is an excellent climate to set profit records, which would add even more to my prestige.

But my emotional barometer, as they say, was set more to storm than fair when we sailed up to the docks. I traded my Evocator's robes for a nondescript costume and slipped away as soon as we were tied up near the Antero warehouses, leaving the business of unloading and port inspections to Carale, captain of our tiny fleet.

It was a warm, sunny afternoon and the streets and taverns were already thronging with celebrants. I cut through Cheapside and the great Central Market.

Drunken farmers reeled down the avenue flush with liquor and coin, ripe for a plucking by the Cheapside's denizens, who regularly harvested a different kind of crop this time of year.

The atmosphere was a heady brew of incense, sacrificial smoke, roasted meats and nuts, and the musk of women wearing masks and little else, who beckoned from dark alleys where curtained carriages awaited. I saw dinksmen playing "find the pea" with greedy-eyed farmers. Shills cried out from gaming taverns, extolling the fortunes waiting to be made tossing dice, or playing Evocators and Demons with cards they guaranteed were the most honest in Orissa. Pickpockets worked the crowds, bumping into people or engaging them in conversation while their mates felt for their purses.

There was music everywhere, and I was hard-pressed to push through the crowds who'd gathered to see troupes of entertainers juggle and vault and balance on ropes strung high across the streets. Small boys threw smoke bombs at the unwary; little girls with solemn faces plucked at their fathers' sleeves, begging to be hoisted up so they could see. Brawny lads flexed their muscles for giggling maids in bright dresses and hair decked with strings of flowers and bells and beads.

The main avenue was roped off for that night's parade, when all would be treated to fireworks and magical displays, culminating in a grand costume parade.

I paid too much money to rent a spavined horse and set off for my brother's villa, about an hour's journey from Orissa. It came up lame about halfway there and I had to lead it along the dusty road. We made a sorry sight; the horse limping, me sweating under the midday sun and rolling back and forth on legs made unsteady by months at sea.

As I approached the long low walls of his sprawling estate I could hear Omerye piping a sweet tune, and I felt the weariness fall away. The breeze seemed cooler and the air had the scent of blossoming vines and fruited trees.

Omerye must have sensed my presence, for the tune shifted to a sailor's welcome home, and my heart stirred and my arms tingled to embrace my family. Amalric himself greeted me at the door and his pleasure was so great at seeing me that for a time I nearly forgot the main reason I'd hastened to him.

After I'd washed away the grime of the journey and donned a clean robe borrowed from Omerye, my brother and his wife led me to the garden and my mother's shrine.

The flowering plants and trees had been one of my mother's greatest joys, and after she'd died, first my father and then Amalric had spent much effort to keep all the way she'd have preferred. Instead of the perfection you see at most grand homes, there was a pleasant untidiness about the garden, making it feel more like a natural glade. The paths were neat, the beds clean, but plants and trees were allowed to sprawl and some things were permitted to grow amongst others to purposefully mar the symmetry.

I was the one responsible for my mother's shrine, a simple stone edifice set under a small rose tree. A spell coaxed a trickle of water down the face of the stone, misting a fragrant moss.

Amalric knew how much I loved this spot, so he had the servants set up a picnic near the shrine. Bees fat with rose pollen and honey buzzed lazily about, and a wasp—drunk from fermenting grapes on a nearby arbor—bumped against the stone, confused that it didn't part before him.

My hosts filled me up with food and drink and family gossip. Omerye was as beautiful as ever, with long, slender arms, a smooth, lovely brow, and tresses as red as Amalric's. She wore a short white tunic with a modest neckline, and the flair of her fine figure was emphasized by a simple sash of pale green.

Then I saw a telltale sparkle in her eyes and knew she was anxious to tell me news of a more intimate sort. Although her belly was as flat as a maid's, I saw that her breasts seemed swollen under her tunic. And when she turned or lifted her arms, she did so delicately, as if her breasts were overly tender. To make certain of my diagnosis, I bent my head, made a small magical motion with my fingers, and listened.

I could hear the flutter of a small beating heart. I raised my head, smiling, and Omerye clapped her hands in glee.

"I see you've ferreted out our little secret, Rali," she said.

I laughed. "I wouldn't be much of a wizard if I hadn't," I said. "Although the blush of your cheeks and the sparkle in your eyes are a surer sign."

Amalric smiled. "You're to be an aunt, sister dear," he said. "If it's a girl, we plan to name it after you."

"You'd better have another child quick," I said. "Unless I've lost my wizardly wits entirely, the little bud Omerye's sprouting is definitely male."

Omerye was delighted. "Then we shall name him Cligus after my grandfather," she said. "I never knew him—he died shortly before I was born—but he left me these pipes." She gestured at the delicate instrument by her side. "He was a court musician, you know. And he'd hoped the child my mother bore would have the gift to carry on the tradition."

Omerye was a daughter of Irayas, the land once known to us as the Far Kingdoms. My brother had met and fallen in love with her when he and Janos Greycloak first arrived in those lands.

"Cligus," I repeated. "That has a nice firm sound to it."

"It means 'forever faithful' in our tongue," Omerye said.

"Now you'll have a son to rear to take over the family business," I told Amalric. "By and by you won't have to take so many long trips away from Omerye."

My brother chuckled. "Planning my retirement already, are you? Well, the boy will have a long wait, for I intend to sail for as many years as my luck holds out."

"O Great Evocator, tell us," Omerye intoned, only half in jest. "Will the gods favor Cligus? Cast his fortune for us, will you, Rali dear?"

I grumbled that I hadn't come prepared, but secretly I was pleased. It'd be an honor to be the first to cast the bones for my brother's heir. I fished out my favorite set of bones given to me by that master Evocator, Lord Gamelan. They were so worn with use that the magical symbols were quite faint. From the pocket in my sleeve I drew out the collapsible casting cup I carry with me everywhere and unfolded it. Gamelan had taught me that the Evocator's art is as much entertainment as wizardry, so I put on a good show.

Frowning in concentration, I blew on the bones, whispered a chant, and plopped them into the cup. I rattled them about, then scattered the bones on a stone table with a flourish.

Caught up by my little act, Amalric and Omerye quickly bent forward to study the bones, although no one but a wizard or a very good witch can read such things. Then both of them looked up at me, faint smiles of anticipation on their faces.

It's a good thing I'd grown skilled in keeping my own features blank during such occasions. For my brother and his dear wife would have despaired if they had seen in my eyes what I knew in my heart.

The faint symbols staring up at me did not bode well. They were all demon horns.

I grinned as hugely as I knew how and swept the bones up. "Your son will be a great credit to you," I lied. "A worthy little fellow to bear the Antero name."

As all now know, Cligus would grow to be an even greater betrayer of my brother than Janos Greycloak. But how could I tell them that? And what could they have done if I had—drown the little bastard at birth?

I think not.

Praying to Te-Date that my casting skills had failed me that day, I quickly buried my fears and let my dear ones chatter on as all young parents do, telling me of their hopes and plans for their offspring.

When the dinner hour approached, Omerye excused herself to oversee the cook and table servants. Amalric poured us both big goblets of that delicious wine my family grew in our vineyards. We eased back in our seats and I filled him in on the general business details of my voyage.

"You've done very well, Rali," he said when I was done. "But I sense you are not as pleased as you ought to be."

I shook my head. "There was a small incident near the end of the voyage," I said, "that troubles me."

His eyebrows arched and he asked me to pray continue.

And so I did.

"The pirates jumped us," I began, "just off Demon's Point. Not far from Antero Bay . . ."

On my previous voyage I'd pressed farther south than anyone had ever gone before. I'd gone beyond the realm of the Iofra, where the parched sands of the desert meet desolate pebbled beaches. Past the farthest point my father sailed in his youth. He'd been the first Orissan to visit the Ice Barbarians. I'd even crossed that mystical divide that seems to girdle the world, where strange starry constellations rule and tornadoes twist in the opposite direction.

In that mission, I'd been concentrating on future trade rather than immediate profit. So I'd charmed, cozened, or cowed many a fierce and hairy chieftain into the Antero merchant's fold. I'd established trading posts, watched over by small complements of our private security forces, all former guardsmen of the highest caliber.

My efforts had paid off handsomely on the fourth trading mission, and as we approached Demon's Point, nearing the first of the southern ice fields, all the ships' holds were bursting with goods. There were two trading posts yet to visit, the most remote of the ones I'd established. The first was at Antero Bay, which I'd named after my family.

As we set course around the rocky shoals that edge Demon's Point, I was in the odd position of hoping that business had not gone as well at those two missions as they had at the others.

"If only we'd taken a fifth ship," I moaned to Captain Carale.

Carale was a dark little man, with fierce mustaches and a morose temperament, who saw ill where others saw gold.

"Aye, 'n' that'd be one more t' lose, me lady," he said. "The devil gods mus' be drunk in their hellish taverns t' let us get this far wit' our skins still whole on the bones."

"Oh, pooh, Carale," I replied. "My brother spent a fool's fortune on sacrifices before the voyage began. And I've made every appeasement to every trumped-up local shaman at every thatch-and-wattle temple from Lycanth to Hells Shoals. The only bad days we've seen were a week's becalming off Shatter Island."

"Mark me words, 'n' mark 'em well," Carale said, black brows crossing swords over his small sharp beak of a nose. "We're in fer a spell o' bad times, me lady. We'll be wishin' we'd a stayed home once the gods sober up."

I laughed. "We've had more good luck than is good for us, is that what you're saying?"

"Laugh all ye like, me lady," Carale said. "But the facts o' the matter are well known t' all th't's been fated to sail the salty seas. A bit o' a blow when the voyage begins spells sunny skies at the end."

"With that logic," I said, "the richest trip you ever took must've started with the death of your mother."

"Twas me sister, lady," Carale answered. "Right bitch she was, if'n ye'll beg me pardon. I was glad t' see her in her grave. But she was close enough familywise fer her untimely death t' see me through t' the best days o' me life."

Despite his gloomy nature, Carale was one of my brother's best captains, and he was a sight to behold in a fight—a regular little whirlwind with a dagger and a sword for edges.

I wanted to laugh again but feared it'd only draw more dark comments. So instead I made a grim face and sighed. "Well, there's nothing we can do but go on," I said. "They'll be expecting us, and we've letters and supplies to deliver."

"Aye, that be our duty, me lady," he said quite mournfully. " 'N' it'll never be said that the likes o' Cap'n Carale ever shirked 'is duty. 'Sides, they's prob'ly lonely so far from home. Seein' us'll bring a bit of cheer int' their lives."

And with that he twisted his mustache points to make certain they drooped downward, then stalked away to make someone else's hours miserable. As I watched him slouch across the deck I thought the men at the outposts were likely to contemplate cutting short their lives if they looked too long on Carale's grim features. I decided to make the visit as brief as possible. Perhaps I could get them to cache the less perishable goods they'd traded for and somehow I'd make room for the rest.

The first place I considered was my own cabin, which was spacious enough, and I could get the ship's carpenter to knock up a little alcove near the entrance where I could store my Evocator's chests. I'd hang a hammock over them and would sleep comfortably enough on the voyage home.

The lookout shouted and Demon's Point hove into view.

It was a bleak hump of land jutting out from a range of desolate mountains. Two dark-eyed caves marked the highest region, separated by a huge black rocky hook that formed a nose. A twisted gash below made a bleak mouth, and two black spears twisted up from the head like horns.

Demon's Point was well-named, although I do not know who first set eyes on it. An Ice Barbarian, perhaps, sailing out from some distant petty kingdom. A fellow with hairy shoulders and a filthy beard and yellow teeth to chatter with when the sight of that awful land struck fear in his savage heart.

I'd been told by local seafarers that it's rare for the skies to be clear enough to see Demon's Point. The land is usually hidden by boiling storm clouds alive with—according to one old salt—crackling lightning that strikes upward instead of down. The rogue waves in that area are as notorious as the storms, and some say an entire fishing fleet was swallowed by waters that reached as high as the Pillars of Te-Date, which mark the entrance to the Southern Sea.

Storms such as those had obscured any view of the point during the three trips I'd made before, although the blows never reached the fury local legend said was possible. This day, however, was as calm as the innocent brow of a novice priestess. A pale sun hung over the point, making the small white clouds hovering above glow with the softness of a maid. The seas were a placid blue, and as we rounded the point a troop of dolphins came out to greet us, leaping high and shrilling their joy at seeing company in such a lonely place.

I was in a peaceful mood, a reflective mood, and for those reasons I was caught unawares.

First the wind gentled and I heard Carale call to his men to make adjustments in the set of the sails. The echoes the men made as they relayed his orders were pleasant haunting sounds playing above the slow crash of the rolling seas. I smelled moist green plant life on the wind and I found myself wondering idly where that delightful odor could be from.

I hadn't seen a speck of vegetation in several days. Only a cold black coastline so thick with rocks and washed by brine that no self-respecting tree or bush would ever consider setting down roots in such a place. I knew a wide desert lay some distance inland. Beyond that were high pine forests and a few valleys where savage farmers might poke the ground with sticks to plant a tuber which they'd leave for chance to rear.

According to some the southern coastline continued like this for many a league. I found later that these claims were mostly true. And furthermore, there is a passage many leagues distant that leads to a great Eastern Sea that no one previously had known existed.

While I stood there on the deck, marveling at the magical scent the winds had borne up, I suddenly heard music.

A delicate strumming of marvelous strings ghosted on the air. They warmed me, beckoned me, reminded me of the hearthfires of home.

It was suddenly most important to see who was playing so sweetly. I turned to ask Carale to set a course that would carry us closer to the point when I heard him order his men to perform the same actions I was about to utter.

His cry stirred a warning in my mind, but my heart had assumed the throne, and for a long time I ignored my mind's pleadings that danger lurked ahead.

It's just music, my heart said, lovely music. Only gentle people could play such music. Civilized people with love in their hearts for all.

My Evocator's senses pounced scant seconds before I saw the first ship.

It was a wide, high galleon of archaic design. But there was nothing primitive about its deadly speed. Triple banks of oars plunged into the sea, hauling the big ship out to meet us at an alarming pace. I heard the oarmaster's drums boom over the mysterious strings. I even imagined I could hear the crack of his assistants' whips as they strode along the benches urging still more speed.

I saw all this as if in a dream. It was a vivid dream, I'll say that. Complete with crouching archers in the galleon's bows and naked swordsmen swarming to the sides.

An immense banner fluttered over the ship. On a field of black a huge silver bear was rising up, fangs bared, claws outstretched to take its enemy.

I broke free from the spell just as two other galleons hauled into sight. I shouted a warning to Carale. But as I did so I knew the warning would fall on spell-stopped ears.

I looked wildly about for a means to fight the magical assault. The first galleon was nearly on us, and I could hear my men shout warm greetings, oblivious to the obscene growls from the pirates preparing to board us.

Battle vision and battle time descended on me, and I saw everything in the most minute detail and all action slowed to a slug's pace. But my mind was racing ahead like a war chariot's desperate drive to force a break in the enemy line.

A shower of arrows fell, miraculously missing all but a ship's boy standing transfixed with a bucket of slops in his hand. A bolt caught him in the throat and he gasped, crumpling to the deck. By an odd quirk the slop bucket fell upright, spilling only a little of its contents.

In my heightened state of awareness a foul whiff of the offal made my nostrils lift, and a mad solution leaped into my brain.

I raced toward the boy and the bucket, dodging another flight of arrows, sixth sense urging me to suddenly step aside, and just as I did, a spear flashed by so closely it plucked my sleeve.

I grabbed the bucket by the handle, swiveled like a hammer thrower, and hurled it high into the air toward the enemy galleon.

As it sailed up and up—pushed higher still by my will—I chanted:

"Fair be foul.
Sweet be cursed.
Foul be fouler still.
Till all is . . . shit!"

I admit it wasn't a very elegant chant. Sometimes my barracks manners and tongue elbow through my wizard's pose. But it was the best I could come up with under the circumstances.

More importantly . . . it worked.

A blast of cold damp wind chilled us, and I saw the offal bucket swell up like a boar's bladder. Then it exploded and the wind sheeted brown and purple filth into our enemies' faces.

We were enveloped in a stench so retching that I nearly fell gagging to my knees. All around me I heard my men coughing and cursing. The pirates suffered the most, and I heard them shrieking in pain and calling on the gods to deliver them from such evil.

I forced air into my lungs, fighting the poisons I drew in. Then I blew out, sending not a spell, but a prayer to any gods who might be listening to rescue us all from my foolishness.

I doubt I shall ever duplicate what came next.

My breath huffed out and at the same instant a blast of wind struck my back. The ship heeled over as a sudden squall buffeted us.

It was gone by the time we'd righted ourselves, but as I struggled to my feet I saw that the galleon had been driven back.

Confusion vanished from our ships as all became fully aware of what was happening. Officers shouted; Orissan warriors rushed to obey and mount first a defense, then an offense of our own.

In times past I would have been hastening to meet our foes with a sword in my hand and fire in my eyes. My arms and legs twitched to join the fray. But I had heavier responsibilities now. The physical fight must be left to others.

I called forth all my resources and cast out my senses. I soon found what I sought. It was a foul, prickly little presence with needle-sharp teeth and claws. It smelled of hot sulfur, like spoiled roasted eggs at a Cheapside market stall.

The creature tried to bolt away and scamper off into the Otherworlds when I approached. But I cornered it. It struck back and my spiritual self felt a nip of sharp teeth. I quickly saw it was only a puffed-up little thing—a demon of some sort.

I called up the image of a large broom and crushed it.

As soon as it squeaked its last, I snapped back to the real world. I saw that my men had won the upper hand and the galleons were fleeing. Carale was poised to order a chase to hunt the pirates down and punish them. He was only waiting for my approval.

I shook my head and told him to leave off. We were too overladen to contemplate a chase. And if our enemy was wily enough to use a small demon to nearly overwhelm us, I didn't want to underestimate him once more.

Then we learned that one of our ships had been heavily damaged in the fray. A boulder fired by a catapult from one of the enemy ships had carried off the main mast. Repairs would need to be made. And with an enemy force so near we'd have to find a safe place to make them. This meant we'd have to cut short our voyage, skip Antero Bay and the other trading post, and retire to a safe position to fix our sister ship.

And when that was done, we sailed home immediately.

"As you said," my brother commented when I was done, "it was a small incident. You dealt with it successfully, and from what I can gather you did everything properly afterward."

He peered at me closely. "Why does it still trouble you, sister dear?"

I sighed. "On reflection, there are several reasons. The first is personal. I was caught napping. That offends my pride. The second is still personal. The magical attack was mounted by such a puny thing, how could it have so nearly succeeded?

"Then it occurred to me that the demon I encountered might be a Favorite. A creature operating under a greater wizard's will."

"Do you think that's the case?" my brother asked.

"Yes, I do," I said. "There were small indications, I realize now. Not proof. But the faint spoor of something larger. More deadly. With a mind and purpose that little demon certainly couldn't have."

"The flag you saw," Amalric said, "rings the chimes of my memory. But I still can't recollect where I've heard of it before."

"That's another thing," I said. "On our return journey I revisited an old shaman I'd befriended on my last voyage. When I described the flag to him, he became very excited. He said the banner was that of the Ice Bear King. An ice chieftain known only in legend. A piratical tyrant who terrorized the region many years before, but who has been dead for at least a century.

"The shaman said some enterprising villain must have adopted the Ice Bear King's ancient standard to cow ignorant fools into submission."

"I think he's probably right, don't you, Rali?" my brother said.

I nodded. "It's the most likely explanation. But it doesn't diminish whoever that rogue is. He's got more than bluff to back him up. He's got wizardly skills, as well."

"You're also worried about the trading posts, aren't you?" Amalric asked.

"I can't help but feel I abandoned them when I turned back," I said.

"Even though they have more than sufficient arms and soldiers to protect themselves?"

"Yes."

"And don't they also have two of Orissa's most skilled Evocators to guard against a magical attack such as you experienced? Lord Serano and Lord Searbe, if I recall."

"Even so," I said. "I fear for them. Especially for the people at Antero Bay, where Lord Searbe is posted. Antero Bay isn't that far from where I sighted the pirates."

"It would be very expensive to make an unscheduled voyage back to those parts," Amalric said. "Especially one that was equipped with enough forces to quickly overwhelm whoever this false Ice Bear King is."

"I know that," I said. "And I don't have enough proof to urge you take such a risk."

Amalric thought for a minute. "I'll tell you what," he said. "I'll send a fast scouting ship out. Something small that will go unnoticed but will have a fierce bite if trapped. They can sniff around, then head for the two trading posts to see if all is well."

I should've been relieved. But I wasn't. My forehead and shoulders were tight and aching with tension.

My brother, ever sensitive to my mood, grimaced. "You want to head that scouting party, don't you, Rali?" he guessed.

"I *must* go, Amalric," I said. "I feel those people are my responsibility."

"Ever the warrior captain," my brother said, grinning. "You'll never get it out of your blood, will you?"

"I guess not," I said. "And I'm not sure I ought to. I opened that area up. I put those people down. And I promised to return."

"But you didn't promise them complete safety," Amalric said. "They're all experienced people. They know the risk in such savage regions."

"I'll put it this way, then," I said. "If you were me . . . what would you do?"

Amalric answered without hesitation. "I'd demand to go," he said.
"Then I suppose that's what I'm doing," I said. "Demanding to go."
"Then go you shall, sister dear," Amalric said. "Go you shall."

Some weeks later the scouting ship was fitted out and ready to depart. But before I left, I made one short pilgrimage.

We of the sisterhood have a small temple at Galana, some three days' hard ride from Orissa. It's a simple little stone building set in a graceful wood—no more than a tree lot, really. The surrounding area consists of rolling hills and farmland, cared for by Guardswomen who are no longer able to fight. Some have suffered wounds of the flesh, some of the spirit, some of both. Old warrior women also spend their final days in Galana, and all who are able see to the needs of the farm and their less fortunate sisters.

It was a hot day, a dry day, a day of crackling leaves and prickly skin when I was escorted through the gates of Galana.

There were many comfortable barracks to house the women, and I noted with professional interest that the encampment included a low hill with a few cave entrances. The whole region was ringed with hills and mountains, and it seemed to me that Galana was well situated to fend off any threats from those heights.

I made polite talk with the silver-haired commander, praising the farm and inspecting the small force she kept ready in case some unforeseen threat arose. I complimented her people and preparations, although I really barely noticed anything or anyone in particular. I was anxious to get to the temple and consult my goddess' oracle.

I went in alone, put a chit into the box near the entrance—promising a fat bullock for sacrifice—and approached the altar.

It was cool in the temple, and dust motes played in the single beam of light that peeped down through a glassed-over hole in the peaked roof. It was a gate for the goddess to enter, or exit.

Old faint frescoes decorated the walls, dramatizing the many trials and triumphs of the Guard over the centuries. To the right of the goddess' idol was a freshly painted picture commemorating my own battle with the Archon not many years before.

I grimaced when I saw the idealized picture of myself, bloody sword in one hand, the Archon's head dangling from the other. It didn't happen that way, and I wished I were as beautiful as the picture made me, with a waist so slender and breasts so high that it must have made many a woman despair of her own figure when she saw such perfection. I know I certainly did. And it *was* me, after all.

On the way to the altar I stopped at a small raised pool. It was enclosed by a low marble wall, and I leaned over the stone to dip my fingers into the water. My image was reflected in the flat, silvery surface and I had to smile at the wavery reminder of just how far I was from being the figure of heroic perfection portrayed in the frieze.

The image broke when I scooped up the perfumed holy water. I sprinkled myself, feeling instantly cool and refreshed, and went to the altar where the idol of Maranonia waited.

I knelt on the steps and gazed up at the statue of Maranonia in her ever watchful, ever truth-seeking pose. I whispered a prayer urging her blessing for the journey I was about to undertake.

I'm not certain of my view of the gods at that time. Perhaps I'd grown cynical, as many Evocators do after they've wrought miracles of their own for a time. Regardless, I remember feeling a little foolish as I made my plea. Wondering for just a moment if my prayers and obedience were being offered to nothing more than a lovely image an artist made from dead stone—no more real than the picture of myself on the temple walls.

But as I knelt there, knees growing numb on the cold, hard steps, the beam of light suddenly broadened and deepened. There was a rush of air, the sound of swishing robes, and the clank of armor.

Then I saw the statue move. First a hand coming up, then a booted foot coming forward. There was a shimmer and the idol glowed into full life.

The goddess gestured.

A sparkling shower rained on her shoulders, and her warrior's garb and weapons vanished, to be replaced by silken robes of translucent purple that swirled about her ivory flesh, clinging to her body's curves and hollows. The robe was cut high on the left, and when she moved, the smooth white limb on that side was tantalizingly revealed from delicate ankle to rounded hip.

I was stunned by the beauty of the goddess. I must've gaped like a poor thing from the deep trapped in a tidepool.

Maranonia laughed at the sight of me, and the air was filled with the scent of her violet breath.

I was frightened and bowed low, my heart vying with my head to knock against the floor. I'd never been visited by a goddess before. In future days, as you shall see, my awe was replaced with less respectful feelings.

"You ask a boon, Rali," the goddess said.

"Yes, if you please, my lady," I quavered.

"What makes you think I can grant it?" the goddess asked.

I'm certain I made a comical sight puzzling up at her like a small child who's just been told her parents were not the ultimate source of power and wisdom. It'd never occurred to me that she couldn't do whatever she wished.

She was a goddess, wasn't she? I thought the only question would be—will she? Not, can she?

The goddess chuckled at my discomfort, and for the first time I thought of the comparison between her laughter and bells sounding the alarm for war.

Her laugh irritated me. My knees hurt and my temper was starting to get the best of me. "So happy to be such a great source of amusement to you, my lady," I said frostily.

This only made her laugh harder. I gritted my teeth until the storm of godly humor faded.

Then she said, "You'll have to watch that temper of yours, Rali. It might cause us both some trouble in the future."

Although she was smiling, her eyes were so steely that I was once again reduced to a properly trembling state.

"Yes, Your Grace," I said.

The goddess crooked a finger, and the room swirled before my eyes and all became darkness except for her glowing form. She spoke and her voice seemed to come from within me.

"I can only tell you this, Rali Emilie Antero," she said. "You must make this voyage. It is vital to the future of Orissa—the people I have chosen to support. I cannot openly side with you, although I will do what I can. There are those who have influence among my heavenly cousins who do not favor the Anteros.

"And I must warn you most severely not to reveal a word about my appearance this day, or what I have said. Your brother, especially, must not be told. His strength must be saved for another time—if and when the final fight comes.

"So it is up to you, Rali, to see your people through this crisis."

Her image started to fade.

"Is that all you can tell me, Goddess?" I cried. "Please. Reveal all you can safely say. I will tell no one."

The goddess' image firmed.

"Your journey will be fraught with difficulty," she said. "Some may die. Some may flee. Whether you are successful or not depends on you, Rali. Not the gods.

"And I will tell you one thing more . . .

"Three ships will mark your fortunes. Three ships will carry your fate. Three ships a-sailing . . . one of silver, one of copper, and one of gold."

Her image vanished and I collapsed unconscious to the floor.

I'd fully recovered by the time we were to depart. When Amalric came to see me off, I was able to display nothing but good cheer. I'd even begun to wonder if the vision had been the result of the sour wine I'd stopped to drink at a tavern near the settlement.

When I thought on it, the whole thing seemed so unlikely, so farfetched.

Amalric embraced me. "May the trade winds always be at your back, sister dear," he said.

I kissed him, then drew away to study him closer. In that moment he looked like the solemn little boy I'd once known and left behind when I'd gone marching off to war.

So I asked of him then what I'd begged from him more than once in those long ago days.

"Smile for me, little brother," I said. "One smile to carry in my heart while I'm gone."

And Amalric blessed me with his brightest, sweetest smile.

I looked at his face, memorizing it. I think he did the same with me. In his eyes I saw a question begin to grow. And that question was—would we ever see each other again?

Ah, by the gods, if I'd known the answer, I'd have kissed him once more.

CHAPTER THREE

THE ORACLE
OF PISIDIA

Before my time and my brother's time our world was a small dark place surrounded by fearful things. We were like mice in a barn stall burrow, poking our heads out when hunger drove us to it, daring the mighty owl in the rafters as we scampered to feed on animal droppings.

Amalric's voyages of discovery opened the East as far as the distant peaks of Tyrenia which overlook the barren lands where the demons and the Old Ones had battled for eons. My expedition against the last Archon of Lycanth unveiled the mysterious West—thousands of leagues beyond the fiery reefs that had once marked the end of the known world.

We'd always traded with the people in the hot regions of the North and had a good idea what they looked like. Although few had personally visited the North, there were detailed maps showing that savage area with reasonable accuracy.

My father, Paphos Anteros, had explored the ice lands of the South in his youth, but he'd been too overwhelmed by the work of expanding our family fortune to exploit his few discoveries. He was an old-school gentleman with courtly manners and a kind and gentle air that masked his shrewd judgment. He was never one to spare his praise, especially for me. I'd perform some small task for him, such as fetching his favorite bowl—cracked and stained with age—so he could pour a little honeyed wine in it and dip his bread for a late night snack. When I'd set the bowl down carefully on his study table, he'd hug me and thank me as if I'd crossed mountains and wild seas to do him this favor.

"Thank you, daughter," he'd say. "And to those thanks add ten thousand more."

You see what I mean? Not one thank-you would suffice. Only ten thousand and one would do.

Although my mother had the greater influence on me—and it was through her that I inherited my magical ability—my father stirred my more noble feelings, forming and cementing my notions of right and wrong and honor. It was also through him that I'd been infected by the Antero family obsession to explore new lands and see new things. And when my mother carried my wishes forward, telling him that above all things I wanted to become a soldier, my father'd made certain I had the chance to achieve my heart's desire.

I was always his darling daughter no matter how rough or boyish my play. When I was a child, I'd sit on his knee night after late night, winding and unwinding my fingers in his beard while he regaled me with tales of his early adventures in the lands of the South.

He told me of the oyster beds along the Straits of Madacar, where the pearls were plump and glowing. He showed me one rare pearl he'd found that was as big as my childish fist and black as the deeps of the deepest sea. He had a little fertility idol, a fat little woman with great breasts and an oversized pudendum, that he prized above all his treasures. He said it came through many hands from the true end of the world and was a goddess to the People of the Edge who lived on the bottom of the earth. It had been his lifelong desire to go to that place, but he'd never had the time to undertake such a journey.

I've been there since those days of pigtails and scraped knees. I've seen what my father ached to see. I remember gazing out on those wild and lovely wastelands for the first time and thinking if things had been different, Paphos Antero would've been the first great Orissan explorer instead of Amalric. Who knows what the world would be like if that had happened?

And how much larger it would be.

I suppose it was because of his dreams and tales that I'd concentrated on southern exploration and trade since I left the Maranon Guard and joined my brother. Perhaps the threat I sensed from the false Ice Bear King made me more anxious to secure those regions for Orissan trade.

As I viewed the matter, any losses suffered to that pirate devil would be as much a blow against my father as myself.

When I set out to investigate the extent of the danger, if danger existed at all, I did so with more resolve than someone seeking mere profit. I'd be damned if I'd let some barbarian upstart interfere with *my* plans. And if he'd harmed any of my people, I'd hunt him down and rid the earth of his flea-riddled carcass.

I was a warrior in wizard's robes, and by the sweet eyes of Maranonia, I swore to have my will in this matter.

We made a fast run south. We flew no flags. We used sails dyed a dawny blue so as not to stand out on the horizon. And we avoided even the most innocent traffic.

My ship was the *Tern*, a single-masted, shallow-drafted vessel built for speed in any waters, from stormy seas to placid river currents. I carried a crew of ten, which was more than I needed to sail her, but all were skilled fighters as well, so we'd make a nasty little force to be crossed. There was a short single bank of oars on either side to get us out of trouble if we were becalmed. And I'd fitted her out with all the most modern devices, such as the small pump just out of our Evocator's shops, that'd keep her dry and light in any weather.

The pump ran on a mild spell of perpetuation, so it never needed manning, other than someone to clear the hose if oakum or some other debris clogged it. The pump was only one of many useful devices Orissans had devised in recent years, combining the magical knowledge my brother brought back from the Far Kingdoms with our native ingenuity for mechanics.

Once again the captain was Carale, whom I was delighted to sail with again. The first mate was Donarius, a big blustery fellow with a bad temper and keen weather eye. He also swung a two-handed sword with impressive and ferocious ease, and although he grumbled some, he always followed orders exactly.

One of the practices I'd instituted since joining my brother was building a stable of men and women trained both as sailors *and* warriors. In my expedition against the Archon, I'd seen the need for such a thing. Most sailors must engage in combat from time to time. But their seamanship is valued over their fighting ability. Anyone who has been in even the mildest storm at sea would never quarrel with the wisdom of this practice.

It seemed to me both things could be achieved, and at a high level of skill if the scale were kept small. And it seemed to be the perfect solution for a commercial enterprise such as ours. My brother had always maintained a crack security force composed of former soldiers or members of elite units. With Amalric's approval, I'd launched the plan and combed near and far for the best people.

I'd promised hard training, high wages, and a clean life that might very

well be short. To that end I'd established a handsome fund for those who
were maimed or became too old, or died and left family behind. I'd been del-
uged with volunteers, so I had my pick. To my delight, many were women,
although I'd had to be especially careful not to impede the rebuilding of the
Maranon Guard, which had been decimated in the war against Lycanth.

All the volunteers were trained as sailors by my brother's most worthy
captains and as soldiers by myself. Later I became so busy, I'd been forced
to turn this duty over to a retired Guardswoman, a steely-muscled sergeant
with a game leg and an educated nose for laggards. Some got even more spe-
cialized training, such as handling caravan animals and desert fighting.

When I left on the mission, most of these men and women were engaged
in other Antero affairs. I didn't have a great variety of people to choose from.
But I was well-satisfied with the men who volunteered, and my only regret
was there were no women available.

Among my men was a set of twins, Talu and Talay. They were blond,
handsome lads so identical in looks, manner, and speech, it was useless to attempt to tell them apart. Therefore we called them both Talutalay. Or Talut
for short. They'd trained for an elite Guards force, but in the army's age-old,
small-minded manner, they were refused permission to serve together. They
left when their first term ended, and I'd snapped them up before they'd
reached the first tavern to drink away their woes.

Another member of the crew worth mentioning was the cook. He was
exceedingly tall and remained thin as a spar no matter how much or richly
he ate or drank. He had a long neck and a small head, and was bald of pate
and chin. He had a nervous habit of licking his lips, a quick dartlike motion
of his tongue. He was a cheery sort, an extraordinary cook, and he could
hurl a spear an amazing distance, using his long, lean body like a throwing
stick. He was the son of a fishing family who'd caught the adventure bug.

I forget his name, but that's because we all called him Lizard, which is
how he introduced himself and was certainly the animal he most resembled.
If you can imagine, that is, a lizard as friendly as an innkeep's pup.

I hadn't told the men the specifics of our mission before we left, saying
only that it was dangerous. Although I'd admitted the pay was triple and the
bonuses among the most handsome ever, I'd downplayed that part and emphasized the danger. I didn't want need or greed to color anyone's decision.

Just before we reached the Pillars of Te-Date I called them all together
to explain what'd happened and what our purpose was.

Carale, the only one who'd been with me on the last expedition,
breathed a sigh when I was done.

"I figgered that's what was up, me lady," he said. His normally dour expression had actually brightened, if you call a storm reduced to mere heavy showers a brightening. "Those poor blighters at the outposts'll be right glad t' see us. I know I'd be."

The others nodded in vigorous agreement. A side benefit of the mission, both Amalric and I had agreed, would be to show our employees that the Anteros were behind them no matter how far away from home our business took them.

"I want to stress," I said, "that we must be careful what we say whenever we go ashore. I don't want this fellow to get his wind up."

"Why, he's nothin' but pig dung, Lady Antero," Donarius said. "Won't take us long to nail his hide to a shed. I 'spect we'll be home in time t' tap the first barrel of spring." He smacked his lips. "I likes me brew a bit green, Lady Antero."

"Like your women, eh, Donarius?" I joked. It was well-known that the big first mate went weak-kneed at the sight of any tavern slut who could still lay honest claim to a girlish giggle.

Everyone laughed appreciatively, perhaps a little louder than the mild humor warranted. I wanted them to become used to my ways. It had been easier when I was a soldier in uniform, wearing my captain's badge: most men would soon forget my sex and accept me as a warrior who was easily their equal on the battlefield or in the tavern yard. But nowadays I was an Evocator, addressed as Lady Antero this and my lady that, until I feared they'd snatch themselves bald from so much forelock tugging.

The laughter sparked a few more jokes at the first mate's expense. He blushed like an overlarge boy, and I raised a hand to bring it to a halt when I thought his good humor might soon dissolve into anger.

I returned to the subject of the false Ice Bear King.

"I don't know if this pirate is just a thief with an imagination," I said, "or if he's a real menace. For all I know, he could be nothing more than a lucky rogue who was shrewd enough to trap that demon into working for him. And when I killed the demon I wiped out what little magical armament he had."

"I fear worse'n that, me lady," Carale said, his expression sour. "It's a well-known fact that where ye'll find one demon ye'll find another."

This was untrue. I'd encountered single demons before—such as Lord Elam, who'd nearly made a feast of me and my companions. But it was senseless to argue with tavern myths and I let it go. Besides, I preferred Carale's wariness to his first mate's overconfidence.

"That's an excellent point, Captain," I said. "I think it'd be safer if we assumed this fellow is the Ice Bear King incarnate. That he's got a whole stable of demons at his command and that his pirates are as fierce as any we've ever encountered. We can't get into trouble with that attitude. Which we certainly can if we underestimate him.

"Also, any self-respecting pirate keeps paid spies at the major ports to sniff out likely victims. We should assume he's at least doing that."

"You needn't worry about loose tongues, Lady Antero," Donarius said. He glowered at the men, his chest and shoulders swelling like a bullfrog's. Putting on his most intimidating display—and maybe getting back at those who'd teased him. "We'll keep our lips clamped tight, won't we, lads?"

All were quick to murmur agreement.

"Actually," I said, "I *want* you to talk. As a matter of fact, the more you babble, the better it'll be."

They all looked confused. Before long that confusion gave way to conspiratorial smiles.

"I propose we look like easy prey," I said. "We'll waggle our soft merchant fannies around a port or two and we'll soon draw him out."

Carale made a sour face. "To what purpose, if ye don't mind me askin', me lady?" he said. "Ain't but one ship here and eleven of us, countin' yourself. I can't make me mind big enough to figger the odds against a whole pirate fleet, sorcery or no. I know ye too well t' think ye'd be proposin' to fight it out toe-t'-toe, as it were. But . . ."

"But what other choice will we have," I finished for him, "if we let him know where to find us?"

Carale nodded. "Somethin' like that, me lady."

"I intend for us to lie," I said. Carale immediately looked relieved. "We'll say we're scouting business prospects and it's rare gems I'm looking for in particular. Which will make us a rich prize, indeed. And then we'll simply say we're going southeast—but we'll go southwest instead. To the trading outposts."

This drew broad smiles. Most people like to think of themselves as potential masters of deceit if only given the chance. This is why they are such easy targets of truly cunning men and women. The thieves play on it, and their victims trip over their own artifice.

The story I'd concocted, however, was so simple that any of the men could carry it off during the brief stops I planned.

If all went well, the men would return home vastly pleased with themselves. And they'd have fat purses and broad boasts to boot.

Our first stop was Pisidia, the great trading center that sits just inside the Pillars of Te-Date and commands the entrance to the Straits of Madacar.

Pisidia was well-named. You could smell it many leagues before you arrived.

I first saw the Pillars of Te-Date on a pearly morn, the seas hissing gently between the great stone columns that reached so high it was easy to imagine they held up the vault of the sky. I knew that just through those columns was Pisidia, whose wide natural harbor made it a crossroads for all trade with the south. But that first view had been spoiled long before, when the stench of Pisidia's huge tanning vats crept in on the night winds.

It was that smell I'd had in mind when I made the counterattack on the pirates—an odor so foul that only sorcery could worsen it.

After the smell, the second thing you noticed about Pisidia was that it always seemed cloaked by massive swirling dark clouds. And the third was the low buzz that seemed to permeate the air, as if the clouds were alive.

To my disgust, I learned they actually *were*. The clouds were composed of huge swarms of flies that hover over the city as if it were a giant, sticky-faced child who'd gotten into her mother's jar of prized jam.

Pisidia was a raw town built of undressed logs from the thick pine forests that covered the mountains that framed it. It was roughly divided into four parts. There was the harbor area, around which were the docks, warehouses, and tall rickety tenements that housed most of the city's workforce. Those buildings leaned crazily over roadways so narrow that it was always dark at street level. To the left were the tanneries—columnlike log buildings where kettles the size of farm carts boiled and frothed and fumed all day and all night. In the yards surrounding each vat building were the places where raw hides were worked and the finished hides graded and bundled for shipment. To the right, on a gently rising palisade covered with gardens, were the plush homes and villas of the people who made their fortunes on all those smelly hides.

They were a pretentious lot with the bad taste of the newly rich, and I found their high and mighty ways amusing, since when the wind shifted, the air over all those gaudy, multicolored homes and landscaped flower gardens became as foul as what the common people breathe. But they didn't notice it. For to live amid such an awful smell was to become as accustomed to it as if the air were sweet as lily fields.

A lovely maid from one of those families once became enamored with me. She made certain that we "accidentally" encountered one another in the garden of the family home. And there she sat amid posies of stunning color in her most revealing costume. She was as dewy-eyed and willing a maid as I've ever encountered, giving me a large goblet of wine and bidding me to sit beside her, saying her family was off to the market that day and we were alone—other than the servants, of course.

Then she'd coyly offered me a flower whose delicate pink and white petals formed a most arousing shape. She blushed, but the blush became a coy giggle as she gave it to me, letting her robe fall open at the shoulder so I could get a peek at her plump milkmaid's breasts.

We flirted for a while, but the day warmed quicker than my passions, awakening all those flies from wherever they go to escape the cool of the night. Thick clouds of them took to the air, along with the tannery smells.

My love-to-be must've been shocked when my nose wrinkled at the odor. And she was probably wounded most grievously when she closed her eyes and puckered her lips for a kiss and I'd turned away at the sight of several flies alighting unnoticed at the corners of that tender mouth.

All I could think of were the heaps of maggots the Pisidians use to clean the rotted meat from the raw hides, which was the reason for all the flies that cloak the city. A fly's larvae is a wondrous creature, I suppose. Healers prize them as well as hide workers. Those ugly little wrigglers devour foul flesh and keep wounds free of infection. And I'll admit the gods should be praised rather than mocked for creating such things.

Still, the image of a maggot is not likely to stir romantic notions. All I could think of were great ugly piles of them squirming on some poor dead animal's skin. My stomach roiled and I quickly got up, made some feeble excuse or another . . . and fled.

Incidents like that tend to make one's life more chaste than a healthy woman would prefer. It might be good for the character, but it makes for many sleepless nights summing up regrets.

Once you get past the smell and rough manners of the Pisidians, however, you realize they are a sturdy lot, more honorable than most, and they have an independent frontier spirit. Their forebears were savage cattle herders who'd turned their skills at hide curing into a fortune. Anyone, no matter how poor the family, could become a person of means in Pisidia.

The port city was also the ideal starting point for my mission.

Once we'd docked, I left two men to guard our ship and set the others loose with a few extra coins in their purses to visit the taverns, spread our gem-hunters' tale, and gather what intelligence they could.

As for me, I planned to visit the Oracle of Pisidia.

It was not so well known then. The grand temple that sits on a windswept hill outside the city was in the early stages of construction. It was to be the only building made of stone for many leagues, and the shiploads of hides it took to finance the undertaking were said to be as numerous as the stars on a bright night. Thanks to the charity and guilt of Pisidia's newly rich families, the temple has become one of the most famous of its kind—dedicated to Te-Date. Supplicants from all over the southern regions visit there, heaping much gold into the temple's coffers to ask a boon or to get a glimpse of their fate.

When I visited that day, the temple was little more than a litter of rubble that workmen were beginning to mortar into the shape commanded by the architect's drawings.

It was late afternoon and only a few stonemasons were about. I pushed past a crew of burly men to the sprawling log edifice that housed the original temple and quarters for the Mother Oracle and her priestesses.

There were only five supplicants waiting their turn inside. Three were young women with swollen bellies—there, no doubt, to ask the Oracle some question regarding their unborn children. The other two were old and infirm. A young priestess attended them, taking each in turn to a black altar stone in the center of the temple. This is the Oracle Stone of Pisidia, a disappointment to many who see it for the first time. They expect some grand, gleaming ebony monolith, no doubt, instead of something so plain as a dark stone about the size of a large cartwheel.

A handsome, middle-aged woman—regal in the yellow, wide-sleeved robe and bejeweled tiara that marked her as the Mother Oracle—tended the faithful. As each approached she listened to their whispered request, nodded, or conferred further if it was necessary to get them to rephrase the question so it could be answered nay or yea.

A price was arrived at—based, I knew, on what the person could afford—and while the young priestess collected the money, the Mother Oracle prepared herself for the casting. When all was ready, the supplicant was handed a flat metal plate painted black on one side, white on the other.

I watched as a pregnant woman, not long out of her childhood herself, gripped the plate and stood trembling as she waited for what would happen next.

The Mother Oracle sprinkled magical herbs on the stone. It glowed into life and the dried herbs caught fire. Pale pink smoke with a pleasing odor whooshed up. The priestess waved a cupped hand slowly through the smoke, wafting it over the young woman several times, mumbling a swift prayer. Then she signaled and the young lady breathed deeply, braced herself, and tossed the plate as high as she could.

Her nervousness showed, for the plate nearly knocked against the ceiling timbers. Then it tumbled down—spinning slowly—and clattered to the floor. I saw the Mother Oracle bury a smile as the young woman saw the white side staring up at her and clapped her hands and squealed with delight. The almost smile shifted into an imperious frown as if she were displeased with such a display in a holy place. The girl stuttered an apology, whirled and fled.

She was grinning hugely, however, when she went past me, and I could see she was eager to tell the good news to her family and friends.

When my turn came, I was the last in the chamber. The little priestess bustled over to me, still full of youthful energy after many hours of tending the faithful.

"Come this way, please," she said. "Mother Daciar awaits."

The priestess was a pretty thing, with snapping black eyes and a coy smile. I'd caught her furtive looks of appreciation and knew she was intrigued.

I must admit I made a rather dashing figure that day. I was wearing a knee-length, dark blue tunic with matching tights. The sleeves were cut at the shoulder, displaying a fine silver shirt with billowy arms. A wide belt cinched my waist—an ornate dagger sheathed on one side, an empty sword scabbard on the other. I'd left that weapon with the bored guard outside the temple. High, tight-fitting boots encased my legs, which I'm vain enough to believe are long and shapely enough to wear such things. Setting the whole outfit off was my finest traveling cape, one side casually tossed back at the shoulder and held in place by a golden pin bearing the symbol of the House of Antero. I knew I looked every inch an adventurous young merchant, with adjustments and decorations here and there as befitted my sex, who relished the road and was open to new friends and experiences.

Before the priestess came to fetch me, I'd seen her adjust her robes to better show off her figure and poke her hair into place so a dark wave swept over a seductive eye.

It was good for my soul to see such a thing, and I couldn't help but give her a wink when she'd finished reciting her piece bidding me to come greet Mother Daciar.

When she saw my wink she blushed prettily and cupped a hand over her mouth to stifle a surprised giggle.

"I hope the Mother Oracle is patient with me," I said, low. "For one look at you and my question went right out of my mind."

The priestess wrinkled her nose in pretended displeasure. "Tsk. Such behavior, my lady. Remember where you are!"

I bowed and murmured an apology, which she pretended to ignore.

She laid a light hand on my arm and led the way as stiffly and properly as she could. But just as we reached the Oracle Stone she gave my arm a quick parting squeeze full of promise.

Mother Daciar's back was still to me when I stepped up. Before she turned to tend to the last supplicant of a long trying day, I saw her rub a weary knot in her shoulder. And I heard her sigh before she said:

"The Lord Te-Date greets thee, wayfarer. If thy cause be true, thy thoughts pure, He may bless thee this day with an answer to what troubles thee."

Quickly, before she raised her eyes, I answered, "Ask Him if you can close up shop early, Daciar, so I can buy you a drink."

She jumped, shocked. Then she saw me and her mouth gaped open in surprise. It snapped shut and her mouth wreathed into a wide smile of delight.

"By the red-arsed fires of the Hells," she growled in a low smoky voice, "if it isn't Rali Antero." She shot a guilty look at the stone, grimaced, then shrugged. "Sorry, O Great Lord Te-Date," she said. Then, to me, "Oh, well. I know He's heard worse."

"If not," I said, "I promise He will very soon if you don't fly away with me instantly to some place where the wine is strong and the will is weak. It's in the bylaws of the Soothsayers' Guild, don't you know? You get time off to sin every hundred years whether you need it or not."

Daciar laughed and embraced me. "You *are* a devil, Rali," she said. "And by the gods whose names we take in vain, I'm glad to see you."

Unfortunately, it wasn't possible, much less seemly, for the Holy Mother Oracle of Pisidia to adjourn to a tavern, low or high. Instead we climbed the several flights of stairs that led to the privacy of her rooms, where she had a good supply of strong drink.

Daciar was an innkeeper's daughter who'd been chosen for her current duties when she was a child. The Pisidians believe that when their Mother Oracle dies, her spirit lingers in the ethers until a suitable child comes along, then the spirit takes up residence in the infant's body shortly after birth.

Daciar was "discovered" by the Temple Elders when she was only ten summers old and was fully invested into office after two years of testing and training. She'd held the post for many years when we'd met, and was so hale and hearty that only accident or plague would keep her from reigning many more. Her people had gotten the best of the bargain, for not only had she proved to be an able soothsayer, she was also skilled in wizardry of all sorts. Among other things, she cast defensive spells to shield the entire city from evildoers. On my last visit we'd worked together to improve on those spells and had become fast friends in the process.

"I suppose it's a great honor to be the Mother Oracle," she'd confessed to me then. "But I still pine for the simple life I led at my family's inn. Those were great times and I was everyone's darling. I was dandled on knees, given sweets and gifts, and delightfully spoiled by one and all.

"I love people, Rali, I really do. And I miss meeting them as an equal on common ground. People look at me now and see the Holy Mother Daciar. When at heart I want to be nothing more than a bawdy wench with a jug to fill up your cup."

This is what she did soon as we'd retired to the privacy of her rooms and I'd sunk into the welcome softness of her old sofa.

The small chambers we were in were slightly shabby but quite comfortable, with all sorts of homey decorations and touches that showed Daciar's common origins: little idealized busts of her parents, such as the kind one has made by a market artist in a brief sitting; scraps of unfinished needlework from the times she felt she'd lost her way as a woman and so got her fingers busy doing "useful things to fill idle time," like her mother'd said was a good matron's duty.

An odd-shaped metal implement kept the pages open in her great Book of the Oracle, which was big enough to kill small demons, if necessary. The metal object, Daciar said, had been her father's favorite keg-broaching tool and she kept it to remember him by. There were dried flowers and herbs both common and magical poking out of pots and hanging by threads from the rafters. Incense burners of all sorts of sizes and shapes squatted here and there, with little sacks of incense of every variety to burn in them. A few pictures of pretty scenes, hung just a little off kilter since she had a weak eye on one side.

A few of her distinctive, wide-sleeved yellow robes were hung from hooks within easy reach of an old porcelain hip bath. And there was a nearby shelf littered with vials of perfumed bath oils and sudsy additives. Next to the tub was a stool pushed up to a mirrored stand for her brushes and cosmetics. On the opposite side of the room was a large fireplace with a broad mantel decorated with a few stuffed, faded-faced dolls from her childhood, as well as a little clockwork device that a copper coin set in motion.

It always made me laugh to see it work. I'd put a coin in the slot, usually good Antero copper with a ship engraved on one side and the sign of the House of Antero on the other. Soon as the coin clicked into place, a fat farmwife would burst out of the little house, pursuing a squealing piglet with an axe. There was an inscription on the base of the toy that read: "It'll be just a minute before dinner, dear."

I thought it was funny. But I suppose I'm too easily amused.

Heaped among all this friendly clutter were books of all sorts: light romances and adventure, poetry and histories and philosophy, and thick technical manuals inscribed with sorcerous symbols.

Just to the side of the crackling fireplace was a curtain of many colors that hid an alcove entirely taken up by a great feather bed.

There were grander quarters attached to the room, her official residence, which was where Daciar received important people and conducted business. Only close friends were allowed to see her here at her untidy ease.

After she'd gotten us our drinks, Daciar plucked off her tiara, unpinned her hair—letting it fall in silver waves over her shoulders—and plumped down in an overstuffed chair across from me. Her yellow robe rode up over her still fine thighs as she stretched out her legs and plopped her feet on the table.

Then she raised her cup in a toast. "Here's to the first of the day," she said, "except for breakfast, which doesn't count, and lunch, which doesn't matter."

It was the cheeriest first gulp I'd taken in many a day. I settled back in the sofa, warm all over from such friendly surroundings.

We chatted aimlessly for a time, emptying one cup and getting a good start into another. Then I told her the purpose of my visit. She listened closely as I described my encounter with the pirates and how the magical music had almost caught me out.

"Except for the ancient tales, my dear, I know nothing of this Ice Bear fellow," she said when I was done. "And I haven't heard of more pirate attacks on merchant ships than usual. Perhaps he's only causing trouble in the regions you visited. If that's so, he's just a local bandit and shouldn't give you much difficulty."

I wanted to believe this. I wanted very much to think that when we sailed to Antero Bay and the other outpost, all would be well. If necessary I could raise a force of sufficient strength from the people I had at the trading posts, pursue the false Ice Bear King, and put paid to his pretensions. But if he were just a nuisance who could be dealt with so easily, why would the Goddess Maranonia have appeared to me and warned that Orissa was in grave danger?

Daciar, who was skilled at reading emotions behind people's masks, caught an inkling of my doubts. "There's something else, isn't there, my dear?" she asked. "Something you haven't told me."

"Yes," I admitted. "But I've been sworn to silence."

"Still," she said, "I flatter myself when I think you want my advice. Only you don't know quite how to go about it."

"That, my dear friend," I answered, "is exactly my dilemma."

Daciar frowned, pondering. Then her brow cleared. She went to the fireplace mantel, mumbled as she dug through the toys and books and flower vases, and finally came up with a large crystal goblet etched with pentagrams and other wizardly marks. She blew the dust off, polished it with her sleeve, and fetched it back.

She stopped midway. "Wait," she said. "I'll need some blessing water. I tell you, Rali dear, sometimes I don't know where my head is when I try to put on my tiara in the morning."

She found a clay jug. She sniffed the contents, wrinkled her nose and declared them to be "blessed enough."

Finally she returned to her chair and sat down. "Let's see what I can learn without violating your oath," she said.

Daciar placed the goblet and water jug on the table, which was draped by an old cloth with faded designs that still pleased the eye. She had me swirl some of the red wine in my mouth and spit it into the goblet, which she quickly filled with blessing water.

She put her hands just above the glass, closed her eyes and chanted:

"Cast the light
On secrets near and far.
Show the path of Mind and Heart.
See the message
The tongue cannot form
And lips cannot speak."

The rosy liquid swirled. Shapes emerged and I leaned closer to look. Daciar, whose eyes were still closed, sensed the motion and waved me away.

Just as I moved back, the liquid shot out of the glass, twisting madly about like a water spout. The scent of blooming roses filled the room. My body tingled with magical force and I felt a soft pressure on my temples like ghostly fingers.

I heard Daciar moan and suck in a sharp breath.

Suddenly the water column vanished and the scent and tingling feeling were gone.

Daciar opened her eyes. "That ought to do it well enough," she said.

She took a quick gulp of her drink, then rubbed her hands together, smiling. "No wonder you were so button-lipped, Rali dear," she said. "You've had a visit from a god."

I almost frowned, giving it away, but she raised a warning hand.

"Don't react to anything I say, dear," she advised. "Otherwise you'll breach your sworn oath. I saw very little. The way was blocked by the holy presence that came to you. I know it was a god, or goddess. Probably not Te-Date, or I'd have sniffed him out. I've dealt with Him most of my life and know his spoor.

"Guessing, not sorcery, tells me it was a goddess who appeared before you ... probably the Holy One you worship—Maranonia."

As I marveled at the results of this rich combination of soothsaying and long experience, Daciar closed her eyes again to concentrate. Then she opened them. This time, however, she didn't smile, but looked quite worried.

"I see much danger," she said. "And I don't think it's only for you and your people. What that danger is I can't say. The good news—I think—is that I also see three ships that may be your salvation. One of copper, one of gold, and finally, one of silver."

Maranonia hadn't put them in that order—she'd said silver, copper, and then gold—but at the time I thought it was only a small slip in Daciar's otherwise perfect casting.

"I also see a bird of some sort," she continued. "I don't know why this bird is important, but it is."

This was new. Maranonia hadn't mentioned birds—or any other creature for that matter.

"There's also a woman," she went on. "A beautiful woman. No, two. One is royalty . . . and one is not. I don't know if either means you harm. But be advised, neither woman is from this world."

Daciar broke off. She remained silent for a long time, staring at me intently. Then she winced and her features paled. She reached out a trembling hand and touched my right cheek. I sat quite still as she explored it, moving hesitantly to my eye. Her hand lowered slowly and touched my left wrist. Her fingers lingered there, then she slowly drew them back.

Tears welled in her eyes.

"I fear you'll be hurt," she said, voice cracking with emotion. "I'm so sorry, Rali."

I pretended indifference although my heart panged with sharp-edged fear. "I've been hurt before," I said. "So long as I live . . . what does it matter?"

"I can't promise that, Rali," Daciar said. "I wish I could. I wish I could look deeper. But the path, as I said, is barred."

"I wouldn't want to know either way," I replied. I meant those words at the time, foolish mortal that I am. "If I die, so be it. I made my peace with the Dark Seeker when I joined my sisters of the Guard."

"I wish I could advise you to turn back, my dear," Daciar said. "And avoid whatever pain it is you must face. But I don't think you have any choice."

I shrugged. "That's the way of it, then," I said. "But tell me this if you can: Will the Ice Bear King be my chief foe? Or is he just someone I have to deal with on the way?"

"I don't know," she replied. "It's been my general reading of late that these are troubled times with all sorts of strange disturbances in the Otherworlds."

My eyebrows arced in surprise. "Oh, really? Strange in what way? Things in Orissa are quite normal, if there is such a state. I've had no trouble with my own sorcery, and none of our magical colleagues have mentioned any difficulties to me."

Daciar chuckled. "Your powers are so great, Rali," she said, "that I sometimes forget how new you are to all this. Of course they wouldn't say anything to you. We're a suspicious and envious breed at heart and we're reluctant to admit our troubles to another mage.

"As for your own difficulty-free experience—why, you are an Antero. And unless my poor wits have fled me, I'm certain the Anteros are the reason for the disturbances. All kinds of things have been frothing up from the spiritual vats since you and your brother came along. It's as if a thousand little cages were opened and mean little things have been scurrying out."

"Like that demon who was slave to the pirate?" I asked.

"I suspect so," Daciar said.

"I'm sorry if we've been the cause of so much trouble," I said.

"Don't be," Daciar replied. "There isn't a wizard in the whole civilized world who doesn't owe you and your brother a debt. We know so much more than we did only a few years ago. It's as if we all woke up one day and realized we'd been blind and brainless the day before. Like the light of understanding that strikes a child and lifts her into awareness."

She said this so sincerely that I couldn't help but feel better.

We chatted on about lesser things after that, exchanging the wine for a fine brandy that cleared the mind of cares and stoked mischief in the body.

"So tell me, Rali," Daciar said, a little of that mischief dancing in her eyes, "how goes the search for the love of your life? Have you found her at long last?"

I grimaced. "I don't even have a decent chart for such things," I said. "To tell the truth, I've just about given up. I've had nothing but foul luck in love since—" I broke off. I didn't want to trot the painful memory of Otara out. She'd been my lover of many years and I'd never gotten over her death.

Daciar, who knew me so well, leaped gracefully over the uncomfortable silence as if it didn't exist.

"Well, you must have had an adventurous affair of some sort," she said. "Come. Tell me all. I could use a sexy tale or two to take the chill from my dreams."

I laughed. "There's been one or two," I admitted.

"Only one or two?" Daciar scoffed. "Where have you been hiding yourself, woman? Why, there must be any number of nubile young things who'd dare all to share your bed."

She laughed. It was a delightful, bawdy sound. "I saw my assistant looking you over. Ilana would think herself blessed by the Goddess of Love if you gave her a tumble. As a matter of fact, why don't I ask her to join us for a drink? And see if you two strike the sparks I think you will?"

"Please, don't," I said. "I admit I found her attractive. I even flirted a bit. No harm in that. But I'm in no frame of mind for any encumbrances just now. And unless I'm very wrong, young Ilana wouldn't be satisfied with anything but complete victory.

"Besides," I continued, "she looks so . . . *energetic*! I couldn't bear all the wriggling about. I'd probably start laughing."

I didn't feel like laughing inside. A sudden loneliness gripped me, but I smiled as broadly as I could so as not to spoil the cheer we'd both created.

But Daciar wasn't fooled. She shook her head and said, quite low, "Poor Rali. All she wants is a little tenderness."

I didn't answer. Instead I found myself looking at Daciar with new eyes. She was perhaps fifteen years my senior. She had fine skin, white and smooth as parchment. Her eyes were large, nearly violet in color, and they seemed to burn softly, like the coals of a carefully banked fire. She'd let her hair down and it was long-flowing waves of silver. She still wore her yellow robes of office, which were made of silk and clung to a soft round figure that I suddenly wanted badly to caress.

My mouth became dry. I was afraid to speak, for my thoughts were far from pure.

Daciar looked at the curtained alcove, then back at me. The coals that were her eyes burned deeper. She rose and drifted over to me like a cloud, taking my hand and drawing me up. I could smell her perfume—hot and lemony like a mulled drink.

"Come, Rali dear," she said.

And she led me to her downy bed.

It was a night of dreams, a night of quiet magic.

Daciar coaxed all the tension from my body, massaging each toe, then working up slowly and carefully, paying close attention to every kink and twist. I became like warm wax under her hands, helpless in my blissful state to do anything but moan and turn this way and that as she commanded.

Then she made love to me, carrying us both off to shaded glades in sunny lands. Afterward we cuddled and caressed for a time, and when we'd recovered, we made love again. I think I called out Otara's name once, but

Daciar only held me tighter and whispered gentle praises, so I knew she didn't mind. When we were exhausted, I fell asleep in her arms.

Daciar had given me a gift worth all the gold in the coffers of the gods.

I awoke just at dawn to the sweet sound of a lyre playing somewhere off in the distance. As I lay there letting the waves of music wash over me, I realized I'd been listening to it for a long time.

It was a most familiar melody.

Then I heard the blast of a great war trumpet. Then bells tolled the alarm. As I leaped up I heard shrieks.

The city was being attacked.

CHAPTER FOUR

THE WARRIOR GIANTS

I leaped naked from the bed, scrabbled madly for my dagger—the only weapon I had—and ran to the window.

We were several flights above the temple grounds, and the window commanded a good view of the harbor and the road that wound up the hilltop to the temple. A cold wind blew in and I shivered. But it wasn't from the sudden chill.

In the harbor was a ship of such size that I became confused for a moment as I wondered how something so far away could seem so large. Fear iced my veins when I fully understood that only giants could sail such a thing.

My mind reeled and then the sounds of fighting drew my eyes to the dockyards. Three immense warriors towered over what had to be a hundred Pisidian soldiers. The giants wore helms and heavy armor and wielded swords with blades as wide as a man and twice as long. The Pisidians were bravely trying to crowd in and overwhelm the giants.

The three huge warriors suddenly charged the soldiers, and many men fell in that furious but disciplined onslaught. Despite their success, the giants didn't seem willing to take advantage of their attack and soon fell back to hold their original ground.

Then I noted a longboat the size of a normal ship drawn up near the shore. It was manned and defended by four other giants. I quickly counted ten double oars and knew there were at least thirteen more enemy warriors on the loose.

I felt Daciar's presence. She'd come up behind me to see what was happening. We watched the scene in silence for a few moments, gathering up our will and our wits. The wind blew colder. Daciar handed me a robe and I fumbled it on, tucking my hands into the deep sleeves. Then I saw the enemy ship's banner stiffen in the same wind.

On it was the sign of the Ice Bear King.

The cold and the sight of that flag seemed to sharpen my wits, and I quickly sorted through a jumbled mass of thoughts and questions.

How had the giants broken through Daciar's magical shield? The lyre music was the answer to that. Which meant, as I'd feared, that there was more sorcery behind the pirate chief than the one little demon whom I'd so easily dispatched.

Why hadn't we slept on, then, blissful slaves to the sorcerous tunes? The answer was simple. Daciar's spells diluted the power of the lyre's assault. Which meant this was magic I could fight and hope to overcome.

Next question: What was the giants' purpose? Take the city? From what I'd seen, that was unlikely. With twenty men ashore, a longboat held in readiness, and a waiting ship, the goal must be something they hoped to achieve quickly before making an equally fast escape. But what could that goal be? The answer came immediately.

I heard screams just below us, then bellowed orders from the roadway. Great mailed figures trotted up the road and then onto the broad hilltop.

The giants were attacking the temple.

There were thirteen. One of the massive creatures dropped back to block the roadway with his steely bulk. He bestrode the breadth of the path, shield held chin high, sword raised. He thundered insults at the Pisidian soldiers who'd followed the group up the hill.

The others trooped up to the building we were in, fanning out as they came.

There were only two temple guards. After all, who would attack such a holy place? The guards were old men; I don't know whether you might consider them heroes or fools, for despite the odds, they immediately trotted out to face the giants.

They fought as well as they could. And they died as well as they could. I think of them sometimes. I recall that scene vividly. Two men decades past their prime wearing a few pieces of hastily pulled on armor moving forward briskly in the path of the enemy's advance. Their duty commanded them to confront a force that was obviously overwhelming. But they did not hesitate. When all seems hopeless to me, when the odds seem insurmountable, I draw

strength from the image of those gray warriors tossing Fate's dice and knowing as they did so that those ivory cubes had been altered. In our childhood
myths their bravery and honor would be rewarded by the gods. Somehow the
giants would be toppled, the warriors spared, the temple saved.

That's not how it turned out.

The heroes died swiftly and with little effort on the part of the villains.
And the only reward the old soldiers got was an easier afterlife for their
ghosts.

As the old men fell and bled, the door to the room burst open and the
frightened priestesses crowded in, crying for Daciar to save them.

She was barefooted, wearing only a yellow robe like the one she'd given
me, and her silver hair was tousled from sleep. But I never saw such a serene
and regal figure as Daciar made when the pleading women pressed in all
around her.

She drew herself up and thundered: "Silence!"

And there was silence.

She gestured to Liana. "Get me my tiara!"

Liana rushed to obey, the women drawing back to make a path.

Daciar held the jeweled tiara high, offering it to the heavens. I felt a rush
of energy flow past as she summoned magical strength—commanding full
powers as the Mother Oracle. Then she carefully placed the tiara on her head
and the flow steadied, then enveloped her until she seemed a fortress.

She flung up her hands to cast a spell. The motion in the ethers was like
the passage of a great creature through the seas, and I felt my sorcerous self
rocked by the heavy, shifting currents.

Just as she was about to hurl the spell, a sudden fist of knowledge
struck me.

"Daciar, wait!" I cried.

Daciar was a gentle wizard who'd served her people well for many
years. An enthusiastic scholar, she was a font of knowledge on magical theory, but her practice had been limited to goodly acts performed for the faithful. She was like a talented Healer who'd devoted her life to the care of
families and common people with common ailments. That Healer might
know much about the killing plagues that sometimes sweep our lands. She
might even have studied defenses and strategies of Healers who'd faced those
plagues in the past. But the difference between knowing a thing and actually
encountering it is like the wide gulf of difference between a kitchen knife and
a broadsword.

Daciar had never experienced war. Never cast a spell in anger, or defended a counterattack, or considered the duplicity of a canny enemy who'd
come to kill. But I had. And I sensed the danger as she cast the spell. She

hurled it with as much force as any I'd witnessed on the battlefields. It was a classic spell, so perfectly faceted that I was in awe of its clean edges and wondrous angles. No Master Wizard, not even Janos Greycloak, could have cast it better. But my admiration was shattered when I saw what the classic counter would be.

My warning shout came too late.

The giants bellowed in pain as Daciar's spell buffeted them. But then her spell blasted back with such fury—the force doubled—that my senses shriveled from the heat.

Daciar screamed and collapsed to the floor.

As the priestesses cried out, I saw a thin trickle of blood leak from the corner of Daciar's lips. She did not move as the women covered her with their bodies and wept.

A giant's voice thundered through the window. "All of you! In the temple! We mean you no harm. We come for the Mother Oracle. Send her out to us at once. Send her out and you will be spared!"

The giant's command brought a hush to the room. The priestesses looked at one another, eyes shifting from face to face. I could feel their fury grow, their common resolve becoming as strong as the roots of a mighty tree. These women would not betray their Oracle. They would not give her up even if she were only a corpse.

I had to act fast.

I pushed my way to Daciar's side. No one said anything as I knelt by her body. The women seemed to understand what I was up to and made no protest when I removed her tiara.

Before I put it on I leaned down and kissed her lips. They were warm, and I hoped and prayed that it was a faint breath I felt when our lips touched.

The giant shouted again. "Send her out, I said. Send us Mother Daciar. Or you'll all die."

I went to the window and leaned out.

The brutes had come closer and we were nearly at eye level. I found myself staring into the huge eyes of their captain.

"I am Mother Daciar," I said. "I am the Mother Oracle." And then I turned away from the window and began my preparations.

I felt like a lamb being led to market as the giants trotted me down the hill in the robes and tiara of the Mother Oracle of Pisidia.

I was alone with them. In Daciar's name I'd ordered the Pisidian soldiers to withdraw, warning that I'd be killed if they made one move to assist me. The roadway was empty, but I could hear shutters being drawn and feel people look out to catch a glimpse of the sad parade.

I felt helpless walking in those massive shadows. You can't imagine how huge they seemed. It wasn't only their length and breadth and weight that was overwhelming. Their smells were strong. Fouler even than the stench of Pisidia. Their stomachs rumbled with digestive gasses, and I could hear the semiliquid contents bumping about like carcass soup in an iron kettle. Their breath wailed in and out like the winds through a sea cave.

When they scratched their greasy waist-length beards, I imagined I saw gray scurrying things of frightening size flee their probing.

The captain caught one between his meaty fingers. There was an audible snap as he cracked it with his filthy nails, and I thought I saw blood gush out. He poked his fingers through his drooping mustaches and sucked them clean of the creature's remains.

He belched loudly, then said, "I likes how you walks, little mother. Betcha got somethin' under them robes that'd make a good meal."

The others cackled. The sound was like ice floes grating together.

"Whyn't we take a look see?" said another. "Got a gold piece she's gotta gash that'd do a regiment of pikemen."

"I got two says she's blond all over," said a third.

"She'll strip nice, that's for sure," said the captain. "Too bad she's so small. Won't last through maybe four or five of us."

I reacted to none of this, concentrating on nothing more than setting one foot before the other. Their crude remarks grew fouler, more explicit, more violent. I couldn't let it bother me. They wanted to humiliate me. Shame me. Bring me more under their power.

I wished I were Polillo. She was strong. She could hate. She'd have shriveled their pricks with her replies. She'd have dared them to drop their breeches, and swear she'd rip off their balls and make them her supper.

And I thought, Polillo, ah my friend, how I miss you. How I wish you were with me now.

And I chanted, low:

> "Ghost. Sweet Ghost.
> Live in me now.
> Leave your spectral home
> And abide with your friend
> Who loves you.
> Come fill me up,
> My Polillo."

She came into me. I felt Polillo's presence swell my veins, thicken my bones, make steel bands of my muscles. I laughed and it was Polillo's laugh.

Bawdy and deep. I rolled my shoulders and felt the rippling of Polillo's strength. I stomped my foot with berserker's glee. And the ground quaked with Polillo's weight.

"Here now, what're you up to?" the giant captain said.

His massive paw engulfed my neck and turned me about.

I made myself demure. "Why, nothing, sir," I sobbed. I made myself tremble and shed a tear or two. "I only stumbled, that's all."

"We just got her all excited, Cap'n," one of his companions said. "Got her knees tremblin' thinkin' of all of us between 'em."

The captain guffawed and let me go. "You won't have to wait long, little mother," he said. He pointed at the crumbled stone seawall where the long-boat and its giant guards waited. It was only a hundred steps away. "Not long at all. You got my promise on that."

Polillo's ghost growled, but I kept her rage in check. I cast a professional eye on the battered seawall. It curved along the shore, sometimes sweeping out so far that parts of the beach were hidden from the longboat's view. If I'd had time, I could have hidden some soldiers in one of those loops. I studied the varied height of the wall, saw the places where it presented an easy climbing surface.

I did all this quite coolly—more of a military woman's intellectual study than anything. For I no longer feared these creatures. They wouldn't harm me. Not yet. They were under orders to take me somewhere, to someone. No, not me. Not Rali Antero. But Daciar. The Mother Oracle.

But why?

By whose orders?

And how long could I maintain this mask?

Polillo's ghost said, "Don't go, Rali."

She was right.

So I let her loose.

The captain pushed me toward the boat and I pretended to stumble again. But as I fell forward I pivoted, recovered, then ran for the highest point of the seawall. I heard the giants bellow alarm and rumble after me, their mail making an ungodly clatter.

Polillo's strength powered my limbs and I bounded up the wall effortlessly. When I reached the top, I dug in my toes to stop.

I caught a glimpse of a startled face staring at me. It was only a quick snatch, but the image froze for a moment. It was an ugly face. A skinny face. Bald of pate and chin. A long pink tongue flickered out in surprise.

It was Lizard.

Then I saw the shadows of the rest of my men swarming up to me.

But I was already fully committed to my next action. As my toes jammed against the stone, momentum carried the rest of my body forward. I swung my arms in the same direction to heighten and control that motion. Polillo's ghost grunted with effort and my legs were powerful springs that absorbed all weight and all speed.

Then I was somersaulting backward. Turning in the air, then stiffening my legs until they were like driving dock poles.

I hit the captain square and we both went over, his armor sounding like a huge collapsing machine of many parts.

He roared in pain and fury. Polillo's ghost wanted me to stop and choke off that sound and break his damned neck. But I sensed an oncoming presence and kept rolling.

I sprang to my feet just in front of an attacking giant. He threw himself back in surprise like a rooting boar that snuffs out a mouse and then fears it'll burrow into his nose.

Polillo's ghost laughed and made me slam down my foot and crush his toes. As he screamed, I leaped up, grabbed his beard, and booted myself away like a sailor kicking off a mast.

I clung to his beard, swinging back just as far as I could, then slammed in—hard.

My feet skidded off an armored thigh and clubbed into the softness it found just to the side.

By the gods, I made it a good kick. A kick for Polillo.

His howl made a lovely sound, my sisters. It started low in that grumbling and grunting place where the beasts strut about and fart between thick, bowed legs. And it ended falsetto high in a tone so piercing that if the heavens were glass they would've shattered.

The memory still cheers me.

But there wasn't time to savor it then. The others were nearly upon me. And their captain had recovered, thundering for them to step aside as he charged forward to cleave me in two with his massive blade.

I should have died then. I should have gone the way of those two old temple warriors. I cursed for not being able to complete my too-hastily drawn plan. And braced for that final blow.

Dark shapes whistled past and a small cloud of arrows struck the captain full in the face.

He screamed and clawed at his face, then screamed again and jerked his hands away. Several arrows protruded from each eye.

As he crumpled, my men burst into the melee. I couldn't help but feel pride. My men shouted wild, bloodcurdling war cries. But there was nothing wild or unruly in their attack.

There were seven of them. The twins and Lizard engaged one giant, dodging and slashing and covering one another whenever a man saw an opening. Donarius and two others took on a second of the armored creatures, while Captain Carale dispatched the giant I'd kicked and ran over to stand beside me and fight. I heard sounds of combat from the shore and knew the rest of my men were taking on the longboat guards.

As proud as I felt, I knew the giants would soon recover from this surprise, regroup, and then easily overwhelm us.

I shouted to Carale, "Help the others."

He whirled and sprinted to the melee at the longboat.

I needed time . . . just a little time.

I knelt and placed Daciar's tiara on the ground. Then I drew her clockwork toy from my sleeve and set it within the jeweled ring.

The little farmhouse with its closed door seemed puny and childish against the sounds of the battle raging about me. But it was all I'd had time to prepare.

I fetched the coin out of my sleeve. It was a good copper Antero coin. I kissed the image of the ship, breathed a prayer to Maranonia, then placed the coin in the slot.

My thoughts skittered about, searching for the proper spell. But my mind went maddeningly blank. I had to slip past the enemies' sorcerous shield, otherwise whatever spell I made would be flung back at me and I'd suffer the same fate as Daciar.

The chant I formed would have to use such innocent words that they'd never be noticed by my opponent. Then a child's rhyme leaped into my mind. I didn't examine it, worry over it, but quickly whispered the words as they formed in my head . . .

"Piggy, piggy, what did you do?
Piggy, piggy, shame on you.
Ate the cream, ate the butter, then
You ate the cat.
Hold still little piggy while I
Give you a whack.
Then I'll stuff you with dumplings
And fry you in fat."

I let the coin fall.

There was a mechanical whirl, and I jumped up as the door burst open and the farmwife came rushing out waving her toy axe over her head.

Instead of running after the piglet, she ran to the end of the toy's painted platform. She didn't hesitate at the edge, but leaped off, her tiny legs carrying her toward the battle.

I made a motion and she grew larger. I motioned again and she became larger still, ballooning bigger and bigger until she was the size of the giants.

She shouted at the brutes, and the shout was like the heavens erupting. But instead of a war cry it was my little rhyme:

"PIGGY, PIGGY, WHAT DID YOU DO?"

The giants were momentarily frozen by the howling apparition.

The huge toy farmwife cackled maniacally, waving an axe the size of a shed. Her voluminous skirts rustled like the winds as she ran. Her eyes bulged huge in that painted face and her fixed grin was so gleeful that it was horrifying.

"PIGGY, PIGGY, SHAME ON YOU!" roared the farmwife. And then she was in their midst, chopping this way and that.

There was no stopping her relentless, untiring, mechanical fury. The giants squealed in terror like massive pigs. One was split in two. Another had his arm lopped off. I saw a huge, hairy head struck from brawny shoulders.

The farmwife rushed about at blinding speed, leaving a river of gore in her wake. The slaughter continued down to the longboat, where the giant guards were soon dispatched.

Then we all stood, stunned by the horror of all that spilled blood, as the farmwife leaped into the sea and began churning toward the giants' ship.

"HOLD STILL LITTLE PIGGY . . ." she cried, speeding toward the enemy vessel like a ship of war, ". . . WHILE I GIVE YOU A WHACK!"

I can't imagine what was going through the minds of the giants aboard the ship when they saw the immense toy coming at them. I prayed that whatever those thoughts were, chaos would reign over all. I felt sorcery crackling in the air and I knew I had them.

A huge ball of magical fire lofted up from the enemy ship. I could smell the sulfur and evil intent from across the distance.

I chanted:

> "I summon the summoned,
> I curse the becursed.
> I cast back the spear.
> Mirror into mirrored
> And mirrored once more."

And I shouted:
"Be done!"

The fireball struck the huge toy, and all disappeared into a vast steamy mist as the sea boiled and frothed.

The surface suddenly became so calm and so smooth that you'd think nothing had happened—that it'd all been the work of a fevered imagination. Then the water bulged as a shape rose up like a ship rising from the deep. It was no ship that appeared, but the sister to the fireball that had been hurled. It hissed and steamed and shot off sparks as it broke through.

The fireball hovered for long seconds, then blasted back the way it'd come. I heard the giants shout the alarm as they realized what had happened. The alarm echoed into hysterical bellows when the remainder of the crew became dimly aware that all was lost.

Then all the sounds that living things make when they're desperate to remain in that state were drowned out as the fireball struck and an explosion rocked the ship.

Flames gouted up from the deck, then ran up the masts and the ratlines, and then the sails caught fire. Some tried to fight it. Others ran for the sides.

But the inferno cut them off and the air was filled with screams of pain.

Then the screams died off and all we could hear was the rumbling of the raging fire. Smoke columned up as the ship burned down to the waterline. It sank with a long slow hiss that could be heard to the very hills.

And all became still except the whistle of the wind and the low crash of the waves.

A few days later I visited with Daciar in her chamber. She looked frail and weak under the covers, still suffering from the sorcerous blast that had felled her. But the bright gleam in her eyes showed she was recovering.

She sent her attendants away so we'd be alone. And then we embraced one another, sobbing all those things people say when they're glad to see that their friend still lives after a great catastrophe.

When emotions had settled, I wet her lips with a sponge soaked in wine. I'd mixed a restorative remedy of wine and magical herbs and was rewarded by color returning to her cheeks.

"Do you know why this happened, Rali?" she asked.

I shook my head. "I haven't the vaguest notion," I admitted. "I've thought long enough on it while you were lying abed. But I keep coming up with more questions than I started out with.

"We know the giants carried the banner of the Ice Bear King, so he must be responsible. We know the giants came specifically for you. And that they'd been ordered to deliver you to some person or persons. Perhaps even the Ice Bear King himself. We can only speculate. With little to base it on."

"Perhaps the enemy thought that without me, Pisidia would be help-less," Daciar said. "And that a large army could march in and take over with little resistance."

"I've thought of that," I said. "It seems the most likely explanation. It wouldn't be unusual for a pirate to get grand ideas, declare himself king, and then set out to seize himself a kingdom to reign over."

"It's so obvious," Daciar said with a smile, "that you don't think it's the case."

"Not entirely," I said. "Otherwise they'd have tried to kill you instead of take you captive."

"But what purpose could I serve?" she asked.

"My only guess," I said, "is that they wanted your power. That some-how they have—or believe they have—the means to tap your abilities to achieve their own aims."

Daciar snorted. "It can't be done," she said. "It's been tried many times in wizardly history. You can make a spell to reverse a spell. To turn it back on your attacker. Which is what happened to me. And I still feel like a fool. But you can't steal magical power. You can't even get it as a willing gift."

"As far as I know," I agreed, "that is the way of things. But who can say for certain? Magic is old but the laws are new. Only since Greycloak have such things been actually tested."

Daciar nodded. She could see my point. Before Janos Greycloak, all spells and magic were handed down from generation to generation. No one questioned the whys and wherefores. Faith was the rule, not reason.

"Pisidia's leaders and generals are meeting now," she said, "to determine what should be done.

"Tomorrow, if I'm well enough, I will add my counsel to the confused hysteria that is going on right now. Tell me, Rali dear, what do you think should be done?"

"I have no right to say," I answered. "It is your homeland that's been vi-olated. Only you and your people know how much you're willing to risk.

"Does revenge need to be exacted? If so, what blood price are you will-ing to pay for revenge or to make certain others don't think you've grown weak and are open to attack?"

Daciar took this in, then said, "My advice will be to wait and see. To arm ourselves and do all we can to be ready for another invasion. But to seek more information before we act."

"That sounds the wisest course to me," I said.

"What will you do, Rali dear?"

"Simple," I said. "My mission was to see how great a threat this Ice Bear King was. Now I know. It's very great. I don't have to sail all over the

Southern Sea to prove that. But is that threat great enough to warrant action from Orissa? From our perspective he's far away.

"I think, like you, I'll advise my brother to wait and see what develops."

"So you'll return home immediately?" she asked.

"Not immediately," I said. "First I'm going directly to the outposts. I can't leave my people in such danger. I'll lift them off, abandon the trading centers to the Ice Bear King if need be, and get back to Orissa as fast and safely as I can."

Daciar smiled. "Such a cautious woman," she said.

I laughed. "My old sergeant didn't used to think so," I said. "She'd lash into me for being such a hotheaded child that some enemy was sure to take it off someday. I didn't listen. Probably because only *my* head was at stake."

Daciar asked me the particulars of my confrontation with the giants and the spell I'd used to overcome them.

"When I was told you'd used one of my toys from girlhood," she said when I was done, "I thought my priestesses had been getting into the wine lockers again. But now I know it's true. And how fitting an end for those creatures." She hugged herself in delight. Then she asked, "What coin did you use to operate the toy?"

"I told you. An Antero copper piece."

"With a ship on it?" she asked.

"Yes, of course," I said. "With a ship on it."

I was confused, wondering why she was impressing this point on me.

Then I realized . . . Maranonia had seen three ships in my future. One of gold, one silver, and one of . . . copper! A copper ship. Like the one on the coin.

Daciar grinned, but didn't push for more, not wanting to endanger my vow of silence. Nothing forbade me from smiling back. She could read into that smile what she liked. And Daciar would read it correctly. Of that I had no doubts.

We talked a little while longer, but then I could see she was tiring and needed to rest. I dabbed more of the restorative on her lips and left the bottle with her for future treatment.

Then we kissed good-bye, whispering little endearments and each urging the other to take great care.

I left the next day.

And I never saw her again.

CHAPTER FIVE

ANTERO BAY

We flew south on fair winds, beneath a sky so blue you'd never know there could be misery under it.

I had countless worries to gnaw on, not the least of which was the safety of our friends at the outposts. My mind frothed with foul possibilities of what might be ahead. But for a time the brisk winds and clear skies kept me off those moody reefs.

There *were* glad tidings to consider. We'd only suffered a few scrapes and bruises in the encounter with the giants, and my men were in high spirits, going about their work with such good cheer that it was infectious.

It was an easy affliction for me to catch. I don't tend to be a brooder. I take life in stride—chart my course for the worst but pray for the best, and let the casting bones fall as they may. For who can really say what the heavens have in store for us? Beware of any Evocator who claims otherwise.

As a wise woman once said, "You want to hear the gods laugh? Tell them your plans."

Life can be good at sea. It's on land where human troubles dwell: a quarrelsome mate, disobedient children, idle relatives, and nagging debt. At sea those troubles are either behind you or ahead of you and there's naught you can do about them until you hail the next port, so what's the point of worrying?

I remember one day in particular during that voyage, when the sea was as clear as the skies. It was like sailing through air, with only the fish below and the birds above to give you any sense of which way was which. We'd shaken out the kinks of land, stowed all that was to be stowed, and had a good fish dinner tucked under our ribs to steady us.

I broke out the grog, a hearty broth made in the Sweet Cane Islands in the west, and passed a good measure around.

A drink or so later Donarius got out his pipes and the twins entertained us with a jig while he played a merry tune. I clapped in time with the rest, delighted to find myself so much at ease in their company.

But the great surprise came when Lizard burst into song. Now as far as looks go, Lizard was not the most pleasing of Te-Date's creations. I'd always imagined Our Lord Te-Date's attention must've wandered when Lizard was squeezed from the common clay. And He kept squeezing and squeezing until He had something so long and skinny there was little room to attach legs and arms—and so smooth that hair wouldn't stick. But as strange as Lizard looked, stranger still was his voice, which proved to be the most melodious baritone I'd ever heard in my life.

I remember my surprise as well as I remember the words of Lizard's bawdy sailor's song:

> "She was the fairest young maid in Orissa.
> So heave, heave me boys, heave.
> She charged a copper each time that I kissed her.
> She said, heave, heave me boy, heave.

> I kissed her high, I kissed her low.
> Heave, heave me boys, heave.
> I kissed her tits, I kissed her toes.
> Crying, heave, heave me boys, heave . . ."

Startled as we were by his rich voice, we all laughed at the song. Not to be outdone, Donarius belted out his own favorite sea ballad in high, wavering tones:

> "They sailed upon a boozy sea, my lads
>   At the Tavern by the Glade.
> They sampled all the joys, my lads.
>   At the Tavern by the Glade.
>   They danced and sang
>   Till the kettles rang
>   Then diddled all the maids . . ."

The song went on like that for a time, each verse descending into another level of obscenity. Some of the men shot me a look as Donarius sang, wondering, no doubt, if their Lady Evocator was offended. But I'd heard much fouler things from my sisters in the barracks, and had even sung a drunken ode or three to fornication myself in my younger days. So I clapped along to Donarius' rhyme with the rest of them, thoroughly enjoying myself.

It turned out that Lizard had an even greater entertainment in store. He'd oiled his voice with grog while Donarius sang, and when the first mate was done, Lizard held up a hand for silence.

He cleared his throat and then he sang a lovely old ballad in tones as deep as the sea and clear as the skies above:

> "There was a lad, a lad so fair,
> And he was the blacksmith's son.
> He loved the inkeep's daughter dear,
> Who dwelt in Castledon.
> Who dwelt in Castledon.

> But she was cruel and she was cold
> And did not believe his boast:
> That of all the girls in all the world
> That he loved her most.
> Yes, that he loved her most.

> His father took great alarm,
> For his mother it was worse.
> They feared their lad would come to harm,
> He mourned till his heart near burst.
> Mourned till his poor heart near burst.

> They sent him to Orissa town
> And for six long years he stayed
> And many a tear came down
> And many a prayer was prayed.
> And many a prayer was prayed.

> But then that lad, that lad so fair,
> Took him to the river and drowned.
> For his sorrow he could not bear.
> And he died for the maid in Castledon.
> Yes, he died for the maid in Castledon . . ."

The tale went on, telling of the maid's sorrow when she heard the news of the lad's demise. Realizing the depths of the love she'd spurned, the maid goes mad and wanders the land until she comes to a tragic end.

When it was done I cried a little. We *all* cried a little. And it was most comforting.

It was an old song, a sad, sweet melody that carried us away to the days of our youth when it seemed the greatest ill that could befall a maid or lad was unrequited love. It cleansed our spirits more than any spell I could've cast to heal the memory of the battle we'd fought and what it might portend.

As I sat there, wiping my eyes and adding my applause to the others, an odd feeling arose in me as if I were on the verge of an important insight or discovery.

I grasped for it, but it was like trying to pick up an object from the bottom of a pool. Soon as your hand breaks the water's surface, it seems like it's at an angle to your arm, and the object itself proves to be not in the same spot your eyes have marked.

Then the feeling passed and I was left with a vague sense of loss and disappointment.

That night Gamelan came to me. In my dream I was sitting on the deck of the *Tern* idly sharpening my sword. None of the men were about, which for some reason seemed quite natural. It also seemed natural when I heard Gamelan's voice greeting me and I looked up, smiling and making a casual reply.

For those of you who've never heard of the master wizard, Lord Gamelan was Orissa's Chief Evocator during the time of my brother's discoveries and had accompanied me on the long pursuit of the last Archon of Lycanth. It was he who'd pressed me into realizing and accepting the magical side of my nature. And it was he who had been my teacher, introducing me to the wizardly arts. Gamelan died in one of the greatest acts of heroism in our city's history, and if it weren't for him, that history would've been bleak indeed.

In my dream Gamelan looked as he had before he'd been blinded by the Archon. Above his long white beard his cheeks were ruddy with health and his eyes were dancing with gentle intelligence. He leaned forward, touching my knee, and the dream was so real I actually felt the warmth of his frail old hand. When he spoke, it was as if we were in mid-conversation, casually discussing the day's events.

"What was the insight you were grasping for, Rali," he asked, "after you listened to Lizard's song?"

In an instant all my thinking of that moment came boiling back.

"It was probably nothing," I said. "But it came to me there might be more to magic than even the great Janos Greycloak surmised."

"That's quite possible, my dear," Gamelan said. "Greycloak broke new ground, to be certain. But there's much still to be learned. What in particular do you believe he missed?"

I hesitated, then said, "I think there might be more to what Janos called the Natural World. More elements that make it up, I mean. Picture the scene this afternoon. There I was, sailing in as serene a setting as anyone could beg from the gods. And I was as engaged with my companions as anyone could be. I'd shed class, rank, and sex to join them. And in that shared moment the ugliest person in our crew was touching us as we'd rarely been touched. With a song, no less. Yet it wasn't really the song but the voice—the human instrument—that caught us, that carried us away. And that human instrument had experienced all that we had, and by subtle tone and measure and by the look on his face, conveyed meaning. And that meaning made us all weep in congress."

"I'm happy you had such a nice time, Rali," Gamelan said. "But it was hardly odd. People come together frequently for such things. From grand concerts and festivals to drunken company in a tavern. What could such events possibly have to do with the laws of sorcery?"

In my dream I sighed as greatly as any weak-minded student who is suddenly stumped by the most obvious of questions.

"For the life of me," I said, "I don't know. Except that the feeling I shared with the crew was so strong that for a moment it seemed to be a force. As much a force as any Janos Greycloak described."

"Let's list them," the dream Gamelan said. "Janos Greycloak claimed that the forces that make up the world about us are light, heat, attraction, motion, and motion in the state of rest. He also claimed that magic, the ability to cause or transform, was as natural a force as any of the others. Most important of all, he said all those forces, magic included, were actually the same thing. The same force. But expressed in different ways."

When he was done, the old Evocator's eyebrows arched high. "Now, once again, Rali," he said, "I ask you to tell me what you think Greycloak left out. What did he miss?"

"That force I spoke of," I said, growing more sure of myself. "The combined spirit of human beings brought together in joy, or sorrow, or adversity. To form a common soul. A common will." Then I thought of all the women and men I'd fought beside over the years.

My emotions bubbled over and my words became heated. "By the gods who bedevil us," I said, "I believe that will can be as great a force as any lightning or raging storm or any spell a wizard can cast. It's a force that is the product of life itself and the supreme desire for all creatures to survive . . . to live."

The dream Gamelan suddenly became agitated, excited.

"Yes, yes," he said. "I see what you're getting at. You're saying that's what Greycloak had left out of his list of forces. Life and its desire to continue in that state. You're saying it's a force, a kind of energy like all the others."

Gamelan slapped his leg in glee. "Go on, Rali," he said. "I do believe you're on to something. Now let's take it forward and—"

Just then Lizard and Donarius and the others suddenly appeared in the dream. They were laughing and passing a ladle of grog around. Gamelan laughed with them, took a sip and passed the ladle to me.

My dreamself fumbled, spilling the spirits in my lap. There was much hilarity at my expense and I couldn't help but join in the merriment.

I woke up giggling.

Then I gaped about, surprised that I was alone in my cabin, my hammock rocking back and forth from the motion of the ship.

My heart lurched when I remembered what my dream had been about. Frantically, I tried to reach back and seize the realizations that seemed to have been bubbling up.

But they were gone . . . if they'd even been there in the first place.

As the days passed I kept trying to go back to that place to search for anything of value that might have been left behind.

I saw a group of dolphins playing in front of our ship and almost came upon the realization again. It was the same on another day when I watched a school of shark thrashing in our wake when Lizard cleaned the galley and dumped the leavings overboard.

But every time I tried to bring the idea to gaff, it slipped the net.

We sailed for many a day, and for a while it seemed we were charmed.

The seas were empty of human life and human strife, and the horizon beckoned us ever onward. Each dawn was a golden wonder, each dusk a rosy treat. Small clouds pranced above like colts at play, and great schools of silver fish swirled and broke and formed again beneath our bows.

As I'd said to Gamelan in my dream, the waters of the south are the richest in the world. They are fished so rarely that the creatures who dwell there have no reason to fear finless things like ourselves. They seemed to view us as oddities and would turn from their course to come up to our ship and look us over. I don't know how many times I gazed into the water, lost in my own thoughts, when I would suddenly find myself staring into a fishy eye. It would study me and I'd study it, and sometimes I swear I saw a glimmer of puzzlement.

Once we came upon a herd of whales—huge animals many times the length of our ship—grazing the waters and blowing towering columns of spume into the air through their breathing holes. It was a calm day, but it seemed as if a storm might be brewing far off. The waters were slate, and here and there chunks of ice roiled in the slow swells. There were birds with immense wingspans swooping about the whales, diving after any tasty morsels their huge presence was stirring up.

I watched for a long time, marveling at how such immense things could be so graceful. A fast-moving squall swept by, spattering me with cold droplets, and I started to turn away to seek shelter. But something drew me back—an odd buzzing at my nerve endings. Not uncomfortable but not wholly pleasant, either.

Then I saw the largest of the whales break away from the herd and come toward us. As the animal neared the ship I suddenly felt a powerful female presence. Waves of sorrow flowed out from her, washing over me.

"What is it, sister?" I asked. "What is troubling you?"

My answer was another piteous wave, so forceful it nearly drowned me. All was blackness, currents both warm and cold swirled about my body. I felt the deck beneath my feet, the ship's rails under my hands, could even hear some of the men moving about. But it was as if only part of me were there with them. The rest was struggling through the rough seas of emotion that emanated from the animal.

I struggled up through it and came gasping to the surface.

I felt Carale's presence beside me, then heard his alarmed voice call out. "What is it, me lady? What's amiss?"

"Go away," I said. "Go away."

I'm not certain he obeyed or even if I really spoke. Thought and speech became tangled. Then were one.

"How can I help you, sister?" I called out to the whale. "Please. What can I do?"

The waves of emotion descended on me again as the whale tried to answer.

Then pain hit me, as intense as anything I've ever experienced. I might have screamed—I can't say for certain if I did. Faintly I felt hands clutch at me. Faintly I was aware of Carale and the others. And I wanted to draw back, to flee that pain.

Just as I thought I could bear no more, the pain vanished.

I felt a gentle probing and knew it was the whale. She was saying she was sorry, that she didn't know, that if I couldn't help, she'd leave immediately. But I begged her to stay, to tell me what was wrong.

Suddenly I understood.

I made my senses into fingers and probed carefully through the great pain she felt. I felt life, so tenuous it was almost a ghost, throbbing inside her.

"Ah," I said. "Poor dear. You're with child."

Help me, she said, using her thoughts to speak, rather than her mind. *Please.*

It was then that I felt the broken spear shaft inside her. In my mind's eye I could see its jagged blade piercing the tube that gave life to the whale child.

I made a spell to give my magical fingers the skills of a surgeon and tried to gentle the spear point loose. The whale shuddered as I worked, but held very still, although I must have been hurting her greatly.

The spear point came loose.

Salty water mixed with blood shot out.

I felt the unborn creature stir, but weak . . . so weak. An infant's heart fluttered. Stopped. Then fluttered again.

And then I felt the whale child die.

I drew away. Angry at my failure. Cursing myself.

"I'm sorry, sister," I said. "So very sorry."

I felt the creature's sorrow deepen as she realized what'd happened. But then fingers of forgiveness touched me. And I knew that at least the great pain was gone, if only to be replaced by a different kind of wound.

And I asked her: "Who did this to you? Who killed your child?"

Beware the hunters, she said.

"Hunters? What hunters?"

An image floated up. It was the flag of the Ice Bear King!

Then she released me. I found myself standing on the deck of the ship, gaping at the huge creature as she slowly made her way back to the herd.

Blood trailed in her wake.

Carale took me by the shoulders and forced me around. His eyes were wide with alarm, his face pale. "What happened, me lady?" he asked. "Are you all right?"

I unstuck his fingers and stepped back. I wiped the perspiration from my brow with an unsteady hand. Then I pulled myself together.

"We'd better get ready," I said. "And we'd better be quick about it. I don't know how much time we have."

I told them all what had happened, but briefly. Sorcery and visions often frighten people; and men tend to become extremely skittish on the subject of pregnancy, especially one that goes awry. I noticed that although I didn't dwell on the details of the whale's agony and what I had attempted to do, they all turned green about the gills.

When I was done, Carale cleared his throat as if something unpleasant had risen up from his innards.

"Do ye think they'll be lyin' in wait fer us, me lady?" he croaked.

"I don't know," I said. "But from what I just experienced, they've clearly been in this area recently."

"Beggin' yer pardon, Lady Antero," Donarius said. "That don't mean they're a-knowin' we're about."

"That's very true," I said. "But we'd best not take the chance."

I had them clear the decks for action while I went into my cabin to investigate further.

I was weak from my encounter with the whale, so I brewed up a thin broth made from fish bones on my little wizard's brazier and added a hefty dollop of grog to give it heart. While it heated I stripped and daubed myself with a restorative much like I'd made for Daciar. In a little while I was feeling much better, glowing inside and out.

I donned a loose robe covered with faded Evocator's symbols and drew my sorcerer's trunk over by the brazier. I opened it and rummaged through the drawers and cubbyholes built into it until I found the proper ingredients.

Night was full on us by the time all was ready. I squatted in front of the small brass stand and puffed on the coals until they winked into life.

I sprinkled incense on them, and a yellowish smoke arose. I breathed in deep, tasting flowers, then exhaled. The cabin walls dissolved and my spirit-self floated up into the starry night.

I knew it to be cold and windy, yet I felt nothing but a rushing sensation. Beneath me the lights of the *Tern* and the white foam of the breaking waves grew smaller. The moon was full and I could feel its chilly tug at my essence. But I resisted easily, coming to a halt just beneath a cloud bank. The *Tern* was a shimmering dot below. At the horizon's edge I could see high ice-clad peaks reflected in the bright moonlight. I pushed my senses in that direction as cautiously as I could. It was like inching forward in a brush-choked gully, sniffing for signs of a waiting enemy.

I felt the ghostly touch of a tendril and nearly bolted. But the motion would have given me away, so I stayed quite still, making my mind as blank as I could. The tendril moved about, touching my spiritself here and there. Then it grew bored and passed on.

I drew back slowly, knowing the slightest motion would signal the seeking presence.

Finally it was safe. I folded in and drifted back down to the ship. The

cabin walls formed about me, and once again I was whole, squatting before the dancing flames in the brass bowl.

I smiled.

Our enemy was waiting. But it was just where I wanted them to wait.

The next morning I huddled with Captain Carale, poring over our charts. With a finger I traced the outline of the nearest land mass, which was about a week's sail to the southwest. It showed as a big bulge of a peninsula, shaped, Carale joked, like a fat man's paunch. Beneath the paunch the coastline swooped downward for many leagues, finally dissolving into small chartmaker's dots where real knowledge ended and guesswork took over.

Before my previous expeditions, nearly the whole chart had been nothing but the lines and dots of a cartographer's imagination. The big-bellied peninsula, for instance, was unknown to Orissans until my first voyage south. The whole coastline beyond had been mapped in my other expeditions.

I jabbed at a point some leagues east of the peninsula. "This is where I saw them," I said.

Carale peered closer. The point I'd marked showed up as a series of small islands, but we knew they were so low that they'd be underwater during heavy seas.

"Aye," he said. "Just as you said, me lady, it 'pears they swallowed our lovely bait."

The bait he was referring to was the story I'd asked the crew to spread about our jewel-hunting expedition. The islands lay just off the mouth of a river that cut west through the peninsula. This time of year the river would be mostly free of ice, and if we followed it, according to tribes I'd befriended in the area, the river would lead to wondrous falls that thundered down cliffs studded with gems.

Carale stroked his chin. "Do yer suppose there really be such riches in that place, me lady?" he asked.

"I don't know," I said. "But remember those emeralds they showed us. Flawless and big as a fist. The chief said he'd gotten them in trade from the tribe that lives in that area."

Carale laughed. "I remember well, me lady. The chief said we'd best stay clear of the place. Nothin' but savages, he said. Wicked fellers. Look at strangers t' see if they be fat 'nough for the village stew pot."

The memory made me laugh as well. The chief who'd deplored the savage habits of the People of the Falls had red fangs tattooed on his lips, and horns similarly applied to his shaven skull, and when we'd greeted him in his hide tent, he was stark naked—sporting a large golden pin inserted through his penis.

"My brother warned me about such talk," I said. "He told me every merchant soon learns that no matter how murderous your customers appear, they'll claim the real savages are just up the river or across the next desert."

Carale nodded. "Good way t' make certain they'll al'as be the middle-man, I s'pose. Gotter deal with them if yer wants the goods."

"Maybe next time," I said, "we'll go look at those falls. We'll see for ourselves just how mean those people are. My bet is we'll be treated like vis-iting royalty. And they'll be sizing us up for fatter profits instead of tender joints for their stew."

Carale turned serious. "Do yer think they'll be a next time, me lady?" he asked. "What with this pirate traipsing about with his giants and all? Might put a pinch in the trade prospects."

"We'll take care of him soon enough," I said. I honestly believed that at the time. "I don't care what kind of forces he has at his disposal, men or mag-ic. This whole region has been benefiting from the trade we've opened up.

"Once we get our people out, my brother can don his diplomatic cloak and talk to our friends about unified action against this so-called Ice Bear King. It won't be the first time—or the last, I suspect—that my brother's dealt with such matters. And they've always worked out before."

"That's true as me dear wife's heart, me lady," Carale said. "But like yer said, first we gotter pluck our friends outter harm's way."

Although the pirates had fallen for my ruse, it wouldn't be that easy to get past them. If we steered a straight course for Antero Bay, the first of the outposts, they'd be straddling our path. The best way would be to merely swing wide around them, make a dash for the outposts, and follow the same route back.

Carale immediately spotted the problem with that plan. "It's gettin' late in the year t' try t' just evade 'em, me lady," he said. "Storm season's almos' on us. Longer we take, more likely it'll be tha' we'll run into trouble. We might be prayin' t' the gods tha' it's only pirates we had t' worry about."

In our present position we were still in the more mild zones. If we sailed due west, the land we'd see wouldn't be much different than one would ex-pect during winter in Orissa. The winters last much longer, but there were trees and sleeping vegetation waiting under the snow for the spring thaw. Farther south, however, little grew except thorny grasses. I've never seen a budding plant below the peninsula. And grasses soon gave way to naked fro-zen rock where the only green that could exist seemed to be a kind of slimy moss in the more sheltered tide pools.

It was not only eternally winter in those regions, but the most vicious winter conditions you could ever imagine. The storms are the stuff of horrid myths they tell around campfires. And the demons who arrive with those storms, I'd been told, were the most evil and powerful demons of all.

At the time I didn't know how accurate those tales were, but I wasn't anxious to find out.

Carale and I had no choice but to lay out a course that would take us dangerously close to the waiting pirates. The trick, however, wouldn't be slipping past our human enemy. That'd be easy enough for a captain as skilled as Carale. It was our enemy's magical allies that most worried me.

The sorcerous net that had been spread was as powerful as anything I'd ever encountered. It had been a raw force I'd sensed the night before, with none of the elegance of our own Evocators.

But raw and primitive as that net seemed, I knew it'd be difficult to slip through.

The day was gray when we approached—as gray as a pot freshly dipped in pewter. The sea and sky presented a solid surface that turned back all vision, leaving us feeling flat, without substance. The only sound was the slap of water under our bows and the flap and snap of our sails. The fog was so thick it seemed to swallow those sounds until all seemed no more than a ghostly rustle. I could feel the tingling edges of the sorcerer's net, and whispered directions to Carale to take us this way or that as we skirted the danger zone.

I'd raised the mist with an elementary spell, so simple I was sure it wouldn't be noticed. Beneath the spell I'd laid in another thin blanket of sorcery that dulled curiosity rather than turning it aside. If a wizard's suspicions were aroused by some accident, such as when the twins dropped a spar, my spell presented a boring answer to the wizard's probing. In that case I made the thunk of wood seem like the pop of a wave against a rocky shoal.

The great flaw in spells of that sort, and the main reason they are rarely used, is that they also blind the wizard who casts them.

In other words, I was as magically sightless as my enemy.

We weren't only dodging the pirates that day, but gingerly threading our way through the barren chain of small islands that sat off the peninsula's coast. My crew's abilities were stretched to the limit as we crept through the mist, all eyes peeled for the sudden appearance of jagged black rock poking out of the water.

When I thought we were opposite the river that led to the fabled emerald beds, I got out the small ship model Donarius had carved during the week's voyage. It was a rough approximation of the *Tern*, about the length of a pike and two hands wide. Fixed to the deck was an emerald bauble from my jewelry chest. It was a small sacrifice for such a purpose. Besides, I'd lost the matching earrings long ago.

I poised at the rail, ship model in hand, and chanted:

> "We are treasure seekers
> Hungry for riches that wait beyond.
> Stones of gleaming green,
> Jewels fit for a king's crown,
> Will soon fill our purses
> And the taverns will ring,
> And the maids will swoon
> At such brave rich fellows as we."

I cast the ship model into the water. A wave caught it, bowling it over, and I held my breath until it righted itself. When it finally did, the little craft slowly turned until its bow was pointing in the right direction.

I whispered a second spell and the miniature *Tern* bobbed away, disappearing into the gloom.

We waited for an hour or more. The hiss of the seas, the rattle of ice against our hull, and the far off cry of a gull made the wait seem much longer.

Suddenly I reeled back as a blast of sorcerous glee shattered the calm. The ship model had tripped the magical trap. Then I heard real shouts roil the mist as the pirate crews were alerted. Those were followed by barked orders from the pirate officers and all was silent again.

Their goal, I knew, would be to follow what they believed to be the real *Tern* to the source of all those emeralds my men had boasted about in Pisidia.

Then the wizard's net was dropped. Moments later we heard the muffled sounds of what the pirates believed was a stealthy pursuit.

My trick had worked. The enemy had been drawn away.

I gave quiet orders and we set sail for the first outpost. If the gods did not fail us, we'd be there in a few days.

We came on Antero Bay at dawn. A spectacular sunrise made the whole coastline glow in welcome. Our expectations were high as we rounded the bend. We were all eager to see our comrades, and those who weren't busy with other duties leaned out over the rail, eyes hungry to take in the view.

I expected to see fields of tall yellow grass spreading from shore to shore, waving in the chilly breeze. In the center would be the dock. Ringing that dock would be the two dozen or more sleepy homes that housed our friends. When last I saw them, they'd completed their quarters and were proud of the colorful roofs of bright green and red and blue they'd added to remind them of home. At this hour I knew a few early risers would be about. My nose twitched for the smells of good Orissan breakfasts sizzling on the hearthfires.

But the gods had not been so kind.

Our luck had changed.

My heart lurched as we closed in on the settlement. Spread out before us were the smoking ruins of disaster.

The outpost at Antero Bay had been overwhelmed and burned.

The scene was ghastly—fit to wrench a soul from its moorings. That it was entirely bloodless made it more ghastly still. The ruins were still warm from the fires that'd swept the outpost. There were no bodies, but there were the white ash outlines of where bodies had once been. Only chimneys stood, fingers of stark stone poking through the smoking ruins. In the black pebbled cores of the homes we found shards of exploded clay jars, runnels of tin from trunks that had melted in the heat, a speck of gold and silver here and there from what had once been jewelry, and bits of bright-colored tile from the roofs.

We were silent as we combed through the ruins for some sign of what had happened to our friends.

My first discovery was that the fire had not been caused by natural means. I quickly sensed, then confirmed, that the source was magical. There were bootprints among the ashes, so many that it was difficult to pick out one from the other. But we had no doubt that a large force of soldiers had come through.

As we investigated the remains, I saw tears in the eyes of my shipmates and once I heard Lizard sob. He was examining a twisted kettle that contained the rock-hard remains of what appeared to be a traditional porridge. None of us thought the less of him for his display of emotion. For as we stood there in that desolation, it felt as if the blow had been against Orissa herself. Our home away from home had been defiled, its citizens terrorized and slain.

There was a nip to the air and the skies were clear, making the desolation seem even more stark. We'd come dressed for the chill, donning furs and warm water-resistant boots. A mild wind brushed away a few wisps of smoke that rose from the larger heaps of rubble.

Carale and I poked through one of the smoky areas—the main trading center where the guards slept. Just as in the other sites, there were no signs of a struggle, only the white outlines of men and women who had died and burned in their sleep.

Adjoining the barracks was the weapons room. It shared a common fireplace with the barracks and was built of stone. The stone walls had been blasted apart by the fire, and the weapons were a melted mass on those stones. The chimney and fireplace still stood, easily twice the size of the hearths in the burned-out homes. The fireplace was double-sided, and a low wind whispered through the opening.

The only sign of life was a hysterical dog that crept out from nearby rocks and barked and howled at us without stop. Donarius, who had a soft spot for animals, tried to calm him but suffered a slashed arm in the process. The dog was so stricken by whatever had occurred here that he couldn't be consoled. He would not eat, would not drink, but only howled incessantly. When he had no more strength for that, he cowered in the ashes trembling so hard we thought he'd break his bones.

Donarius finally killed him out of kindness. After that it was many hours before he could speak again.

Down by the charred heaps of what had been the docks, we found scores of footprints in the mud where the attackers had disembarked. These were much clearer than the others. There were also the heavy marks of long-boats, at least half a dozen of them. The enemy had come by sea.

Carale put his boot alongside one of the footprints. They were about the same size.

"Weren't giants this time, me lady," he said. "Unless we got giants with very small feet."

"I'm not surprised," I said. "After all, how many giants can there be? When the gods made them large, they kept their numbers sensibly small. I doubt if there's enough in all the known world to make up a city the size of Orissa."

"What's sensible abou' it, me lady?" Carale protested. "There was no sense to makin' giants in the first place. And in the second . . . why, it's plain daft, I say. Daft!"

"You wouldn't say that if you were a giant, my friend," I murmured.

Carale didn't hear. He was puzzling over the footprints.

"What's this, me lady?" he said, pointing at an area near the shore.

I looked closer, saw the mass of confused prints, and almost turned back to ask Carale what in the hells did he mean. Then I saw the pointed toe outline leap clear from the muddle. On the heel was the symbol of the Evocators' Guild. I bent down, waved a hand over a set of pointy prints, and felt a faint magical tingle. I knew the scent.

"They be Evocator's prints, me lady—'less I've gone as daft and blind as the gods," Carale said.

"You're right," I said. "And from the scent of them, they were made by none other than Lord Searbe. The Evocator I left in charge."

"Don't look like he put up much of a fight," Carale observed. Then he hastened to say, "Course he probably had a sword point at his throat."

I nodded, although I knew threats probably hadn't been necessary. Searbe had been a bit of a disappointment. Like me, he'd come late to wizardry. And like me, he'd started his adult life as a soldier. He had a big personality—big voice, rough manners, and as plain-spoken as anyone could ask. He made much over honor and seemed to live by that code. I'd quite liked him, had been refreshed by his lack of social graces and frank way of speaking. It was quite a change from the dry lordly types who usually became Evocators. So when Searbe volunteered to head one of the outposts, I'd enthusiastically agreed. But when I'd landed him at Antero Bay, he'd instantly taken on such a self-important air with all the ordinary workers that I'd felt it necessary to admonish him. He'd apologized profusely, said he didn't know what had overcome him. I'd accepted his apology. But after I left I'd thought of him from time to time and wondered if I'd made a mistake. Such a prickly and bombastic personality, which on reflection also seemed self-centered, might make life difficult for others in such conditions.

As I stared at the prints, that doubt came crawling back. If I'd been mistaken, then it could be a very large error, indeed. If a man like Searbe—who made such a point of honor—was all a bluff, then I had a weasel to deal with, not a man.

And if so, that weasel was in the hands of the enemy.

His footprints, along with four other pair, broke away from the others and trailed along the shoreline. The prints were flanked by the other sets, apparently those of his guards. But the boot marks were so widely spaced that the guard seemed casual. The prints were heavy, with iron-edged boot heels and single spiked tips, scooping down like a cat's extended claw and cutting into the mud or scraping the mossy rocks.

The shore and the prints curved into a broad field of the tall yellow grass that favors that region. It's thick and saw-toothed and seems to thrive on the frigid winter blasts. Several animals—including a large flightless bird—made their nests in that grass. When we came to the field, I saw the grass had been flattened and was littered with still smoky campfires and mounds of animal dung.

"It looks like a large caravan of some sort camped here, captain," I said to Carale.

He scratched his head. "Aye, me lady, tha's so." He looked back at the docks where we'd seen the marks of the enemy boats. "Seems they was two groups of 'em. One come from the sea. Th' other traveled by land t' meet 'em."

"And for some reason," I said, "the group that came by sea handed our Evocator over to the caravan. I see Searbe's footprints lead into this field, but for the life of me I don't see them coming back out."

I looked across the heavily trodden field and saw the trail the caravan entered and exited from. It led off into the stony wilderness that surrounds Antero Bay.

I turned and started trotting back toward our boats. My captain followed.

"We'd better get to the other outpost," I shouted to Carale. "Just as fast as we can."

By the time we'd reached the shore, the skies had gone from fair to stormy black. Without warning a wind came whistling in from the bay, growing stronger and colder by the minute. I shouted for the others but my voice was made suddenly small by the winds.

Then the storm struck full-strength.

And it didn't relent for a month.

CHAPTER SIX

THE STORM

It slammed down on us like a black steel curtain, ringing us in on all sides so we couldn't escape.

It was as if the hells of the ice demons had been opened up. The wind ripped the surface off the sea and flung it at us in long needles that tormented the flesh. Then it turned colder still and the seawater became sleet, then became sharp pebbles of hail.

The *Tern* was lost in the first few minutes.

I remember its going as if it were only yesterday. For in that awful moment all hope was crushed along with the lives of our three comrades who'd stayed behind.

When the first fury of the storm hit us, we all flung ourselves on the ground and scrambled for cover. I found a low clump of rocks and hugged the earth to escape that icy fist.

I raised my head—cheeks instantly going numb. I could barely see through the stinging rain, and had to use spread fingers for a shield. First they lost all feeling. Then they began to burn as if I'd plunged them into liquid fire.

But I had to witness what was happening. I gritted my teeth and peered through the fence my fingers made.

My eyes went up, up, crawling up the stormswept shore. I saw a gray boil of foam and rock and sand where the land met the sea. I tried to make sense of the confusion, then oriented myself and forced my eyes along the surf line.

In horror I saw our longboats shatter against the shore, the pounding sea swiftly carrying off the timbers.

It was all so quick that it could've been my imagination, but I knew it wasn't. And I knew worse would soon follow.

Then I couldn't stand the elements anymore and ducked down, sucking in air and rubbing feeling back into my fingers and face. I recovered, breathed a prayer to gods I knew weren't listening, and raised my head again.

My eyes were gulls in a hurricane, fighting forward, surging over the bucking winds.

Out at sea there was a white sheen flat on the horizon. It shone through the darkness like a grimace.

And in that grimace I saw the *Tern* heeled over, struggling with her anchor.

A loose strand of hair lashed my cheeks, drawing blood. The droplets blinded me and I had to duck down again to clear my eyes and draw breath. When I came up, only the white grimace remained. The *Tern* was gone.

I sagged down, struggling with the enormity of what had just happened. There were eight of us left. The next outpost was many days' sail away. And we had no ship to sail to it. Even if we had, that camp might already be in ruins. There was no help elsewhere. The storm might be early, but winter would soon descend and it would be many months before anyone could come and look for us.

In other words, we were marooned.

If we lived, that is.

I pushed away all but thoughts of survival. My first duty was to see that we all made it through the storm. Then I'd take stock.

Urgency fired me. If I didn't act soon, we'd all die on this shore.

I pushed my senses out, seeking some magical solution. But it seemed as if they'd become as numb as my fingers and I could barely grope ahead. Clumsily I felt about in the ethers. At first the storm seemed a raw natural force. Then I caught an undercurrent of sorcery. Then cold, both real and magical, closed in and I had to snatch myself back. I tried to think through what I'd experienced, but the gale fogged my brain. It was apparent that for the time being I'd have to depend on my physical abilities.

Very well, then.

But what should I do?

I thought . . . shelter first. I must find us shelter.

The largest and strongest buffer I could recall in the desolation behind me was the chimney and fireplace in the destroyed trading center. With some difficulty I got my intentions across to the others and we slowly withdrew.

It took a long time to reach that shelter. And to call it an agony makes light of it. It was all done in darkness, with the wind's hands tearing at us, grabbing us and shaking us about and flinging stones on us and drenching us with a freezing mixture of sea and sand. And by the gods it was cold. None of us had ever felt such intense cold. Even Carale and I, who had experience in these lands, had never encountered such a thing.

The storm swooped in off the sea as if it had rolled down from the highest, coldest mountain range that any demon king could conjure. It cut through our parkas like they were the lightest summer wear instead of good sealskin fortified by a firm spell of warmth.

There was some relief, but not much, when we finally got behind the chimney. The storm howled through the eye of the fireplace and tried to crush its fingers around the stone sides. There was no sense trying to speak over the wind, so I made signs to convey my orders: we needed rocks, piled just so.

I don't know how long it took. It seemed like days or even weeks, although I wouldn't be writing this now if it'd taken more than a few hours. Eventually we stopped up the hole with a rough stone wall. Wind shrilled through the cracks, but it was better. Then we stacked more rocks along the sides, building up a low wall to keep the storm from pinching in at us.

We were all exhausted but I knew we didn't dare rest—not just yet. I was so stricken with the cold sickness that I could barely make out the details of my surroundings. I was becoming weaker by the minute. I thought that soon the core of me would be frozen and I'd lose the will to live. And I knew the others must feel the same.

I had to keep moving. All of us had to keep moving.

I organized teams to creep out into the frigid blast and grab what hot timbers they could from the ruins of the center. We did it in stages. First one team—the twins, for instance—would reconnoiter a smoky pile. They'd drag back what they could, fighting the winds and deadly cold all the way. Speech was still impossible—the roaring winds swallowed all other sound. So if they had something to communicate—some danger, say, for the next team to avoid—they had to signal with their hands. But sometimes they'd be so chilled they couldn't move their fingers and we'd have to spend precious time and fuel to thaw them out.

Then the next pair would take its turn in the freezing, body-and-mind-battering maelstrom.

We made a shallow bed of the coals, just wide enough to hold the eight of us if we stayed close together. We covered the coals with pebbles and stretched out full-length on that rocky mattress. The warmth rising up was like heaven, but we found ourselves turning constantly as the side exposed to the elements quickly became numb.

There was more I wanted to do, but I could see the weariness in the lined faces of my comrades and knew I couldn't drive them or myself much longer. We had to eat and rest.

Expecting a short stay, we'd only brought rations for the day—one large meal at most. For that reason I had to make my next, and perhaps most crucial, choice. Either we went on short rations and tried to stretch out the little food we had for as many days as we could. Or we could do what I finally decided. Which was to eat all the food while we still had strength to draw nourishment from it. Then we slept as if we'd joined the dead, the storm howling around us and rattling the stone.

It was the last deep sleep any of us enjoyed for many a day.

I came awake as the storm's great hammer battered down on us harder than ever. Wet debris spurted through the holes in the walls like water through constricted pipes.

I woke Carale, who prodded the others up, and we got to work making our shelter more substantial.

I had no idea how long the storm would last. But an old hand from these regions—a shaman from a fishing tribe—once told me that the only way to fight the elements was to assume you might have to spend what remained of your life in whatever situation you found yourself. Nothing can be temporary. And every gain must be as if snatched from the jaws of a tiger shark.

I had the men make the walls of the rocky shelter thicker and higher, but not so high as to let what little heat we could produce rise out of reach. We made a roof of flat rocks held up by piled rocks that turned the interior of the shelter into small rooms, if you can picture rooms inside a structure about the width of a goat shed and the height of a tall person's waist. You had to kneel inside and crawl about, clambering over the forms of your comrades.

We stopped up the cracks between the rocks as best we could with bits of debris and earth. This turned out to be a constant job, as the wind seemed to find new places to pierce every time we got one gap plugged. A small hole was left in the roof to carry out the smoke. We had to make the fire small— there was no way we'd find enough fuel to maintain that rocky bed of heat. Each trip out to find more bits to burn was an ordeal that left us near dead. Only four could huddle around the fire at a time. One side of you would be barely warm, while the other side was like ice. Meanwhile, your comrades shivered and chattered as they waited their turn at that little space of choking smoke and feeble warmth.

After warmth—such as it was—food was next. This was even more difficult. The fire had destroyed all the outpost supplies, so there were only scraps to be found, consisting mainly of a few leftovers from our comrades' last meals. It was the greatest misery imaginable to crouch in the middle of that ice storm and paw through the hearths for such poor leavings.

They tended to be scorched and so hard that we mixed them with water from melted ice to make a gruel. It was barely palatable, and hungry as I was, I came to dread the feel of the mush against my tongue. The only blessing was that the scraps weren't spoiled. Even without the storm, in that area of the south it's always too cold for rot or decay.

Perhaps a week passed, a week of increasing misery, before Lizard came to me.

"Beggin' your pardon, lady," he said, voice barely distinct over the wind. "But I've been thinkin' about the garbage."

Cold as I was, there was life enough in me to wonder what in the hells he was talking about.

"There is no garbage, Lizard," I said. "If there were, we'd eat it. So what's the sense in worrying about stuff we don't throw away? And if there was a surplus, there'd be no need to worry about spoilage or sanitation. It's too damned cold for that."

His fur parka bobbed as his head went up and down in what I supposed was a nod of agreement. He could have been grinning as well, but who could tell? It might be nothing but the permanent grimace we all had on our faces, fixed there by the bone-grating chill.

"That's what got me thinkin', lady," he said. "Nothin' spoils here. Which means any garbage thrown away by the others'd still be in a pit. And it'd all be as fresh as the hour and day the cook made each meal."

The thought of eating garbage did not revolt me. Instead my mouth spurted with juices in anticipation of a messy feast.

The trouble was, how to find the garbage pit? There was no telling where it might've been dug, especially since the settlement was nothing but rubble now. If there were no storm, we could hunt about and eventually find it. But each trip outside the shelter was a lifetime for the traveler, a lifetime that could be measured by grains falling in a glass.

My Evocator's faculties were nil. The storm's natural force, combined with the underlying spell of confusion, had fuddled my magical wits so there was little force I could bring to bear on almost any detail. I could have made a fire, for instance, if ours burned out. But I couldn't have drawn enough energy to fuel it. Even the spell of warmth on our cold-weather gear had faded to nothingness. And that spell had been especially formed and cast by skilled Evocators who worked with the Chandlers' Guild. My chest of sorcerous goods had been lost with the *Tern*, so there was no way I could test to see if those materials had been affected, as well. I suspected they would have been, so there was no real reason to mourn their loss.

Which brought me full circle to my dilemma: how to find the garbage pit. A physical search was out. Only magic would do. How could I accomplish such a thing considering the circumstances? I felt very small against the might of that storm.

Then it came to me that smallness might be the answer. The more I thought about it, the more it seemed that the less magical surface I presented, the better off I'd be.

Our last foraging party had come back with a great prize, the frozen body of a ship's rat found beneath a hearthstone. Donarius had clawed it up as he was searching the ashes for blackened crumbs of food. We'd all made much over him for his find and were eagerly anticipating the rat's body being boiled into a broth, and that broth and the creature's ground-up bones added to our next batch of gruel. Now that would be a feast indeed.

You can imagine the frowns I got when I asked for the rat. Even men trained like these couldn't resist the very human feelings of suspicion that I might be demanding more than my share. I paid them no mind, trusting in their professionalism to keep their heads fixed tight to their necks.

I withdrew to a corner and the men went back to taking turns around the fire. They did their best to ignore me, giving me privacy for my wizard's work. It wouldn't be hard. The wind roared all around us, making normal speech impossible. It was easier to let the sound swallow you as you crouched before that fire for the small time allotted each person. For a few minutes you could enter a state of dreamy exhaustion where the outside world was faint and far away.

I laid the gray body before me. I fumbled my firebeads from my purse and draped them across the small corpse. I didn't bother breathing the little chant that would make the beads glow into life. I'd attempted it before, and knew even that simple spell—which every Orissan child knows—wouldn't work. But I thought I might use the beads as a focal point like a magnifying glass. At least that was my theory. It remained to be seen if the theory could be made to work.

I concentrated on the beads lying against the dead creature. I made my will a narrow beam, slender as a needle. I held that image, made the magical needle sharper still and narrower, with a wide eye to receive the thread. I slipped the needle forward as delicately as I could.

I felt a hum in the ethers. Something had been alerted! I felt inquisitive little particles of magic waft toward me. But the interest was mild and there were only a few bits—like a gentle puff of snowflakes—swirling about. I kept still until they were gone.

When it was safe, I prodded with my magical needle again. I pierced a firebead, felt a minuscule glow of power, and pressed on through the bead and into the rat's body. I left the magical needle fixed in the body and slowly withdrew, unreeling a thin magical thread from the needle's eye as I drew back.

In my wizard's eye I could see the thread unspool, a silver bit of gossamer waving in the etherous breeze. My mental fingers gripped the thread and I chanted:

> "Fur and fang,
> Squeak and quarrel.
> Scurrying, always
> Scurrying . . .
> Busy in the burrow.
> Fur and fang,
> Squeak and quarrel.
> Seek in death
> As ye did in life.
> Scurrying, always
> Scurrying . . .
> Busy in the burrow,
> Seek . . . Seek . . . Seek!"

The rat stirred. First its whiskers flicked, then its nose twitched and pink little eyes fluttered open. The pink dots darted about, then the rat suddenly leaped to its feet. It didn't wait, didn't linger, but dashed for the base of the rock wall. There was a slim depression there between a ground stone and the hard-packed pebbles of the floor. I held onto the thread, made myself small, and let the rat carry me with it.

I tugged hard on the thread and then I became that rat diving at the depression. My paws flashed and the floor was scooped away and I saw a hole emerge, but it was small, too small. But my little rat mind began to squeeze and squeeze and then I was through that hole, jamming myself deeper and deeper, swimming through pebbles and sand as if they were water. Then the pebbles fell away and I found myself dodging out from under an earthen shower and then scurrying along a narrow tunnel.

My wizard's self felt cobwebs of magical suspicion fall away as I hurried along the tunnel. I was too small to be noticed by our unknown enemy. But

I didn't let myself dwell on it: the wrong mental activity might raise an alarm. I became as ratlike as I could.

I thought, "Eat. Eat. Find eat."

And I scampered along, burning with rat's energy, every nerve end seared by a multitude of sensations. I could hear the storm raging above the burrow but it meant nothing to me. I was warm, I was quick, I was hungry. And suddenly I *knew* the way and I was taking a fast turn to the left as another burrow loomed up. I could smell eat. I could sense others like me thinking eat, eat. Scuttling along other tunnels like mine. They were full of challenging scents. I was measured for fierceness, so I made myself the fiercest of all. A ferocious scent rose from me like smoke and I felt my challengers shrink away.

Except for one.

She burst out of a large tunnel and shot toward me, fast as a cat, agile as a snake.

She had one eye, a scarred ear, and long teeth that could bite through steel. She was the Queen Rat and had borne and fed and guarded many litters through her long lifetime. She had her pick of the males, the best food from the garbage pit that I smelled just behind her. I knew this Queen Rat had killed many rivals, maimed twice as many upstarts, and was now determined to do the same with me.

I feinted for her right—the blind side—but struck left. My teeth sunk into fur, then flesh. I ripped her snout, then shifted my attack downward, slashing at her belly. I felt sharp teeth sink into my back paw but I paid no mind, twisting around her until I found the spine. I snapped it in my teeth. The Queen Rat gave a squeal of pain, then went still.

I dived past her body into the tunnel she'd guarded. And there I found treasure—the outpost garbage heap.

I snapped the magical thread, breaking the spell, and I was myself again.

Every bone and muscle ached as if I'd just performed the greatest and most strenuous feat in wizardly history. I grimaced. So much effort just to be a damned rat.

Then I went to tell my comrades the good news: There was a banquet waiting for us nearby. A feast of old rinds, moldy peels, and gobs of grainy fat.

Their mouths watered when I described it.

We suffered much to raid that pit, but we ate every filthy scrap of it and mourned the last meal when that dismal moment came.

After that was gone the fuel was next. Our supply dwindled until only enough remained to make a cup of hot water for each of us at the beginning and ending of each day.

During those weeks, the storm never ceased. Sometimes it was a blizzard, burying us all in snow. Then it would sweep the snow away with winds as dry as desert gales that'd suck all moisture from you, turning your lips into rims of dried flaking sponge.

I don't know how we survived those weeks in Antero Bay. I've heard of other mariners who've suffered such things. Some of them, I've read, became closer to the gods and praised their names until the day they died for saving them from such misery. I can't understand why. As far as I'm concerned, they deserve a good cursing for tormenting me so.

I can't describe how cold that storm was. At first I thought it was like knives, and then I thought it was like a leech, draining me of all power, all will. I also can't describe how hungry we got. Again, those knives were first in mind. But then I thought, no, it's like something was *eating* me.

The other senses were assaulted as well, but after time only the cold and the hunger meant much. In a way, they even obscured pain.

We became like automatons whose clockwork was slowly winding down. Every motion was measured, carried out slowly and painfully. There were no flares of temper or hysteria, not because we were all so brave but because we had no energy left for such displays. A low growl or a single tear would have to suffice.

Then one day we awakened to find that we were one less. Priam had died. He was a good-natured seaman but had become even more withdrawn than the rest of us during the crisis and so no one could remember when he'd spoken last. One day he was a cup thrust forward for a ration of hot water, and the next day that cup wasn't there anymore. We all gaped dully at one another, wondering what had happened. Then we realized what was missing.

We found Priam curled up like a child in his parka. Cold and dead.

I suppose there was some sorrow, but shortly afterward I felt a change in the air. Men kept looking over at the bundle that was Priam's corpse. I knew what was on their minds.

I called everyone together. Fortunately there was a rare lull in the intensity of the winds and I could make myself heard.

"Let me speak plainly," I said. "There's no sense in polite dodgings about the issue at hand."

I pointed at Priam. "One of our mates is dead. And we're all sorry for it. Meanwhile, we all intend to live. Priam doesn't have any use for his body any longer. But we could make use of it, thereby letting us all live a little longer."

I looked around but no one would return my gaze. They all hung their heads as if ashamed. I could see the tension knotting in their jaws.

Carale cleared his throat. "I 'spect we was all thinkin' along those lines, me lady . . . and wonderin' what yer opinion would be."

"Of cannibalism?" I pressed. "Let's give it the proper name. You can't duck it by making it sound better."

"Yes, my lady," Donarius broke in. "And I'll also call it meat, if yuz don't mind. For that's all old Priam be, just now. Meat."

I shrugged. "I agree," I said. "And I don't have any scruples about making use of it."

Everyone smiled and I could almost feel them inch forward, itching to get out their knives. I raised a hand and everyone froze.

"But I think we ought to consider what we're about to do," I cautioned. "If we eat poor Priam, it'll give us a meal or two. Then we'll be without once more. Except this time we'll know where there's more meat to be had. We'll start waiting eagerly for the next person to die. Then we might even start encouraging it."

"None of us be murderers, me lady," Carale protested.

"But could you be?" I asked. "What if we made it easy? What if I suggested that next time we draw straws and that the one with the short straw sacrifice himself? We'd kill him and eat him. It's been done before, you know. Sometimes there has even been a survivor or two."

Donarius shuddered. "I've heard such tales, Lady Antero," he said. "We all have. 'N' none of 'em have been pretty."

I said, "And all of the . . . volunteers, shall we call them . . . didn't necessarily go bravely, did they? A few screamed and begged for mercy. But it didn't stay the butcher's hand. For they'd become . . . just meat."

I grabbed up a tin cup and a handful of pebbles.

"Instead of straws," I said, "we could use pebbles for our lottery. I could mark a number on each stone. Drop them in. One by one."

I did so, and the rattle of each falling pebble made the men flinch. I stopped at seven. Then I shook the cup about, making a loud clatter.

"Then all we have to do is"—I held the cup out by way of demonstration—"draw a stone."

Everyone shrank away from the cup as if the drawing were real and their lives had actually become mere stones in a tin cup.

"But I think we ought to decide what to do together," I said. "We should vote on whatever course we take."

I looked at the ground and let the tension build.

"Well," I said. "What shall it be? Do we eat Priam or not?"

The twins said, as one, "Not!"

Then Donarius and Carale: "Not!"

The others weighed in as well, and all voted no.

Someone sighed, and the men relaxed as if a great burden had lifted. One man even made a joke; I don't remember what it was or even if it was very funny, but we all laughed as if it were from the Jester of the Gods himself.

The storm's respite continued, and normally we would've used the lull for a hurried foraging mission. After Priam's body had been taken away for later burial, I called the men together again for a much needed talk.

"We've all discussed our situation," I said, "but it's been in bits and pieces. And I'm not even certain we've all been together in one group so all know the same things."

"We'd 'preciate a word or two from yer, me lady," Carale said.

"Here's how it is," I said. "We can do nothing until the storm stops. When it does, we'll still be marooned. The closest place is the other outpost. But I think we'd better assume they've also been wiped out."

" 'Pears we're gonna have a long walk home, lads," Carale said, trying to be jolly about it and failing miserably.

"And cold as the hells, too," one of the Twins said. The other grunted agreement.

"When do yuz think the bleedin' storm will let up, lady?" Donarius asked.

I answered carefully. As their Evocator, as well as leader, I had to make certain they understood but did not fear. Sorcery sometimes makes even the spell maker's skin crawl.

"I keep getting signs that it'll end any day now," I said. "There's a feeling of slackening—like this lull we've got now, for instance. Then it picks up again. Harder than before. But there's time between each lessening, so that gives me hope."

"Is hope all we gots, lady?" Donarius growled.

"Meaning, why can't I stop the storm or at least weaken it?" I said dryly.

Donarius nodded. "No disrespect intended, lady," he said, "but I been wonderin' that . . . from time to time."

"The storm might be early," I said, "but it *is* natural. Not even all the Evocators of Orissa and wizards of the Far Kingdoms could create such a storm. And it's so strong a storm that my magical powers have been . . . limited. It's like they were flattened . . ." And I murmured to myself, half in thought: "Flattened in a curve and close to the horizon . . ."

"What was that, Lady Antero?" Donarius broke in. "About bein' close to the horizon or some such. What was close to the horizon?"

"Never mind," I said, "it's something a scholar will have to figure out. Back to the point. The storm has limited my powers. Why, I can only guess. But I also sense something *not quite* natural about the storm."

"Another sorcerer, me lady?" Carale asked.

"Almost certainly," I said. "But the presence I sense is more like a . . . chorus . . . a faint chorus at that. And this magical chorus is somehow using the wind to make its influence stronger."

"Chorus has a sorter friendly ring, me lady," Carale said. "But you haven't talked 'bout it in such a friendly manner."

I shook my head. "It isn't even vaguely friendly," I said. "No, it's looking for something, all right. It's looking for magical presences, and anything it finds will be . . . burned out, is the only way I can describe it."

I'd never experienced such a thing, but I'd instinctively felt my magical flesh squirm each time my enemy's presence had made itself known.

"That's why I've had even less use of my powers," I said.

I paused. Then, "Anything bigger than a rat trick will bring it down on me. And if it gets me, then it'll know where you are. And it'll know your business. And it's likely to disagree."

Donarius grunted. "I gets yer point, Lady Antero," he said. "I gets it very well."

"Pardon, lady," came Lizard's voice. "What do we do when the storm's over? And you get your powers back? What do we do then?"

"Conjure up a bottle of grog," I said, "and get you to sing us a good drinking song."

The men chuckled. It felt almost warm in that chamber of frozen stone. Someone started to tell a story. I leaned closer to listen.

Then the storm howled in on us again and we all scurried back into the snowbanks of ourselves.

I dreamed I was standing on a long blue shore and a silver ship came swooping out of a cloud bank. I didn't find it remarkable in my dream, although I gazed with interest at the straining sails, thinking to myself that it was a windless day. Then I saw—quite clearly—a woman at the wheel of the ship. She was the color of ivory, and an ivory gown whipped around her, showing every curve and hollow of her figure. She had long auburn hair that streamed behind her and she made quite a heroic figure as she steered the ship through the sorcerous gale.

Then I saw her turn, one hand still on the wheel, and she peered toward the shore. Our eyes met and it was as if we were a mere breath apart, and I felt thunder shudder through my bones. Her eyes were dark pools that drew me down. Then they widened in fear and she was back on the silver ship and I was on the shore.

I heard lyre music swell the clouds, saw the distant figure in ivory wrench at the ship's wheel, and then the ship was soaring away in desperate flight. I watched until it fled over the horizon.

The lyre music stopped and I woke up.

I rubbed my eyes. I looked around, feeling oddly out of place. Disoriented. Bewildered. Something was wrong. Something was different.

And then I realized what that difference was.

The storm had ended.

DEATH OF AN EVOCATOR

We came out blinking into sunlight and calm. The sky was eye-searing blue, and the ground—thanks to the snow-lashing we'd received in the last blow—was heaped with mounds of dazzling white powder. The sea was smooth, patterned like gray tiles, and at the shoreline the foamy surf was clotted with lumps of ice.

I shuddered in breath, feeling remarkably free. I might be starved and frostbitten, but, no thanks to the gods, I was alive!

I drew in three more quick gulps of air, then cast my senses out. Delicately at first, then stronger and soaring high into the ethers when I met no resistance or traps.

I rubbed my hands together. "Let's have a fire," I said. "A nice fire."

The men chortled and gathered about. With a flourish I swept my hands into a parting circle, indicating a space the size of a large campfire. The men shuffled out of the way.

I chanted:

> "Hearthfires—
> Fires of home—
> Come where I beckon
> And burn warm and bright."

I gestured, making a good Evocator's show of it, boosting their spirits along with my spell. Then I flung my closed fist forward, opening it wide at just the right moment as if I were hurling dice. A small ball of flame leaped out, startling the men so, they jumped back. Then the ball fell to the ground, steaming and hissing as it sank through the snow. I threw my hands wide and the glow grew higher and larger.

Then I clapped my palms together and it became a large cheery bonfire crackling in the snow. It gave off the scent of burning leaves—leaves from familiar trees in Orissa.

The men cheered and we gathered close to the fire. We were truly warm for the first time in weeks. I had to be careful not to scorch my flesh, I enjoyed the flames so much. Soon the spells on our winter clothes even wavered into life with a little help from me and we were as toasty as the day we'd landed.

The next problem we had to solve, and quickly, was food. *That* I couldn't produce by magic—not by snapping my fingers, at least. Certainly I could command a meal to appear, as luscious as one could imagine. I could summon an entire banquet, for that matter. But there would be no substance in the food. No taste, no nourishment, and no matter how much one ate, she'd never feel full. If you consume a banquet plucked from the spirit worlds, you will leave the table as hungry as when you sat down.

I found a quiet place with sheltering rocks, made a little fire, and crouched down before it. I made a sea hawk in my mind, a hunting hawk with a hood drawn over its head. I plucked the hood off and let my spirit soar with the hawk as it flew through the air.

I could see the men gathered at the larger campfire. None of them saw me, although my spirit hawk self swooped over them low enough to ruffle their hair. I swept across the mounds of snow that marked the ruins of the outpost, glided along the shoreline to the broad field where the caravan had camped. I swung out from the flattened area, which looked like a depression in the high rolling blanket of snow that covered the tall grasses.

I caught a flicker of movement and instinctively tucked in my spirit wings and shot downward. I was a shadow, less than a shadow, speeding a scant few feet over the white field. Then snow exploded in front of me, and I heard a squawk as I climbed away from the explosion.

I circled about to see what prey I'd found. First I saw the fox, mottled gray, snapping at the mouth of a large burrow. A flightless bird nearly as big as the fox and armed with a long heavy beak was striking out at his attacker. The bird wasn't afraid, which must have been a surprise to the fox or he'd never have attempted the attack. Instead the bird was angrily clubbing the fox with its stubby swimming wings and pecking at him with its beak. The fox broke and fled, leaving the bird muttering to itself and clearing away the debris that'd fallen into its burrow.

I brought the spirit hawk back gently, not wanting the shock of a suddenly broken spell. Then I was back into myself, rubbing my hands in front of the fire. My stomach rumbled.

We would eat.

The flightless birds were delicious. They were a bit stringy perhaps, and fishy, but I don't think I've ever tasted anything as good as that first bite of roasted flesh. They also made a tolerable stew, which improved in the next few days because Lizard made liquors from their organs to flavor the food. I'm afraid we hunted out those fields in short time, digging into the grasses and dragging the birds out of their burrows. We clubbed them, skinned them, ate our fill and butchered out and preserved scores more.

Then Lizard came up to me with a shy request. "Remember your promise, lady," he said. "About the first thing you'd do when the storm ended."

I did indeed. I'd promised a jug of grog if he gave us a song.

How to produce that grog, however, was a different matter. I told Lizard the problem, seeking his assistance.

"I can get grog," I said, "but it'll be like imaginary grog. You'll see it, feel that it's wet, but that's about all. However, if I have something similar to exchange, I can get the real thing."

"You mean grog for grog, lady?" he said. He scratched his head. "What's that get us? If we had grog, we wouldn't be needin' any, now would we, lady?"

"It doesn't *have* to be grog," I said. "Just something fermented like grog. Anything will do. If we had vinegar, as a matter of fact, I could make a decent enough wine."

Lizard brightened. "Aye, lady. Vinegar, you wants? Why'n't you say so?"

"Fine." I grinned. "Then I'm saying so. We need vinegar. But for the life of me, I don't know where to get it. We have no supplies, if you recall."

"Certain we do, lady," Lizard said. "Not old supplies but new ones."

He dashed off and returned in a little while with a bloody object glistening in one fist. He shook it at me, a big grin splitting his homely face. "Here's our vinegar, lady," he said.

The bloody hunk he displayed was some kind of bladder. Lizard pierced it with his knife and squeezed out a clear stream of liquid. I caught some on my finger and tasted.

"It's a bladder from one of them birds, lady," he said.

"And it tastes exactly like vinegar," I answered.

By dusk Lizard and I had squeezed about a gallon of the stuff from the bird bladders. Not much longer after that, I'd cast the necessary spell and we were all sitting about the fire toasting each other with the most pleasing and heady wine imaginable.

Although it did taste a little fishy.

The next day we got busy laying plans for escape.

"Here's the size of it," I told the men. "We could try for the other outpost and pray they still live."

"That's not likely," muttered Carale.

"And we'll be worse off than we are now," I said. "We'll use up what strength we have left to get there, and if a miracle hasn't saved our friends and there is no one waiting for us with fuel and supplies, we'll be doomed."

"Where else can we go, Lady Antero?" Donarius asked. "Nearest place we know's more'n twice distant. 'N' that's a nomad camp. Mightn' even be folks there, either."

"Unfortunately," I said, "the nearest civilization is ruled by our enemy. We don't know exactly where his lair is, but we've seen the marks of a caravan that went through here. And we've seen the trail it took. It has to end someplace. More than likely that place will be civilization . . . for better or worse."

"Worse, more'n likely," Donarius muttered. He looked around at the stark landscape and the frozen bird corpses piled up like logs for a fire. He shivered. "Maybe not," he said.

"So what do you think, lads?" I asked. "Do we go right to the heart of the enemy? Take a chance that we can steal a ship and sail home with our skins still on our bones?" Then I indicated the same bleak landscape that had caused Donarius to shiver. "Or do we stay here? There'll be more storms, I'm certain. We've yet to face winter."

I gestured at the crackling fire we were all enjoying. "I can't keep that up," I said. "It takes sorcerous energy that I'm drawing from someplace else, as well as from myself, and I can't keep it up forever. Also, if I use more energy than I can quickly replenish, if some emergency occurs, I might not have the power to respond."

"Don't mind the stray witch tha' might pop out, me lady," Carale said. "It's the lack of fire that got me. If stayin' here in this cold got me six months more of life than I face on the trail, I'd rather move on than stay, if it's all the same to you."

"You've got tha' right, Captain," Donarius agreed. "I say we see how far sneakin' can carry us. Maybe even get to whack a head or three afore I go. Better'n swingin' at the wind out here."

Everyone agreed, with no little vehemence. An uproar erupted over what preparations should be made, the terrain that might be faced, the things that needed making, the supplies that should be brought, and on and on. It was like old times. Like being in the barracks readying for a long march that'll likely end in battle and quite possibly death.

It cheered me immensely.

It took us a little over a week to prepare. We were growing stronger daily. The weather remained mild and we had plenty of time to do the job right. Only Carale and I had any winter training, although all the others knew the theory of basic survival in any land.

I had no qualms about tackling this wilderness. At least it wasn't mud. I've fought in mud, and it's worse than snow.

We made snowshoes out of the bird carcasses, using their feathered hides for the base and the bones for frames. They worked quite well. If you've ever seen those black and white birds skim across the snow on their bellies, you can imagine how easy it was for us to get about. It was like skating on snow rather than crunching awkwardly about on clumsy shoes.

We also used the bird hides for packs, stitching them together with gut from their innards and needles from their bones. We found two small timbers we'd overlooked when foraging for fuel. We turned those into a sled to carry our supplies, which mostly consisted of bird meat and unused hides. We'd strung the timbers together with rope made from tendon, suspended hides over them for a carrying bed, and that was that. Our reworked costumes also became heavily dependent on bird skins and feathers. Holes were patched with feathers, our clothes were stuffed with them for insulation, and we made hats of the stuff, perching them on our pates like black and white nests. We drew our parka hoods over the feather hats, drawing the strings tight so no cold air could get in.

We'd become obsessed with matters involving warmth and cold. Finicky about the most minute details, like old soldiers at a grogshop. Always going on about how the socks ought to go over the boot top and then the breeches tucked in. As if these small things were the most interesting and absorbing topics in the world.

I wasn't displeased with our armament. Each of us had swords and daggers. We also had bows and slings and battle-axes. There were various other arms, but not many. We'd only planned, after all, to spend that one day on shore. But we'd come better prepared to fight than eat, so I didn't think we were that bad off when we finally set out.

We must have looked an odd group as we shuffled out of the ruined outpost: scooting along the snowy path on bird skis, with black and white feathers sticking out of our clothes. But none of us laughed and none of us looked back at the place that had nearly become a desolate haunt for our ghosts.

Finding and then following the caravan trail was not as hard as it might seem. True, a month had passed; the area had been swept by a massive storm and then left covered with snow. But all of us were skilled trackers. The twins were especially good, brushing away the snow in likely spots and finding physical signs to follow. Added to that was the magical spoor left behind by the caravan drovers and their animals.

The terrain we traveled was strange. From a hilltop it looked like slow rolling waves of white. The waves seemed like lacy clouds clinging to jagged peaks of black and brown and gray. Those peaks clawed up, malformed by wind and time, looking like demons' talons. Meanwhile the sky was an ever-changing swirl of thick clouds of white and black and gray. Here and there a patch of blue would break through and a column of sunlight would hit a point of land and make it leap out with startling clarity.

That was the view from a hilltop. It was different close up. To begin with, the snow was not an even blanket. Some areas were smooth enough and we could make good time, skating along on our bird pelts. But other areas were as treacherous as the worst reef-edged coast.

I remember being a day or two out, on point, charging along the trail at top speed. The men were strung out behind me—with the twins guarding the rear and Carale and Donarius paralleling us on both sides to watch our flanks.

The physical signs of the track had been faint, and I'd taken the lead from the twins—sniffing for magical signs. I'd caught a strong whiff of Searbe, our captured Evocator. The scent aroused mixed feelings. First, I was glad he'd still been alive when the caravan passed this way. On the other hand, I was worried about why he'd been captured and how much he'd cooperate and to what purpose. Still, the scent of him had given me a surge of energy and I charged along the trail at a high rate of speed.

Then I grew tired. The physical signs became plainer and I waved for the twins to relieve me.

As they came forward I dropped back, intending to let the others pass so I could take up the rear and rest for a while. The twins grinned as they flashed by, raising their thumbs to signal that they'd spotted Searbe's spoor, as well.

Then they turned it into a boyish race, with Talu gradually edging out his brother and straining some yards ahead. I watched their sport with a smile, ready to bring them to heel if I thought their high spirits would tire them out too soon.

Talu spurted ahead, aiming for a boulder the two had obviously chosen as a mark. As he neared it he leaned into a graceful curve, showering snow as he skidded to a stop. Then he raised his arms and shouted a mock battle cry to claim victory.

The snow suddenly collapsed under him and the cry shrilled into fear. He clawed the air for balance, then started to sink from view. I ran toward him as fast as I could, but there was no way I'd get there in time.

At that moment Talay hurtled up, shouting his brother's name. Talay dived forward, grabbing his twin's wrist and stopping his fall.

But just as I was sighing relief the terror continued. Talu's weight overbalanced them both. And now the two of them were sliding to their doom. He called out to his brother to let go, to save himself, but Talay ignored him, clinging harder.

Then I was diving forward, grabbing Talay's legs. I clung to his ankles, digging in my toes to anchor us. They skittered across icy ground, and now I could feel myself being dragged along, as well. Then Donarius' strong hands gripped my calves, his heavy weight dug in behind me, and we stopped.

We clung together like that for a long time. At last our comrades caught up and reeled us in one by one; and soon we were all on our feet gaping at the hidden ravine we'd nearly fallen into, marveling that it had happened so fast. Within a few blinks of an eye all three of us had nearly been killed.

After that incident we traveled with more care. It was a good thing the accident had occurred early on. We soon saw that the whole region was laced with deep ravines, lying hidden between the rolling waves of snow.

The caravan track was some help. Naturally, it took the easiest route. But the weather had rearranged many things since the caravan we followed had passed. Sometimes the trail across a ravine would be barred by rocks that had collapsed from the sides. The most treacherous places tended to be those that looked the safest. The way ahead would appear smooth and safe. But lurking just beyond might be a deep ravine that had been bridged and hidden by a thin sheet of snow-dusted ice. Waiting for you to set your foot down so it could swallow you up.

We were in a hurry, so by necessity we sometimes had to trust luck and our growing experience, poking at suspicious places with our spears or swords and moving quickly along other areas with nothing but prayers to guard us.

I saw scores of avalanches, thankfully always from a distance.

I'd be looking at a mountain's smooth, serene face when suddenly I'd hear a rumble. Then snow would break away and spill down the mountainside like a thick white waterfall, fountaining clouds of foamy dust as it plummeted to the ice below.

Visibility was strange under those swirling skies. Sometimes the trail would seem like a river of cloud shadows that moved so swiftly along the ground that you'd lose your bearings and suddenly find yourself clutching madly at the air to regain your balance. Then the next moment you'd be moving under a blue patch of sky with light so dazzling that you'd become confused and stand there gaping like a dumb beast suddenly set upon a different world. Colors were brighter, objects clearer, but just in that swatch of light. All else would appear fuzzy and surreal.

Game was scarce. I could sense small animals about, little burrowing things. But nothing large. From time to time we came upon frozen streams, or ponds. At those places, I used a trick I'd learned from a nomad to fill our cookpots. It took no magic to perform the trick, unless you consider the wonders of nature sorcerous. But there was enough guesswork involved to edge it close to a wizard's art.

There are freshwater fish in the far south that are frozen rock-solid in the winter. When spring comes they thaw out and swim away as if nothing had happened. The nomad claimed the fish can remain frozen that way for many years without effect.

The trick was to guess where they'd be beneath all that ice, and then chip away the area and see if you'd guessed right. The nomad said you had to imagine you were a fish yourself and look at the breaks in the banks and the bends in the shallows to see where your favorite fishy hiding place would be. I'd guessed wrong the first few times—at the cost of much nasty labor and scowls from my mates, who were wondering if perhaps Lady Antero had lost her mind and her good magical sense.

But I worked on, spurred by memories of Gamelan, who had been a skilled fisherman himself and used similar methods to catch our finny cousins.

And when we finally struck through to the right place, my friends' scowls turned to broad smiles and loud compliments. A school of about two dozen were in the first find, and nearly that number in the second. Then my companions caught on to the trick and it became as certain a dish as if we'd cached supplies in advance of the journey.

Fuel was a constant problem, although we managed well enough picking up bits of brush and frozen grasses as we went. Growth was spotty and sometimes the day would end with nothing but ice over frozen rocks for our beds. A few times, when we were caught out like that, I drew on my magical resources to keep us warm. Other times we actually dug up the frozen animal droppings from the caravan and burned those for heat and cooking.

Water was also not easy to come by. There were no free-running streams, and we had to melt ice or snow to get it. This took time we could ill afford, and we were continually amazed that such big potsful of snow produced so little liquid.

The magical landscape was as severe as the natural. The dogs of sorcery unleashed by the storm had killed mercilessly. All creatures with any magical senses had been slaughtered or crushed, no matter how small or innocent. It may surprise you to know that some plants and even a few lowly worms have small abilities that allow them to tap into the ethers to sustain their life processes. For a wizard, the ethers are always abuzz with such presences, like insects in a garden. But as we trod that frozen land, the ethers seemed silent and lifeless, like a desert is at first glance. Only the spoors and faintly glowing husks of what had been left behind were evident.

Little by little, however, the etherous landscape began to change. I felt magical presences pop back into existence like flowers blooming in the mud after a brutal spring deluge. Like myself, some of my lowly cousins of the sorcerous world had gotten warning and had been quick enough to go to ground and remain there until danger passed.

Although the caravan track twisted and turned, it generally headed south toward a ragged range of snow-covered mountains.

We experienced a few squalls during the early days of the journey, but nothing like the storm that'd nearly killed us. Each time inclement weather arrived, I thought our enemy might be returning. We'd hunch down in a gully or dig holes in the snow to shelter us until the storm was over. Within hours the front would have passed over us without any real danger. I began to wonder if I'd been mistaken about the storm that had marooned us. Perhaps it really had been nothing more than an early winter blow.

"Yer've never been wrong afore, me lady," Carale said one day, when I'd confessed my doubts.

"Still," I said, "it makes better sense if this time I was. If there was an enemy behind the storm, where is our enemy now? Why hasn't he come back? Leaped on us with something new and even more deadly?"

Carale shrugged. "Maybe he thinks he's done the job, me lady," he said. "Yer say yerself tha' ev'n the smallest critter suffered. So maybe this wizard thinks he's done all that's necessary."

"The question is," I said, "what did he have in mind besides slaughter?"

"Yer certain he didn't know we were here, me lady?" Carale asked.

I considered a moment, then nodded. "I'm positive," I said. "That was a blind attack. There was no single target."

" 'N' yer thinks this ice pirate we was after has somethin' to do wi' it?" he said.

"I'm not so certain of that," I said. "The enemy left no sign of identity I could decipher."

"But yer inclination is t' suspect the ice pirate?" Carale pressed.

"Yes," I said. I sounded more sure than I was. But that short flat answer leaped to my tongue without prodding.

"Then tha's probably who it probably is, then," Carale said. "Take yer first guess and stick with her is my advice, me lady. Works as well as anythin' else."

"Yes, but why hasn't he returned?" I asked.

"Who knows, me lady?" Carale said. " 'N' does it really matter that much? We'll find out by and by."

"There's another thing," I said. "It's nearly winter. Yet the weather still seems mild for these parts." I gave a rueful laugh. "The cold and gloomy skies we see about us are fair weather down here. More like spring."

Carale grimaced. "Why look for trouble, me lady?" he asked. "Why dare the gods with such questions? Winter'll be on us soon enough. And if it's late this year, why, let's bless the gods for favoring us."

"Somehow," I grumbled, "I don't think it's got anything to do with favors, especially from the gods."

Carale's eyebrows shot up. "Yer think there's magic behind that as well, me lady?" he asked, worried.

I shook my head, exasperated. "I don't know. And that's what's troubling me the most. I just plain don't know." ·

Carale clapped my shoulder. "Cheer up, me lady. We'll find out soon enough . . . one way or the other."

He poked at the fire with a twig, suddenly gloomy. "Still," he said, "I'd feel much better if I had a deck under me feet. I'd not be revealin' a deep personal secret to yer, me lady, if I told yuz I don't much like walkin'."

I smiled. It was the old argument between sailors and soldiers.

"I admit I've grown to love the sea," I said. "But I was a soldier too long to trust my fate to a small enclosed space."

"Aye, yer've said that afore, me lady," Carale said. "But yer'll have to admit we can't walk home."

"No," I said, "that's true. But think what would have happened if we'd have remained on the *Tern* instead of being on land. We'd have been dead along with the others. No ship could have survived that storm."

Carale pursed his lips, considering. Then he said, "Tha' may be true. But we'll never know, will we, me lady? I've always trusted in me seaman's skills, and they've never failed me yet."

He rubbed one of his feet, wincing when he hit a sore spot. "The gods had a most evil sense of humor when they gave us these, me lady," he said.

"Clubby, ugly things. Nothin' so ugly as a foot, if yer thinks on it. 'N' yer toes are so tender, like twigs. Yer can break 'em. Yer can freeze 'em. Yer can plain wear 'em out.

"If a deck timber goes bad, yer can just patch it up with a piece of good wood. Can't do that with toes."

"No, you can't," I agreed. "But you can put your shoes on and run like the hells," I said.

Carale nodded. "Yer right, me lady," he said. "But yer can't run very far. The hells catch up to yuz quick enough when yer afoot."

Several weeks out we came upon a frozen oasis.

There was nothing to mark it at first. A storm seemed to be brewing beyond the horizon, and the sky was an eerie swirl of thick gray and black clouds, making visibility difficult. All color had been reduced to bleak whites and grays and blacks, making us feel like insects crawling across a page of ink-blotched parchment. We'd been marching for hours and were looking for a place to rest our weary bones.

We came upon a valley sheltered by broad shouldered hills of volcanic rock. The caravan track led through a parting between two of those hills, and we followed it to a place where another trail intersected and seemed to blend in. From all signs, the second trail seemed to have been made by another caravan. The track was fresher than the first but not by much. Although we entered the valley with caution, it was only good habit that bade us to do so, for there was no sign of life.

If it weren't for the trail, we might have missed the squat building in the center of the valley. It was covered with snow and looked like just another small hill to pass by. The caravan track led directly to the building, curving around to the south side, where we found an entrance, more of a broad tunnel than a door or gate. The archway was of dark, hand-hewn stone blocks.

We chipped away ice and snow and found that the rest of the building seemed to be made of the same material. We went inside, threading our way through a series of cantilevered walls that I guessed had been thrown up to block winds coming from that direction. The deeper we went, the stronger became the stale smell of animals and the more sour odor of unwashed humans.

About halfway down the passage dim lights winked on. The light came from little piles of crystals heaped in small stone cups set in niches in the tunnel walls. After inspecting them, I saw the crystals were similar to the stuff we make our firebeads from. Only our presence was needed to set them alight, much like the way we light the gloomier recesses of our own public buildings in Orissa.

As we entered the low-vaulted central chamber, light bloomed from overhead. The chamber was about the size of a dockside warehouse. The walls and floors were all of dark stone, but the stone had been stained and badly worn from many years of use—centuries was my guess. The ceiling funneled upward into what I assumed was an elaborate chimney that would draw out any smoke, yet wouldn't allow the raw elements to get in.

On one side was a large stone corral where the caravan animals had been kept. I noted there were plenty of old droppings littering the corral, assuring us of fuel. There were two main sleeping areas evident, with raised stone pallets for perhaps a hundred or more people. Many of the pallets had little warming ovens built into them. All you had to do was heap your bedclothes on top, stuff in the fuel, set it alight, wait until the pallet got nice and warm, then crawl into your blankets for a blissful sleep.

All of us immediately saw their purpose. We were drawn to them greatly, as if by a spell, but we pressed on in our exploration, although for a time there was so much yawning and gaping that Donarius said we all looked like "a great lot of lazy camels."

There were alcoves of various sizes opening into the chamber, with raised stone platforms set inside. We guessed they were used to store caravan goods in, although all we could find were a few broken leather harnesses and a frayed belt with its buckle removed. In one chamber we found a split sack of grain. Lizard immediately started scooping the grain up and we all had visions of hot porridge for dinner.

We kept circling, spying out this sign and that. When we'd nearly completed the circle, I caught a sudden whiff of sorcery. I waved the others back and moved forward, all my senses alert.

I came upon a room with an odd-shaped entrance easily twice my height and breadth. I stood back from the entrance a moment, puzzling at the shape. Then I realized that it was formed like a rearing bear with outstretched claws.

I entered, wary and sniffing about for a wizard's trap.

The room was empty.

Then on the far wall I saw chains. Hanging from those chains was a corpse. I looked closer, trying to ignore the gross mutilations that had been inflicted on the body. Tears welled up when I saw the familiar clothes.

They were Orissan.

I was saddened but hardly shocked. I'd been worried that we'd encounter such a thing ever since we'd left Antero Bay.

The only surprise was that Searbe seemed to have put up a struggle before he'd been killed. I was angry at myself for misjudging the Evocator. He'd been tortured by our enemies, but had apparently refused to aid them.

The others helped me get the body down and respectfully laid out. The men muttered at the treatment Searbe had suffered, and I knew if we caught up to the guilty party, there'd be more than professional enthusiasm in the fight. I sent them all away to make camp, except for Carale, who stayed behind to help me get the body ready for burial.

We worked at this grisly task in silence for a time. Then Carale scratched his head and murmured, "Seems t' have shrunk a bit."

"What did you say?" I asked.

Carale gestured at the body. "Wasn't Lord Searbe taller, me lady?" he said. "Had a potbelly on him, too. Liked his dram 'n' a brew, he did. Don't mean t' be disrespectful of the dead, but he bent his elbow more like an old tavern lush 'stead of a wizard."

I smiled forgiveness. "He likely lost the gut to exercise and short rations," I said.

"Tha's true, me lady," Carale said. "But he wouldn't a gotten shorter, would he, now?"

I looked at the corpse's features again. Although mutilated, they still looked familiar. Then I checked the rest of the body. Gradually it began to dawn on me that Carale was right. Searbe had been a little over six feet, although he had a silly little lie he told that claimed he was taller still. He also had a long trunk and short stubby legs with feet so small that he seemed to stagger when he walked—sort of a mincing stagger, actually, like a blowzy washerwoman trying to act like a delicate milkmaid.

The body I was studying was a good two hands shorter, was split high, and the feet were proportional to his size.

Still, he looked familiar. Just as the few remnants of magical energy lingering about the corpse were familiar. This was definitely the corpse of an Orissan Evocator.

It was then that the delayed shock hit.

"It ain't Lord Searbe, is it, me lady?" Carale growled.

"No," I said, low.

"It's the Evocator from the other outpost, ain't it?" he said. "I was there when yer dropped him off. Lord Serano, was his name. Little feller. Bold he was. Heart like a lion."

"Yes," I answered. "It's Serano, all right."

"Now we know for sure," Carale continued, "tha' the other outpost was hit. 'N' mos' probably destroyed. Not only tha', but everybody was killed, 'cept for the Evocator. Just like at Antero Bay. An' him they took captive."

I made no reply. Carale tenderly tucked the ragged parka around Serano's brutalized features. "Poor bastard," he said. "He was a brave one, he was."

We gave him the best rites we could under the circumstances. I led the others in prayer that Serano's ghost would find peace in the afterlife, if such a thing exists. And we heaped rocks over his body since it was impossible to dig a grave.

Then we withdrew to a campfire Lizard had built near the sleeping platforms. He was making dinner, and the area was filled with the rich odor of porridge made from the grain the previous occupants had left behind. It was bran, might have even been meant to feed the animals, but it tasted like nectar to us. While we ate I conferred with each of the men, adding what they had found to my own discoveries.

Then I said, "Here's what I believe happened, and please feel free to stop me if you think I have something wrong."

The men nodded, so I continued.

"Both of our trading posts were attacked and wiped out. In each case the attack came from the sea. But we know they were probably carefully timed because caravans soon came on the scene. The attackers captured and then handed over both of our Evocators, Lord Searbe and Lord Serano.

"The two caravans then struck out for this oasis. From all evidence, the one carrying Lord Searbe reached here first, with the other caravan arriving no more than a day or so later.

"Is that the way you two see it?" I asked the twins.

They both agreed, adding that the two groups had camped here for some time. At least a month.

"Which means," I said, "they were waiting out the storm. If it were only one group, I'd say they were lucky to reach here in time. But since there were two, and the timing of the attack and the journey was so close, I'd suspect they knew the storm was coming and made for this place as fast as they could. If this is true, it was a prearranged meeting at a predetermined time.

"When the storm was over, they moved on as a single, enlarged group. I can only speculate that they're headed for the same place, but I think it's as good a guess as any."

Carale broke in. "If they went t' so much trouble t' capture our Evocators, me lady," he said, "why'd they end up killin' one of them?"

"I don't know," I said. "Not for certain, anyway. But I'd say it was a fair guess that they wanted some magical feat performed."

" 'N' Lord Serano refused?" Carale said.

"Yes," I said. "He refused."

Left unsaid was that Searbe must've complied. Otherwise we would have found his corpse here, too.

"But why'd they go t' so much trouble, lady?" Donarius asked. "I can understand wantin' t' wipe out our tradin' posts. But why go t' all the trouble to catch our Evocators 'n' carry 'em away?"

"The same reason the giants attacked Pisidia," I said. "And the sole purpose for that, unless I'm wrong, was to carry off the Oracle Mother, Lady Daciar."

"But tha' don't answer the why of it, if yer'll be beggin' me pardon, me lady," Carale said.

"No, it doesn't," I said. "But it does show a pattern. These pirates want much more than booty—at least the kind that you can spend. Someone is going to no end of trouble to get their hands on as many wizards as they can get. For what purpose, I can't say. If it were only to weaken their opponents, why, they'd just kill them. But each time it seems they are most anxious to keep the wizard alive."

Everyone's eyes glanced over to the other side of the chamber at the rock heap that was Serano's grave.

"Didn't do too good a job keepin' *him* alive," Lizard muttered.

"That was probably a mistake," I said. "They got their blood up and tried to force the issue. Whatever that issue was. Unless I'm very wrong, they'll be the hells to pay when they get where they're going and are one Evocator short."

"Shows to go ya," Donarius said, "tha' it's savages we're up against, lady. They can fight. I'll give 'em tha'. But they ain't so good at followin' strict orders."

"I hadn't thought of that," I said. "That might be a weakness we can exploit."

"Aye, we'll be doin' tha', lady," Donarius growled. "Tell the truth, I figger we ain't got much hope a gettin' home. 'N' if that be the case, I'd like to get a few good exploitin' type sword strokes in."

"Let's not be foolhardy," I said. "We've all been in fixes before. We'll get out of this one."

"Never been in one wi' such a tight fit," Lizard muttered.

"Well, I have," I said. "I was lost in the West for nearly two years. The people I was with, other than my Guardswomen, were poorly trained and motivated. Tell the truth, if I wasn't the only hope they had of getting back, they'd of slit my throat in the night. Although that was tried when it looked like we were nearly home.

"We're in a much better position here. We *know* which way home is. All of us are here freely, and we've had no lack of training. All we need to do is keep going. If we find a port, we'll find a ship. Then it's only a question of how we get our hands on that ship.

"So let's not fix on the idea of revenge just now. There'll be plenty of time for that. And plenty of help to carry it out in Orissa."

Carale waved a hand, taking in the chamber of stone. "If savages they be," he said, "they got more brains than most. 'N' from the looks of this place, they've been around for a longer time'n most, as well."

"This wasn't built by the current crop," I said. "Just as you judged, this is an ancient place. From the shape of the doorway where we found poor Lord Serano, it was constructed during the time of the First Ice Bear King."

I picked up a broken piece of paving stone. "There was magical labor in the making of this, as well as physical. But it's old sorcery. I'm not saying our enemy isn't capable of doing the same thing. It's just that I don't think he's been around long enough to accomplish a project so grand. I'd bet a fat purse of gold that as we travel we'll find other such comfort stops.

"My guess is we're still dealing with an upstart. Someone trying to wear the mantle of a great and legendary king who spent his whole lifetime adding to the work of another great king who came before him.

"This is the remnant of an empire, my friends. An empire someone is attempting to rebuild."

PEOPLE OF
THE ICE

Our first sight of them was through a swirl of fog rising off a broad
frozen lake.

The mist had enveloped us as soon as we'd set foot on the ice.
We were four days out of the oasis when we came upon the lake. The caravan track vanished at the edge and we lost many hours examining the shore
in both directions before we were certain they'd headed out across the ice.
Even though a much larger group had crossed before us, we were uncertain
as we made our first timid steps on the lake's frozen surface.

It seemed as solid as true ground, but the knowledge that we could
break through at any weakened point made us nervous. A person could die
in a few short minutes in water so cold. Our whole group could be gone just
as swiftly if we all went in.

The proper way of crossing would have been to stretch out in a long
line, rope ourselves together, then move along with as much distance as possible between us. If one went in, the others could instantly drag him out.
Even if that plan failed, at least only one of us would be lost.

We didn't have enough rope to take such precautions. We got together
what line we could, which was barely sufficient for three people with seven
feet or so between them. Those three took the lead, testing the treacherous
path for the others. But the fog became so thick that even that small precau-

tion proved useless. We were forced to stay within a few feet of the person in front or we'd all be lost.

We must have strayed from the path during the early part of our effort, because at one point we all walked out on a weakened area.

The first warning was a sudden series of loud pops and cracks, like the breaking of bones. The ice shifted under us so suddenly that no one even had time for a warning shout.

We stood still for what seemed like eons as the surface buckled beneath our feet, tilting crazily this way and that. What made it even more frightening was that we couldn't see the danger. I heard the splash of open water somewhere in front of us and smelled the musty odor of lake bottom.

Then all became still. The shifting and crackling of the ice ceased.

We waited as long as we could, then gingerly made our way around where we imagined the break to be.

About an hour later, to our vast relief, I picked up Searbe's faint sorcerous scent. Then the twins found some castoffs from the caravan. More certain of our direction, we struck out at greater speed, following the trail.

The fog billowed around us, making us feel like we were in a world of bleak dreams and smothering nightmares. The wind was slight but seemed to whistle a ghostly song in our ears. The waves of fog formed monstrous shapes, broke apart, then reformed to even more ghastly images. We had no idea how far we'd come or how much longer we had to go before we reached the other shore. We were tense, sweating under our parkas, imagining that unseen danger would erupt at any moment.

I was at point when we saw them.

I felt them first—a heavy pressure in the air of a large moving presence. Then the fog parted and I saw something broad and gray cut through. It swung toward me, then away.

I heard a strange voice shout an order, and we dropped flat on the ice. Then I heard another shouted order and a distinctive rasping sound, as if something heavy was being drawn along the ice.

The fog whooshed to one side, and to my amazement I saw what appeared to be a ship tack a few yards in front of me. The ship leaned to one side, steadied, then righted itself and disappeared into the fog bank.

I waited until all was silent again. Then I gave two sharp tugs on my rope, signaling the others to stay where they were. I untied the rope and crept forward. I'd seen a ship and thought that at any minute I'd come to the edge of the ice and find water. Instead the surface remained steadfastly firm and frozen. My hand struck a ridge in the ice. I stopped and came to my knees, peering down at what I'd found.

There was a large slash in the ice about three hands wide. I moved along the slash for a short distance and saw that it was more of an unbroken track than a cut. Using the track as a starting point, I crawled away on a diagonal. About ten feet from that point I came to a second track identical to the first. I signaled and the others moved up.

Just as they reached me, I felt a shift in the air pressure, like pillows pressing in. I heard a heavy presence grate on the ice and we all dived out of the way as the fog parted and a shadow bore down on us.

I lifted my head as the ship went by, sailing across the ice on great wooden skis.

The ship looked spectral, haunted, with fog billowing all around and the mast and sail and lines all faintly aglow. They looked like the trails heavenly bodies make on starry nights—a whisper to the eye to sketch a pattern that might not really be there. Ice particles shimmered within that sketch, making the ship appear more ghostly still.

I saw a large shape at the tiller, heard barked orders come from that shape, saw other manlike shadows scurry to carry them out. No one was looking in our direction, and I doubt if they could have made us out if they did. Then the fog shifted again, obscuring all but the figure at the tiller.

A trick of light made his face suddenly glare into startling clarity. It was long and pale as new ice, and the eyes were painted black circles, rimmed with dark blue and white. Blue streaks highlighted the long cheekbones, and the chin was pointed and tipped with black. The lips were stained blue, and there were black streaks to indicate fangs.

I tensed as the man's eyes swept over me, ducking my head so I wouldn't draw attention. Then they moved on and the ship was gone.

Lizard was nearest, so I tugged on his sleeve to pass the word for us to move back and regroup. A few moments later Lizard tugged my sleeve in return. Everyone was ready.

We started to slither back, but then stopped as a big bell tolled from that direction, the tones rolling and booming through the frigid air. I flattened on the ice again, hesitating, wondering which way we should go.

The bell took up a steady toll, about once every two breaths. Then I heard other sounds coming our way—headed toward the bell.

This time I could make out many voices, barking dogs, and much movement. Quickly, I cast a spell of confusion to aid the fog, then I signaled Lizard to tell the others to spread out. As he moved away, lights bobbed into view all around us, flitting about like monstrous fireflies.

Two shadows hurtled toward me. I shifted on my side to present as small an edge as possible. The shadows became hooded, fur-cloaked men drifting across the ice at high speed. They were only a few feet apart, and I tensed, hand clawing out my knife as I braced for one of them to stumble over me in the fog.

I caught a glimpse of wooden skates, and then the men moved smoothly past on either side. One of them brushed my parka with his skate, yet didn't notice. I heard one man say something to the other. It must have been humorous, because his companion laughed.

Dogs yipped, a whip cracked, and then a whole line of shaggy figures plunged into view. A dog-drawn sled rushed down on me, and I thought for certain the animals would sense me and howl the alarm. The whip cracked again and I had to roll to the side as the dogs and then the sled shot past.

A whole group of voices followed in the sled's wake. I barely breathed as a crowd of fur-cloaked people skated by me. Their conversation was casual. I heard snatches of gossip. Remarks about market prices. Complaints about husbands and wives and lovers.

We remained flat on the ice for hours. Cold crept into our bones, tweaking the painful scars we'd suffered at Antero Bay. At least a score of dog sleds passed, perhaps a hundred people or more—both in groups and singly. Two more ice ships sailed past. Yet during that whole time no one saw us, or even suspected our presence.

If the fog had lifted, we'd certainly have been discovered. It was like hiding out in a great field of tall wheat that was about to be harvested. While we waited, dreading that moment of discovery, a large group of people we feared might be our enemy was passing through that field like a gap-toothed rake. Only luck could keep those gaps spaced wide enough so no one would find us.

Our luck held, and finally the crowd thinned to a few stragglers. And then the bell stopped.

I took my best guess on which direction would lead to safety, and we withdrew as quickly and as silently as we could.

We barely got off the ice in time. Just as we reached the rocky shore, a wind came up, sweeping away the fog in long, lingering wisps, and we had to sprint for the cover of a low boulder-covered hill.

I skittered over the top, flipped around, and as my men swarmed past, I raised up on my elbows to get a good view of the area from which we'd retreated.

The landscape was a scene out of a devil's dream. The lake was a broad plane of ice rimmed with ugly black fingers of ruination. As far as the eye could see, the southern and northern shores appeared as if they had been gouged by giant claws.

Hills had been pared down, mountainsides blasted with fire. Dirty snow and ice ringed those wounds, and here and there I could see jagged roads and paths slicing through the rock. They led to the mouths of huge caves that seemed shored up by hand-hewn rock. There was no sign of activity on the roads or near the caves, although I thought I could make out vaguely familiar equipment scattered about here and there. I could also see clumps of large stone buildings with huge, black-streaked chimneys. Fire glowed in some of the chimneys but there was little smoke.

Then I heard a whoosh in the air, and from around a bend in the lakeshore came a graceful ice schooner. It was built for war, with a heavy ram fixed to the front and shields hanging from the sides. I saw fur-clad men with spears and other weapons standing on the deck.

Fluttering from the mast was the flag of the Ice Bear King.

The ship tacked for the point where the lake bowed into a bay. There was an ice port there, with dirty brown docks and a jumble of warehouses. Several smaller ice schooners were pulled up at the docks, and I saw figures swarm along the longest one to meet the incoming ship.

Crowded around the port was a warren of homes and buildings that made up what appeared to be a small city. The town was easily a mile long and was ringed by hunched mountains of gray, streaked with fingers of bare black rock. The homes and buildings were narrow and seemed to be constructed of rough timber, with high, sharply peaked roofs to shed snow. Other than the figures on the docks and ice schooners, I couldn't see anyone about.

Then the big bell tolled again and my eyes swiveled and found the source of the sound.

At the far edge of the city was a huge shaggy shape, easily twice the size of any of the buildings.

I jolted back.

It was a bear. A giant bear, reared back on its hind legs, jaws gaping wide for the attack.

The bell tolled again and I suddenly realized the sound was coming from between those massive jaws, which looked like they could engulf a ship. Then my breathing steadied and the bear came into better focus.

It was carved from stone and there was a wide staircase that led from its feet to big gates set in its paunch. The gates were open and I saw people swarming through.

"What in the hells is it, me lady?" Carale said. He'd come up beside me.

"Some sort of temple, I think," I muttered, but my mind wasn't on the answer. Instead I was gathering myself to cast out my senses. I motioned for him to be silent, then carefully slipped a feeler forward, like an eel slithering from its den and tasting the water for some sign of prey.

I caught a few magical particles drifting in the etherous breeze, noted they came from Searbe—our kidnapped Evocator—and followed that trail. The particles became fresh clumps of spoorsign the nearer I came to the town.

I pulled back, took a few deep breaths to moor my physical self, then turned to Carale. "He's still there," I said, pointing toward the town.

"Lord Searbe, ye mean, me lady?"

I nodded.

"Do we try t' go in and get him?" he asked.

I hesitated, then said, "I don't see how we have any other choice."

Carale nodded glumly. "I afeared as much, me lady," he said.

He peered out at the city and the bleak landscape surrounding it.

"Minin' town from the looks of it," he said. "Filthiest people in the world, mine owners is. 'N' it 'pears they been diggin' away here since Te-Date was a babe in messy blankets."

I could see he was right. The caves were obviously entrances to mines. The equipment scattered about was digging and hauling equipment, including wagons and hand trolleys to haul the ore along wooden rails set into the roads. Some of the buildings, I was now certain, were places where the ore was crushed and separated from the mined rock. Others—the ones with the towering chimneys—would be where the ore was processed into metal ingots.

The bleakness of the landscape now made much more sense. It had a purpose, ruinous as that purpose might be.

The only thing that still puzzled me was why there was no apparent activity in the mines and foundries. From what I could see, nearly the entire population was gathered inside the huge, bear-shaped structure.

Perhaps it was a festival day, a religious celebration of some sort. Whatever it was, it had to be of great importance. Mine operators are not known for such kindly gestures of devotion as closing their foundries and tunnels to give their workers time off to honor the gods.

Then from out of the ethers came a blast of sorcerous energy that seared my Evocator's skin. The pain was ferocious. I tasted blood and realized I'd bitten my lip nearly through to keep from crying out. I quickly quashed all my magical senses, pulling all feelers back like a squid folding in its tentacles to avoid a sea lizard's attack.

I felt Carale's hands gripping my shoulders and realized I was doubled over from the assault. I weakly waved him off and raised my head to get another look.

Then I heard the roar of many voices shouting in unison, and my head jerked to the right, eyes sweeping for the bend where the ship had appeared.

There was a roll of big-bellied drums, the rhythmic clang of swords hammered on steel shields, and then from out of the mist that still girdled the bend came score after score of fur-clad warriors.

They shouted again, and the shout was like thunder. Hundreds of savage warriors poured around the bend and skated toward the harbor in long, deceptively slow strides that carried them an amazing distance in a short time. Their beards were thick and frosted white from their steaming breath. They wore peaked helmets draped with the pelts of small beasts with the heads still attached and jaws fixed in permanent fang-rimmed snarls. They had knee-length capes of rough fur that billowed out behind them, showing off their light mail, metal bracers, and wide, hook-fisted gauntlets.

As they skated they hammered on their shields with short swords roaring this chant:

> "Magon is coming—
> The enemy trembles!
> Magon is coming—
> The enemy flees!
> Magon is coming—
> Hearts be glad!"

The soldiers fanned out into an ever-widening phalanx that was soon joined by other warriors, except these men had their swords sheathed, their shields slung over their shoulders. They beat on heavy, scoop-bottomed drums with padded clubs and joined in the thunderous chant . . .

> "Magon is coming—
> The enemy trembles!
> Magon is coming . . ."

An ice ship hove into view, then two, then three. They were larger than the first, painted in blinding colors and draped with dyed furs. There were soldiers on the deck who seemed to wear richer costumes and armor than the skaters and who brandished finer weapons, as well. All the ships flew the flag of the Ice Bear King.

Long canoelike craft shot out, all filled with warriors—pikemen and bowmen mostly—and all powered by burly men in ragged furs and gaunt, haunted faces, who skated alongside, pushing at heavy poles protruding from each side of the canoes. Men with whips skated around them, lashing and cursing any miscreants they thought were lagging.

Then the most amazing craft sailed into view. It was an ice galleon, double decked and with a flying bridge jutting above the decks. The wind was quite brisk now and the galleon's sails were straining, carrying the ship swiftly across the ice on its massive runners.

A huge bearded warrior posed on the flying deck, helmet removed and long hair streaming back. He wore a great white bearskin cloak thrown over shining armor of black specked with gold. In his left hand he grasped a long black spear, planted into the deck butt first. In his right, cradled in the crook of a brawny arm, was a woman.

I was startled when I first saw her. Despite the cold, she seemed to be wearing little more than scraps of colorful silk draped across tawny hips and breasts. The wind made the silk flutter, revealing more of that tawny skin. The woman was small and delicately formed. Her hair was gold, like mine. Her bare arms were long and slender, and in one hand she held a staff with a crystal globe mounted on top. The globe was a swirling glow of magical power.

I had no doubt who the warrior was: Magon, the Ice Bear King.

But who, I wondered, was the woman?

There was one other thing that alarmed me.

The ice ship was made of gold.

It took a while for that fact to sink in. I'd been so shaken by the magical assault that my mind felt numb. But when it finally sank in I immediately remembered Maranonia's prophecy of the three metal ships. The thought was fleeting, a mere observation, noted and put away for future consideration. My second reaction was marvel.

The entire galleon seemed to be built of gold, a smooth shimmer of metal from stem to stern. Even the sails seemed to be made of the stuff: a skin of gold that fluttered and billowed in the breeze as if it were cloth. It wasn't the ostentatious display of riches that amazed me. Barbarian kings do things like that. Thrones and palaces and even comic objects like chamber pots are likely to be of gem-encrusted gold in a barbarian court.

What made me goggle was the mechanics of it. Even if the ship were gold-plated rather than solid, the weight would be so extreme that the ship would collapse on its golden skis. And even if it didn't, the greatest storm wouldn't be able to move such weight even a foot.

Then the great bell tolled, drawing my attention to the town and the Bear Temple. People poured out of the gates and swarmed to the shore. They were carrying banners and flags, beating on drums and blowing on trumpets. They swarmed to the docks—thousands of people—but in an oddly orderly fashion: forming up in lines, with small knots of richly dressed folk in the front, who I guessed were officials.

We watched for nearly two hours as the crowd greeted King Magon and the mysterious woman I took to be his queen. There were speeches, although we couldn't hear them; there were shouts of praise, which we could.

Big tubs of incense were set on fire, sending out thick clouds of smoke whose perfume eventually drifted over to tickle our noses. Kites with exploding tails swooped through the sky, glowing balloons were lofted, and music blared from the city's savage orchestra, a cacophony of drums and horns and bone rattles.

Carale tried to get my attention, to pull me away so we could discuss the situation with the others. But I shushed him and made signs that no one should speak.

Even in all that noise I could sense something hovering near—listening.

The dockside ceremony ended and the crowd marched back into the Bear Temple, with King Magon and his queen leading the way. His soldiers remained by the ships, some squatting down to rest, others skimming about the ice in squad-size patrols.

A few moments later steam hissed from the Bear Temple's nose and its stone eyes shone fiery red. I had a sudden sense of urgency and signaled my men to withdraw from the hill.

I took one last look before I slid down to join them and saw soldiers break away from the dock. They were headed in our direction.

I skittered down the slope and leaped to my feet. Silence was no longer a factor.

"They're coming," I shouted to the men. And I led them away in a mad dash through the snow and away from the lake.

They hunted us for hours. We tried every trick we knew to shake them: dodging into boulder-strewn gullies and leaping from rock to rock, dashing across barren lake inlets where we'd leave no tracks on the ice, shifting direction and doubling back over our own prints to add confusion, hiding while patrols passed and then using their tracks to hide our own.

In the end they pinned us against a high ridge. We were on the ice, looking for a way up that ridge when twenty soldiers skated into view. Then twenty more joined them, and as they formed up, so many more swept in to swell their ranks I lost count and knew we were doomed.

They shouted a challenge and skimmed across the ice to meet us, pounding on their shields with their swords. There was no time for sorcery so I drew my blade and rallied my men.

We were few in number but we made a long fight of it. The twins were killed first. They'd charged into a mass of men, breaking their formation and leaving nearly a dozen lying on the ice dead or mortally wounded. But then the men they'd charged had regrouped and overwhelmed them.

I didn't see how Lizard died. But I saw his corpse on the ice, throat slit. That lovely voice stilled forever.

Then only Carale and Donarius and I were left. We were exhausted, but we fought on—elbow-to-elbow, our blades bloody life-taking wands wavering before us.

The enemy made a final charge. A solid wall of armored flesh overwhelmed us. I was on my back, sword ripped away, and a huge figure towered over me. He raised up his sword to strike. Then I heard music. Lovely music. The tones of a heavenly lyre.

And then all was blackness.

THE ICE BEAR KING

I awoke to darkness so impenetrable that for a moment I was seized with fear that I'd been blinded. I remembered how helpless Gamelan had become, his Evocator's powers failing along with his eyesight.

I raised a hand before my face but could see nothing, no matter how close I held it to my face. I touched my eyes, felt the lashes fluttering under my fingertips, but found no wounds. I felt stickiness on one cheek, which I assumed was blood. My head was throbbing, every bone and muscle aching, and I could feel the sting of cuts and scrapes when I moved. But all my injuries seemed minor.

My feet were bare and my parka had been removed and I seemed to be wearing nothing more than my tunic and leggings. I was wet through, my clothes sticking to me uncomfortably. At least it wasn't cold. In fact it was just the opposite: the atmosphere was steamy and I was sweating profusely.

With dim hopes I whispered, "Carale?"

There was no answer.

I was alone.

The stone floor was warm beneath me. The walls were also of stone and warm to the touch. I heard water dripping as if in a pool, and slithered in that direction, hands outstretched for protection. I groped about until I found the pool, nothing more than a skim of water over a stopped-up drain.

I felt around until I found the source of the water—a slow trickle of condensation running down one of the walls and splashing into the pool.

I dipped up water and sniffed it. It seemed musty but not unclean. I tasted it. It had a muddy flavor—not entirely unpleasant. Suddenly I felt so thirsty I became sick to my stomach. I scooped up water and drank, to no ill effect.

Then I searched my person. All my weapons and other possessions were gone. But I did find an overlooked kerchief tucked into my sleeve. I dipped it into the water and washed myself as best I could.

When I was done I examined the rest of the chamber, inch by blind inch. It was small, made of old stone blocks with crumbling gaps where the mortar had rotted and fallen away. A small door made of thick wood bound with broad bands of metal was set in one wall. I assumed there was a corridor on the other side of the door, although I could hear nothing but the sound of my breathing and the drip, drip, drip of the water. At the bottom of the door was a grated opening just large enough for a food pail to be passed through.

I fell to my hands and knees and tried to look through the grate. Nothing. Only blackness. Flat, soul-smothering blackness. I poked my fingers through the grates. They stubbed into wood. A panel had been drawn across the grate.

I searched the room further, carefully examining every crack and rough spot.

There was no bed platform, no blankets, no furniture of any kind. In one corner I found two empty buckets. Their purpose was obvious. One smelled of human waste. The other had the stale scent of old food.

I knew what to do—I'd been in dungeons before. I placed the food pail next to the grate to be exchanged for a full one, if and when the turnkey came to feed me. The other I placed in the most distant corner, to be used when I needed to relieve myself.

I did light exercises to stretch my muscles. They were sore but seemed to work well enough, so I ran in place for a few minutes, inhaling and exhaling as deeply as I could until my nerves calmed and my heart beat a steady rhythm.

Then I crouched, leaning back against one wall, found my Evocator's center and chanted:

"What is dawn?
What is night?
What is day?
What is bright?

> What is moon?
> What is light?"

I rubbed my hands together briskly, then opened them, palm side up.

A faint glow appeared.

I could see.

By the dim light I created I found a large protruding stone in the wall about chest high. I rubbed the wall with my hands, leaving smears of light. I continued to rub until the whole block glowed and only a few particles of magical light were left on my palms. I snapped my fingers and the light brightened. Not much, but enough to make out the stark gray emptiness of the chamber. I snapped them again and the light winked off. Once more, and it returned.

Good. If someone came, I could quickly extinguish the light.

I didn't know how long I'd been unconscious. Hours? Days? Not more than one day, I thought. I dipped a finger into the glowing particles on the stone and made a single mark for that day on the dark space below. Then I made another for this day.

Then I settled back to think and wait and prepare.

Someone would come eventually.

I wanted to be ready.

Six more glowing marks joined the first two before they came for me. I assumed that meant eight days from my capture, although there was no real way to tell when one day ended and the other began. I had to rely on the number of times the grate was opened and a food pail was passed through to be traded for the empty pail and my slop bucket. So much time seemed to pass between each visit that I assumed each one was a new day. The food was typical dungeon filth and not to be commented on, except to say it was plentiful enough.

The first time I was fed seemed to be a few hours after I'd regained consciousness, although that was a guess. Minutes can sometimes seem like hours when you're alone and confined in a hot dank cell.

There was little warning, no boot heels echoing in an outside corridor, no clank of warder's keys. All I heard was the scrape of the grating being pushed aside, and I quickly snapped my fingers to darken my cell. The glowing stone had barely blinked out when I saw a gleam of dim light at the grate.

I remained crouched in the corner I'd chosen to sleep in, silent. I heard breathing, but nothing more. I had the distinct impression that someone was peering through the grate. Then a long, glowing rod was pushed through. It poked this way and that, a brighter beam of light spearing out from the tip like a single eye. It finally pointed at me and became still. I was being observed.

I said nothing and did nothing. Then the rod was withdrawn.

"You want eat?" a voice growled.

"Yes," I said.

"Give to me pail," was the reply.

I complied, fetching the old food pail and pushing it through the opening. My nostrils curled at the sour smell of spoiled meat, and then a bucket of food was passed through. I set it aside.

"You go latrine yet?" the voice rasped.

"Yes," I said. "I've done my business."

"Give to me," the voice commanded.

I sent through the bucket I'd used. It was traded for an empty one.

Then the grate closed and that was all.

I knew from my experience in the bowels of the dungeons of Konya that I had to eat no matter how disgusting the meal. But the food smelled spoiled and I didn't want to get sick. I'd learned from my father that in a savage place it's best to eat your food as hot as possible if you want to avoid illness. So I cast a spell to make a little fire and boiled the contents of the food pail. Soon the cell was full of the strong odor of rotted cabbage and butcher's castoffs.

I thought of other things and forced myself to consume all I could. I had no implements, so I had to use my hands. When I was done there seemed enough left over for another meal and I saved it for that purpose.

I fished through the contents of the greasy stew and found a slim sliver of bone. I tried to guess what animal it came from. It wasn't fowl, of that I was sure. Nor was it from a pig or a cow. Then I became certain it was lizard. I tucked the bone into my sleeve for later use. After my next meal, I examined the empty metal pail in some detail. It was rusted and had a carrying handle. I knew I couldn't use any piece of the pail or handle to make a weapon because my keepers would immediately note anything that was broken off. So I flaked away some of the rust—making a little pile of it—and wrapped it in a scrap I'd torn off from my kerchief. I tucked the packet in my sleeve along with the lizard bone.

I exercised, blanked the light, and slept.

When I awakened I exercised again, then settled down on my haunches to consider my circumstances.

I pushed out with my Evocator's senses, met the wall, pressed through the stone, then was stopped. The blocking spell felt thick and spongy. I pressed harder, but the sponginess absorbed all my attempts. I gave up. I was on the home ground of an enemy wizard, which is difficult to overcome in any circumstances, even if that wizard is an ignorant shaman. I cast my own protective spells, however, shielding myself as best I could from a surprise attack.

That attack came soon after I'd fallen asleep.

I was back in the long ago days when I'd pursued the Archon and was lost in the Western Sea. I was in my quarters, swinging in a ship's hammock, soothed by the steady roll of the ship in gentle waves.

Then Gamelan came rapping into my dream with his blindman's stick. "It's time for another lesson, my friend," he said.

He threw the stick to me and it became a large winged serpent, hissing and dripping venom from its fangs.

I wanted to leap away. Every nerve in my body urged me to jump, to roll out of the hammock and flee those deadly needle points. Instead I caught the serpent behind the neck and turned it toward Gamelan. I squeezed two fingers into the pits on each side of the snake's neck and green poison squirted out.

The venom splashed against a shimmering surface just in front of Gamelan. He cried out and the sound of his pain made my heart wrench for doing such a thing to my mentor and friend.

Then his image melted, streaming down the shimmering surface like heated paint running down a mirror.

I jolted awake, pulse hammering, every tendon quivering like strummed wire. My mouth was parchment dry, my lips thick and crusted from thirst. I snapped my fingers to make light and went to the corner where the water dripped into the small pool. I scooped up water and drank. The muddy taste of it coated my tongue, but my thirst was eased. I returned to my corner and crouched there for a long time until I had myself under control. Then I went to sleep again.

The warder came. Pails were exchanged. I made another mark, exercised until I was exhausted, then slept.

I dreamed I was in Amalric's garden. Omerye was playing on her pipes. My brother was pouring me a goblet of wine.

"I love you, sister dear," he said. "You know I do. And I've always admired your courage. But I think you're beaten. Admit it. Then we'll have a drink and you can go home."

I took the goblet from his hand. It held good Antero wine, the very best vintage from our very best orchards. Its perfume made me long for Orissa. I was suddenly so homesick that a sob boiled up and nearly burst forth.

Amalric spread his arms wide. "Come embrace me, Rali," he said. "I miss you so."

I smashed the goblet on the garden bench and was left holding a long crooked shard of crystal. Amalric held out his hand as if pleading with me. I slashed the hand with the shard. He cried out and blood streamed from the wound. I came up from the bench and he tried to run, but I caught him before he'd taken more than a few steps. I slashed out with the glass dagger.

And he fell to the floor dead before a weeping Omerye.

Tears were streaming down my own face when I returned to wakefulness. I stifled my sobs, wiped away the tears, and went to the pool to once again quench that sudden, awful thirst. I quelled all feeling, all emotion, and made my mind blank as a lazy schoolgirl's slate.

Time passed. The warder came and went. More glowing marks were made on the stone. My dreams were untroubled. But I knew my opponent would return.

I made several more marks on the wall before the next attack.

Once again I was in Amalric's garden. Omerye was weeping over my brother's body. My hands were covered with his blood and my white tunic was drenched with it.

Suddenly my mother appeared and I was a small girl, dripping blood, wrenched by guilt so strong that I wanted to die myself.

"What have you done, Rali?" she cried. "How could you kill your own brother?"

I still had the crystal in my hand.

I did what I had to.

Quickly.

And when she was dead, I killed Omerye, too. The blood flowed over the garden path and flooded the roses.

I shuddered out of the dream. I had to run to the slop pail to vomit.

It took me hours to recover. And when I had, I knew I'd suffered the last assault from afar.

I made ready for what I thought might come next. I got out the lizard bone and sharpened it against the stone, honing the tip into a needle point. I used a bit of my food to smear over the bone and make it sticky. Then I sprinkled the rust particles over it until the bone was coated. I made a spell, then hid the bone in my sleeve.

Before I slept again I washed as thoroughly as I could. I untangled the knots in my hair and clawed it into some kind of shape.

It's not good to be left alone with your private ghosts. All the old sins and failures gather to humiliate you. Compulsions you gave in to, petty acts you committed, forgiveness you refused to grant. You trot them out one by one. Examine them, weep for yourself, lash yourself, then put them carefully away—all unresolved and unsolved—so they'll be ready when the next time for self-torment comes. I suffered those things, crouched in my corner until I became hollow-eyed and empty-hearted.

The warder came with the food pail one more time. I made yet another mark and dully wondered how many more light smears would be added to that crude calendar of my imprisonment.

I was eating, trying to think of other things, when the cell door was suddenly flung open. Light flooded in, and as I shielded my eyes from the glare, two large shadows burst through that light and rushed down on me. They bore a net of shimmering gold between them, and as they came at me they spread the net wide.

I had my plan, such as it was, and I made no resistance. They flung the net over me and I was enveloped in the glittering mesh. It clung like the web of a great spider, trapping my arms and legs so tight I couldn't have hurled it off if I'd tried. I slipped the lizard bone from my sleeve as they rolled me up in the net as if it were a carpet. I gripped it tight in my fist, but made no other motion—lying absolutely still.

Then the men grabbed either end of the net and unceremoniously lifted me up and carried me away.

No one said a word as I was rushed along dungeon corridors and up dungeon stairs. I saw barred cell doors, hulking guards as slovenly as swamp beasts, naked prisoners hanging by chains from corridor walls, and the huffing bellows and spark-spewing furnace of a torturer at work. I was relieved as they swept past that room, but then my chest tightened when I heard someone scream. I couldn't tell if it was a man or woman—as if that mattered.

We came to what seemed like a landing at the top of the longest flight of stairs. As we climbed I automatically counted the steps. There were one hundred and seventeen. I remember that useless number to this day and have recounted the steps many times in my dreams.

When we reached the top I saw that the stone walls ended at the landing, to be replaced by bare, gouged-out rock. I twisted my head slightly to look as my captors hauled me toward what appeared to be a wooden-gated shaft.

They hoisted me up as if they were tilting a log on its end and carried me through the gate onto a wooden platform with slatted sides and an open roof. I craned my head back to look up and saw some kind of chain hoist mechanism that led into a yawning darkness that had a pinpoint of light at its end.

The heat was nearly overpowering, steaming up all around the edges of the wooden cage. Perspiration rolled down my face, stinging my eyes and cracked lips.

One of the men yanked a cord and I heard a far-off bell ring. The platform jolted under me, and then with a huge groan and rattle of chain we were slowly drawn upward. The cage's journey began clumsily, jerking and jolting and bumping into the walls, but then the rhythm smoothed out, the jerking motion stopped, and the pace speeded up.

Stone walls flashed past, moisture and bits of metal flashing in the light of the small glass pots of glowing crystals hanging from one of the cage posts.

The shaft's surface was broken now and then by tunnel openings, where men waited for transport and blinked in surprise as we rushed by instead of stopping. The openings, I realized after a time, led into mines. And I realized just how deeply my cell was buried beneath what later proved to be the deepest of all the mines.

As we were drawn past the mine tunnels, I heard the roar of fire, the clash of metal tools, the crack of hammers breaking rock, the rumble of wooden cartwheels, the curses of overseers, and the moans and cries of forced labor.

The ascent took several hours, and during that whole time the men never exchanged a word with one another or even glanced at me. After a time I nodded off, dazed by the stifling heat.

I felt a blast of cool air and the platform jolted to a stop.

My eyes blinked open, but I immediately had to squint against the light. Guards swung the gate open and I was hauled out into a cold gray day.

Before I could look about, a black bag was drawn over my head. A heavy smothering odor filled my nostrils, choking me. I fought for breath and drew in more of that nauseating gas.

Blackness descended once more.

I dreamed I was in a leafy bower in the arms of a lover. She was strange and familiar to me at the same time, her face and form shifting whenever I looked closely at her. She was sweet and kind and all the things we want a lover to be, and when our passion climaxed, a delicious joyful languor enveloped me. In my dream I dozed off, my head pillowed in her lap.

I awoke to sounds of faint pipes playing a peaceful tune. Perfume and incense drifted on the currents of the air and I felt the delicious softness of deep pillows beneath my body.

As awareness returned I realized my fist was still clenched tight over the lizard bone. Relief washed over me. The weapon hadn't been found.

Someone said my name and I opened my eyes to find two young maids bending over me. They were pretty things with skin like fresh cream, and they were dressed in short sheer gowns with golden ties belted about narrow waists.

They had sponges to wipe my brow with perfumed water and a jar of light wine to slake my thirst. Gently they roused me from the comforts of a wonderful bed, with deep brocaded pillows and rosy-hued curtains that could be drawn to shut out the light.

They called me Lady Antero and said I must get ready to be presented to the king. I let them lead me through the chamber, paying no attention to their gentle chatter, which mostly consisted of gossip about their young friends.

I looked about curiously as I padded naked across deep carpets. The walls of the room were hung with fabulous tapestries covered with delightful scenes of field and forest and stream. There were scenes of beautiful young people at play. Chasing a deer, dashing across a meadow, or tenderly embracing under the trees. Although they were naked and some of the love scenes were quite explicit, all was done with much taste, so you were charmed rather than enticed or repelled.

The maids led me to a pool-size stone bath filled with steaming perfumed waters. I walked down the steps to enter the water, which came about waist high. They took my elbows and helped me settle down; then they clapped their hands and several other maids—each lovelier than the next—appeared from behind curtains. They were all so young, girls really, and it did lighten my mood to hear their innocent squeals of pleasure as they shed their clothes and climbed into the pool with me.

There, I was treated to the most marvelous bath. Gentle fingers probed here and there, sponging and massaging and pouring steamy water over me. They washed my hair, kneading my scalp and treating the damaged parts with conditioning oils.

It was as if I'd never left the dream but had been whisked away to a small paradise where my every need was catered to. A paradise with danger peeping from every corner of the stage where I was the featured player in a charming scene. I went along with it all, laughing at small jokes, tickling a giggle from a girl now and then, using the actions to shift the lizard bone about so it wouldn't be discovered.

The maids didn't notice my crafty movements. They praised my looks, wept at my battle scars, and said, tsk tsk, poor thing, as they gently tended my weary body.

They toweled me off, rubbing my skin until it glowed, then draped me in more thick towels and settled me down before a small table where delicacies had been laid out to satisfy my hunger.

There was a clear broth, toasted bread dripping with butter and honey, rashers of bacon, eggs steamed in wine, and slices of iced fruit of every variety. I ate my fill, smiling and answering the maids when they asked me what I needed, but saying nothing else except please and thank you very much, my dears.

Then it was time to dress, and they drew aside a curtain, revealing a closet the size of a small room. There was every kind of costume imaginable in that closet, with shoes and sandals and boots to match each one. I looked them over, remarking on the quality of this and the pleasing color of that. I didn't have to ask or try the costumes on to know that each one would fit me perfectly.

The whole atmosphere was casual and natural. We were all sisters together, getting ready for a grand affair. I said nothing or did nothing to spoil that atmosphere, letting events carry me forward and storing up all the will and energy I could.

I chose a simple tunic and matching leggings with a floppy-sleeved blouse to wear under the tunic. As I drew it on I hid the lizard bone in the sleeve.

There were doeskin boots for my feet and a belt of silver chain for my waist. The maids opened a velvet-lined chest with all kinds of clever drawers filled with all sorts of jeweled adornment from tiaras to plain gold bracelets and earrings.

I demurred, saying I really didn't like jewelry, which was a lie. But I knew better than to wear metal and crystal given to me in the realm of a strange wizard.

The maids were completely unconcerned with my decision, and when they shut the chest I wondered if I was wrong and the jewelry safe. I touched the lid, pretending to help fasten the catch, felt a warning buzz of sorcery, and knew I'd been right to refuse.

Finally I was ready. I looked at myself in the mirror as the maids fussed over me, rearranging the tuck and fold of my clothing and pushing stray curls under the jaunty cap I'd chosen to top off my outfit.

Hard knuckles rapped on the chamber door. One of the maids opened it and two mailed soldiers stepped in.

It was time to meet the king.

We moved along many corridors, ascended and descended many flights of stairs, passed through more halls and chambers than I could make note of, and finally came to two great wooden doors guarded by sentries with spears.

Raucous noise came from behind the huge doors, wild music and laughter and loud indistinct boasts bellowed from drunken throats. Then the doors opened and I was escorted into King Magon's feasting hall.

It was long and narrow, with rough tables and benches set on either side of a broad aisle. Chaos reigned at those tables, where burly warriors sat, stabbing up joints of meat with daggers and shortswords, swilling enormous jugs of ale—brew foaming down their beards as they drank—and brawling over small delicacies.

Servants of both sexes darted in and around the tables, carrying jugs of spirits and trenchers of meat and roasted vegetables, dodging blows and clumsy caresses. Entertainers pranced among the tables and along the aisle, juggling knives and pies, tumbling and somersaulting over the tables, balancing on wires stretched over the heads of the celebrants. The warriors jokingly jabbed at the wire walkers with bread sticks and even swords.

The sound of carousing was deafening, and the music, which came from a small group of long-suffering musicians set up in one corner, was somehow less distinct with the doors open.

My escorts prodded me forward and I walked down the long aisle, gradually gaining the notice of the celebrants, and was showered with leering comments about my physical characteristics that I'm sure some of the men thought were complimentary. If it'd been another time and place, I would've paused to teach them better manners. Instead I concentrated on putting one boot in front of the other, dodging tipsy celebrants and weary acrobats, but at the same time not making the guards nervous about my intent.

I kept my self cold, casually unrevealing. I kept my magical senses tight about me, giving nothing away. Above the din of the brawling men, I could feel the distinctive buzz of a sorcerous presence.

The farther I walked along that aisle, the stronger that feeling became.

Near the end of the feast hall the crowd cleared and I saw the king.

Even sprawled in the big thronelike chair set before his dining table, the king was as big as I remembered from my first distant view. He was dressed in a loose white shirt, stained red with wine, and he had a royal robe pulled carelessly over his shoulders. The heavy, gem-encrusted crown had a dangerous tilt to it. His boots poked out from under the table, one big foot propped on top of the other. His high-backed chair carried the carved head of an ice bear.

There was a small crowd gathered about the king, who was bellowing so loudly that I could hear him above the din. As he spoke he thumped the table with a meaty fist to underscore some deeply held royal opinion.

Then I saw a small delicate man lean toward the king and whisper in his ear. The king nodded, and as he looked to see what the small man was pointing out, he wiped greasy fingers in his beard. Magon's eyes found me as I reached the stairs leading up to the platform where his dining table was set. One of the guards tugged my sleeve and I stopped.

The king bellowed for quiet, but you couldn't hear the words plainly much beyond me. He flushed with impatience, hauled himself to his feet, and pounded the table with a wine jug.

"Silence!" he roared.

The jug shattered, wine flooding out everywhere. But he got the silence he'd commanded.

All turned to look at the king.

"Boys," he said, his voice rough with drink and manly cheer, "we've got a special guest tonight. Down here to see us all the way from the North country."

He gestured at me, and everybody craned to get a better look. I searched for the source of the magical buzz as he talked. It wasn't him. The king was no magician. It wasn't his aide—the small delicate man. And it wasn't any of the people around him.

As I searched, the king was saying, "She's from a real rich family, too, boys. From what I hear, it's the most important family in all the North. Brother's a big merchant prince or something. Explorer, too. At least that's what they tell me."

He smiled at me. "Do I have it right so far?" he asked.

I bowed slightly. "As right as you can be, Your Highness," I said.

"You're also a witch, I'm told," he said—but loudly, so all could hear.

"Actually, I'm an Evocator, Your Highness," I said. "Which in my city is an official post."

"No matter how you cut it," he said, "it's still the same thing."

I smiled, accepting his kingly correction. "Yes, Your Highness."

The king nodded, absently thrusting out a hand for a wine mug. There were none within reach, but a servant instantly scooped up a full goblet and thrust it into the king's fist. Magon, without acknowledging that the goblet hadn't been there a moment before, clasped it and drank the wine down. He dangled the goblet, then let it fall. The same servant snatched it out of the air so the crash wouldn't disturb his majesty's serenity.

Magon belched and wiped his beard. Then he leaned forward slightly, looking me over for some reaction. I made none. Although I did note that much of what I was seeing might be a pose.

Then he asked, "What brings you to our kingdom?" He waved a hand, indicating his warriors. "We're honored, of course. Such an important person traveling so far. Isn't that so, boys?"

His men shouted good-humored jeers and mock compliments.

The king looked at me, his beard split by a sardonic grin. "You see how honored we are?"

This brought another thunderclap of jeers and laughter. I let it wash over me, keeping a calm smile fixed on my face as if all were normal.

When they were done, I said, "I hope you won't take offense, Your Highness, but until this voyage I'd never heard your exalted name."

The king frowned, his heavy brows dipping over his forehead like two longboats nearly colliding in heavy seas.

"Never heard of King Magon?" he thundered.

"No, Your Highness," I replied. "As you said, I come from far off."

"And I suppose you've never heard of the Ice Bear King?"

I glanced up at the carved bear head on his throne, then shrugged. "Not until recently, Your Highness," I said. "I was told he was a legendary monarch in these regions. Hundreds of years ago."

Rather than getting angry, Magon smiled at my answer.

"You see how it is, boys?" he said to his men. "You see how those rich stuff-robes on the outside lie about us? Legend, huh? Hundreds of years gone, huh?"

His warriors shouted drunken insults at the unnamed "stuff-robes."

Magon turned back to me. "King Magon," he said, "and the Ice Bear King are one and the same." He thumped his chest. "You're looking at him."

I dipped my head in a slight bow. "I'm honored to be sure, Your Highness," I said. "Thank you for enlightening me."

"But you're not amazed?" the king asked.

"Amazed, Your Highness?" I said. "Why should I be amazed?"

Magon frowned. "Why, to see a living legend in the flesh!"

I shrugged. The king's frown deepened. Shrugs were the property of the monarch in this court.

"Sorry if I somehow gave offense, Your Highness," I said, not sounding very sorry at all. "If I expressed amazement, it would be a lie whose only purpose would be to curry favor from the throne. After all, I only just learned you existed. Just as you only recently heard of me. So we come to this meeting as equals in ignorance."

The king's humor was restored. He wagged a finger at me. "Not that equal," he said. "I know quite a bit about you, Lady Antero."

"I'm relieved to hear that, Your Highness," I said. "For if you know about me, you know the innocence of my purpose."

King Magon barked laughter. "Innocent?" he bellowed. "You hear that, boys? Did you hear what the witch said?"

His men rumbled appreciatively.

Then the king's mask of humor vanished. "Do you deny that you traveled down here to exploit my kingdom?" he thundered. "That your city—this . . . this Orissa place—is in league with my enemies? And your allies?"

"I have no allies, Your Majesty," I said. "Nor does my brother. We're merchants, not officials of state. And our purpose is to trade, not conspire."

"If trade was your wish," the king said, "then why didn't you come to see me? To ask permission, pay tariffs and duties and whatever."

"How could I, Your Highness?" I said. "I'd never heard of you, remember? And now that you've raised the subject of duties and permissions, why, the whole thing has just become simpler. We can open up talks now. Work out some kind of agreement I can take home to get my brother to approve."

"It's a little late for that, isn't it?" the king said.

"How so, Your Highness?"

"There's blood between us," he said.

"A tragic error on both sides, Your Highness," I said. "I'm sure we can reach some kind of compensation agreement to help the widows and orphans of my men. Along with a suitable apology from you that such a terrible—although unavoidable—accident occurred. After all, we wouldn't want such a thing to sour future relations between us.

"So, if you'll just return my men to me, Your Highness, we'll put all behind us. Work up a little trade pact between you and the Anteros. And we'll be on our way. We'll need credit, of course. So we can buy a ship from you and return home. But mutual credit is the sort of thing usually set up in any trade agreement. And I'm sure that if you've learned anything about the Anteros, it's that their credit and word is sound."

"Just like that"—the king snapped his fingers—"and all is forgiven and forgotten?"

"Why not, Your Highness?" I said. "It's the way of civilized people."

"Are you saying we're *not* civilized?" the king rumbled.

I made my brows arch in surprise. "*Me,* Your Highness? I never said such a thing, sir."

"But you implied," he said, "that if I didn't agree I'd be no better than a savage." He looked at his men. "Isn't that what she said, boys?"

His warriors shouted agreement.

"You see?" he said to me. "There are no savages here."

"Good," I said, deliberately misinterpreting and twisting the scene. "Now that we've settled that matter, Your Highness, I'd be pleased if you'd reunite me with my companions immediately. So they, too, can rejoice in the news that they are in the gentle hands of such a wise and civilized king."

The king flushed heavily, his features purpling above his ragged white beard. As I looked more closely at him, I thought his face seemed younger than the whiteness of his hair implied. His skin was coarse, roughened by the elements and heavy drink. But his brow was relatively unlined, the scratches at the corners of his eyes faint.

Then he said, "We, er, have other matters to discuss first. *Then* we'll talk about your men."

I acted surprised. "I'd be a poor commander, Your Highness, if I didn't put my men above all other things." I glanced around at his warriors, sweeping their faces with an amused look. "I can see from the loyalty and devotion of your own men, Your Highness, that you agree with such matters of soldierly honor."

The king sputtered, but then covered his angry confusion by draining another cup of wine.

"And after I see to my men, Your Highness," I said, "I'd like to presume to raise another concern—a concern, I think, that is a danger to both of us."

"Danger?" he said. "How am *I* endangered?"

"There's a gang of bandits in your kingdom, Your Highness," I said.

He reacted massively. "Bandits? What bandits?"

"Why, the ones who attacked my trading posts," I said. "They're a murderous group. Monsters of the worst sort. Our people were killed in their sleep."

The room was hushed. The king glared at me, furious. But for some reason he was intent on keeping up the pretense.

"I've just come here," he said. "I don't know anything about such things. My capital is on the sea and many leagues away. You're lucky I was touring my kingdom. Otherwise I wouldn't have been here to stop my people from killing you. We don't trust strangers much, I'm sorry to say. You were all armed and, frankly, lurking about. Seems pretty suspicious when you think about it.

"Damned suspicious. Don't you think, boys?"

His men muttered darkly. Magon turned back to me. A stern kingly frown furrowing his brow. "Why didn't you just come up to us and state your business?" he asked.

I raised a hand, pleading ignorance. "We were lost in the fog, Your Highness," I said. "I don't even know where I am now. What city is this? What is your kingdom called?"

"The city is Koronos," Magon said. "My people mine rare metals here. The kingdom is Lofquistina. Which means Land of the Bears in our ancient tongue."

"Thank you for enlightening me, Your Highness," I said. "When I return home, I'll praise your name and your kingdom to my people.

"Now, here is how I come to be in your realm. My family had established two trading posts near the sea some weeks' march from here. We dealt with only the local people, trading for furs and things.

"If we were in your territory, I apologize. The people there are wild folk and perhaps didn't think to tell me who their king was. But we were new to the area and I'm sure we'd have learned of this oversight soon and come to you with proper gifts and ceremony to beg your largesse."

"You say these two outposts were attacked?" the king asked. He acted shocked. I kept wondering why he continued the lie.

"Yes, Your Highness," I said. "And they were clearly cowardly assaults whose purpose was plainly to rob my people."

I spat.

"Murderous pirates," I said. "An honest opponent who resented our presence would merely have demanded we leave. If we'd have been so foolish as to refuse, there'd have been a fight. But it would have been an honest dispute. And there'd have been no shame in the action. Although we'd all mourn those who fell."

"And then what?" the king asked abruptly. "What happened after you visited your trading posts and found them destroyed?"

"I only went to one post, Your Highness," I said. "I'm only guessing the same thing happened to the other. I've seen some evidence of that. But I can't know for sure."

"Go on," the king said.

"We were caught in that great storm that surely bedeviled Your Majesty, as well," I said.

The king nodded. "Yes. I know which storm you mean."

"One of our men," I said, "was taken captive. An Evocator, like myself. He was put on a caravan. When the storm was over we followed the caravan trail. On the way we found the body of our Evocator from the other post. He'd been killed. Tortured first, I might add. Must be the same group of bandits, Your Highness. For who else would torture and kill a helpless man?"

The king glowered but said nothing.

"From there, Your Highness," I said, "we continued following the trail. Hoping to rescue our comrade. We were engaged in that pursuit when we became lost in the fog and stumbled upon your people. And unfortunately alarmed them.

"Perhaps you could help me learn the whereabouts of our friend, Your Highness," I said. "From the signs I saw before we became lost, he's somewhere in this region. His name is Searbe. Lord Searbe."

The king leaned to the side and whispered in the ear of his tall aide. The aide whispered something back. The king nodded while he spoke, looking at me the whole time.

It was then that I discovered where the magical buzz was emanating from. Just beyond the king—at the edge of the curtained platform his table rested on—was a graceful musical instrument sitting upon an ivory stand. It was a wondrous lyre, beautifully curved and with delicate strings that glistened in the torchlight.

The king finally spoke, and I had to drag my eyes away from the lyre.

"It seems we do have your friend," he said. "He's safe. And well."

"I'm relieved to hear that good news, Your Highness," I said. "I can be rejoined with dear Searbe when you bring me the rest of my men.

"Or tell me where they are, Your Majesty. I shall go tend them this instant. You needn't trouble yourself with issuing a lot of tiresome orders."

The king jerked back, the skin around his beard purpling. He stammered. "Oh, uh, you couldn't do that, uh . . ."

"I'll bring them back to this hall," I said. "And we can all join in the feasting. What a great moment to celebrate. Our rescue by such a great king. I have a troubadour among my men. A marvelous balladeer, Your Highness. I'm certain he'd be honored to make us a song about this great event."

I turned in the direction of the lyre, widening my eyes as I pretended to notice it for the first time.

"Why, he could even play the new ballad on that lyre, Your Highness," I exclaimed.

As I did so I jabbed my finger to indicate it, shooting a spark of seeking magic from the tip. It struck the lyre and I felt the burn of returned sorcery and snatched it back.

I smiled at the king, bland as could be. "You *do* like lyre music, don't you, Your Highness?"

Before King Magon could answer, the lyre suddenly began to play. The strings trembled as spirit fingers swept over them and glorious music sounded through the king's feast hall.

Then a blinding light blasted from the lyre, filling the room so completely that all color was washed away.

The music swelled louder still, and I looked toward the lyre, shielding my eyes as best I could.

Now the instrument was a great fountain of light, strings thrumming faster, music and light pouring all around and through us.

Then the lyre became a bird with marvelous glowing wings and a widespread tail filled with all the colors of the rainbow. The bird shimmered as the music continued to play, its wings beating in slow, steady time.

Then the music stopped and the feast hall dissolved around me, and I suddenly found myself standing in a room rich with tasteful carpets and pillows and tapestries.

King Magon was stretched out on the deep pillows of a low-backed couch. A large white bearskin hung on a wall behind the couch, framing him.

I looked about. There was no one else in the room. But I felt a presence and glanced at the curtained alcove next to the bearskin. As I looked, the curtains parted and a woman emerged.

She paused, gripping the curtain edges for just a moment, posing briefly so her beauty could be appreciated.

It was the woman I'd seen on Magon's ship. She'd traded her colorful silks for scraps of gossamer that shimmered over her nude form. She was small and delicate, as I'd observed before, and so gracefully made that the nudity seemed more of an artful costume than a blatant display of her charms.

Her skin was lightly tanned, as if she'd lived all her life running free under a warm sun. Her breasts were full and high and well-shaped. Her waist was so narrow I could have put both hands around it, and her hips flared out like the magical lyre she played. Despite her small height, her legs were long and slender, from dainty feet to where her shapely thighs met in the golden downy triangle of her sex.

She smiled at me, then stepped lightly away from the curtains, letting them sway into place.

The king groaned, pulled off his crown, and rubbed his brow with thick hairy knuckles.

"Thank the gods you came, Novari," he said. "My head is killing me."

She gave me a glance, pale eyes blank, and made the shrug of one sister to another: Forgive me while I tend to this *man*.

"You poor thing," Novari murmured as she ankled over to him, the air stirring with the faint scent of a most marvelous perfume that made all the senses tingle—a touch of a delicious tension.

She stood behind him, took his head in both her hands and began to massage his temples. The king closed his eyes and groaned in appreciation.

Then he said, "Novari's been mad at me."

She kissed his head and tinkled laughter. "Well, you have been a naughty boy, my sweet." She pouted. "Making poor Rali wait in that filthy dungeon." She shuddered. "That was very rude of you, sweetness. Admit it. You were rude. And I think you should apologize this instant."

The king raised his head, rolling his eyes up to see her as she continued to massage his temples.

"I think we should just kill her, Novari," he complained. "She's just going to be trouble."

Novari hugged the king's head against her breasts. He squirmed in pleasure. "Have I ever advised you wrong, my sweet?" she murmured.

He wagged his head from side to side, nestling in the tawny mounds of her breasts. "Never."

"Then do this little thing for me, will you dear?"

The king turned his head up again. A sly grin. "You want her as a gift?" he murmured.

"Yes, darling," Novari said. "A gift."

The king's answer was to draw her around the couch until she stood before him. "Then you shall have her," he said.

He plunged his face into her belly and began kissing and nibbling around that small, tawny plain. Novari stroked his head, then turned and looked at me.

"You'd better go," she said. She motioned toward a far door. "There'll be someone waiting there to take you to your rooms."

The king pulled her tighter, and I left. Just as she'd said, there were guards waiting on the other side of the door.

As they closed it behind me I heard lyre music again.

And I heard the king groan as if he'd come upon paradise itself.

When I think back to that time, I'm amazed at how cold I'd become, how deeply I'd burrowed inward—drawing all emotion and feeling in after me. I reflected not at all, avoided all thought of the future, concentrating fully only on the immediate path before me. I'd been ambushed by the storm, blindsided by the sorcerous scorched-earth attack by my enemy, and I'd never had the chance to fully recover.

I'd seen what had nearly happened to Daciar, and knew that any large spell performed by me would instantly blast back with disastrous results. Now that I was completely in my enemy's power, I'd have to be even more cautious.

Nor could I reveal the extent of my power and abilities so that I might have the element of surprise if I ever got the chance to use it.

Meanwhile all I could do was look for a crack in my enemy's defenses and then exploit that crack, smashing at it with all I could bring to bear until it parted.

For two more weeks I lolled in splendid imprisonment in the lush apartments assigned to me. I was fed the finest food, served gracious wines and spirits, and was pampered endlessly by the serving maids. I gathered strength, hoarding every speck, quietly rebuilding my powers with every passing hour. I didn't see this as a mistake on the part of my enemy.

I had no doubt that I was being fattened for the kill. Although for what purpose was still a mystery.

As the days passed I stole small moments to myself. Only a minute or two each time. But those minutes were enough to gradually piece together a spell I could cast so that not even the most wary and sensitive wizard would notice.

Using that spell I turned the lizard bone into a long golden hairpin. I buried the pin in the jewelry chest, then pretended to find it one day. I made much of it, saying it might be just the thing for my hair.

The maids all agreed, and one of them even thrust it through my hairdo herself and held out a mirror for me to see.

I looked it over as if unsure. The maids declared it perfect. They made such a to-do about the pin, insisting it was so lovely that I must wear it at all times, that I knew I'd been right to refuse all metal objects offered to me. I teased them, pretending I wasn't certain. But then relented.

From then on I wore it in my hair every moment, night or day.

One evening after dinner the maids suddenly burst into activity. While one pretty trio cajoled me into taking a bath—liberally spicing the water with sweet oils, lemony perfumes, and dilutions of warm wine and honey— the others fussed over the apartment, making certain all was tidy and perfectly arranged.

They draped me in a simple but elegant robe, and while my hair was dried and brushed until it glowed, some of the maids fetched refreshments on a tray and placed them by the hearth, where they spread out pillows and poked up the fire until it gave off a warm, cheery breath. They fixed my hair, adjusting the golden pin so all was just so.

I didn't ask what was happening but took note that there were two ornate goblets on the tray of spirits they'd brought in.

Then they dimmed the lights and drew aside the curtains against one wall—it was the first time they'd done so—revealing a large window overlooking the frozen lake. The night sky was clear, filled with thousands of stars, and a full moon glittered on the frozen lake surface.

The strings of a lyre, low and coming from far away, drew me to the window to stare out at the stark wintry beauty.

I heard silken rustling and out of the corner of my eye saw the maids withdrawing silently.

The music grew louder, but pleasantly so, a shower of wondrous notes falling all around me.

In the distance I saw a small cloud drift across the face of the moon. It was winged, like a bird. Then the cloud became a bird and it swooped across the ice, dipping low in a long dive until it skimmed over the gleaming white surface, then shot up toward the window.

It flew straight for the glass—but spread its wings an instant before collision and hovered there.

The music swelled as the creature's tail fanned out, revealing all the glorious colors, the feathers shimmering with song as if they were the strings of a harp.

It was the Lyre Bird.

The one I'd been awaiting.

The Lyre Bird fountained light, and as I shielded my eyes, it drifted through the glass. The music stopped. The light vanished.

And Novari was standing in front of me.

She posed for a heartbeat, letting her heady beauty radiate out like a rare musk. Silk veils of many colors swirled around her perfect form. A thin tiara pebbled with diamonds held in her long fair hair. She smiled prettily, white teeth flashing through soft lips the color of a new rose. She took a flowing step forward, raising a dainty hand to touch mine in greeting. As she moved, the silk veils parted, revealing glimpses of honeyed flesh.

I shivered as her fingers brushed across my knuckles. The shiver drew another smile, and she looked deep into my eyes as if acknowledging a mutual attraction. Her eyes were pale mirrors, urging me to see whatever I might desire.

I let her lust-magic coax a smile in return. Let my loins tingle with the warmth she intended. Felt my skin pebble in response to her seductive aura. But beneath it all I kept all my defenses up, guiding myself by feel through the perfumed thicket she'd created.

Novari tensed and I caught a pout of disappointment because I was apparently unmoved by her charms.

"How kind of you to come see me," I said. I gestured at the trays of spirits and delicacies set by the fire. "Although it seems I was expecting you."

I felt a boil of energy as she came to full life and she threw back her head and laughed. The sound was rich, her breath smelled of poppies.

"You want truth, Rali," she said. "That's my specialty. I speak nothing but the truth. I cannot do otherwise." She gave me a wink, bawdy and conspiratorial. "Come, my sweet. Ask me what you will. I find the prospect so, so—" She paused, shivered as if she'd just had a sexual climax, then finished: "—so full of delicious surrender."

She looped her arm through mine, squeezed my wrist against her softness, then guided me toward the hearth where the refreshments and soft pillows waited.

She made a big fuss over me as I sank down onto the pillows. She rearranged the pillows, plumping them up, then personally served me a little plate of tasties and poured out a goblet of brandy.

I let her fuss. I *made* her fuss more. I'd play her own game—throw it back at her, demand subservience to my femininity and exaggerate those claims.

I complained about small things, saying some of the tasties were liver and I disliked liver as a food above all the creations of the gods. Although, I confessed to her in sisterly tones that when I had my monthlies I did like a good piece of heart.

I primly pushed away the brandy, saying I'd much prefer tea. But while I did I let the top of my robe fall open and saw the hunger in her eyes. I blushed and pulled it tight, casting my eyes down, letting my long eyelashes flutter like delicate wings.

And all the while I was secretly laughing at her—a full-bellied soldier's chortle, if I could've given it voice.

Novari became flustered, face flushing from irritation and no little lust.

"You know," I said, as she handed me a cup of tea she'd brewed herself over the hearth, "perhaps I will have a little brandy after all." I shivered. "It *is* a chilly night."

I dumped a hefty slug into the teacup, sniffed its fumes, then drank. Then I looked her in the eye with a flat soldier's stare.

"*I* can play princess," I said harshly, "or *you* can play princess. So long as we both know that either way it's only play."

Her pale eyes flickered, and although her face remained a gentle mask I could see that my small dart had struck home.

She recovered, tinkling laughter. "You are an amazing woman, Rali Antero," she said.

"As much woman as you'll ever meet, my dear Novari," I replied, mock toasting her with my brandy, then drinking it down in one long swallow.

I hooked up the jug with a crooked finger and refilled the cup. Easing back into the pillows, I crossed my ankles and rested the goblet on my chest.

Then I eyed her, one lip curled in amusement. "You claim you're bound to speak the truth," I said.

"Yes," she said.

"I won't say whether I believe that," I said. "We'd only get into a lengthy and useless discussion about ancient riddles and philosophic terms: When truth can be a lie . . . and a lie the truth."

"Shall I tell you my story, Rali?" she said. "And then you can make up your own mind?"

I shrugged. "If you like. I'm yours to command, and all. But I still won't know if it's the truth, will I?"

"I'll tell the tale anyway," she said. "And see if you say the same thing when I'm done."

The fire had died down. I made a magical gesture and it flared into life again, crackling merrily.

Novari laughed, and the sound was that of lyre strings.

"I'll take that as acceptance," she said.

She frowned, lovely brow furrowing in concentration. Then her brow cleared and she began.

CHAPTER TEN

THE LYRE BIRD'S TALE

"I am one of a kind," she said. "So far as I know, there are no other . . . *presences* . . . like me.

"I came into being long before the first Ice Bear King—perhaps a thousand years ago . . . or more. I was created by a powerful wizard to be the slave of his prince. Through me the wizard intended to command his master and his master's kingdom.

"To create me, the wizard scoured the countryside for the perfect clay. He sought the most beautiful intelligent virgins. I don't know how many were swept up by his hunters. Two thousand. Or more."

She drank. Not a dainty sip like before, but long and deep. I saw her perfect cheek twitch in painful memory. It wasn't an act: The memories she was dredging up were not pleasant.

"When he was certain he had enough, the wizard sacrificed the girls in a temple he'd had specially built on the palace grounds. The blood flowed like a river. The screams of the dying girls, it was said, could be heard for so many miles that villagers shuttered their windows and barred their doors, thinking a terrible storm was brewing.

"Then the wizard—using their substance, their souls, their torment, their everything—created a single creature. A sexual slave who delighted in her slavery."

Novari dropped her eyes. "Me," she said.

"Did the wizard do all this on his own?" I asked.

"No," Novari said. "He'd made a bargain with a demon. A rogue, who'd broken away from his brothers."

I'd guessed as much. The demon sounded like Lord Elam, a powerful wild demon I'd encountered in the Western Sea.

"What happened to the demon?" I asked.

Novari laughed. There was no music this time—only harsh cynicism. "What else?" she said. "The wizard killed him. He tricked the demon when he was done and stole his powers to add to his own."

"Now the wizard was not only powerful," I said, "but he had you."

"Yes. He had *me*," Novari said. "But to get me, he had to put my essence through several stages. First he created a magical lyre, because the lyre is the most pleasing and sensitive of all musical instruments. A breeze can pluck song from the strings. Even a soft breath. And the music it produces stirs emotion, *commands* it under some hands.

"Then he used the instrument to create a magical bird. A Lyre Bird. For its beauty. And its ability to mimic any cry from any creature on earth. In its magical state it understands the deepest motivations and cares and sorrows of those it is close to.

"Finally he used the Lyre Bird to make me. A spirit whose primary form is a woman. Although I can shift among the three—lyre, bird, and mortal—at will."

"And so you were created to service the prince," I said.

Novari answered: "Yes, to *service* the prince. But my most important duty was to *serve* the wizard.

"When the prince made me his slave, he also enslaved himself. I could—and did—bring him every delight. I was all the wizard promised and more. There was no sex act I didn't perform or even suggest. From the moment of first penetration each day—when I bit my lip from the pain of being deflowered—I became more bawdy and imaginative by the hour. And by day's end I'd participated in the foulest of acts. But the next day I was fresh again. Innocent in the eyes of my prince. Ready to be seduced and deflowered once more.

"As the perfect courtesan, I serviced his pride, as well. I praised his imagined strengths, ignored or denied his too many failings. He trusted me totally, for I was all things to him.

"Part of the spell used to create me required that I must always be truthful, so he trusted me even more. Of course, truth can wear many costumes, some more pleasing than others. And my wizard master made certain I was skilled in the art of coloring the truth to fit his aims.

"At the wizard's instructions, I sparked ambition in the prince. I fanned that spark until it was a willing blaze. The prince set out to be a great conqueror. Armies marched. War spells were cast. And many a kingdom was forced to lower its banner and hoist his.

"All this he accomplished without ever leaving the pleasure palace. I kept him happy. I kept him pliant, while the wizard directly waged the wars and ruled his growing kingdom."

"And then it went wrong," I said.

"Oh, yes," Novari said. "Fairly swiftly, too. The wizard overextended the armies, and the kingdom suffered a humiliating defeat. Several enemy monarchs united, invaded the realm, and captured the prince and his wizard."

"And you?" I asked. "Did they catch you as well?"

Novari's features darkened at some shameful memory. "Of course," she said. "I was a possession. How could I flee?"

"What did the kings do?" I asked.

"They held trials and convicted the prince and his wizard of crimes against nature and the gods. I was a big part of that trial, portrayed as the evil enchantress—the succubus—who possessed the prince to bend him to the wizard's will.

"The public hated all of us. But they seized on me as a symbol to hate most of all. I was blamed for all their monarch's sins.

"All of us were found guilty and condemned.

"The prince was the lucky one. He was killed quickly, without pain.

"The wizard was tortured for many weeks. Then they cast a spell to keep him alive while they cut him to pieces and forced me to eat him scrap by scrap."

She stopped. Her chest heaved. A single tear rolled down her cheek. Then she sighed, and the sigh became the most mournful music I'd ever heard. It wrenched at my heart, strummed my emotions as if they were strings.

I cast a shield and the lyre's sigh faded.

I said, "And then?"

She seemed not to notice my cold tones. "And then they raped me," she said flatly. "Mass rape. And I was a virgin for every man who assaulted me."

Another long silence broken only by the crackling fire.

I said nothing. I refused to imagine the humiliation and pain she'd suffered. But I knew she spoke the truth. And that realization was as powerful as if she'd conjured a great spell to rock me.

I said, mouth suddenly dry, "But they didn't kill you. Somehow you survived."

Novari smiled grimly. "Before, I was always under the wizard's power.

I was incapable of doing any magic that he did not command. I had no control over anything . . ."

She touched her breast. "Not my body."

She touched her head. "Not my mind."

She caressed the air. A soft sprinkle of strings. "Not my magic."

Novari let the sound fade. "But while I was . . . being tortured . . . I found a spark of myself. And from that spark I forged a will. And I took something—a small something—from every man who raped me. I added that to my store, gathering strength and self-purpose. I cast a spell causing much pity. I made it bigger until the pity became a certainty that anyone who slew me would suffer a terrible curse for killing such a beautiful spirit as myself.

"Even so, there was still strong feeling against me that I couldn't overcome. So the wizards gathered to seek a solution. They couldn't kill me. But I must cease to be a danger to anyone.

"So they took me to a small rocky island where I was exiled for all time. They advised me to take on my spirit form so I wouldn't die from the elements or starvation.

"There I remained until not many years ago. I was a solitary spirit wisping across a bleak island a mortal would need no more than ten minutes to cross. I knew every inch of that island to the point of madness. Many times I so despaired that I nearly took on mortal form so I would die. But I knew that wouldn't end my exile. For much wrong had been done to me.

"And I would be condemned forever to be an angry ghost, raging eternally against nothing."

She looked at me. "Can you imagine anything worse?"

I shook my head. I honestly couldn't.

Novari said, "With that peace denied me, I turned all my efforts on my magical abilities. I became quite good. Quite powerful." She giggled. "After all, I had plenty of time for improvement."

I said, "And brooding."

Novari nodded, solemn. "Oh, that I did. I brooded for centuries."

"And you swore revenge?"

"Yes," she said flatly.

"Those who harmed you are long dead," I said.

Novari shrugged. "I have more ambition than mere revenge in me now," she said.

"You're using King Magon to carry out those ambitions?" I asked.

"Yes," she said.

"As a succubus?" I asked. "I mean, that's what they accused you of. But that's what you are, am I right?"

"More or less," she said. "It's more complicated than a simple yes or no."

"How did you come upon King Magon?" I asked.

Novari grinned. "He came to me, actually," she said. "He was a minor warlord who was trying to make a name for himself. He visited the island during a pirating expedition he'd raised."

"And you entered his dreams and possessed him," I said.

She giggled, girlish. "It's not all *that* bad for him," she said.

"And he just *happened* to wander onto your island?" I asked wryly.

Novari shook her head. "I caused him to," she said. "Not *him*, specifically. But someone like him."

"How?" I asked. "You said you were far away. Too far for such a spell to reach."

"I cast the spell before a storm," she said, with just a touch of pride shining through. "I've learned to use storms for such things."

Now I understood what had happened when the ice storm caught us by surprise at Antero Bay. Still, a spell to lure a fool from his distant home is quite different from the magical firestorm she'd hurled across the land. I was certain no single wizard could accomplish anything like it.

"Now, you've heard my story," Novari said.

I didn't answer. I stared into the fire—waiting. The long seconds ticked away. She became frustrated.

"Don't you want to ask me anything else?" she snapped.

"Yes," I said.

Again I waited.

She squirmed. Then: "What a maddening woman! Ask me! Ask what you will."

"Where are my men?" I demanded.

She sighed. "Is that all you can think of? Your precious men?"

"They are that," I said. "To me, anyway."

"What about yourself?" she asked. "Aren't you interested in what plans I might have in store for you?"

I shrugged. "I'll worry about that after I've seen to the welfare of my people."

She raised an eyebrow, mocking. "Such loyal concern touches me," she said. "Pity they aren't so loyal in return. One of them has betrayed you already."

I didn't question the truth of her declaration, as bitter as it was.

I made a sour face. "There's always one," I said. "I assume you're accusing Lord Searbe. My Evocator."

"The very one," she said, eyes glittering.

"I'm surprised it's only one, actually," I said. "You're a succubus, after all. That's what you do. Magically seduce men . . . or women."

Novari's lips parted, moist, mocking. "You know me, sister," she said archly.

"More than I want to," I said.

She pouted. "You needn't be cruel," she said. "Besides, your precious Evocator didn't need seduction. He was willing the instant my captains seized him."

I leaped at this breach. "You admit it!" I snarled. "You admit you deliberately attacked my people. Slaughtered them. Tortured one until he died. And kidnapped another." I sneered. "And you speak to me of cruel wizards and kings!"

Instead of becoming angry, Novari flushed, embarrassed. "I'm sorry," she said. "I didn't cause it out of cruelty. It was necessary."

"Torture was necessary?" I snarled.

"That was not my fault," she snapped. "He was supposed to be brought to me unharmed. The men who took him were savages. They got out of hand. And if it's any satisfaction to you, it cost them their lives. Your Evocator has been revenged."

I nearly lost my temper. Not by half, he hadn't!

As the anger rose to scorch my throat, I felt her tense, felt the ethers swirl as she drew in power to strike me first if I should be so foolish as to attack.

I fought for control. Regained it. And felt her tension drain away.

I said, as mildly as I could, "What has Lord Searbe told you? If it's the purpose of my mission, why, that was to see what kind of a threat your slavish king was to us. That's not so innocent a purpose as I first claimed, to be sure. But it's hardly a crucial revelation."

Novari laughed, waving a dismissive hand. "Oh, he babbled about all those things right off," she scoffed. "Frankly, the particulars of your expedition were of no interest to me."

"Then what did interest you?" I asked.

"Why you, of course," she said. "Rali Emilie Antero. Soldier. Wizard. Adventurer. And more importantly, a woman."

She leaned forward eagerly. "I had to meet such a woman," she said, glowing with excitement. "To dare and accomplish so much. As a mortal, not a spirit. Why, when I learned of you, I knew immediately you are the one I've longed for all my life."

A light hand touched my knee. "We could do such great things together, Rali," she said. "Such great things!"

I pushed her hand away and laughed harshly. "If you see me as your life's mate," I sneered, "you have a poor way of wooing me. I suppose you can't help it. You're so used to relying on magical seduction, you make a horrible comedy out of pleading your love as a mortal."

I curled a lip. "But you tried magic first, didn't you?" I accused. "You tried to invade my dreams. You came to me as my brother. And then as my brother's wife, my dear friend. Then you had the gall to try to use my own dead mother against me.

"But you failed! In *all* attempts."

She nodded. "That pleased me," she said. "It would have spoiled it if I could have overcome you so easily by sorcery."

"And so now you fall back on such charming tools as threats and intimidation?" I mocked.

"Look beyond my clumsiness if you can, Rali," she pleaded. "In those matters I'm still very much a child. I have no social skills beyond a girl's training for court.

"I am those hundreds upon hundreds of young girls with awkward ways and awkward expressions that it took to make me. My magical powers are so great you might mistake me for your equal in human experience. I'm not, Rali. But I can grow. I can learn. Give me that chance!" She glowed with youthful sincerity, with a tender heart too easily and innocently displayed.

I sipped my brandy and turned my eyes to the fire, saying nothing.

She sat quietly for a time, hands gracefully folded in her lap. Then she said, "I've come upon a great thing."

I remained silent.

"I had hundreds of years to experiment and learn by those experiments," she went on. "I had no books, no teachers, no term of apprenticeship. The island was barren of all life, other than shellfish in the pools and the fish in the seas. In other words, I only had raw nature to work with.

"I had light, heat, cold, air, earth, water, and the forces created from their . . . motion. I'm uncertain of that word. But motion is the only one I can think of that describes the particles I sense flowing this way and that in all elements."

I couldn't help but let my eyes be drawn back to her. Her discussion was treading into the realm Janos Greycloak opened. Greycloak, who thought all natural and magical forces were merely different expressions of a single force acting in different ways.

How could she have come upon an insight so grand that until Greycloak no other had considered it? And in complete isolation, at that?

"You know what I'm talking about, don't you, Rali?" she said.

"Yes," I answered.

"Your loyal Evocator told me you would," she said. "He told me all about Orissa. Janos Greycloak. Your brother and mother and family. The Far Kingdoms. Your battle with the Archons. All of it. It was quite a stirring tale. Inspiring, as well."

Lord Searbe, I thought, had been a busy little coward these past few days. She shifted subjects. "You know there are other worlds, don't you?"

"Yes," I said.

"Lord Searbe said you'd entered some in your battle with the Archons."

"If you know," I said, "why ask?"

"I can draw on those worlds for power," she said.

"That's what magic is," I said, shrugging. "We reach into the Otherworlds and draw out the means to cast our spells."

"No, I mean *real* power. I mean enough to blast a mountain."

"*You* can't do that," I said. "You said yourself that you used natural forces such as an already brewing storm to carry your biggest spells. And you can't focus that. It's sort of like casting bits of paper into the wind. You have to have a blizzard of those bits to make certain you hit your target. Like a shower of arrows on opposing troops."

"I can't do it now," she said. "But I'll be able to when I'm done. And more. Why, the power is unlimited. Whole ranges of mountains could be turned to dust."

"If you could," I said, "which I doubt ... for what purpose? Why would you want to blast all those innocent mountains?"

She laughed. "Don't be silly," she said. "What do *I* care about mountains? It's the power I want. The delicious power. Why, it's the stuff that makes all wizards' dreams."

"Not mine," I said.

"Come now," she said. "How can you say that and claim it's true? Look how hard you've struggled to reach where you are. Look at how you have been treated by the men who rule this world, who command all women to keep their place and do their bidding like slavish animals with convenient orifices to please their masters."

"Ah, I see," I replied. "All you do is in the name of sisterhood. You attack your neighbors, stalk the trade routes with pirate ships, kill my friends or lure them into betrayal, violate my dreams, and all in the name of our dear sisters, martyred in the temple of brute men."

She became angry, her lovely features swelling with fury. "Why do you insist on arguing with me?" she demanded. "I've *explained* everything to you. Every word I've spoken is the truth! You know it's the truth. And you still argue. You still mock. You still turn away. Why is this?"

"Where are my men?" I demanded.

She huffed. "That again!"

"Yes," I said. "That again. Where are they?"

"Dead," she said.

"*All* of them?" I asked, keeping all feeling under heavy rein.

"Except for your Evocator," she said. "I needed him for something else."

"And if I spurn you," I said, "I suppose you'll kill me, too."

"That's not going to happen," she said. "I need you alive. Willing or not."

"For the same purpose as Lord Searbe?" I asked. "And Daciar? And my other Evocator, Lord Serano?"

"Partly," she said. "Although I have more need of you than all of them, including the others I've captured. I've gathered quite a collection of wizards since King Magon began his raids."

I made no response to this. To do so would draw me deeper into her sphere.

"Don't you want to know why I've gone to such trouble to collect them?" she pressed.

I remained silent. She had to tell me freely. Only then would the knowledge come without spell-tainted strings.

She finally said, "I'm doing with them what the wizard did with all those girls. Except the presence I'm creating will be commanded by *me*!"

Now I knew how she was able to cast such a deadly spell on that storm. She'd somehow seized the powers of all the wizards she'd captured and molded them into a creature of her will.

I gave no indication of my understanding. I casually drained my goblet and tipped in an inch or so more brandy. I was also remembering my conversation with Daciar when I'd declared that it wasn't possible for a wizard to steal another's power. Novari, it seemed, had certainly proven that statement false.

"It appears to me that I have two choices. Join all those wizards in whatever hells you've condemned them to. Or side with you."

She tilted her head, a coy smile on her lips. "I had more intimacy in mind than merely choosing sides," she said.

I primped my hair with exaggerated femininity, touching the pin in my hair as if making certain it was in place. It was my only weapon.

I dimpled a smile as coy as her own. "Why not?" I said.

Then I turned the smile into a broad grin. I gulped my brandy and set the goblet down. I made my voice rough as I said, "I like a good fuck as well as the next woman."

Novari winced at my crudeness. "Please," she said, voice trembling.

"What more do you want?" I said.

She slipped toward me, body glimmering in the firelight. I lay there motionless, watching. She sank down beside me. She looked deep into my eyes, and I could see emotion boiling in her own. Her lips were swollen, soft. Her perfume a heady musk that warmed me as I drank in the air.

She touched my arm. "Please," she said again.

I did nothing.

She touched my breast. "Please." Softer now, almost a whisper.

She leaned over me, her hair brushing my cheeks, making my skin tingle. Her lips were inches from mine and her breath was as sweet as a field in flower.

"I can't give you what I don't feel," I whispered.

She nodded. "Let me help you," she whispered back.

Her face still mere inches from mine, she stroked my temples and looked deeper into my eyes. The spell of her perfume increased, and it was as if I were drifting in warmed honey. I could feel the heat grow where her body was pressed against mine.

Lyre music swelled, soft and washing against me like gentle waves. The strings spoke to me of past loves, old regrets.

I wasn't frightened but let the song take me where it would. I nearly cried out loud when it found Otara.

My dear Otara. My only real love. The woman who had been all to me and whose loss was a wound that would never heal.

"Oh, Rali!" Otara cried. "I've missed you so."

And she came into my arms and all the years between us vanished.

We embraced.

We kissed.

And we wept.

The tears came like rivers, and the more we wept the more joyous I felt, and then we were laughing and tickling like schoolgirls. Passion flared and we were clutching each other, caressing each other, and I felt all the sweet lust that only Otara could arouse in me.

Then we were moving toward our bed, our great, soft familiar bed which we'd shared for so many years.

Just as we reached it I stopped. I unpinned my hair, letting it fall in waves across my shoulders.

"You always liked my hair this way," I said.

Otara laughed, low and throaty. The laugh I loved so much. Then she drew me into the bed and began undressing me, kissing each place she unveiled.

My heart was hammering so hard I thought my ribs would crack. My limbs were like jelly, pliant to her every touch. Her every caress.

But I had the golden pin clutched like a dagger in my fist.

Otara embraced me, twining her limbs around me, and I could feel the heat of her loins against my thigh.

I took all the love I had for Otara, all the great emotion Novari had roused with her succubus spell, and I made it my strength.

And I plunged the golden pin into her back.

She screamed, and her scream was shrill lightning, scorching my hearing. She arched her back, struggling to escape the agony of the magic pin. I held tight, trying to press the pin deeper still.

Suddenly I was buffeted by huge wings. They lashed my head and my sides like great padded clubs. The Lyre Bird shrieked and fought and clawed at me with her spurs.

I struggled to hold on, and then a blinding flash exploded in my face. I felt an immense force push at me and my arms were ripped open. The Lyre Bird's weight suddenly lifted and I heard the thunder of wings and felt the blast of wind they stirred up.

I leaped to my feet, half blind, naked, and fighting for breath, waving the golden pin in front of me.

Dimly, as if through a haze, I saw the Lyre Bird's glowing form against the far wall of the chamber. She shimmered and my eyes cleared and the spirit bird became Novari.

She sagged back against the wall, then came up, leaving a smear of blood on the stone from the wounds I'd caused. Blood trickled down and pooled at her feet.

I reached deep in that shadow of a moment and grabbed desperately for some of my old power. With all the spells cast over the palace, it was like scrabbling in flowing mud for a lost object.

As I searched I could see Novari's face turn from shock to a mask of hatred. Her naked body shot off magical sparks of anger. She reached out to revenge herself, and I grabbed what power I could, scrambling back before she had me trapped.

Novari gestured and a spark arced out. The spark became a lightning ball hurtling at me as if from a ship's catapult.

I cast a shield with the golden pin, and the lightning ball exploded against it. White-hot globes splattered the walls, cracking the stone, while the force of the explosion itself blasted back at Novari.

I dropped the shield, hurled a spear of fire, then raised the shield again.

Novari was quick. She flung up her own shield, shattering the force of the blast and diverting my spear.

I didn't give her time to recover, but charged forward, slinging my magical shield at her eyes—it sliced at her, a red-hot wire of force, and she flung up her shield to block it.

I came up under her guard, saw her eyes glow with power, and I struck at them.

She snapped her head back and the pin sliced her cheek, leaving a long smear of blood across those perfect features.

Novari screamed and I stabbed again, striking for those eyes—striking for her power.

But the killing blow stopped short as heavy hands grabbed me from behind, dragging me back. Heavy blows rained on me and I fell to my knees.

I fought them—three, perhaps four guards. I broke one man's knee trying to get up. But the others clubbed me down again.

While I fought I desperately tried to form another spell. I had to strike before Novari recovered.

I had the spell half formed when an explosion lifted me up and I was slammed back against the walls of the chambers. Heavy objects hit me. I was stunned, lying in rubble. I tried to come up, woozy, drained. There were dead guards beside me.

Novari loomed over me. I blinked at her. Helpless. Burned empty by her attack.

She said nothing, and I heard heavy boots as more guards arrived. Novari gestured at me and they hauled me up.

I hung there between two of the guards, unable to hold my weight on my feet.

I saw the pretty maids rush up to Novari, weeping at the wound on her cheek and wiping at the blood. She stood there, staring at me as they dabbed at the wound and pulled a robe onto her.

Then she flung them off and stalked forward, her strides long and slow. She stopped in front of me.

"To think I believed I needed you," she said.

I didn't answer. I couldn't have if I'd wanted to.

Novari touched the wound on her cheek. Her eyes filled with tears. She wiped them away. Then she said, "You went for my eyes."

In the silence that followed I saw a flicker as she made some sort of a decision.

Novari hissed at me, "Bitch!"

Then she turned to the guards. "Take her to the mines," she said. "They'll find useful work for her there." The guards started to drag me away.

"Oh, yes, one more thing," she said. The guards stopped. Waiting.

And Novari said, "Bring me back one of her eyes."

Again she touched her right cheek where I'd cut her.

"Bring me the right one," she commanded, voice hoarse with rage. "Make certain of that. Only the right eye will do."

CHAPTER ELEVEN
THE MINES OF KORONOS

I can't say much about what happened next. The days and weeks that followed were a blur of constant shock and pain. It was all a mad chariot ride through a nightmare that had no beginning or end.

I don't remember how and when they took my eye. I only remember through a thick haze my first awareness that it was gone.

It was like floating up from the bottom of a muddy lake of misery. I emerged gasping and choking in hot sooty air that seared my lungs. I found myself stooped at the head of a line of creatures dressed in filthy rags. I felt stiff scratchiness on my own skin and knew I was dressed the same.

I heard fire roar and bellows pump and I tried to turn my head to look.

The world spun and I lurched into someone. That someone cursed me and I felt a hard tug and heard the clatter of chains. I muttered an apology and became dimly aware that I had a steel band about my waist and that I was linked together with the rest of the group by a heavy chain that ran from belt to belt. My feet and arms, however, were free.

I heard the iron slap of a hammer against an anvil—a slow, steady measure. I tried to look again. Everything seemed strange, distorted and flat-dimensioned, making it difficult to make out the edges of things or how far or near they might be.

I tentatively touched my face. A bandage was looped across my forehead, covering the right side. Beneath the bandage I felt the throb of a hol-

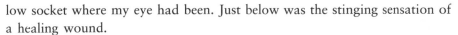

low socket where my eye had been. Just below was the stinging sensation of a healing wound.

My thoughts were a dim-witted babble: "My eye? That's right. Novari has it. She ordered it taken out."

I had no feelings about the mutilation, other than dull interest. I was too numb. Too much in shock from hard treatment.

Someone bellowed. A heavy hand struck my shoulder. I shuffled forward on aching legs. The others followed me, chains rattling.

Another blow brought me up short. Someone stumbled into me. I automatically snarled a curse, and got a muttered apology in reply. Why I knew to do this, I couldn't say. But it came to me that I'd been in these circumstances for some time. Somehow I'd learned what to do in order to survive.

I was streaming sweat and it was hard to breathe. My mouth was dry from dehydration. I tilted my head and cautiously peered about with my good eye.

I was in a large blacksmith shop. The walls were covered with hunks of iron and chain and racks of implements in various stages of repair or construction. I heard the hiss of metal being plunged into a tempering bucket and smelled steamy oil.

The bellows resumed their pumping and I located the forge. A blacksmith with a fire-scarred apron covering his bare torso manned the bellows. To one side of the forge was his anvil. On the other was another man dressed in clean expensive robes. He stood before a small table with a few medical devices on it and a pile of dirty rags folded like bandages. A Healer of some sort. I didn't think that when I saw him. I was too fuzzy to make even such a simple guess. I just *knew* it somehow.

Someone had told me. I didn't recall when or who.

A guard with a piggish face unlocked my chain, freeing me from the others. He shoved me forward and I tottered up to the forge. I was dragged to a stop in front of the Healer.

"Let's see your arm," he said, bored.

I didn't have to ask which one. I automatically lifted my left.

I gaped. The arm stopped short at my wrist. A ball of rags stained with blood was tied about the end. The Healer peeled off the rags, unwinding them swiftly and with no thought for the pain he was causing as he ripped them away.

I found myself staring at a pink stump where my left hand used to be. There were two metal bolts driven through the stump with threaded ends protruding on either side.

The Healer held my arm by the bolts, turning it this way and that so he could get a good look. He sniffed at the flesh, smelled no corruption, and nodded in satisfaction.

"This one looks ready," he said to the blacksmith. "I did a pretty good job, even if I do say so myself."

The blacksmith sneered at him. "Takes no talent to whack 'em off," he said. "Any butcher can do that. The real work's makin' 'em new again."

"Don't be stupid," the Healer snorted. "She wouldn't be any use to you if her stump was rotted, would she, now?"

He let go of the stump. I held it there for a while, squinting with my single eye to see it better. All emotion was at great distance. My only wonderment was that I thought I could still feel my hand. Absently, I tried to wiggle my fingers. But there was no sensation other than a burning at the stump.

The blacksmith grabbed it roughly and pulled me to him. It hurt and I tried to pull back. The guard slapped me on the back of the head.

"Stay still, bitch," he said. "He's not done with you yet."

I did as I was told.

The blacksmith looked the stump over, paying more attention to the bolts than to my flesh. He daubed the threads with an oil mop, then shouted over his shoulder to his apprentice.

"Size seven ought to do it," he said.

I watched a fat young man waddle to a rack. On it I saw scores of black metal hands. The fat apprentice searched among them until he found one he thought would satisfy his master. He fetched it to the blacksmith, who burred and polished the fittings with a round file, then directed the apprentice to hold my stump.

"Steady, now," he said to the apprentice. "Last time you flinched and ruined a perfectly good stump." He gestured, indicating me. "Don't mind if it pains her," he advised the apprentice. "She ain't nothin' more'n an animal. Got no feelings we need to think on."

The apprentice got a good grip, and the smithy greased the interior of the metal hand, then forced it on the stump, twisting back and forth to do so. The pain was incredible. I think I moaned. I'm not certain.

"Good rough fit," the smithy said approvingly. "Won't need much touching up."

He yanked hard and the metal hand came off. I nearly fainted from the pain. I must've staggered, because the guard slapped the back of my head again and snarled for me to straighten up.

The smithy clamped the hand in tongs and thrust it into the fire, heaving at the bellows until the fire roared white-hot. When the metal hand got good and red, he withdrew it, laid it against the anvil, and used a small hammer to tap here and there—making adjustments, he told the apprentice.

When he was satisfied, he plunged the hand into a tempering bucket. Steam and oil fumes hissed up in a greasy cloud. He withdrew the hand; it was glistening and dark.

Once again the apprentice held my stump while the blacksmith twisted the metal into place. It was still hot from the forge, and through the pain I was dimly aware of the smell of my burning flesh. I heard the Healer say something about there being little chance for infection now.

The threaded bolts in my stump jutted through openings in the metal hand. A drilled band was placed over the bolts and heavy nuts were cinched into place with a wrench, then welded so they couldn't be removed.

I fainted while they were doing the welding.

I suppose I eventually came to. But I'd returned to that hazy world of misery, drifting about as if heavily drugged.

The next time I became even vaguely aware of the world about me, I was working beside a short, heavyset woman. I was helping her pull a solid gold rod from an extrusion machine. It was smoking hot, still soft and nearly ten feet long. We were using our metal hands to hold the rod, and I was amazed when I realized that I was clutching the object as if the hand were real instead of artificial. It felt like someone else's hand, acting out my wishes from a great distance.

The woman and I lugged the rod across a wide room that seemed to have been carved out of rock. The walls and floors and jagged ceiling were grimed with grease and oil and soot. The room was hot, hotter than anyplace I'd ever been. And there was a constant thunder of heavy machinery at work. I saw other slaves, both men and women, shuffling about the room, going from one strange machine to another, barely moving out of the way when a furnace unexpectedly belched steam or fire.

All of them had metal hands like mine.

The heavyset woman and I dropped the rod on a large pile. We stopped, panting for breath.

I looked at my iron hand. I moved the fingers in and out, bent the thumb across my palm. It performed all these tasks slowly but very smoothly on greased bearings in the knuckles and joints. I could feel a small ball of warmth in the palm and knew it was magic.

Soon as I caught the scent of the spell, my senses widened—although only slightly—and I could smell the ozone stench of powerful magic at work. The machines reeked of it; the stone in the walls and floors were slippery with it. The very scorched air I sucked into my heaving lungs had the foul tang of demon's breath.

Somewhere a heavy gong echoed and the machines went silent. My fellow slaves began lumbering into long lines that stretched across the immense chamber to massive barred doors. I became confused. I didn't know what to do.

"We have to go, Rali," the woman said, taking my arm.

Suddenly she seemed familiar to me. Her name popped into my head without effort. I nodded and went with her, saying, "Where to, Zalia?"

"Where we go every night, dear," she said, her voice gentle, as if she were speaking to a child. "To our cells."

"That's right," I said, vaguely remembering.

I got into line with her. Orders were barked. We all shuffled forward—hundreds of us—and whips cracked and slaves cried out.

"Where are we?" I asked.

"I've told you before, dear," Zalia said. "But I'll tell you again. We're in the mines of Koronos."

Emotion boiled through the haze that enveloped me. I felt tears well up and I thought, The gods help me, I'll never get out of here.

I must have sobbed, because Zalia patted my shoulder to comfort me. Then all manner of what seemed like new sights and sounds and sensation pummeled me as I was led at a dog trot through the mines.

It was a bewildering warren of horrors. Hammers cracked at rocks, molten gold spurted from pipes into big vats, machines ground and clanked and spewed fire, and everywhere I looked laborers moaned in pain. Sometimes we had to wait as other columns of slaves passed. Other times big ore cars blocked our way, with slaves hitched up like oxen to drag them along wooden rails.

At last we came to a corridor with barred cells on either side. Zalia guided me into a cell, and I slumped on a stone bench.

She went to a bucket of water and wet a rag. She returned to sit beside me and gently lifted the bandage that covered my empty socket. She sponged around the wound.

Although I remembered nothing, not even meeting her, the tender routine had a familiar feel to it. I felt I could trust her. Somehow she had become my companion and possibly a friend.

When she was done she tucked the bandage back into place, saying, "There you are, dear." She went to the bucket to clean herself up.

I studied her as she lifted her ragged tunic to scrub soot from her legs. Awareness was trickling slowly back and I examined her closely. I *knew* this woman. But until that moment, it seemed to me, she'd only been a tender voice emanating from the shadows.

Zalia was squat, with calves the size of my waist. Her hair was a butchered auburn mop and her face was large and round, but with a small nose and bowed lips that looked out of place. There was also an odd aura about her that aroused me further from the dullness.

I tried to slip out a probe to test the edges of her aura. I was alarmed when nothing happened.

I tried again. I felt resistance, then whatever was holding my magic back began to give.

I pressed harder, felt something like fabric rip, and I tasted just a whiff of sorcery—and then pain suddenly gripped me. It shot up from my metal hand, wracked my elbow like it was struck by a sledge, and then my shoulder and neck and back were seized with such agony that my stomach heaved.

I vomited on the floor.

Zalia was suddenly beside me, holding my head and rubbing my back as I spewed my guts on the cell floor.

"Poor thing," she said, "poor thing."

Then the pain and sick feeling were gone. She pushed me back on the stone bed. She cleaned me up, put a cold wet rag on my forehead, and then mopped up the mess I'd made.

I lay there silently, and the only pain remaining was the throbbing of my eye socket. I closed my good eye.

Sparks and glowing shapes drifted through blackness.

I slept.

There was a clack of wood against metal. I awoke to see Zalia carrying a pail of food through the cell door. A large wooden spoon with a hooked handle bumped against the side.

I was suddenly very hungry. I sat up, licking my lips as she scooped up a thick yellowish gruel and dumped it into a wooden bowl. Odd bits, colored the greenish gray of spoiled meat, floated up as she stirred the bowl's contents with a tin spoon.

The gruel smelled delicious. My mouth watered, and I got up to find my own bowl.

"You can't eat this, dear," she said. "I've told you that before." She was dipping up some for herself as she said this.

"Why not?" I asked.

"It's not good for you, Rali dear," she answered.

"*You're* eating it," I accused, trembling like a child being unfairly denied something everyone else was enjoying.

"It'll make you fat and ugly," she said. "Like me."

"I don't care," I said. "I'm hungry."

"Just be patient, Rali," she said. "I'll feed you tonight. Just like I always do."

I struggled for some memory of this but no images came. I went back to my bench and sat.

I felt petulant, pouty, and full of resentment. As I became aware of these feelings I became unhappy with myself. And I thought, What's wrong? This isn't like me.

The haze lifted further and I became more certain of my surroundings. The door to the cell I was in was open. From where I sat I could see down the corridor outside. The other cell doors were also open and I could see lumps of humanity going about their slave's business. They were eating or quarreling or playing games with bits of rock and bone. I saw a man and woman coupling in full view of others, rutting and grunting like dogs.

I turned away, shaken—the hunger in my belly frothing into sickness.

I heard the slap of bare feet on stone and turned back as several men led by a shambling brute pushed into our cell.

Zalia looked up at them but continued eating. Her thick body seemed relaxed, easy. But I could feel tension suddenly thicken the air.

"I'm here for your answer," the shambler growled.

Zalia raised an eyebrow in pretended surprise. "And what," she said, "was the question?"

"You know," the shambler rumbled. He jabbed a thick, crooked digit at me. "Whatcha want for her?"

"Oh, *that* question!" Zalia widened her eyes as if in sudden recollection. Then she shrugged. "I thought we settled that before," she said. "Rali's not for sale. I didn't refuse you the first time to get a better price. There is no price, my friend. Understand that and you'll sleep easier."

She indicated the cell door. "Good-bye. It was nice to chat with you." She smiled blandly and resumed eating.

Shambler came forward, flexing his muscles and extending his metal hand.

Before he could reach her, Zalia exploded up from her bench, flung the bowl into his face, then grabbed him by the neck with her metal hand. She pulled his head down and a thick knee snapped upward, colliding with his chin. She let go and he crashed to the floor.

The others were coming for her, and she spun to face them.

Anger swept away the last of the haze and I leaped from my bench and grabbed one of the men. My iron hand seemed like it had the strength of a giant and I gripped him by the throat, squeezing until he gurgled and slamming my other fist into his gut.

I heard Zalia dispose of the other man, and my opponent suddenly went limp. Overcome by my anger, I kept squeezing, and then enormously strong arms were pulling me away and I let him drop.

I swung around, tears of hatred streaming down my face, and I tried to grapple with Zalia. She embraced me, pulling me so tight I could do nothing but pound on her strong back.

"Easy, Rali," she said. "Easy, dear."

The anger drained away and I went limp. She lifted me up and placed me back on the bench.

"Wait here, Rali dear," she said. "I'll be back."

She dragged the men into the hallway one by one and returned. As she sat beside me, I saw the men recover and then slink off.

Zalia stroked me, saying, "*That* was a surprise, dear. I've never seen you so aggressive."

"Aggressive?" I said. "Those sons of poxed whores don't know what aggressive is!"

Zalia sighed. "I wish it were a sign that you were getting better," she said.

Then she got up and went to her own side of the room, squatting down on fat haunches to clean up the spilled gruel. When she was done, she settled on her own bench and closed her eyes. She wasn't asleep, but I didn't disturb her.

An hour or so passed. I tried to think, but the process that had once been automatic seemed clumsy—like rusty gears trying to jerk into life. I kept at it, and the more I tried, the easier it got. I couldn't make sense of my predicament, but I had a vague feeling that large, unwieldy puzzle shapes were beginning to fit into place. I became tired, so I stopped. For the first time I noticed that the light had dimmed and only a few firebeads glowed along the corridor. All was silent except for the snores of the other slaves.

Hunger burned in my belly, and I looked over at Zalia just as she roused herself. She scraped the food pail until she had a good-sized lump and stuck the lump next to a hole in the cell wall. She squatted there for a long time, as motionless as if she were stone herself.

Finally, whiskers wriggled in the hole. Then a sharp nose poked out. The nose twitched, sensed no danger, and a moment later a large fat rat emerged and nibbled at the bait.

Zalia's metal hand blurred forward, snatched up the rat, and snapped its neck.

I remembered doing something similar long ago. It was someplace cold: a storm raged outside, and I was catching rats so my friends and I could eat.

The memory faded.

Zalia, meanwhile, had pulled a loose rock from the wall, revealing a fairly large hiding place. There were several small bundles inside. She took them out, unwrapped them one by one, and set them up. Soon a little fire was burning beneath a pot, and she'd skinned and cut up the rat.

When it was done cooking, she served it to me in a bowl, and I was so ravenous I devoured every drop, scraped the bowl, and sucked the marrow from the bones. As soon as I was done I felt remarkably full and strength flooded through my veins.

"What happened to my hand?" I said. "Does Novari have that, too?"

Zalia grimaced, weary. "I've answered that question before, dear," she said.

"Tell me again," I insisted. "I don't remember."

"You never do," she said.

"Just tell me."

"They cut off everyone's hand," she said.

I nodded. "I saw the others."

"And they give us these instead," she said, raising her own iron hand.

"Yes. Go on."

"The flesh and bone they take from us are given to Novari's wizards. They use them to cast spells to power the metal ones. The slave hands."

I thought about that. And came to a clumsy conclusion. "So Novari doesn't have my hand," I said.

"No, she doesn't, Rali," Zalia answered. "Otherwise your hand wouldn't work. And you'd be no use at all in the mines."

Something else occurred to me. "Why did it hurt," I asked, "when I tried to make magic?"

Zalia shook her head. As if she'd been through this many times. But her voice was patient.

"The hand controls all of us," she said. "If you try to escape, the hand will sense it. It will hurt you in order to make you stop. And it will kill you if you don't. The same with magic, Rali. If you try to cast a spell, that hand will become your worst enemy."

"All right," I said. "I understand now."

"I wish you really did," she said. "I tell you the same thing every night. You say you understand. But by the next day you've forgotten. And the next thing I know you're hurting yourself trying to cast a spell."

"Don't worry, Zalia," I said. "I'll remember this time."

I suddenly felt sleepy. I yawned, stretching out on my bench.

"Sure you will, dear," Zalia soothed. But I could tell she believed otherwise.

"Honestly," I insisted. "I'll remember."

"Oh, Rali," Zalia said, "I wish it were true. I wish you'd rise up tomorrow and tell me that you remembered all you witnessed today. But I know that won't happen. Not for a long time, if at all."

Through my dimness it struck me that her voice was cultured and musical. It seemed odd and out of place coming from such a hulking body.

Then the thought vanished and I mumbled, "You'll see . . ." and closed my eyes.

I slept. I didn't dream, although I woke up once to relieve myself in the slop pail. I heard Zalia breathing heavily, but I didn't disturb her. I went back to sleep.

Much later a gong rang and I sat up. I swiveled, turning my single eye on Zalia, who was yawning awake. I spoke, my voice hard, "I think you'd better tell me who you are."

Zalia blinked, jolted from half sleep. "I'm *Zalia*," she said. "Don't you even remember that?"

I said, "I remember yesterday, at least. You acted like a friend then. But I don't know that for a fact, do I? Because everything is a blank from the moment I was condemned to this place to yesterday in the shops."

Zalia lit up—delighted. At least she was acting delighted. But at that moment I trusted no one.

"Thank the gods!" she said. "You're returning to normal."

She started to get up, but I raised my metal hand to stop her.

"Sit back down," I said.

She did as I commanded, but her eyes seemed to be sparkling with interest instead of resentment.

"Listen," I said. "You're strong. I can see that. But there isn't much I don't know about killing, so your strength won't do you any good. Do as I say, and if it turns out I'm being rude, I'll apologize profusely."

"Fine, Rali," she said. "I'll do as you say. And gladly."

"Good," I said. "You can begin by accounting for yourself."

"I don't think we have time for a full accounting," she said. "They'll come to make up the work parties in an hour."

"Tell me how I came to be in your company," I said. "That's a good enough start. If you're still alive in an hour, you'll know I believe just enough to let you live until tonight. And then you can tell me the rest."

Zalia shrugged. "Maybe I just felt sorry for you," she said. "You were wandering around bumping into walls like you were drugged. The guards shoved you from one task to the next. You nearly fell into a furnace once. Then some of the other slaves got some ideas about you. Perhaps I took pity on you and took you under my wing."

She glared at me. "If that's the case," she said. "I'm now being poorly paid for my sympathy."

"Is it the case?" I demanded.

Zalia trembled with anger. "Maybe it wasn't," she snarled. "Maybe I had designs on you myself. Maybe I wanted to make you my own slave, make you labor for me in the day and pleasure me at night. And the fight you took part in yesterday was because I was protecting a possession."

"That's *not* the worst possibility for your motives," I said.

Zalia's eyes widened in surprise. The surprise turned into a cynical sneer. "Oh, I suppose you think I might be a spy?" she said. "That I might be working for Novari and plotting to win your trust so I can betray you?"

"That's one possibility," I said. "You could also be Novari herself, for all I know."

"That's stupid," she said. She swept a beefy arm about, indicating our surroundings. "Can you imagine Novari submitting herself to these conditions?"

"I've seen harm come to people," I said, "for ignoring stupid possibilities."

"Well, that can't be proven one way or the other," she said. "You'd need sorcery to do it. And that hand will kill you if you attempt it."

"We'll have to rely on your powers of persuasion, then," I said. "And I'll only ask you one more time: What did you intend with me?"

"To get you well, if I could," she said. "So we could both escape." She gave me a long fixed stare, as if daring me to brand her a liar.

I stared back, just as long and just as hard.

Then I said, "That's good enough for now. You can tell me the rest tonight."

"To the devil with you," she growled. "Believe what you want. I don't care. Get out! Find your own place. I'll have nothing further to do with you!"

"We'll talk tonight," I said again. "And then we'll see what happens next."

The day that followed was one of the strangest in my life. It was like awakening from a nightmare and finding yourself actually living that nightmare. All sensation was familiar and alien at the same time.

To begin with, I was seeing through only one eye, which distorted reality until I became used to the loss and learned to compensate for the absence of my other eye. While I'd been in shock, I'd somehow formed a habit of letting my head flop to one side when I wanted to look at something. I kept having to jerk it up again, which made the guards nervous at first, then made them laugh at my silly antics. Their mockery was spur enough to correct that habit.

The strangeness was compounded further by the artificial hand. It was an unfeeling object hanging from the end of my left arm. The hand acted like mortal flesh, reaching for things when I willed it, gripping them and releasing them at my command. But for a time the actions lagged behind thought, as if the thoughts were fingers trailing through water. When the hand finally moved, there was a slight hesitation at first, then it would shoot forward as if my commands had just caught up with it. Sometimes I had to actually will the device to slow down so I wouldn't knock something over.

The hand was also much stronger than its mortal cousin, and I had to be careful not to crush things by mistake when I gripped them. It was also impervious to heat, and we were expected to make use of this function by plunging it into molten vats or picking up white-hot metal bars. Each time I was confronted with such tasks I had to force myself to overcome instinct. I knew it wouldn't hurt, but knowing and doing can be two different things. The guards made me suffer until I learned to overcome those natural fears.

Oddest of all was that everything I was now experiencing I'd experienced before, but I had no memory of it. Yet there was a shadowy familiarity about my surroundings, as if I'd once been a ghost in this place.

Which is what I'd been.

When the guards came to take us to our labors, those ghostly impressions guided me and I automatically followed Zalia out into the corridor. We lined up with about thirty other slaves from our warren, which is what they called each grouping of cells. When I joined the line, I knew without thinking that Zalia would fall in behind me. Somehow I'd become accustomed to that position. I felt more comfortable with her there, although I couldn't say why I felt that way.

When I realized that it unnerved me. And I wondered how long I'd been in the mines and what else had happened to me.

Then the full realization of the violations that had been committed against me struck and my heart went crazy, slapping against my ribs like a trip-hammer, and I suddenly found it hard to breathe. I nearly blacked out, and then I felt Zalia's thick arms surround me and squeeze—pushing in, letting out, pushing in, letting out—until I could breathe normally and my heart steadied . . . and the panic passed.

At that moment the guards barked and cracked their whips and we all shambled into motion and marched out of our warren.

Instead of returning to the shop I'd awakened in the day before, we were marched a short distance to a huge elevator cage and were herded inside. We descended for perhaps ten minutes and then the cage groaned to a halt.

The cage door rattled up and we were prodded out into an underground yard where empty ore carts were lined up on tracks. Sledgehammers, long iron bars, and other miners' tools hung from the sides. We were split up into groups, with each group assigned an ore cart.

Zalia helped me put on a leather band that held a reflector with a single firebead mounted in the middle so the light was cast in a narrow beam. All the other slave miners were similarly equipped.

Then we were hitched to the carts and long whips snaked out to bite us and we were forced into motion, dragging the heavy carts along the rough rails.

I labored for nearly an hour, legs and shoulders aching from the load, my chest pinched so hard by the harness that every breath came as a gasp. When a halt was finally ordered, I thought I'd reached the end of my strength. But that was only where my day began.

First we had to fill the cart with gold ore.

Next we had to drag it back to the yard and unload it for the crusher.

And then the process started all over again.

Just filling the cart took an enormous effort. We had to crack away hunks of rock from the face of the tunnel using sledges and the long pointed bars. The hunks had to be broken up into smaller pieces with sledges. And the rubble had to be heaped into the cart.

Each task required all your strength—and more.

Zalia pushed one of the bars into my hands, took up a sledge, and led me to the rock face. The gold vein was plain even in the dim light of the torches and firebeads. It was a broad, glittering band about shoulder high. Zalia showed me a crevice to slip the tip of the bar into and told me to hold it steady.

I did as she said, only dimly aware of what was going to happen next. I turned my head and saw her draw back with the sledge, handling its weight in her iron fist as if it were a twig. Then I saw the sledge slam forward, aimed right at me and blurring from the speed of her blow. I had no time to react, much less jerk aside. Instead of hitting me, it slammed into the iron bar. The bar bit deep into the crevice and a big chunk of rock broke off and crashed to the floor.

Zalia grinned. "You should see your face," she said with much satisfaction. "Now you know I could've killed you anytime I'd wanted."

I licked dry lips. "Doesn't prove anything," I said.

Zalia laughed. "No. But it'll make you think. That's good enough for the moment . . . Now," she commanded. "Hold it steady."

And she drew back to strike again.

"Don't flinch," she said. "Or there could be a most regretful accident."

She swung.

And I didn't flinch.

When the day ended, we stumbled back to the yard where we were made to stand in deep troughs while other slaves hosed us down with water so cold it seemed like it came from ice fields.

The shower wasn't for our benefit. It was to wash off the golden grime that covered us all. Our skins and faces sparkled with the stuff at day's end. Eyes and teeth gleamed eerily through the sparkle. The troughs carried the glittering grime away to shallow pools where other slaves panned it so there was no wastage.

When I finally reached our cell I was so weary that I nearly looked at it as a cheery home. I sighed with relief when I sank onto my stone bench, falling back as blissfully as if the stone were soft as a down bed. I immediately plunged into a deep sleep. I awoke much later to the smell of cooking meat and found Zalia preparing my evening meal.

Although I still didn't trust her, I took the bowl without hesitation and ate every scrap, sucking the bones dry of all nourishment. While I ate I studied Zalia, who was lying on her bench, eyes closed, arms folded across her big bosom. I knew she wasn't asleep. I thought, If she thinks she's softening me up, she's got a great deal more to learn about Rali Antero.

When I was done, I said, "You want to tell me your particulars now?"

She spoke, eyes still closed. "I've been here for seven months. One month longer than you. You've been in my care for three of those months."

I was stunned. "So long?"

Zalia sat up. "Yes, Rali," she said, the hostility gone from her voice. "You've been here for six months. Six months in which you were as helpless as a dim-witted child. I would have helped you sooner, but I had to learn enough about this place so I could manage it. There were rules to be bent. Favors to be done."

She waved at the cell around us. "Why, I paid a week's worth of rations to get us this palace."

"That was good of you," I said dryly.

Zalia sniffed. "If you think I'm lying, others will bear me out. Ask anyone you like."

"You can be sure I will," I said.

"Good," she said. "You'll see." She wiped her eyes with a meaty paw.

"How did you come to be here?" I asked.

"I was captured," she said. "I was on a mission for my queen. Novari and her toy, King Magon, had been giving us much difficulty. But during my mission I was caught in a storm. I alone survived."

She wiped an eye as the recollection made tears well. At least that was the impression she wanted to convey.

"Then Magon's soldiers came on me and I was captured."

"You saw Novari?" I asked.

"Yes," she said.

"What did she ask you?"

"She wanted to know the nature of my mission," Zalia said, "and many details about my queen."

"How did you answer?" I asked.

Zalia curled a lip. "As you can see," she replied, "whatever I may have said won me no favors from Novari."

I ignored the sarcasm, pointedly staring at her, waiting for her answer.

She finally sighed and said, "I told her nothing. Novari tried to force me with magic, but my queen had placed a guardian spell on me that blocked it. I was able to maintain my pose as an innocent who'd strayed into Magon's waters. In this kingdom, that sort of innocence gets you a life sentence mining the king's gold. The only bright spot is that no one lives very long in the Mines of Koronos."

I thought for a moment, searching for a means to test her. Then I said, "Tell me a lie."

Her heavy brows furrowed in puzzlement. "A lie? Whatever do you mean?"

"Novari can't lie," I said. "If you're Novari in disguise—"

Zalia broke in, "*That* again!"

"Yes, *that* again," I replied. "Foolish or not, it *is* a way I can test you. Now, tell me something we both know is a lie."

"I can prove more by telling you a truth," she said.

"Such as?"

Zalia leaned forward and said, "I was told when I met you I should mention . . . the ship of silver."

That nearly bowled me off my bench. No one other than a goddess and Daciar knew that term would have any meaning to me.

"Who told you to say that?" I demanded.

"In my kingdom," she said, "we worship the Goddess Maranonia. Before I set out on my mission, I consulted her oracle."

She hesitated, then said, "There are some things I was forbidden to say. But I can tell you that Maranonia appeared to me. That she gave me instructions. And she predicted I would meet you. When I did, she said, I was to use the phrase 'ship of silver' to introduce myself. So that we could work together."

"For what purpose?" I asked.

"Why, to defeat Novari," Zalia said with some surprise. "What other purpose could there be?"

I almost snarled, *Why didn't She tell me that?* but checked myself. The goddess had given me strict instructions that I was to say nothing of her appearance to me. But it was damned maddening to learn she'd appeared to someone else and seemed to have told them more.

Zalia said, "Maranonia appeared to you as well, didn't she?"

I shook my head. "I can't answer."

Zalia nodded. "That tells me she did. Otherwise you could've simply said no."

I pushed past that, saying, "Tell me about the escape."

"Then you believe me?" Zalia said.

"I don't know if I do or not," I answered. "For the time being I'll lean toward belief—but with severe hesitations."

"Thanks," Zalia snarled.

"It's the best I can do," I said. "I'm sorry. I'm a suspicious woman. And I always shall be."

Zalia's angry features cleared. She wrinkled her little nose. "I suppose I can't blame you," she said. "You've suffered much."

"The escape," I pressed. "I'd rather hear a plan than pity."

"Very well," Zalia sniffed. "If it's facts you'd rather have than my sympathy, you shall have them. Although if it weren't for my pity you'd be a sorry mess, and that's for certain."

"Just tell me," I said.

"Here's how it is," she said. "Before I was captured, I knew Magon's soldiers were coming for me. So I hid my ship. If we can make it out of the mines and reach her, we can easily get away." Her tone became proud as she continued. "It's a very fast ship. Once under way, no one can catch us. Not with *me* at the helm."

"How far away is your ship?" I asked.

"Three days' travel," she said. "Perhaps four. We have to strike west across the lake to a group of low mountains. The sea is just beyond that range. Once we reach it, my ship is hidden nearby."

"That's all very well," I said. "But first we have to escape the mines. How do we accomplish that?"

Zalia paused, then said reluctantly, "I haven't been able to figure that out yet."

I'm afraid I sneered when she said that. "A lot of good the ship is going to do us."

Zalia's face reddened. "I've been busy keeping *both* of us alive," she said. She started to say more—to really blister me, I suppose—then stopped. Her anger faded and she sighed. "You're right. I've wracked my brains for months and haven't come up with a single idea."

Her head dropped. "I've been starting to wonder if it might be impossible."

Her confession of doubt had the odd effect of stirring hope in me.

"There has to be a way," I said. "Anything you can get into, you can get out of . . . given time."

Zalia laughed. "We have plenty of that," she said.

"I'm not so certain *I* do," I said. "Novari could send for me at any moment. She could suddenly decide this punishment isn't enough. Or she may discover a new and interesting way to attempt to break me to her will."

"Then you'd better get busy," Zalia said sharply.

I mocked her. "What?" I said. "Where's the sympathy?"

Zalia shrugged. "You'll earn it back," she said, "the day you learn to trust me."

"That could be never," I shot back.

"It could, couldn't it?" she said with a decided lack of concern. She lay back down on her bench and closed her eyes. "From now on," she said, "you can make your own dinner."

She meant it as a final sarcastic dart before she slept, but soon as the words were spoken, she bolted up again.

"I forgot to tell you about the food," she said anxiously. "The gruel we're fed is magically enhanced. Although it's the foulest sort of swill which you wouldn't feed to hogs, it's made to taste and smell delicious. So much so that it's addictive, and those who eat it want nothing else. It makes you strong—even fat. But the food binds all prisoners to the mines. Even the thought of being without creates an uncontrollable longing that will paralyze your will."

She indicated her metal hand. "It also somehow acts on this. Making the obedience spell stronger. Unbreakable."

"So that's why you kept me from eating it," I said.

Zalia nodded. "When I took you in," she said, "you were already addicted to the stuff. I had an awful time breaking you of the habit. I think the food was responsible for making you helpless for so long. And I saw that as I gradually weaned you from it, awareness slowly returned."

"What about you?" I asked. "You eat the gruel without apparent fear."

"The spell my queen cast to guard me," she said, "keeps it from acting on me. It's a good thing, too. If both of us were on diets of rat meat, the guards would soon notice we weren't eating our food or trading it away. One person is hard enough to cover for. Two might be impossible."

She laughed. "Besides, I don't mind getting fatter. It's the strong part I want. I want to be as strong as I can possibly be when we finally make our escape."

I looked at my artificial hand with its ugly bolts jutting out of my wrist. I remembered the pain it had caused when I'd attempted a small spell. Yet Zalia was telling me that the sorcery controlling the hand, and thus me, was lessened because she'd denied me the rations all the other prisoners were required to eat.

I shuddered when I realized what might have happened if she hadn't solved the riddle of the food.

I looked at Zalia with new admiration, although still begrudged. "Thank you," I said.

Zalia nodded, satisfied. "That's a good enough start," she said. "And who knows, by the time we get out of here we might be friends."

"We'll see," I said.

"Yes," she said, "we will, won't we?"

With that, she turned away and fell instantly asleep. A few moments later I followed her into that darkness. For now it was the only escape offered in the Mines of Koronos.

Tomorrow I'd see if there were another way.

CHAPTER TWELVE

THE ESCAPE

Whaten hatching an escape plot, time can be the greatest enemy or the greatest friend.

I've interviewed Orissan prisoners of war after the army had won their release, and all swore they'd been determined to escape from the moment of capture. They said, however, as you test and ponder and test once again to come up with the perfect plan, days can become months, months can become years. Meanwhile, they said, a peculiar lethargy sets in, and with that comes confusion and lack of confidence, so every idea is dismissed too quickly.

In other words, the longer you wait to escape, the less likely you'll have the will to do it.

On the other hand, your captor is at her most wary in the early period of your imprisonment. Escapes launched within days or weeks of capture almost never succeed. Usually death results because your captor is likely to want to use you as an example to others.

Later, however, the enemy is likely to let down her guard. To be lulled into believing you're incapable of ever being a threat to her again.

This was the point I thought I was at when I awoke from my long stupor and found myself in the Mines of Koronos. Although I'd been there for months, my will to escape was still keen.

Time had been my ally in other ways. The months I'd spent as a shambling, nonthinking wreck had the odd effect of shielding me from the horrors of the mines. The emotional shock of being maimed had been cushioned because I had had no memory of the assaults. That cushion had also given me an unconscious period of mourning for my crew.

They were my friends and had died bravely in my service. I was deeply affected. But the wound had partially healed during that time of dim awareness.

I also thought I'd been handed a singular advantage. By now, I thought, Novari was certain to have dropped her guard. It was only a slim advantage, but I was determined to make the most of it.

Many days passed before I discovered the first glimmer of a plan. In the meantime I was nothing more than another hunk of unwilling meat to be fed into the gristmills of the mines.

We were whipped from one dangerous, mind-and-soul-numbing task to the next. We staggered back to our cells each night, bowed down by exhaustion. It took tremendous effort to keep my mind on track and my goal in clear view. All I desired was to collapse into sleep. Sometimes I was so weary that self-pity would strike and tears would unaccountably well up.

I came to appreciate just how great Zalia's will had been during those long months while she nursemaided me. This didn't mean I trusted her fully. Despite all she said, she could still be Novari's spy. I had to accept that I was taking a dangerous chance with her. Once I'd done so, however, there was no holding back natural emotion—and growing admiration was one of those feelings. My main problem was keeping those emotions in check so I didn't reveal too much to a woman who was still a stranger to me.

Regardless, it was immediately apparent that Zalia's will was as strong and stubborn as her squat powerful body.

I saw her save a woman's life one day when we were working in the smelting chamber. Somehow a stack of heavy gold rods toppled onto the woman, pinning and crushing her. Several burly slaves tugged at that mass to free the screaming woman, but to no avail. Zalia rushed over, swept them aside, and lifted the bars off—joints popping and crackling loudly at the effort. Unfortunately, the woman was so badly injured she was of no further use to our masters, and the guards hauled her away some days later to be disposed of like a broken-down cart animal.

When we worked as miners, Zalia could crack ore-bearing rock with a single blow, exposing new veins of gold as thick as her meaty wrists. When we lugged the ore carts up steep underground inclines, it was Zalia who muscled us safely to the top and then acted as an anchor to get us down again. I lost count of the times when someone stumbled, letting go of the ropes, and Zalia saved us all from following that hapless one into the disposal pits.

She could also be remarkably tender. Like when she bathed my wound each night, softly dabbing away any grime that got under the bandage and cleansing the eye socket with a touch so light I barely felt it. More importantly, she gave no indication of the horrors my wounds must have presented. She went about the task as if it were the most natural thing in the world.

Once, I wanted to examine the extent of the wound for myself and hunted for a mirrored surface to study the injury. Few reflective objects existed in the mines—everything but the gold was scored and pitted.

Gold itself is a poor surface. It absorbs all images and gives only shadows back. That ought to be warning enough for all seekers of gold and what they dream it offers. It is only the luster that beguiles them, not the substance.

One day I found a large shiny spoon and tried to peer at myself in its bowl, sweeping off the bandage as I looked. But Zalia intervened, gently plucking the spoon from my hand and tucking the bandage back into place.

"You don't want to do that now," she said.

"Am I so ugly?" I asked. My voice trembled, which surprised me.

"I'm the only ugly woman in this cell, Rali," she said. "Just wait a while longer. Until you've healed more."

She put the spoon in our hiding place behind the loose stone. "We'll get it out later," she promised, "when the proper time comes."

I was comforted . . . and relieved. I'd wanted to look at my ravaged face, but a fearful child lurked beneath that desire. I was too frightened to look—and equally as frightened not to. Zalia wrested that decision from me and put it away for another time when I might be braver.

That day came soon enough.

She finished bathing my wounds one night and said, "This is coming along nicely, Rali. You should see. You really should."

My heart lurched when she said that. But before I could stutter a response, she threw the rag bandage away. She went to our hiding place and pulled out the spoon along with a tiny bundle. She returned, unwrapping the bundle and holding out its contents for me to see.

It was a golden eyepatch hanging from a golden thong.

She draped it over my head and adjusted the patch until it was comfortable. It felt light and soft as the finest silk, and it seemed to form itself naturally over the socket. Soon as it was in place, the throbbing and empty feeling vanished and I felt oddly whole again.

Zalia polished the spoon with her tunic sleeve and held it up so I could look into it. I broke out in a cold sweat. My heart fluttered like a hummingbird's wings.

But I looked.

My face was unfamiliar at first. I was thinner than I remembered, much more care-worn, and my hair was a ragged mop like Zalia's. Then I recognized the long features and fair skin and the single blue eye staring back at me. It had the intent stare that marks all Anteros.

I shifted my gaze and saw the golden patch covering the place where the other eye had been. Just beneath the patch was a small crooked scar where the surgeon's knife must've slipped.

"You look kind of piratical," Zalia said, voice light.

I gave her a nervous smile then looked again.

It wasn't nearly as bad as I'd imagined.

"Very dashing. And romantic," Zalia said, still trying to bolster me.

Actually, I thought as I peered for a last time into the bowl of the spoon, she was right. With the hair swept so on one side, tight breeches, loose floppy shirt, and a wide sash, I could cut quite a dashing figure.

I was too timid to admit it right off. "I don't know," I said. And then I tried to make a joke of it. "I look scary enough to send half the maids in Orissa screaming hysterically into the streets."

Zalia laughed. "And the other half," she said, "and the most interesting half at that, will want to linger for a while. To see if your bed is as thrilling as your looks."

"Sure they will," I said. "And if you believe that, I have a mine I want to sell you in Koronos."

Secretly I was relieved. I even went so far as to embrace her and thank her for the gift. It was an awkward moment for both of us, and we broke the embrace quickly.

I touched the eyepatch, marveling at its effect on me.

"Wherever did you find this?" I asked.

"I made it," she said. "During the time you were bumping into walls. I was only waiting for your . . . face to heal . . . before I gave it to you."

"Made it?" I said. I fingered the material. "How? And what's it made of? It looks like gold. It feels like silk, but of a quality I've never seen before. My family has been trading in silk for years. So I've seen every kind there is."

"It's made from the gold we're mining," Zalia said.

I was astounded. "Gold? This doesn't feel like gold!"

"But that's what it is," Zalia said. "You told me you saw King Magon's golden ship before you were captured, right?"

"Yes," I said. "I wondered at the time how it could bear up under its own weight. I also wondered mightily about his golden sails."

Zalia pointed at the eyepatch. "That's exactly the same material," she said. "One of these days you'll see for yourself how they make it." She shuddered. "It's the worst detail in the mines. Our turn will come soon enough."

Then she said, "From what I've been able to gather, the process used to make the material dates back to the age of the original Ice Bear King. It was lost when his kingdom was destroyed."

"Just sitting there all those centuries," I murmured, "for Novari to come along and rediscover it."

Zalia nodded. "She found it when King Magon reopened the mines to mount his campaigns and to pay allies and mercenary armies to fly his banner. But the magical process to create the material proved much more valuable than mere gold. Now all the gold we dig from these mountains goes into the ancient machines Novari brought back to life."

She leaned forward. "And it takes many ore carts heaped with pure gold to make just one ounce of that stuff."

"That'd require a tremendous amount of power," I pointed out. "I don't know of a wizard in the world who could do it."

"Not alone," Zalia said.

"Ah, yes," I said, recalling Novari's kidnapping raids that'd swept up my own Evocators.

"The things they make from this material," Zalia said, "are as close to miraculous as you can get in the real world. Weapons that never shatter or become dull. Shields that are impervious to any blow. Huge ships as light as if they were made of pine veneer but are actually as indestructible as steel.

"From the quantities we're turning out here, Novari must be preparing to equip the greatest army in history. And she's got an empty-headed man toy to lead it."

I felt like a fool when I recalled my brave words to Novari. I'd dared her to attack Orissa and suffer the wrath of my people—who, I'd believed, had such superior forces that no mere ice barbarian like Magon would stand a chance.

As if she were reading my mind, Zalia said, "Both our homelands are in grave danger, Rali. That's why I came here."

"Why you were sent, you mean?" I said.

She hesitated, then said, "Yes. That's why . . . my queen . . . commanded me to undertake this mission."

"Isn't it about time," I said, "you told me about your kingdom? I don't even know where it is. Or know your queen's name or her looks or her desires. Or any other details about your homeland, such as why your people worship Maranonia.

"She's a war goddess. And war is only popular in its beginning stages. When the blood flows, only a soldier, and a special kind, at that, has stomach enough to praise Maranonia."

"I'll have to disappoint you," Zalia said. "And I'm not sorry for it. I'll tell you nothing until the day comes when you swear you trust me."

"You have the word of the Goddess Maranonia herself," I said, "to swear to my honesty. According to you, she appeared in a vision and said to seek me out."

Zalia sneered. "First off," she replied, "you know very well I can tell you nothing more about the vision than what I've already said. You also know I'm forbidden to tell you whether she said to trust you or merely to make certain I met up with you and to speak a certain phrase. 'The silver ship,' Maranonia said. 'When you meet Rali, mention the silver ship. She'll know what I mean.' "

"You're begging the point like a royal politician," I said. "It's this. It's that. It's whatever it pleases you to believe at any given moment. Maranonia's visit to you clearly implies that you are commanded by her to trust me."

Zalia curled a scoffing lip. "*You're* the one who sounds like a politician," she said. "You brandish the word 'trust' too easily when it applies to you, and not easily enough when it applies to *me*.

"You can't have it both ways, Rali. The trust has to be mutual. Otherwise I could place my queen and kingdom in peril on what could prove to be your slippery word.

"No, I think I'll rely on a captive soldier's pose. You know all about that so you shouldn't object. It's name and rank you'll get from me and that's it. Novari got nothing more. You'll get the same. In the meantime I'll tell you what I choose you to know and when I think it's best advised you know it.

"And that, my dubious friend, is that."

I fingered the eyepatch and decided to slip past the quarrel if I could, for the sake of the gift. "Thank you for this, anyway," I said.

I started to take it off and hand it back. "And you can be sure that when I put it on every night, I'll thank you for it again."

"Leave it," she said, surprised at my action. "Why use it only at night? I made it for more than cosmetic reasons. It's mostly to promote healing and keep dirt and infection out. You'll notice it has magical properties that make it shed dust and grime and all other sorts of nasty things. That's why I went to so much trouble and no little danger to steal the material for it."

"But the guards will notice the eyepatch immediately," I protested. "Not even a dunce could miss it. It's gold, after all. And magical gold at that!"

"It's only the color you have to worry about," she said. "And that can be fixed easily. All you have to do is think a particular hue, hold the thought for a moment—and the patch will become that color. Think black and it'll be black. Red, and it'll shift to red.

"It's the nature of the material. And since it was produced here, using Novari's sorcerous machines, even the most sensitive wizard will miss it. No power was stolen, but only . . . borrowed . . . and then returned in a different guise."

I was intrigued. "Any color I like?" I asked.

"Try it," she said.

I peeled the eyepatch off and dangled it in front of me. I pictured it black and instantly it shimmered from gold to black. I tried red and green and the other pure colors, and each time it shifted to those hues the instant the color came to mind. I turned it back to black—a rather grimy black, to match the conditions of the mine—and put it on again.

It felt smoother and even more comfortable than before. And I no longer felt the urge to let my head flop to my shoulder to study things with my good eye.

"I always wanted to be a pirate," I said. "Now at least I can look like one."

Zalia looked me over, measuring. "What you really need," she finally said, "is a pair of earrings. A stud on one side and a big loopy one on the other. That'd really set the eyepatch off.

"It's what only the most discerning pirate would wear."

The eyepatch changed more than my image. As the days went on I noticed that objects seemed clearer and possessed more depth. I no longer suffered a dizzy feeling when I looked at a thing too quickly.

Although I only had one eye, the missing one—thanks to the eyepatch—seemed to serve some ghostly purpose. As if it were peering into the ethers to help my remaining eye focus on the physical world and give me two-eyed perspective.

Then one day I realized I could also "see" more clearly in the Otherworlds.

It was at night, just after my rat stew meal, and I was cleaning grime from my metal hand while Zalia slept. I got dust in my eye and winked a few times to try and clear away the irritating speck.

When I shut the eye, however, a strange image floated up—seemingly from nowhere.

I opened my eye and the image vanished. Was it only my imagination?

I shut my good eye again and up floated that faded image. I could make out a vague outline, a skeleton really, of fingers and a thumb. I wriggled my artificial hand and saw the ghostly image wriggle in return.

I opened my eye and saw only the metal hand—the slave hand. But now I could definitely feel the shadow of the real one—the part of me that'd been lopped off for Novari's magical stew pot.

I shut the eye once more, turning my head this way and that. All kinds of glittering things seemed to be fluttering about. I realized I could see into the ethers with almost no effort. I only had to shut my eye and *shift* my view, and the sorcerous world made itself plain.

"Zalia," I said. "Wake up!"

She bolted up from her stone bed. "What's wrong?" she said, alarmed.

"Nothing's wrong," I replied. "I have to talk to you."

Zalia groaned, weary from breaking rock all day. "Can't it wait?" she said.

"Not a single moment," I replied.

"What do you want?" she asked, yawning but resigned.

"Tell me how you made the eyepatch again," I said. "Every detail. Leave nothing out. And while you're at it, I want you to think very hard."

"About what?"

I fingered the eyepatch. "How we can get onto the right work detail and steal more of this stuff."

It took fearfully little time for Zalia to do what I'd asked.

The two slaves we approached eagerly grabbed the small bribe she offered. They readily agreed to switch places with us. They swore they'd not whisper a word and would assist in every way to cover up the small bargain we'd made. They were so fervent in their assurances, I had no doubt they'd keep their word. I growled a few appropriate threats about what'd happen if they betrayed us, but it wasn't really necessary. They were two very happy slaves.

This was my first sign that Zalia hadn't exaggerated when she'd said it was the worst work detail in the mine.

Confirmation came a day later when a guard poked his head into our warren and shouted: "Two for Hellspoint! Antero! Zalia! Get yer arses out here."

We stumbled from our cells and I shot Zalia a look, whispering, *"Hellspoint?"*

She grimaced. "It was *your* idea," she whispered back. "And don't forget it!"

I didn't.

Her whisper hung over me like a demon jester, mocking me, as we were pummeled into line with another sorry group of slaves. As each chain was linked to each belt, I heard the sound of the locks snap shut with unnatural clarity.

Whips cracked and we shambled forward. Slaves in other details looked at us as we passed and shook their heads in pity or grinned at our misery.

We were marched for about an hour, winding through a series of tunnels and corridors and going up and down several lifts. Finally, a gate clattered open and we staggered out of the mines into the shock of sudden sunlight.

For the first time in months I was not enclosed by tons of hollowed-out rock. The air was crisp and cold and my muscles twitched uncontrollably at the elusive scent of freedom on the wind.

I heard other slaves mutter curses and nearly snarled myself, but bit my lip when Zalia gave my arm a warning squeeze.

The guards roared and charged the ones who'd cursed, quickly beating them into submission. They did it with such practiced ease, I knew that the incident was a routine occurrence on the way to Hellspoint.

It was only a sip of what was in store for us.

We were herded through a large yard, which was cut into the face of a mountain that rose above us for as far as I could see without craning my neck and earning a lash from a watchful guard. The yard was hatch-patterned by wooden rails, and carts were being lugged up and down the rails by slaves. Our route took us through the yard to a rubble-strewn road that wound down the face of the mountain.

When we came to it, I caught a glimpse of the Bear Temple in the distance, saw the docks jutting out into the frozen lake and ships with billowing sails skimming freely across the lake. Overhead the sky was a shocking blue.

The immense vistas were enough to make me want to bolt—to leap over the cliff face if necessary.

Zalia clutched my arm and I breathed deeply to steady my nerves.

While I calmed myself I remembered seeing the yard and the mountain road from another perspective. I peeped out at the lake and saw the familiar rocky far shore where I'd hidden with my men so long ago and had observed the mines and foundries of Koronos for the first time.

I looked at the docks again and noted the absence of Magon's golden ship. I guessed he'd left, and I wondered if Novari had returned to their capital with him.

Thinking about Novari helped me steady myself, and I was soon able to plod along passively with the others. A dull shambling slave on the exterior, while on the interior my mind was ablaze with curiosity, observing and storing every detail for possible later use.

As we came around one bend I saw the Bear Temple towering over the city. It seemed quiet. Maybe even empty. Then I felt a buzz of magic and knew wizards had to be at work. Not Novari, though. I would've sensed her immediately. And I wondered: Where was she? What was she up to?

It was about a mile's walk to the bottom and about another mile to our destination.

The factory they took us to was built of plain, rough stone blocks. It had no chimney or any remarkable features at all, other than the big, double-gated doors we were heading for. The building was long and extremely low, but as soon as we entered I saw that the bulk of it was underground. Six floors in all, I learned, for that's how many flights of steps we descended to reach the main forgeroom.

It was a terrifying place. The dim light had an eerie orange cast to it, and the whole building throbbed rhythmically as if an immense heart was beating just beyond the walls. The sound was a big drum backdrop to the shriek of hot metal plunged into water, hissing steam, chains clanking, hammers hammering, and—so distant it could be from the Otherworlds—what sounded like faint screams.

We shuffled through huge rooms with racks of golden swords and spears and shields. I could feel sorcery radiating from them and knew they were made of the same material as my eyepatch. Once, we swung close to a rack of swords and I snatched a hungry look at their keen edges and apparent light balance. I ached with the impulse to dash for the rack, grab a weapon, and lay waste to the guards.

The impulse was replaced by sudden foreboding that those weapons might soon be wielded by the enemy against my own people. The anxiety made me quicken my step. I had to act—and soon.

I bumped into the slave in front of me and he snarled, "What's your hurry, sister? It's to Hellspoint you're goin'! What'ja think it was, the chow line?"

I slowed my pace but continued to shift my head about, studying the might of my opponent, my anxieties growing with each thing I saw.

On the sixth and final level, we came to immense golden doors set in stone that were stained black with grease and smoke. The doors were so dazzling, so polished and clean-looking, I knew they had to be made of Novari's magical material.

We stood there waiting as the guards unlocked our chains.

"Remember what I told you, Rali," Zalia hissed. "Do exactly as I say at all times."

I nodded and two huge guards, naked to the waist and streaming sweat, muscled the doors open.

A blast of heat nearly knocked me over. I gagged at the acid stench of the air. It burned my throat and seared my lips.

Before I could recover my wits, we were all kicked and pushed through the doors. Bewildered, I saw the guards step swiftly back outside. They screamed for us to get to work, then slammed the doors shut, closing us in.

Hellspoint was so hot you couldn't toil there for more than an hour at a time. Each shift in that chamber was limited to an hour. Then you had an hour's rest while another slave crew suffered inside before you were forced back into the forgeroom to take their places.

Slaves were worked to the point of collapse, driven by special guards who changed crew every fifteen minutes. Other slaves dragged you out to recover while a second group manned the forges. During our rest periods we were given copious amounts of cold water to drink and pour over ourselves. This was not a sign of kindness in our masters. It was a necessity. Without the rest and the water, we'd have died quickly, and then who would do the work?

The chamber was huge, filled with machines belching fire and steam. Slaves staggered past pushing wooden platforms on rollers stacked high with long, thick bars of natural gold.

The rods were hauled to an immense machine that commanded one whole side of the forgeroom. They were loaded onto a wide, clattering conveyor shaped like a shallow trough; it carried the rods into the machine's fiery maw. Another conveyor swept out from behind the machine through a large area that glowed and shimmered so it looked like the conveyor was emerging through curtains.

But instead of golden rods, the bottom of the trough was covered with a film of glittering dust.

It was from this dust, Zalia later told me, that the magical material was formed. That the material Magon's ship and weapons were made of—and my wondrous eyepatch.

Slaves moved along the final leg of the conveyor, hauling big portable bellows on rollers that were valved so they reversed the flow of air. Flexible hoses sucked up the gold dust, which was drawn into large gray jars that Zalia later said were made of sugar. The jars were fed into another forge, the sugar vanished, and the dust became a thin golden sheet that could be stitched like cloth or worked and reshaped like metal. The swords, for example, were formed of many layers, turned back on one another repeatedly until the blades were perfect.

I saw the chamber in dim snatches stretched out over what seemed like the eternity the gods reserve for the condemned. Guided by Zalia, I loaded and unloaded bars. Helped pump out the dust and lugged the filled jars—which were amazingly light—to other slaves who carried them away for storage.

The heat and noise drained every speck of energy, so you felt like you were swimming in hot porridge. It was an effort just to lift your arms, much less the murderously heavy rods. I was doubly punished because the sorcery pouring out of the magical forge seared my senses, withering them with blast after powerful blast.

Somehow I managed to get through the agony. At the end of the day one slave was not so lucky. It was the fellow who'd cursed me for being in such a hurry. He'd suffered a seizure in the final hour and lay there flopping on the floor until a bored guard lazily motioned for us to haul him away. He breathed his last as I lifted his arms. It was a long sigh, and in my imagination it was filled with the sound of vast relief.

When I heard it I thought, May the gods be with you, brother. Wherever you're going, it can't be worse than this.

They hosed us off with some sort of chemical that stung the nostrils and made the skin look as red and chafed as if we'd spent a week under a desert sun.

The man's sigh still echoed in my thoughts when the day was done and I finally staggered into the cell and collapsed on my stone shelf.

I heard Zalia moan as she sank down on hers.

"Now what in the names of all the gods who curse us was that worth?" she groaned. "Except to dig our graves deeper and longer."

I wrenched myself up, favoring sore muscles I didn't even know I possessed until I'd entered Hellspoint. But my spirits were returning, so I managed a grin as I said, "Cast your eyes on this, my friend."

And I extended my mortal hand.

Zalia's eyes widened when she saw the gold dust packed under my nails.

"Should make a nice little pile when I clean them," I said.

"I thought you wanted to steal a piece of the finished material," she said, puzzled.

"I did," I said. "But I saw right off it wouldn't work for what I have in mind. Besides, it would take too much in its finished form. Novari or one of her minions would notice its absence."

"You're going to use the dust itself?" she asked, giving me an unbelieving stare.

"That's exactly what I plan," I said. "And it ought not to take more than a dozen trips to get enough."

Zalia was aghast. "A *dozen* trips!"

"Maybe more," I said. "Although I hope not."

"I *pray* not," Zalia breathed. "I pray to all the gods past, present, and future—if there is a future worth having."

I laughed, trying to make light of our ordeal, but it had a hollow sound to it.

Later, when I cleaned the gold dust from under my nails, it made a heap that was depressingly small.

* * *

As Zalia had feared, it took more than a dozen trips to Hellspoint to obtain what I needed. It was easily twice that number, and each hour we labored in the forgeroom was a torment I dislike to recall.

I consoled myself by thinking that at least I was alive enough to curse the experience. Although why Novari had let me live still puzzled me.

Did she really feel more revenged by condemning me to this miserable existence? And how long would this humiliation satisfy her? Also, if she was using the mines to soften me up so I could be bent to her will, how soon would she come for me? There were many other questions, all variations on the same theme, which was wonderment that I lived at all.

Zalia had still another theory. "Perhaps Novari can't kill you," she said. "Not without coming to some harm herself."

At first I scoffed at this. "I don't think so, my friend. She was perfectly capable of killing me any moment she chose. Why, she nearly slew me when I attacked her. Several of her own men were killed when she cast that spell. And since I was on the receiving end, I can swear on any holy object you choose that it was *definitely* not only death-dealing but meant for me."

"Ah, but you attacked *her*," Zalia pointed out. "That only proves she can defend herself against you. But maybe she's forbidden—if there was some sort of curse, say—to act directly. She can't command your death. But she can put you in circumstances that would certainly be guaranteed to lead to your death."

"That's a possibility," I admitted. "But only a vague one."

"It's as good as any reason *you* have," Zalia said. "Perhaps even better. I've had much more time to study her. It's my kingdom that's threatened directly, after all."

I cocked my good eye at her. "*Your* kingdom?" I said.

"I, uh, mean my queen's," she stuttered. "Queen Salimar's."

"Aha!" I chortled. "So that's her name? By the gods, woman, I finally got *something* out of you!"

She flushed. "What of it?" she mumbled. "I was getting ready to tell you anyway."

I gloated. "Riight!"

Zalia clamped her lips and said nothing more that night.

I knew my victory had been a childish one. But in Koronos it seemed as pleasing as any other I'd had in a long time. And I was childish enough to take satisfaction in recognizing just how infantile Zalia had been as well when she'd whined, "I was getting ready to tell you anyway."

Well, the laugh's on you, woman, I thought.

The laugh's on you.

* * *

While I gathered the dust I also gathered information about our prison.

I immediately noticed a certain looseness in the mine's security. Certainly there were guards everywhere. And we were frequently chained together, especially when we exited the mines and were herded for Hellspoint.

Yet it seemed to me the reasons for being chained had little to do with fear that we'd escape. The artificial hands would ultimately stop even the most determined slave. Plus there was the sorcerous gruel that all the slaves, except Zalia and myself, were addicted to. No, the chains were to protect us from harming the guards or ourselves when freedom was dangled before us and hysteria set in.

Mostly, if we kept to our own warren, we were left alone during the hours we were allotted each day for eating and sleeping. And it was fairly easy to visit other nearby warrens. All you had to do was walk past a few warren guards, who would give you a bored glare, then wave you on. Many times those guards would be momentarily absent or even asleep. No one seemed to care. The metal hand bolted to your wrist would prevent any real mischief.

You especially tended to be ignored if you were an "old-timer." The death toll was so high that those who survived a year were marked by their sheer endurance as being safe. An old-timer could talk from the corner of her mouth and be heard or observed by no one but the person she was speaking to. An old-timer knew how to absorb a blow or a lash and suffer the least harm. An old-timer knew how to snatch a few seconds to rest, how to study the guards' moods and know when a little blatant shirking might be in order. Old-timers knew the system. And the system worked best if you rolled with the punches and watched for small openings to grab a bit more food, a bit more comfort, a bit more life. You could add up the little store of extra life that you gathered second by second.

Like the grains of sorcerous gold I was stealing from Novari's forgeroom.

While I gathered the dust, I made a tool. It was an ordinary rat bone; long, thin, and quite straight. I cleaned the marrow out so it was nicely hollow. Then I polished the hollow with a rough thread I'd taken from my smock. Night after night I pulled the thread back and forth through the bone until it was nearly paper thin. For a while Zalia watched me, curious. But I made certain she knew I'd turn away any question she asked and she soon lost interest.

Daciar was right. Secrecy comes as naturally to a wizard as the ethers she commands.

One night I returned from Hellspoint so exhausted I could barely eat. The magical blast from the forge had been particularly intense that day, and my mind felt like crushed ore being fed down a rock slurry chute.

I fell asleep before I even cleaned the precious dust from under my nails. I simply sprawled on my stone bed, and darkness leaped up and carried me away.

I drifted, dreamless, for what seemed like a long time.

Then a soft cry crept into my peaceful slumber. It was faint and echoing and full of pain, like the cries you heard when entering Hellspoint. In my dream I had a sudden desire to investigate, to find that person and comfort them. I reached out with my good hand—the hand with the gold grime under the nails—and I felt a force drawing me like the moon draws the seas and makes the tides.

I let it take me, and my spiritself floated free, hovering over my slumbering body.

Again I heard the faint cry. I ghosted toward the sound, slipping through the stone walls, moving as freely as if I were rising from the bottom of a deep pond.

I burst to the surface, coming out under a full moon. I felt the moon tug at my hand and I lifted it and saw my fingers were all aglow. I marveled at the glittering power of it, feeling energy surge and purpose grow.

I floated down the mountain road invisible to the sleepy guards and continued along the path until I came to Hellspoint. It was black under the bright moonlight, low and menacing like an iceberg broken off from some evil field.

The forgeroom drew at me more powerfully than the moon, and I kicked free and went to it, wisping through stone and metal doors until I came to the great machine itself.

The chamber was empty and the conveyor belt was still. But the sorcerous fires continued to roar, drawing me to the shimmering curtain that divided this world from the ethers.

I stopped there, pulling back against the outgoing tide of energy.

Once again I heard the scream. It seemed closer. And then another scream joined the first, and then another and another until there was a whole chorus of tortured souls howling from the hells.

I closed my good eye and found I could see through the curtain. It was like looking through a telescope into the Otherworlds with an ethereye.

All was wavering fire at first, then the scene came into sharp focus.

There were scores, perhaps hundreds, of souls twisting in agony as flames of blue and green and yellow licked at them from every side. They were kept in place by long magical chains which they fought against cease-lessly. Some were twisted in coils of chain, sobbing to get free. The souls were of men and women and creatures whose form I couldn't make out, and they were all screaming and moaning in horrible pain.

I knew immediately that they were wizards and other beings with sorcer-ous powers. And the chains were spells created by Novari to hold them captive.

Those wizardly souls were all slaves laboring in Novari's special hell—just as I labored in her mines. But by the gods, it was worse. Worse than I have powers to describe.

One of the spirits saw me and cried louder. I looked closer with my ethereye and saw with a shock the familiar face of Searbe.

My missing Evocator was missing no more.

He struggled toward me, crying my name. I wanted to help him but I couldn't let myself be drawn into Novari's private hell. He stretched the chain, struggling to come closer.

Then he screamed in greater agony and powered himself forward until the magical chain was taut and he was hanging just beyond the shimmering curtain. He was so close that if it were the real world, I could've reached out and touched him.

"Save me, Lady Antero!" he cried. "Save me!"

"I will if I can, my friend," I said, as calmly as I could. "But I won't tor-ture you by promising. I don't know that I can even save myself."

Despite his pain he had a sudden crafty look on his ghostly face. "I can be of much value to you, Lady Antero," he said. "I know Novari's plan."

I'd forgotten how transparent Searbe could be. And I wondered mightily at my own judgment for ever trusting him.

"Then tell it to me," I said. "The knowledge may help me free you."

"Oh, you can't trick me *that* easily," Searbe said.

"Why would I do that?" I said. "You're one of my own."

"Because I betrayed you," he said, with only a tinge of shame. "And I betrayed Orissa."

"You were forced," I said. "I won't hold anything you revealed to Novari against you."

Searbe hung his head. "I was weak," he said. "I was afraid. And then she promised . . . she promised . . ."

"You don't have to tell me what sort of promises a succubus makes, Searbe," I said. "I wish you hadn't succumbed so easily. But all of us are not as strong as others. I, for one, won't judge how much forcing another can take."

"I'm no coward!" Searbe protested. "Don't think that of me!"

"It doesn't matter if you are or you aren't," I said. "Tell me her plan and all your sins will be washed clean. In my eyes at least."

He hesitated, weaving back and forth behind the glowing curtain. Then the flames shot higher, the screams became more shrill, and there was a hard yank on his chain. Searbe pulled back against it, fighting to stay in place.

"I'll tell you!" he shrieked. "But you have to free me . . . after."

"Quickly," I said. "Before it's too late."

"This machine is the source of all her power," he babbled. "All of it comes from these hells. She's feeding every wizard and witch she can capture into this machine. She can draw on it at will from any place and at any moment she wants. And every day more souls join us to become her fuel, making her stronger than ever."

I didn't have to guess what she wanted to do with that power. Those who seek such a thing are all mad and single-visioned. The more power they get, the more they desire. Combine that with the eternal succubus itch to consume all emotion for their own pleasure, and you had that most original of all dominators—Novari, the Lyre Bird.

"She didn't know about . . . Orissa until I . . . told her," Searbe said. He seemed shamed and spoke hesitantly, as if it were a difficult confession. "Not anything important . . . But she became . . . interested . . . when she heard about all the . . . the . . . discoveries we've been making."

"Orissa is far away," I said. "She has many other kingdoms to threaten before our people have to face her."

"No, no, no," Searbe wailed. "That's not so! There's another way. To get to Orissa. A portal or something. I'm not sure. But it goes through one world and comes out at Orissa."

"Why doesn't she just do it, then?" I said.

"She can't," Searbe said. "There's another . . . kingdom or something . . . in the way. A powerful queen. She's got Novari blocked. Novari thought she'd beaten her for a while, but the queen escaped. Novari doesn't know where she is. She's afraid to attack until she finds her—or gathers enough souls so she can just blast through and strike Orissa."

Then he said, "I was just . . . uh . . . put here a little while ago. A week, maybe. Gods, it feels like a thousand years!"

"Really?" I said, sympathy fading. "Only a week or so, is it? And what did you do, my friend, to earn her wrath?"

"She just didn't . . . she said she didn't . . . I mean I was of no further use to her. So she threw me in. Pointed her finger and blasted me here.

"But I think she's getting desperate, Lady Antero. The king's got kidnap parties combing near and far, trying to come up with enough wizards to feed this infernal machine. That's why she threw me in. She needed my power. More than she needed me alive."

"Tell me this, my friend," I said. "Why aren't I in there with you?"

"Because you're an Antero," he said, gritting his teeth. Not in pain, I noted, but in barely disguised hatred. "*You* have to come here willingly, be seduced into it. She said you had some power that prevented it. An ancient power that could only be passed down by a family through many generations.

"She admitted she was . . . hurt . . . the first time she really tried to get at you."

I remembered the attack on my dreams while I was in the dungeon armed only with my bit of lizard bone. And I knew now that when I'd slashed into the images of my brother and Omerye, I'd wounded Novari.

I imagined her pain. And it pleased me.

"That's all I know," Searbe said. "Now. Get me out of here. Like you promised."

"As soon as I can, my friend," I said.

There was another hard tug on his chain and he was yanked back toward the leaping flames.

He screamed, fighting to return to the curtain. "Please, Lady Antero!" he wailed. "Save me now!"

"I can't," I shouted. "I can't!"

The sorcerous fires boiled up more furiously than before, and Searbe was dragged back—shrieking in pain and fear—into the mass of tormented souls.

"I'll try!" I cried. "I'll try!"

Then I was being shaken awake and Zalia was holding me in her powerful arms and I was weeping uncontrollably on her shoulder.

After I'd recovered, I told Zalia all that'd happened. She accepted without question that it had been a real experience, although it took place in a dream or a vision. When I was done I said, nicely as I could, "It's your kingdom he's speaking of, isn't it? That's why your queen—Queen Salimar—sent you on this mission."

"Yes it is, Rali," she said. "And I'm not from this world, if that's what you're getting at. My kingdom is on another . . . plane, is the only word I can think of. We were already under much pressure before she heard of you or Orissa. Now it must be even worse."

"Your queen is missing," I said. "What could be worse than that?"

Zalia shrugged, seemingly unconcerned. "Not finding her, I guess," she said, voice light, almost cheery. Then she became grim. "We've *got* to get out of here, Rali!"

"I know," I said.

"Novari might launch her attack at any moment."

"I know that, too."

She slammed her metal hand against the bench. Stone crumbled.

"I feel like I'm blind in here," she said. "I don't know what's going on! What she's doing! What she's thinking!" Now it was her turn to weep. They were angry tears. Tears so bitter they'd turn a lake to salt.

I held her, comforted her, until she stopped. She lay in my arms quite still, oddly light despite her bulk.

I said, low, "Tell me about your kingdom, Zalia. What sort of land is it?"

And she murmured, "It's called Khalilow. And it's a land where it always seems like summer. Trees and flowers everyplace you look. People and animals roaming free. The sky is always blue there. The sun always bright."

"What of your queen?" I asked. "Is Salimar wise? Is she beautiful?"

"Perhaps you can see for yourself one day," she murmured. "But I'll tell you this: she lives in a crystal palace with flowing fountains and fruited trees and a library. I remember the library best. It has books—more books than a woman could read in a thousand lifetimes."

"I like her already," I said. "Crystal palaces are nice. So are flowing fountains and fruited trees. But books? Ah, now that's a treasure I'd give my left—" I stopped. Then, with a laugh, "I don't know exactly what portion of me I'd willingly donate. I can't remember which side of me has the most left."

Zalia giggled. "Oh, Rali, my dear," she sighed. "If only we'd met . . . another time."

Then she closed her eyes and fell asleep. There was a small smile on her lips. She looked almost pretty.

And I thought what a pity it was that I could no longer concentrate on our escape.

It would've been nice to have gone to Zalia's land. Seen palaces and gardens and books and the gracious Salimar. And perhaps even have come to know Zalia better in more pleasing circumstances.

But escape was no longer at the top of my list.

Somehow, some way, I had to stop Novari.

I had to destroy her machine.

I told Zalia nothing. I felt guilty about it. For I was now certain I could fully trust her.

But what if I were wrong? The mistake could cost the lives of many Orissans. So I buried the guilt. It was a large graveyard and nearly full, but I found a small corner to squeeze in another of my sins.

First I had to solve the problem of the ugly lumps of metal that enslaved us: the artificial hands.

I had enough of Novari's gold dust to do the job, but the spell I had in mind was so strong that it was guaranteed to alert Novari's wizards.

To avoid discovery, I had to have Zalia's cooperation. She shamed me more when I revealed that part of my plan.

She clapped her hands in delight when I told her, saying, "Finally! You've decided to trust me."

She sniffled and wiped her eyes. "I knew you'd come around one of these days, Rali," she said, making me feel lower with every word she uttered. "I kept telling myself you were still suffering from all that'd happened to you. And if I were as patient as I could be, you'd finally see we *had* to trust each other."

She gave me a sheepish grin. "I have to admit I wasn't always that patient, Rali. I know I've said quarrelsome things to you. And I hope you accept my apology."

I ducked my head, mumbling, "No apology necessary," then quickly veered back to the main subject.

"The problem," I said, "is that we'll need more than an hour in the forgeroom. The work will take at least that long. So my question is this: Is it possible for us to last two hours?"

Zalia frowned. "I can't imagine going that long," she said. "Each time we leave that chamber, I think I'll die if I have to stay a single minute more."

"That's not my question," I said. "My question is, can it be done? Do *you* think you can do it?"

"I won't know," she answered, "until I try."

"Are you willing?"

"By the gods, yes!" she said, eyes blazing. "I'd do anything to get out of here."

I took her at her word. Arrangements were made, and a few days later we joined a work gang headed for Hellspoint.

When we exited the mines that day, the air was especially sweet, the light clear as I'd ever seen it. I heard shouts from the lake. We all turned to see what was going on, slaves and guards alike.

Out on the frozen lake bed I saw a golden ship sailing for the docks of Koronos. Soldiers skated in front of the ship, hammering on their shields and chanting a familiar song:

> "Magon is coming—
> The enemy trembles!
> Magon is coming—

The enemy flees!
Magon is coming—
Hearts be glad!"

Although it was too far away to make out the figures posing on the great ship's deck, I knew Novari was among them. I could smell the perfume of her sorcery drifting on the winds. My memory responded to her magical scent and I could feel her soft succubus caresses on my thighs and breasts. I shuddered. Disgust rose, and the feeling became a sickness in the pit of my stomach and I turned away, gagging.

I felt Zalia's arm about my shoulder. "What's wrong, Rali?" she said.

I shook my head. I couldn't answer.

Finally the moment passed. I pulled myself up and wiped my face with the sleeve of my smock. Just then the guards became alarmed that we'd tarried too long and they lashed us back into line and hurried us down the mountain to Hellspoint.

As we rounded the bend overlooking the Bear Temple, its huge bell swung into life, tolling greetings to the arriving King Magon and his consort, Novari. The golden ship was already docking, and I saw officials scurrying out of the temple and down the road to hail their king.

They must not have known their rulers were coming, I thought. Or the bell would've already been ringing and there'd be a grand display to welcome Magon and Novari.

Zalia tugged my sleeve, whispering, "Does this change our plans?"

I shook my head. Actually, I wished I could accelerate them. But I didn't see how.

When the forgeroom doors boomed open and the hot stinking air fouled my lungs, I forgot all about Novari. I steeled myself as the doors crashed shut, locking us in.

Now I faced two hours in the bowels of Hellspoint.

A guard's whip snaked across my back and he bellowed for me to get to work.

I plodded toward a stack of golden rods. Every step I took tested my resolve. Within minutes I doubted I'd even be able to survive an hour, much less two.

Zalia helped stack the rods onto a pushcart. We hauled it to the conveyor feeding Novari's machine.

I'd noticed before that all of us, guards and slaves included, tried to stay as far away from the machine as possible. The closer you came, the more intense the heat and misery became. Our practice was to roll the carts to the far edge of the conveyor, load them on as quickly as possible, and then rush away from the sorcerous blast.

It was the only time in the forgeroom anyone moved at a pace above a slow shamble. There was a narrow passage between the conveyor and the forgeroom walls. No one went down it—we all used the wider apron on the other side. I'd examined it closely, however, and seen the eerie leaping shadows formed by the sorcerous curtain.

On my last visit I'd tested the depth of those shadows. When no one was looking, I'd given an empty cart a hard shove and it'd rolled down the narrow passage and bumped to a stop against the edge of the forge.

My heart leaped when I saw that the cart was completely hidden by the dancing images cast by the glowing curtain. If Zalia and I crept into those shadows, I thought, no one would see us. We could do anything we liked as long as we remained there.

But that had been a mere test. Actually entering the area proved to be a different matter.

The killing rays pounded us as we approached the conveyor. I looked about, saw no one near, and signaled Zalia. Instead of stopping to unload, we quickly pushed the cart down the narrow passage and into the shadows.

Gritting my teeth in pain, I looked to see if anyone had noticed. I saw a guard's gaze sweep past us without pause and knew we were well hidden.

My skin felt like it was being flayed by the blast and my ears were howling with the song of rushing blood. Breathing was difficult. I had to force my ribs to heave in and out to drag in each stinking breath of air. My limbs felt like jelly and my heart was an open wound that hot pokers were being thrust into.

I heard Zalia groan, saw her face turn so pale that she looked like a bloodless night creature. I motioned for her to squat beside me. She nodded, gulping air like a fish, and crouched.

I slipped a bundle from my smock and rolled it open on the floor. It contained the hollowed-out tube and a small pile of Novari's dust. Zalia tapped my shoulder for attention and passed me a short blunt file we'd stolen from the quarries.

I gripped one of the conveyor legs with my metal hand—the left one—locking it into place. With my right hand I began to file at the bolts, holding it to my stump. Each motion was an agony, a slow death. I ground away relentlessly, like a miserable clockwork toy.

It was frightening how quickly I tired. Zalia took over, grunting with effort as she sawed at the bolts. Soon she sagged back, gasping, unable to go on. I resumed cutting, although I nearly despaired when I saw how little headway we'd made.

I had to continue. The only safe place to remove the hand was in the sorcerous shadow of the great forge. No wizard, no combination of wizards, no matter how powerful or numerous, could sense what I was doing beneath that deadly blanket.

I got one bolt off and was cutting through the last thread of the second when the shift changed. We saw the other slaves exit and a new group being driven in.

An hour had passed. And there was an hour more to go.

I cursed time, I cursed myself, I cursed Novari and all the people I could think of to hate. And from that anger I drew strength enough to go on.

No one would miss us. The guards were too tired from their own, much briefer shifts and never made a final count until the day ended and we were led back to our warrens.

After all, who in their right mind would stay in the forgeroom longer than necessary? There was no reason to suspect someone would deliberately linger behind, forgoing the badly needed rest period.

I yanked my stump out of the metal hand, leaving the thing still gripped to the conveyor leg.

I held the stump in front of me. It was an ugly sight, but I was too numb from the sorcerous assault to be appalled by what had been done to me.

I closed my good eye, shifted my "view" to what I now thought of as my ethereye, and saw the ghost fingers float up.

They seemed firmer than before, enhanced by being in the presence of so much sorcery. I mentally ordered the ghost fingers to spread and flex, and they did all I asked. Just as when they were alive.

I opened my eye, got the bone tube, and knelt over the pile of gold dust. I sucked up some dust into the tube then closed my good eye again so I could see the ghost fingers. In the Otherworlds the tube was transparent and I could see the transformed gold glittering inside.

I blew gently, coating the fingers with dust.

The dust adhered to them, forming a golden shadow of a hand.

When I filled the tube again, I noticed that its real world outline was beginning to take shape. It appeared like a hazy cloud that seemed to form fingers and nails and even a palm with a familiar lifeline when I turned the ghost hand over.

I tried to move it.

Nothing happened.

But I was heartened and I continued on, filling the tube and emptying it three times before I was done—coating the living flesh above the ghost hand so the bolt holes were covered and all blended in nicely with my wrist so you couldn't see where one stopped and the other began.

Under my living eye, however, it didn't look so fine. Instead of smooth gold, my left hand appeared like a mottled, grainy golden glove. It still refused to obey me except in the Otherworlds. In that place it moved, but in the real world it was a dead lump at the end of my wrist. It was so light, however, I could barely feel it.

I had an elegant spell all worked out. Artful words about the light beyond the sinister, or some such. But when I went to whisper them, my mind was so numb from the beating I was taking that all the words remained frozen fast.

Instead I growled, "Be a hand, damn you! Be a hand!"

It was enough.

I felt a surge of energy, and the hammering of the furnace suddenly seemed more bearable. My whole left side felt incredibly powerful, and when I looked at my new hand, it seemed like such a slender golden marvel that amazement jolted me out of my stupor.

I made to clench my fist and the fingers moved smoothly, without hesitation. I spread them apart, turned them this way and that, and if not for the strength and shimmer of golden material, I wouldn't have been able to tell it apart from the one I'd lost.

I looked up at Zalia, who nodded and did her best to smile.

A heavy burden fell from my shoulders, and I felt free for the first time in what seemed like ages. The furnace was still an agony, still sucking away my life. But I didn't care. By the gods, if I died now, at least I'd be free of Novari's slave spell.

I grabbed Zalia's metal hand and began sawing at the bolts.

I had power enough now to make a cutting spell to aid the file, and in a short time I had it off and was blowing gold dust over her own ghost hand.

This time I didn't bother trying to remember the words of the spell, and simply commanded the hand to be a hand, dammit, and Zalia was free, as well.

Then I heard the great doors to the forgeroom boom open.

The second hour had passed.

And we not only lived, but were stronger than before.

Quickly Zalia grabbed a rag she'd hidden in her smock. It was smeared with thick black grease.

Our plan, at least that portion I'd revealed to her, was to hide our magical hands by coating them with the grease. No one was likely to notice what was in front of their faces if we made them look as dirty as our slave hands.

Then we'd join the group leaving the forgeroom, praying that an hour's respite was enough time to recover for the next shift. We'd continue through the rest of the day as normally as possible. After that we could plan the rest of our escape in the relative privacy of our cell.

Zalia threw me the rag and jumped up, urging me to hurry. Instead, I dropped the rag and rose to face Novari's forge, probing with my ethereye.

I could see the hellsfires burning beyond the shimmering curtain. I could see the writhing souls and I could hear their terrible screams.

I jumped up on the conveyor. It jolted forward.

I cried out to Zalia: "This way! Novari awaits!"

I saw her hesitate. Saw shock turn to decision turn to resolve. Then she shouted a war cry and leaped up beside me.

We gripped our living hands. Held our golden fists high.

And we rode through the flaming curtain into Novari's hell.

CHAPTER THIRTEEN

KINGDOM OF DREAMS

Fire gouted. Thunder crashed. Smoke tornadoes roared on every side. The air was a demon's fetid breath, stinking of corpses and burning flesh. All color had collapsed into garish hues of red and black.

The wails of lost souls were dark tides of pity sucking us deeper into Novari's machine.

The conveyor was sweeping us toward a flaming whirlpool of power. Screaming and flailing around it were hundreds of spirit slaves. They were chained to the grated floor with sorcerous links which they tore at with bleeding nails.

I saw Searbe among them, heard his tortured screams, saw flames char flesh and bone which became whole again for misery's next roundelay.

Above it all was the song of the Lyre Bird. But the strings did not sing of promised pleasures and seductive dreams. The music was a mad dissonance of notes forming and shattering and reforming into shrills of greater and greater intensity.

The souls all writhed and danced in time to that mad music, their agony feeding the whirlpool of fire.

Ahead I saw a stack of gold rods carried through the whirlpool. Sparks exploded in every direction. On the other side of the whirlpool I saw the conveyor emerge again, the trough glittering with a fine layer of Novari's magical dust.

I gripped Zalia's hand tight, drawing in power with every forward jolt of the conveyor. I was a magical sponge, sucking up sorcerous energy until my body and soul were completely infused with it.

I felt a jolt of power jump from Zalia to me, and I was suddenly drawing in more energy than I thought possible. I was too full of surprised joy at this new source of strength to question it. To wonder how Zalia had suddenly become my wizardly sister.

I threw back my head and shouted my spell into the fires of Hellspoint:

"She who plays pain's melody;
She who strums strings of perfidy;
She who drains all love from passion,
All grace from ardor,
All that is tender,
All that is life.
Hear me, Novari! I am your foe!
I am the sword at your throat.
The boot in your back.
The wizard bitch
Who will haunt your dreams
For all eternity
Unless you slay me!
Come, Novari!
Come face your final test!"

I hurled the spell into the ethers. Fire blasted from our golden fists. Lightning arced down from the skies to mate with that fire and our magical hands glowed and crackled with energy.

My strength was enormous. I could feel Zalia's power surge as well, transforming into something else. I heard her shout defiance. A glorious incense suddenly turned the foul air sweet. And her thick-fingered grip became slim steel bands cutting into my palm.

But I felt no danger. Her strength was still my strength. And mine was becoming hers.

Just as we swept into the furious whirlpool, Searbe spotted us and screamed to me for help. He surged forward, fighting his chain, and I reached out with my golden hand and lifted him onto the conveyor effortlessly. I broke the magical chain with one yank of my etherhand, freeing him.

And we were all carried into the very eye of Hellspoint.

Then I was floating in a stark white void. All was silent except for a faint echo of lyre strings. The music was softer now, moist with enticement. But the enticement wasn't meant for me.

I was alone, yet I could still feel Zalia's fingers clutched in mine. I looked around, but saw no one. Then her ghost grip tightened as if in alarm and a huge crab scuttled into view.

It was twice my size and had one mighty claw that snapped open and shut with ferocious speed. Its shell was mottled armor of greenish gray perched on yellow saw-toothed legs. A viscous liquid oozed from its mouth.

The crab's eyestalks moved back and forth in time with the faint music. Then they swiveled and found me.

A loud sharp note twanged on the lyre.

The crab scuttled for me, its powerful claw clack-clack-clacking as it came.

I reached into the Otherworld with my etherhand. I envisioned Novari's armory with its racks of golden weapons. I snatched up a sword, and pulled it through. I struggled as if against quicksand that was trying to draw me down. Then the sword came free with a loud pop.

I struck out just as the crab leaped. The magical blade bit deep, cutting through the crab's armor. I heard an all-too-human scream. Slime and blood spurted from the wound and the crab jumped back.

A man's head and torso burst out from between the wavering eyestalks like an erupting boil.

It was Searbe; part crab, part man, part Evocator—and wholly Novari's willing slave.

"I'll kill you, Antero," he gibbered, his big claw clacking madly.

"Let me help you, my friend," I pleaded with him. "She's got you in her power. But if you give me a chance, I can free you once and for all."

"You're no friend of mine, Antero," he railed. "You cheated me!"

"When?" I said. "When did I cheat you? I gave you a high position. A position of respect. You were Chief Evocator of an important outpost. Your future was assured. Your possibilities endless."

"You always thought I was nothing but a rude boor," he screamed, bordering hysteria. "A worthless boaster."

"You have faults," I said. "But I was willing to overlook them. I thought you had talent that outweighed those faults."

"You're an expert at rewriting history, Antero," he babbled. "You stuck me on that outpost and abandoned me to whatever evil might come along. You refused to show me any of your own powers so I could at least protect myself."

"I've never refused you anything," I said.

"That's not true," he screamed. "It's a lie! And you shall pay for all your lies."

"Listen to me," I persisted. "I just saved you in one world. I can do it here as well. Don't work against me. We're comrades. Friends. Fellow Orissans. We can work together to solve this."

Searbe suddenly became calm. He leered at me. "I've been working in my own self-interest for some time now," he snarled. "Just as *you* have. Just as all Anteros do."

The lyre music swelled louder, filling the void with a song of mockery.

Searbe waved his crab claw. "Do you hear that?" he crowed. "Novari says she's sorry. She loves me. She's always loved me. She didn't want to hurt me. But she didn't have any choice.

"You forced her, Antero! You made Novari hurt me!"

I wanted to protest. To give him one more chance before he made his move.

The great claw suddenly swept out to crush me.

I stood firm, letting it come.

Then at the last instant I struck. My golden sword sliced through the claw as if it were cloth instead of shell armor.

Searbe howled, trying to draw the stump back.

I slashed to the side, and the howl became a gurgle as the blade cut his throat.

I slashed again to make certain he was dead, but in midstroke the void dissolved in a sudden blast of light.

I found myself standing on a boulder-strewn plain, Searbe's death rattle echoing in my ears and his blood staining my sword.

Zalia's hand had been ripped from my grasp and I turned to find her. I saw a woman's shadow stretched long under the cold white light radiating from boiling skies.

I called out, "Zalia?"

I thought I heard her reply. Thought the reply came from the womanly shadow. I heard lyre music and the shadow vanished.

I turned toward the sound. Far across the plain I saw a black mechanical shape humped on barren ground. Its center spouted fire, and beneath the torrent of lyre notes I heard the clank, clank, clank of the conveyor.

I heard Novari call, "Come to me, Antero. Come to me, my sweet. I'm waiting, Rali. Waiting for your embrace."

I tightened my sword grip and started toward the machine.

A blinding light blossomed in front of me. And out of that light stepped the goddess, Maranonia, spear held aloft, its needle point glowing with heavenly fire.

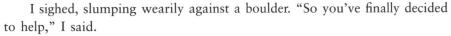

I sighed, slumping wearily against a boulder. "So you've finally decided to help," I said.

The goddess laughed. The sound was like breaking glass.

"At this moment," she said, "most mortals would fall on the ground and abase themselves and praise my name and beg my forgiveness for all sins, real or imagined."

"Look at me," I said. "Aren't I missing enough parts to make up for any transgressions? Or do you require my other hand and complete blindness?"

The goddess laughed again. It was cold and sardonic and felt like the blast of winter wind.

"I'll grant you the right to be angry with me, Rali," she said. "And I'll forgive you for it. To do otherwise would make me a poor goddess, indeed."

I wanted to tell her what she could do with her forgiveness. But I had more pressing business.

"What do you want me to do now, my goddess?" I asked. I pointed across the plain at the hunched black shape. "My goal was to destroy that infernal machine."

"That's the wisest course, Rali," she said. "Destroy that and Orissa will be saved."

"I could use a little help with it, if you don't mind," I said. "Maybe you could level the damned thing with a godly blast. Then I can finish off Novari."

"I can't aid you in that directly, Rali," she said. "If I did, more than Orissa would be destroyed in the backblast. My enemies are prepared for any intervention on my part."

"That's great. Really great," I snarled. "Then what are you here for, O Great Goddess? An eve before the battle speech to rouse my blood? After which you can retire gracefully to the Halls of the Gods and watch the action with a good vintage from your heavenly vineyards?"

Maranonia ignored my sarcasm. "My purpose, Rali," she said, "is to warn you. And in all fairness I must offer you a choice between what may be two evils."

"And they are?" I asked.

"First," she said, "let me fetch our sister."

She gestured with her spear and a warm wind blew up and then a shimmer of light rent the air. A woman stepped through that shimmering gap to stand before us.

As weary and soul sick as I was, I couldn't help but marvel at her beauty. She was tall and willowy, with ivory skin, a heart-shaped face, and eyes as wide and dark and mysterious as a starry night. The wind made her long auburn hair stream behind her like the mane of a great wild mare, and her smock was pressed against her body, displaying every curve and hollow.

It was the woman I'd seen in my dream long ago. The woman who'd sailed the silver ship through the skies over Antero Bay, pursued by some terrible force.

The woman stretched out a golden hand. And when she spoke, she spoke with Zalia's voice: "Don't you know me, Rali?"

"Zalia!" I breathed. "How could it be?"

Maranonia chuckled. "Queen Salimar," she said, "is as good at disguises as you are with weapons, Rali."

I gaped so wide I'm afraid I must've looked like an old mud-spitting pond fish.

"Queen Salimar?" I said. "You mean, Zalia is really—"

"I'm sorry," Salimar said. "I thought the deceit was necessary."

She gave Maranonia a cold look. "You nearly made us both enemies, Goddess," she said, "instead of natural friends."

Rather than being insulted, Maranonia seemed pleased. "Such spirited women!" she said. "No wonder the battle tends my way. What other god can boast of two such as you?"

"I heard Rali ask you for help, Goddess," Salimar said. "I also heard your answer. What choices are you speaking of? And what are the stakes?"

Salimar's cultured and melodious voice, which had sounded odd in her coarse disguise as Zalia, now seemed entirely natural. There was no mistaking that Maranonia was being addressed by a queen.

The goddess stabbed her spear twice into the air and two glowing portals popped into view. The portals rested side by side, windows opening out onto two different worlds.

The closer portal looked down on Orissa from a great height. My heart ached to see the lovely river flowing past my city. I saw the docks and ships bearing the Antero flag. I saw the great amphitheater where I'd both fought and been honored. I saw the Evocators' Palace on the hill overlooking the city and the magical glow of the Evocators at work. Far beyond that, past the winding road and gentle woods, I saw the outline of Amalric's villa. I smelled the rosebuds blooming around my mother's shrine. Heard the fountain play. And the soft tunes of Omerye's wondrous pipes.

I saw my brother and Omerye playing in a nearby meadow, laughing and tossing a small child about. Their son, I thought. The one Omerye was carrying when I left home. I marveled at how much he'd grown. And I wondered if they'd named him Cligus as they'd planned. I remembered my foreboding when the name was mentioned. I yearned to be with them, to help guide that innocent child past the shoals I feared his soul might founder upon someday.

I felt tears on my cheek and wiped my eye. Beside me I heard Salimar weeping softly and knew she was seeing similar things in her own homeland. I went to her and put a comforting arm about her shoulder. It was the oddest sensation. My stocky friend was gone, replaced by a woman of great beauty. The person I touched was strange and familiar at the same time. She sagged against me for a moment and I held her tighter.

I looked through the portal at her world: Khalilow. It was all she had said, from the graceful palace and gardens, to the blue skies and buttermilk clouds of eternal summer.

Then Maranonia whispered, "Begone," and both portals vanished.

I felt like I'd been hanging from a thread and nearly fell. Salimar steadied me. I gazed into her eyes. They were wet and full of longing.

"I think that was our last look at home," she murmured.

I turned to the goddess. She seemed sad, which was frightening, for I knew the sadness was meant for Salimar and me.

"What do you want of us, my lady?" I said. I was more respectful now. Her sadness made me feel sorry for her, though I knew it was stupid to feel that way. *We* were the ones who seemed doomed to suffer, not Maranonia.

"I want you to do exactly what you set out to accomplish, Rali," she said. "I want you to destroy Novari's machine."

"You said something about choices," I reminded her. "What are they, please?"

"The first choice is this," the goddess said. "I can send you both home now. You can gather your armies separately and hope you will eventually defeat Novari when she comes. The chances of defeat or victory are exactly equal at this time. I don't know about later. The Lyre Bird is a primitive force, a savage force. But she grows wiser and more powerful each day.

"But win or lose, you'll at least have the comfort of being with your family and friends."

"What's the other choice?" I asked harshly.

"You can fight," the goddess said. "If the machine is destroyed, the threats to both your cities will end. And the gates through the ethers that link Orissa and Khalilow will be permanently broken."

She hesitated. "But it's unlikely either of you will live through the destruction."

My answer was a shrug.

As far I was concerned, there was no first choice. But I wondered what Salimar would say. Would a queen accept a soldier's fate so easily?

I heard her snap, "Then die I must. My people's future is at stake. I will not risk it. Besides, my kingdom can continue without me."

Maranonia nodded, smiling. "I chose well with you two. I am greatly pleased!"

The goddess snapped her fingers and a mailed chariot appeared; four black war-horses snorted and pawed the air. She tossed me her spear. I caught it clumsily with my living hand. The spear throbbed with power and I felt my blood suddenly boil with berserk rage.

"Go," Maranonia commanded. "And do battle for your fates."

I passed Salimar my sword, shifted the spear into my golden hand, and leaped aboard the chariot. Salimar jumped up beside me as I took the reins, and the horses suddenly surged forward.

We flew across the plain at a fantastic speed, skimming over rocks and boulders as if we were on a surface of hard-packed sand. The great machine bulked larger, flames spouting higher, and then an army charged out of the flames.

Their standard was the Bear Flag and they were Magon's soldiers, spewing out to meet us, a rolling wave of armor and swords and spears.

We struck the wave dead center. I heard screams and stabbed out with the spear, shouting for the horses to go on. Sorcerous fire arced from my spear, searing all it touched. Melting armor and flesh and bone.

Salimar slashed and jabbed, and blood sprayed all around us, a grisly rain.

Then we were through, crushing men under our wheels, and the glowing forgegate was just in front of us, the big conveyor rattling into its maw.

I formed a spell and jabbed forward with the spear. A great blast crashed into the forge, tearing away the conveyor and showering molten metal in every direction.

We roared through the forgegate—returning to Novari's special hell—and once again all was flame and smoke and groaning souls.

I shouted for Novari. From far away I heard her call out in surprise, "Rali?"

Then I heard another disembodied gasp. "Salimar? Where did you come from?"

"Beneath your nose, bitch!" Salimar shouted.

Novari shrieked fury—it was like the cry of a vulture.

The forgeroom suddenly melted around us, and then the chariot and horses were gone and my stomach lurched and we were falling through air. The fall was short and my breath whooshed out as I slammed into hard pavement.

I bounced to my feet, Salimar coming up beside me at the same moment.

We were standing in Novari's armory in Hellspoint. Racks of weapons hung from every wall. A shriek of discordant lyre strings rent the air, and

King Magon burst through a door. He was the size of a giant and his armor clattered like a siege machine being rolled toward the enemy's walls.

I stabbed out with Maranonia's spear. A ball of lightning blasted toward the onrushing king.

His armor and shield absorbed most of the spell's blow. But it rocked him hard, nearly knocking him to the floor. He staggered, dazed, smoke rising from the surface of his mail.

As I readied another blast he lifted his head and cried out, tormented, "Novari! If you love me, help me!"

I heard Novari laugh. There was no returned love in those mocking tones.

Then the lyre strings shrieked again as if they were being clawed by a taloned hand. Weapons shot off the racks. Swords and spears were lifted up by Novari's power and hurled at us.

But I was ready and it was my turn to laugh.

The weapons were absorbed by my magical shield and then backblasted across the room.

Magon screamed horribly as a dozen or more ripped through his armor. He crashed down. Dead.

I felt suddenly empty, drained of all power—more helplessly mortal than I'd ever been. I slumped, catching myself on one knee, fighting as much for breath as strength.

I felt Salimar's hand on my shoulder. Light glared from somewhere and I felt her grip tighten.

Novari stood before us, sweetly innocent in a flowing gown of virginal white. But there was no innocence in her face. She looked at me, sneered, then turned to Salimar.

"Pig you were," she said. "Pig you shall be."

She lifted a slender finger and Salimar staggered back as the sorcerous blow struck. She fell to the floor, mortally wounded.

And for her final humiliation her body had been transformed. Lying there on the floor was Zalia, my poor ugly Zalia. Squat of body. Elegant of soul.

Novari turned to me. "Now for you, Rali."

I reached for my power, felt threads of it snaking to me. But it was too late.

Novari cast her spell.

A cold blue wave rolled out at me.

Just before it struck, Zalia suddenly came up, diving in front of me.

She caught the full blast, screamed, then fell back. She shuddered once. Then was still.

I looked at Novari and felt a grin stretch my lips. I could sense her emptiness. I knew she'd drained herself trying to kill me. And now it was the Lyre Bird who was scrabbling for power, racing against time as I gathered mine.

I took a chance. I grabbed the last bit of energy I could and cast Maranonia's spear.

It left my hand, but instead of shooting forward it seemed to float. Slowly. So damned slowly, pushing through my enemy's shield.

Novari was gaining power. She transformed into the Lyre Bird, great wings beating up a gale as she rose from the floor. The spear, still moving slowly, shifted its flight, following her as she rose to the ceiling.

I saw a glow bloom out all around the immense bird. Heard the lyre music swell to a great crescendo.

The spear struck just as she cast her deadly spell. The two forces met, competing tidal waves of raw power.

The world went white. There was no other sensation but that glaring whiteness. No sound. No touch or taste or scent.

The whiteness cleared. Sensation returned. I found myself standing on the frozen lake outside Koronos.

The great Ice Bear Temple was a smoking ruin. The town was nothing but a charred heap of wood and stone. The docks had collapsed and Magon's golden ship was engulfed in flames. The foundries and forges, including Hellspoint itself, were nothing but rubble. The mines had all collapsed and there was smoke hissing out of hundreds of gaps in the face of the mountain. I saw no living thing, although a few smoldering corpses were sprawled in the litter.

Beside me on the ice was the still form of Zalia.

I heard the Lyre Bird scream. I looked up and saw the huge creature plummeting out of the sky, tumbling madly in a long death fall. The bird transformed into Novari. She screamed my name as she fell, white gown streaming like a falling kite.

"Rali," she cried. "Rali!"

And then she was gone.

Vanishing in midair.

I knelt beside Zalia. She was still breathing . . . faintly. Her eyelids fluttered but didn't open. I took her hand in mine. Her fingers twitched—a weak squeeze of recognition.

She tried to speak, lips barely moving. I bent low to hear.

"I love you," she whispered. "I always have."

And then she went limp.

I was empty of all feeling and had no tears to shed.

Then a billowing cloud blew across the lake, and out of the cloud emerged a silver ship. It was the dream ship I'd seen Salimar sailing in my vision. Maranonia was at the helm.

The slender ship came to rest in front of me.

The goddess motioned to me. "Come," she commanded. "Bring Salimar with you."

I looked down and the still form of Zalia had become the lovely Salimar once again. I lifted her up and she was warm and light in my arms.

I carried her to the ship but my legs dragged, weary. Maranonia gestured and I floated onto the deck with Salimar in my arms. I put her down as tenderly as I could.

The goddess stretched out a long slender hand and touched her—eyes narrowing in concentration. She shook her head and withdrew her hand.

"She can never awaken from Novari's spell," Maranonia said. "She'll sleep like that until all mortal functions cease. And then her ghost will sleep on forever."

Salimar groaned, her face twisting with pain, and I knew she was suffering.

"Her dreams are not good, Rali," the goddess said. "Her long sleep will be a torture, I fear."

"What can be done?" I said, numb.

Maranonia looked at me and once again her eyes were filled with a sadness that frightened me.

"I can give Salimar her kingdom back," she said. "Although it will only exist in her dreams. But those dreams will always be joyful, full of summers that never end."

"Then do it," I said. "She deserves nothing less for what she's done for you."

"And you, Rali," the goddess said. "She saved your life."

"And a worthless thing that is," I said. "I'm weary of war and pain. Of death and magic." I waved my hand, taking in the icy wasteland. "I'm sick of all of it."

Maranonia smiled gently. "Then will you join her, Rali?" she asked. "Will you join her in the long sleep? It's the only way I can make her that gift of peace. You must be at her side.

"I promise you this if you do: it will be a paradise. Or at least as much of a paradise as the two of you can make of your common dream."

I looked down at Salimar, wondering about my own feelings toward this beauteous queen. Was this the woman I wanted to spend eternity with? Then I saw Zalia behind that lovely mask. Saw the coarse features in my memory, small nose and bowed lips and strong arms that were as gentle as a maid's.

"Well, Rali?" Maranonia pressed.

"Please," I said. "Grant us that gift."

I saw tears glisten in the goddess' eyes. Then she nodded and turned to take the ship's helm.

The sails filled with a magical wind and the silver ship whooshed off the ice and into the sky. We flew across barren lands and frozen seas. We flew forever and flew in no time at all. And soon we came to a huge ice citadel, glittering and translucent under a pale sun.

The citadel's gates boomed open and we sailed inside.

Then we were standing beside the ship in a vast chamber. Salimar was in my arms.

There were racks of golden weapons on the walls—Novari's weapons. Mine now. The spoils of my victory.

Set in the center of the chamber was a large tomb with a rounded lid made of clear ice. The lid was open.

I carried Salimar to it and laid her out on the soft snowy pillows. She sighed and smiled, mumbling my name in her sleep.

I crept up beside her and she shifted so I could hold her in my arms. She fit, just so.

Then Maranonia was standing over us, her hand on the tomb's cover.

She smiled. "Now Rali, you may go to your reward." And as she swung the lid shut, she whispered: "Sweet dreams, my warrior woman. Sweet dreams."

Darkness came swiftly. And just as swiftly dissolved into light.

Salimar and I entered her dream kingdom together. Where the sun was always warm, the breezes gentle and perfumed. We courted there and in time became lovers: a love built to last an eternity of dreams.

Then the Goddess Maranonia returned and woke me up and took away the dreams. She said Novari lived.

That she'd killed all the Anteros, save one.

And she was hunting that child now.

A child named Emilie.

BOOK TWO

EMILIE

CHAPTER FOURTEEN

SIGNS AND
PORTENTS

I had much time to consider those events. For I was sailing to Orissa from
the very bottom of the world. I broke the incidents apart, examined each
segment from every angle, and put it all back together again to ponder
the whole. I learned much and found some peace and considerable purpose
while going over the tale from beginning to end.

Even Novari herself no longer remained as much an enigma.

I've called her evil. Actually that term gave her more human qualities
than she in fact possessed. The Lyre Bird was more like a plague. A plague
lives by killing. When all within reach are dead, it rides ships and caravans
to other lands where it can resume its feasting. Eventually, when the potential
victims are too few or too far, the plague burns itself out. And waits for its
chances again.

Novari had waited for centuries once before. This time, it seemed, she'd
required less than fifty years. She had every reason to be a vengeful spirit. It
had taken mass murder to create her. She was the repository of hundreds of
innocent girls whose ghosts must all call out for revenge. I understood that.
A part of me even sympathized. Insanity begets insanity. It was logical and
understandable that all her thoughts and actions would be centered on revenge and a determination to have so much power that no one could harm
her again.

She'd tried once but had failed. Betrayed, from her point of view, by a woman. A woman she believed she loved. And that woman had spurned her, then brought her down.

This time Novari would be even angrier and more vengeful than before. And she'd be cannier, I thought. Much cannier. I doubted if she'd go at things so directly. She'd try to come in from the side, weighing her actions and tempering them.

The last time, I'd required all my strength and wit to defeat her. I'd grown in power during my long sleep with Salimar. I could feel an enormous pool of sorcerous energy within easy reach the moment I required it.

But would it be enough?

I saw no other mortals for a long time. Encountered no other intelligence as I sailed the icy, storm-swept seas of the far south.

Then one day, some weeks out of Pisidia, I was skirting an enormous iceberg with towering clifflike edges that had been wondrously sculpted by the winds and seas. The iceberg was pale green, and as I sailed by I marveled at the fantastic forms carved into it.

I swept around the 'berg, swinging wide to avoid an outcropping. I adjusted my course and peered north, studying the way ahead. In the distance I saw a waterspout. Then there were other spouts spewing up and I saw long gray shapes and knew it was a pod of whales.

I smiled to myself, then put them out of my mind. But the whales veered toward my ship, curious, no doubt. As they approached I saw one huge, gray animal move away from the others and come closer.

She seemed as old as time itself, with barnacles clinging to her sides and seaweed trailing off in every direction. She moved smoothly alongside my ship, peering at me with a single eye.

I looked closer, saw the glow of intelligence, and felt a vague flush of recollection.

Immediately a warm presence formed about me. A voice came into my mind, rich and deep. *I know you, sister.*

And I know you, I answered, using my thoughts to speak rather than my voice. The ability somehow came naturally in that wise old female presence.

The whale's voice came into my mind again: *You came this way many song seasons ago. When I was in difficulty.*

I remember, sister, I said. *It was a terrible time. You lost a child to Magon's hunters.*

The hunters have not come for many song seasons, she said. *Not since you killed him.*

How did you know about that, sister?

We speak to the seals and the sea lions, she answered. *And they speak to the birds. Who speak to everyone . . . Birds are such a nuisance. They talk too much. Although I was friend to an old albatross for many song seasons. He'd light on me when he passed this way. A wise old bird. But very talkative, like all birds. He became forgetful, alas. And less wary about where he alighted and to whom he spoke. I haven't seen him for some time, now. I fear a shark may have eaten him.*

There was a pause. A feeling of slight embarrassment.

I'm old, the whale said. *At least fifty song seasons older than when I saw you last. When you went to slay Magon and the Lyre Bird. Since that time all has been peaceful in these waters. And the land animals say all has been at peace there, as well. Life is good on both the sea and tundra with Magon dead. There are many who praise you for this, sister. Mothers tell their children of the warrior woman who saved us from Magon's savagery.*

I said nothing. I sensed the meeting was not accidental. I had a feeling of great distances crossed and mighty currents traversed to bring about this rendezvous.

I have been seeking you for some time, sister, the whale said. *I was told you hunted the Lyre Bird again. I came to find you. And tell you that one of my granddaughters saw her not many song seasons ago.*

Where was she seen, sister? I asked. *And when?*

I don't know exactly when, the whale said. *My granddaughter only recalled it when we heard the news that you hunted the Lyre Bird. It was perhaps seven or eight song seasons ago.*

My granddaughter said she saw her near the black shoals a half season south of here. She said she saw a ship caught on the reefs. The sharks were happy, drunk with blood. So everyone on the ship must have fallen off.

My granddaughter said there was a big golden bird perched on the highest mast. She said the bird called to her with music. Beautiful music. Almost as beautiful as whale song. But my granddaughter became frightened so she didn't come close like the bird wanted. She left.

I questioned others and found a great-niece who was also near the black shoals during the time of the shipwreck. She said she'd been north of the black shoals after the wreck. She didn't know how long after, but said she doubted many tidefalls had passed. She said she saw a ship going north coming out of the area of the wreck. She remembers it because she, too, heard wondrous music. She didn't think it was meant for her, but for the men on board the ship.

And she didn't see a golden bird, but she did see a woman playing music on an instrument. There was much excitement in the air. Mating season excitement, she guessed. Although it was her opinion the woman had no inten-

tion of mating with any of them—that she found no human bull among them worthy of her.

That certainly sounded like Novari. She'd apparently enticed the sailors to take her off the wreck. She'd have used them to carry her to a place where there were richer and more powerful victims. And from there she'd have leaped up the chain and across the leagues until she reached Orissa.

It might have taken a few years to get there. However, when she did, she'd certainly have found more than enough greedy men of power to feast on.

I questioned the wise old creature for a time, but she knew nothing more that would aid me. Finally I thanked her and wished her farewell.

As I sailed away she sent her blessings after me. And long after I'd lost sight of her and the others in her pod, I could hear their song throbbing in the ship's silver deck.

In not many weeks I came to Pisidia. It was mid-morning, the sun was bright, the sea surface was small chop, and the wind was steady and brisk. I came on the city without warning, sailing around a coastal bend where all had been forests before.

Pisidia had changed vastly over the years. I almost didn't recognize it, reflexively glancing at my charts to see if I'd somehow made a terrible navigational error. The first great change was the remarkable absence of the smelly atmosphere, that awful odor from the tanneries that in times past had greeted mariners many days before they reached the city. The air was pleasing now, full of the rich scents of a healthy port town. The reason was that the tanneries were gone.

Over the years the city had also grown immensely, spreading its wings wide along the coast, sweeping through the forests to leave clumps of homes and villages in its wake. The port was much larger as well, and quite busy. I looked among the merchant ships and was disappointed when I saw none flying the Antero flag.

But the main reason I could still recognize Pisidia was the imposing temple sitting on the familiar hill overlooking all. The old wooden structure that'd housed Daciar, the Mother Oracle, was gone. The stone temple replacing it was the one that had been under construction when I'd last visited here. It was very old-looking now. An imposing reminder of how many decades had passed since Daciar and I had faced Magon's warrior giants.

I'd hoisted a nondescript Free Merchant's flag and cast a spell to disguise my silver ship so it seemed to be made of normal timbers. I drew no undue attention when I docked, and the port officer was only interested in the size of the bribe I gave him to assure my ship of a good, secure berth.

I'd dressed with care. My tights and tunic and heavy cloak were of fine quality, but quietly so, mixing grays and blacks, and I'd shunned all jewelry except for simple golden loops dangling from my ears. I wore elbow-high gloves to hide my golden hand. The eyepatch gave me a rakish look, so it was easy to fall into the same pose as before: I was a merchant adventurer, scouting for new trading opportunities.

It was no trouble at all to blend into the new Pisidia. There was a business fever in the air, and everyone seemed to be dashing about with much purpose. Most of the homes and shops now catered to a wealthier clientele, and there were many new neighborhoods of middle-class homes for all the artisans and shopkeepers. There were also many graceful homes lining the hillsides. Pisidia had apparently not only become richer, but more mature.

I found a tavern near a popular chandlery where expensively dressed captains seemed to care nothing for the prices they paid to equip their vessels. Younger merchants, many dressed similarly to myself, frequented the tavern, and I noticed with delight that several of them were women.

The tavern was abuzz with sea trader's gossip, and I squeezed myself into an empty space before one of the long, rough oak tables. A pretty tavern maid, flushed from dashing from table to table, finally brought me a jug of good wine and a tasty beef pie. It'd been years since I'd had such fare, and I relished every drop of wine and crumb of gravy-soaked crust.

To tell the truth, I was a bit dazed from being in so much human company. The sounds of the heavy traffic outside, bawling animals, and creaking carts, combined with the loud conversation in the tavern, made me feel oddly alone and out of place. But as I listened to the talk swirling about me, I gradually regained my bearings.

"What's the word on the hide trade?" I asked the neighbor on my right, a ruddy-faced youth with a bristling mustache and a friendly smile.

"Not so good if you're short of investment funds, my friend," Ruddy Face said. "Price per bundle's higher than it's ever been. But there's big profits to be made if your overhead's low and your market's distant."

The young woman on my left heard what he said, shook her head in disagreement, and broke in. "I wouldn't put a nicked copper into hides if I were you, sister," she said. "Quality's off this year. Especially if you're buying in small lots. They'll spoil if you're trading far. Open your hold and find nothing but maggots and stink for your trouble."

"Oh, it's not so bad," Ruddy Face said, defending his views. "You just have to know what you're looking for. You have to know hides."

"Didn't used to be that way," the old portly fellow across from us said. Although his merchant's robes were wine-stained, they were of obviously rich quality, and he had heavy gold chains hanging about his fat neck. "In my day hides was king," he went on. "Highest quality in the world, they was. Prized the world over. Not a green'un in a thousand." He gulped wine, his frown signaling that he believed the days had grown bleaker since his time.

"But then they moved the tanneries outta the city," he said. "Moved 'em all out to New Pisidia. Miles away over the hills. And all quality went to the hells after that. New process, they say. Magical process. Don't need flies and privy water to tan hides, they claim."

He glowered at me. "Takes a ripe smell to make good leather," he said. "And no one can tell me any different."

My companions laughed at him. "Who cares?" the woman said. She was a small woman, and fierce in her views. "The city stunk something awful then, my granny says. It wasn't worth living in. Now we've got more trade than we can handle. And hides make up only a small part of it. Look about you, old man. The air's fresh. The streets're clean. And there's opportunity for all in Pisidia these days."

She gave me a wink. "Bet your mother was as surprised as mine," she said, "when you went a-merchanting. A woman couldn't do that sort of thing in Pisidia's good old smelly days."

I smiled and nodded in agreement. "I'm not certain where I'll put my money," I said. "I was thinking of consulting your oracle."

"A wise decision, friend," Ruddy Face said. "Our oracle is still the best in the world." He glared at the portly man. "No one can dispute that."

"That's true enough," the old man said. "Although the chief priestess ain't anywhere near as good as Mother Daciar." He shook his head. "Died when I was still a lad, she did. We've had two Mother Oracles since then. And this one's a little young for my comfort. And I don't mind saying it for all to hear."

Ruddy Face grinned at me. "Don't pay him any mind," he said. "You go see the Mother Oracle. She's no younger than me and ten times as wise as any man or woman in Pisidia. She'll put you on the right path—whether it's love or profit you're after."

"Or both," the woman chortled. "If you're lucky enough to be able to combine business with pleasure."

A handsome serving lad went by carrying a tray. The woman gave me a bawdy wink and made a pinching motion with her fingers as if testing ripeness.

Times certainly had changed—in Pisidia, at least.

I'd intended to visit the Oracle all along, but I pretended to be persuaded by their advice, consulting them about the custom of making such an approach and getting the price and the Mother Oracle's name, which was Hana.

I was too weary to attempt the visit that day, so I rented good rooms near the tavern. I gave a boy a coin and sent him to the bookstalls to find a copy of my brother's final journey. I'd seen the most crucial segments of his adventures with Janela Greycloak in powerful visions. But I wanted a firmer grounding than that. And what could be better than Amalric's own words?

The boy returned with a battered, dog-eared copy. It had obviously passed through many interested hands. I bathed and ate a light supper, reading all the while. I was so deeply drawn into my brother's spell that I read half the night. I relived his agony with Cligus, the son whose betrayal I'd sensed when I cast the bones in Amalric's villa so many years ago. I struggled with him and Janela Greycloak across the unexplored wilderness where Tyrenia—the real Far Kingdoms—lay. I shared his despair when he was nearly defeated and his joy when final victory was won over Ba'land, the Demon King. And I wept when I read his last loving words, moments before he and Janela sealed their lovers' pact and took their own lives. I prayed that they'd truly found the glorious Otherworld they sought.

When I finally did sleep, I dreamed that I traveled with them in that world, and the sights we saw together in my dream were so marvelous that they'd spoil in the telling.

I slept late, dawdled in unaccustomed landside luxury, then dressed as I had before. I hired a litter and was carried up the hill to the temple.

When I arrived, the day was nearly done. The last of the worshipers were leaving, and after making a handsome donation to subsidize sacrifices for the poor, I was ushered into Mother Hana's presence.

Her rooms were on the far side of the temple, and as I was led across the holy place, trying not to sneeze from all the incense, I noticed that the walls were elaborately carved with scenes depicting the history of Pisidia and its Oracle. I tried to get a closer look when we paused before the Mother Oracle's door, but as soon as the priestess knocked, a voice called for us to enter.

She was a busy Mother Oracle and was hastily drawing on her holy robes of office to greet me. I could see that she'd just been preparing to relax before attending to her evening duties. Then I'd arrived and made a donation deserving of a private audience.

Mother Hana was a handsome woman of some thirty-five summers. She was regal, with dark brows, a patrician nose, and piercing eyes. She had that forced smile holy people paste on their faces when they sniff riches for their poor boxes.

I knew she was thinking, I'll be nice no matter how big a rich boor she is. Just think of all the starving babies to be fed and smile, Hana, smile.

I bowed low. "I'm deeply honored, Holy Mother. And thank you for making a stranger welcome on such notice."

She murmured a polite reply, but as I came up from the bow she gave me a sudden odd look. I dismissed it, thinking it was my golden eyepatch that'd caught her attention.

"I've reached a crossroads in my life, Holy Mother," I said. "And I've come to seek your sage advice. If you think my goals are worthy, perhaps I could persuade you to consult the Oracle to help me choose the proper path."

Instead of answering, she peered at me more closely. Then she suddenly bolted to the door, saying, "Wait here!"

I was alarmed. What was wrong? Had I offended her? Or was it something worse? I was considering that it'd been a mistake to leave all my weapons at the door when Hana burst into the room again. The look on her face was one of wonderment.

"I *knew* there was a resemblance!" she exclaimed. "You're an Antero, aren't you?"

I nearly sputtered a weak evasion, then thought better of it. "How did you know?"

"Why, even with that, uh, eyepatch, I could tell." She grabbed my elbow and tugged me to the open door. "Look," she commanded, pointing to the largest frieze on the near wall.

There, in twice lifelike size, was carved an idealistic scene of a warrior woman fighting giant soldiers. The woman's face was clearly mine—sans the eyepatch, of course. Another woman fought beside her. It was Daciar, wearing her holy crown and robes.

"You could be Rali Antero's twin!" Hana said. "Come now. You can speak honestly, my friend. If you've come to us seeking sanctuary, I'll grant it without question. All Pisidia will consider it the greatest honor to protect the last Antero from any who might harm her."

My heart stopped. "What do you mean, the last Antero?" I said. "There was a child. Emilie Antero. My nephew's daughter."

"I fear she may be dead, my poor friend," Hana said. "I thought all the Anteros had been slain by those wicked Orissans.

"But look! Here you are! Clearly an Antero. Perhaps there are others, dear. Perhaps the child really isn't dead. Orissa is far, and news is slow and sometimes becomes garbled and twisted on end from traveling through so many mouths."

Rumor or news, I was haunted by the possibility that I'd lost before the battle had even begun. Hana guided me to a comfortable couch and fetched me brandy to steady my nerves.

It would take me months more to reach Orissa to discover the truth for myself. If Emilie were dead, I'd have to make another plan. A bitter laugh echoed in my mind. I thought, What plan, Rali? You haven't even reached the "commence planning" stage.

Hana sat across from me on a stuffed chair. We were in the marble receiving room, a traditionally cold place. But she'd taken the trouble to put comfortable furnishings and a few soothing tapestries on the wall. I suspected that her personal quarters would be less cluttered than Daciar's but just as welcoming.

"Tell me your name, please," she said with a warm smile. "I can't go around just calling you Antero. It sounds so . . . I don't know . . . military!"

I made a wry grin. "You don't know how close you are to being correct, Holy Mother," I said.

"Call me Hana, please," she admonished. "Or I shall take away the brandy."

"Then Hana it is," I said. And held up my cup to beg more.

My emotional balance had returned and I was considering how best to answer her question. Finally I decided to tell the truth—although in a circuitous wizardly way.

"I think it'd be best if you learned who I am for yourself," I said.

I tilted the cup, slowly pouring the contents into the palm of my gloved hand. The brandy came out as a shower of silvery flakes. It made a small shimmering heap in my palm. Then I poured it back and it became brandy again, splashing into the cup. While I did this little trick I felt Hana's magical senses recoil in surprise, then creep out to taste the ethers.

She grinned, eyes glittering with wisdom. "So that's how you escaped," she said. "You're a wizard! Like your great ancestor Rali Antero."

"I'm more than that," I said.

I dropped all shields, laying myself open to her. Inviting her to probe for truth. I sensed her recognition of my offer, then felt a gentle presence enter my aura. Quizzical fingers slipped here and there, tenderly skirting the edges of old wounds and older sins, until they came to the center of my auraself. They quivered, startled by what they found there. Tested again. Then slowly withdrew.

Hana's eyes were great moons of amazement. "You're Rali Antero herself!" she said. "How can this be? Am I dreaming? If so, don't wake me, for I am clearly insane!"

"All the crazy ones dwell in the heavens and sit on godly thrones," I said. "I won't speak their names for fear of lightning bolts striking too near."

Then I topped up our cups and told her my tale. The crier called the hour many times before I was done.

Hana wiped tears from her eyes. "Such suffering and tragedy," she said. "And yet, the first thing that comes to my mind is your dear Salimar. How lonely she must be without you. How miserable you must be to be torn from her side. And if you fail, you might never be rejoined again."

"That might be so even if I don't fail," I said, barely disguising my bitterness. "Victory may well require my death."

I shrugged. "I'd thought I made my peace with the Dark Seeker long ago. Death wasn't something I sought eagerly. And I certainly had a normal fear of it. But now . . ." My voice trailed off. I shook my head.

"Now you have something personal to lose, Rali," she said. "You have Salimar. Before, you fought for your homeland, your family. But you had nothing that you'd gained for yourself.

"Money? I don't think money means anything to you. Power? I know your history. I've read your book and both of your brother's books and saw no such ambition in either of you.

"But your brother found love. Long-lasting love. And until Salimar—you had nothing but sad memories of your first real lover."

"Otara," I said.

Hana nodded. "Yes, that was her name. I recall it now—Otara. After you lost her, it was quite plain in your journal that you never expected to find such a love again."

"That's so," I said.

"Then I must make sacrifice tomorrow," Hana said. "All of Pisidia will participate. And we'll demand that the gods assist you in your mission. Rali Antero deserves no less."

"Please allow me to decline that gracious honor," I said. "No one can know that I've returned. I don't want Novari to have the slightest suspicion that I live."

Hana sighed, but nodded. "I understand," she said. "But if all must be done in secret, what can we do to help you? Just ask and it will be done. I'll see to it that no questions are asked."

"What I would welcome most right now," I said, "is information from someone I can trust. Tell me what you know of the events in Orissa, please. And how it's affected the rest of the world."

"The last is the simplest to tell," she said. "The whole civilized world is in shock. For your homeland has been torn by a bloody civil war that has disrupted all trade, shattered all alliances, and has many a villain scrambling for the dark profits that come from such things.

"We are so distant from the troubles that the only effect it's had on Pisidia is increased trade from merchants seeking new routes until things settle down. But we listen closely to all the news we hear because our sentiment is naturally with the people of Orissa, and especially the Anteros."

"How long has the civil war lasted?" I asked.

"More than two years," Hana said. "It began when a rogue Evocator—Kato—won election to the Council Of Magistrates. He immediately purged the council of all but his cronies and seized power as Chief Magistrate. He declared martial law and made himself War Director, freezing the rights of all citizens."

"My people wouldn't take kindly to that kind of yoke," I said.

"They didn't," Hana replied. "In fact, the majority of the citizens revolted. They were led by two men. The first, and the most popular with the masses, was your own nephew, Hermias Antero. The second was your Chief Evocator, Lord Palmeras."

I blinked in recognition of the name. Palmeras had been Chief Evocator when Amalric set out on his final voyage. From my brother's journal I gathered that he thought highly of the man.

"One of Kato's first actions, you see," Hana said, "was to seize the Palace of the Evocators. He wanted the workshops, of course, where new discoveries are being made every day advancing Janela Greycloak's discoveries. Palmeras was forced out, but he took a small band of Evocators with him."

I smiled a sad cynical smile. "I'm not surprised it was only a small band," I said. "We wizards are such a greedy breed."

Hana nodded. "What they seek," she said, "is iron control of what the scholars among us call 'Greycloak's Law of Unification.' "

I couldn't help but chuckle. Scholars can make the most stunning ideas seem drab by their titles.

"The Evocators' ranks split badly for Orissa," Hana said, "but most of the people supported your nephew and Palmeras. There were many rallies and incidents, which for a time threatened to make Kato's reign a short one.

"Unfortunately, the Director's minority included the most influential men in the military. So he had a good portion of the army under his control."

"But not the Maranon Guard," I said. "They'd never go along with such a thing."

"Then you'll be pleased to know your sisters didn't disappoint you. They joined forces with the rebel army groups—special troops, mostly, from what I understand. Mountain fighters and other highly trained soldiers. They are the much smaller force, but so fierce and so able that for a short time it looked like they might win the upper hand. Alas, the latest news I have is that Kato has been gradually overwhelming them.

"First Hermias was killed leading an assault against the Palace of the Evocators, where Kato holds court. It was an assassin, not a soldier, who slew him, I'm told.

"Then a major battle was lost at the outskirts of the city and the rebel army had to flee. Palmeras and most of his Evocators escaped. As did your sisters of the Guard. The rest of the army suffered badly. They were led from the field of battle, it was reported, by a man named General Quatervals. It was called a textbook retreat and was spoken of admiringly by those who know of such things."

That was another name I recognized. Quatervals had been my brother's strong right arm during his expedition to Tyrenia—then known as the "Kingdoms of the Night." Quatervals had also been among four people who'd taken on the special mission of carrying Amalric's journal back to Orissa.

"All of Orissa and most of the surrounding countryside are now under Director Kato's rule. I was told he used the term 'pacified.' Which meant all who opposed him were hunted down and slain. And all their family and all their friends. The Anteros were atop that death list.

"You should know that all Pisidia has been shocked by the assault on your family, my dear. We've wept and said many prayers for your ghosts. Men and women, even infants, were slain. Until all Anteros, the rumors claim, were wiped from the face of the earth."

"But what about Emilie?" I said. "My grandniece. Do you know for certain that she's been slain? Have you even heard her name mentioned?"

My heart sank when she nodded yes.

"That is a tragic tale in itself, I fear," she said. "One of your brother's most trusted captains died trying to save your little Emilie. Her name was Kele—you may recall it from your brother's journal."

Yes, I knew it well. Kele had been his most loyal and able skipper. She'd commanded the fleet that took them to Tyrenia. And her father, Lu'r, had skippered my brother's first voyage in search of the Far Kingdoms.

"Kele spirited Emilie out of the city when the collapse came and the assassins were hunting down your family. She carried her up the river to the rebel stronghold, dodging Kato's forces for weeks. I believe that stronghold is called Galana. Perhaps you know of the place?"

I nodded. It was in the small temple of Galana where my journey had truly begun fifty years ago. It was also the Maranon Guard's private retreat for old soldiers and would be an ideal place to withstand a siege.

"Captain Kele," Hana continued, "was cornered before she reached her goal. She turned to fight, sending others ahead to Galana with little Emilie. In the end Kele was slain and the girl was safe. But only temporarily so. At least that's the last news I heard. As I said, it was as much rumor as news.

"The account making the rounds now is that the rebel defenses at Galana have been breached, and although they were not overwhelmed, the child herself has been taken."

"And killed?" I asked. "Do they say she was killed?"

Hana gestured helplessly. She didn't want to arouse false cheer. But she didn't want to alarm me unduly, either. "Yes, they did. However, it's speculation, I'm sure," she said. "Although . . . what else could you expect her fate to be?"

"If Novari's got her," I said, "I'm not sure. Death may not be so bad an end if that's the case."

Hana grimaced. Besides my own tale, I'd told her what Maranonia had said about the child's innate power. A power that Novari desperately wanted. And Hana could guess what means the Lyre Bird would take to achieve that aim.

"Even with a child?" she asked.

"Yes," I said. "Even with a child."

Then I asked, "What of Novari? What role has she played, other than the power behind the scenes, of course."

"I'm afraid your assumption is in error, my dear Rali," she said. "The Lyre Bird is very much onstage. In fact, she takes the center. Wait, I'll show you . . ."

She got up to rummage in a chest and brought back a roll of blue cloth. She unrolled it, saying, "A merchant brought this to me a few weeks ago."

She held it up. Emblazoned on it was the picture of a wondrous golden bird perched on an ancient harp.

It was Novari. The Lyre Bird.

And Hana said, "This is the flag that now hangs over your city. She's been declared a living goddess in Orissa, and it's her banner that Kato flies—that he commands all to fight and die for."

She crumpled up the flag and hurled it to the floor, then kicked it to the side and slumped back into her chair.

"Many have become convinced of her godhead, I'm sorry to report," Hana said. "Her magic *is* very powerful. Especially with the Evocators' workshops in her hands. The Law of Unification is a staff she is increasingly learning to wield. It's amazing that Palmeras and the rebels have been able to hold out against her for so long."

"It's Emilie," I said. "Little Emilie is shielding them from the full force." I looked up at her. "But if she's dead . . ."

Hana sighed. "Yes. All is lost. But we'll pray that it's otherwise. And if the gods be willing, you'll reach her side soon."

I sailed the next day with the bells of Pisidia tolling at my back. I could still feel Hana's farewell kiss on my cheek and hear her whispered prayer fluttering in my ear.

The winds were with me and the gods' attentions were elsewhere, for I sailed without incident for many a day and many a night. It was a dismal experience. Day after day I agonized over what had happened to my city. I was even more devastated as the reality of what had happened to my family sank its claws deeper and deeper with each league that I traveled.

All my kinsmen had been slain, Hana said. So many lifetimes, so much struggle and pain, to make the Antero name.

Wiped out by Novari.

I brooded over the long journey. And polished my weapons and kept myself fit for what was to come.

RETURN TO ORISSA

It was late summer coming on to fall when I reached the mouth of the Orissan River.

I approached with extreme caution. I'd already dodged swarms of patrol craft flying the Lyre Bird's flag. They were bristling with armed men, and each carried an Evocator to sniff for magical contraband. But I knew the delta region well: where the fog banks and hidden coves were most likely to be; where the coastline was most deserted and would offer the most ideal cover.

I leapfrogged from fog bank to cove to fog bank. Several times I slipped into a cove and climbed a hill to spy on the patrol ships. Once, I saw a patrol run down a petty smuggler. They boarded the ship, searched it, and seized some cargo from the hold.

This was not so unusual. All civilized people have regulations to protect their trade. Under Orissan law—the Orissa I'd last seen five decades before—the ship, its captain, and the crew would have been arrested and made to stand trial. The penalties would range from heavy fines to imprisonment. Perhaps even banishment, if the smugglers were citizens.

What happened next, however, was not only unusual but appalling. Through my telescope I saw the ship's Evocator order the goods placed under special seal. Then the captain and crew were beheaded on the spot and their corpses were dumped into the smuggling ship, which was burned in place.

I shadowed another such patrol craft for two days. I watched them board ship after ship. Almost all were allowed to pass without harm when the search was completed. But a few were as unlucky as the first group I had seen.

If I wanted to avoid the same fate, I'd have to approach Orissa by land. It was a week's walk from the delta to the city. Four days on horseback. Whatever means I took, I'd also need a disguise that would pass muster at the many checkpoints I assumed Novari and Kato would've posted along all the main byways.

The most wrenching part of my decision was realizing it was unsafe to leave my ship behind. There was no hiding place I could trust completely. If someone stumbled on it, Novari's Evocators would soon be swarming all over the ship and quickly pick up my spoor, which to the Lyre Bird would be unmistakable.

I found a likely inlet to do the deed and ran the ship up on the shore. I cut a splinter of silver from the mast. If by chance I survived, I could re-create her from the splinter and fly home to Salimar. I didn't think that circumstance was likely, but I did it anyway.

Then I said a prayer of apology to the ship's soul and cast the spell that would destroy it. Cold blue flames licked up all around her. There was no smoke, but as each piece of the ship caught fire, the air shimmered, then there was a sharp crack as it vanished into nothingness.

When I departed, all that remained was the depression on the beach where I'd driven her ashore.

Two days later I came out of the hills and found the main road leading to Orissa. I was riding a fat old war-horse whose best days were behind her. She fit perfectly with the disguise I'd adopted.

I was posing as a Guardswoman who'd been pensioned off because of the wounds she'd suffered fighting for Orissa. To that end, I'd removed my golden hand—wrapping it in clean white rags—and stashed it in my saddlebags. I covered the stump with a wooden bowl carved for that purpose. It had an attachment fixed to it so I could grip the bow I carried slung across my back. I made the magical eyepatch appear like sturdy leather, tanned a deep brown. And I rubbed a little rouge into the scar below to make it stand out more.

I demoted myself to sergeant, and to avoid untimely slips of the tongue, I kept my first name—Rali. I wasn't worried about arousing suspicion. After all, many Orissan children were named for me after my victory over the Archons. And if anyone thought of it, they would assume I was one of those children who happened to follow her namesake into the Guard.

My costume was an appropriate mix: military cloak and boots, civilian shirt and breeches, topped off by a battered bowman's cap with a wide brim. I cast spells to make my sword and other weapons seem more like those of an ordinary sergeant. Besides sword and bow, I had various knives and daggers stashed about me. And a good many other nasty surprises in my saddlebags and pack.

Keeping the riverbank on my left, I rode for an hour or more with the road to myself. I savored that short time. It was one of those rare moments in life when, amidst the greatest adversity, all your cares are suddenly swept away and you find peace.

I was riding under a warm Orissan sun, with the smells of the familiar river wafting on the breeze. A few fishermen plied their nets in the middle, and birds were circling, calling out to their brothers and sisters to come see this marvelous feast. On my right was field and forest and farmland. Small animals would dart from the brush, be startled by my presence, and freeze for a moment, then dash back. Cattle moved close to the fences, lowing as I passed. The scent of olives and grapes and oranges mingled with the river wind to make that most unique of perfumes—the scent of home.

I basked in it all like a simple animal taking pleasure when and where she can get it. Then I saw a farm cart coming toward me, and the real world came crashing back.

But just before I reached the wagon I whispered to myself: "Welcome home, Rali."

The heavily laden cart was drawn by a resentful mule. A graybearded farmer walked beside it, tapping the mule behind the ear with a stick whenever the notion took him. Each time he was tapped, the mule curled his lips as if to bite—which would make the old man mad and earn the mule another rap behind the ears. As I came close I could see that both were near the end of their tempers.

"Good mornin', Granddad," I said.

The old man and the mule jolted up. They'd been so deep in their feud they hadn't noticed me. Both gave me a wary look.

"Mornin'," the farmer replied abruptly.

"Is there a village near here, Granddad?" I asked. "A place where an old sergeant can rest her feet and work her parched throat, if you know what I mean?"

By now the farmer'd seen my battle scars and noted my military bearing. He grinned, suddenly friendly. "There's a right enough place about an hour on, Sergeant," he said. "But watch the innkeep's pour. He's tight-fisted with strangers."

"He better not skin me short of a decent drunk," I growled. "I've had enough of liars and cheats. May Te-Date strike down all the fat-arsed bas-tards who rob poor soldiers of their due."

"I know whatcha mean, Sergeant," the farmer said. "I was a soldier once. Just a lad then. And nothing so grand as bein' a Guardswoman like yourself. But I did my part. Yes, indeedy I did. And all I got was grief when I mustered out."

"Damned paymasters," I snarled. "Cheatin' me out of my proper pen-sion, they are." I indicated my stump. "Supposed to get extra for that." I touched my eyepatch. "And more for me ruined glim. Half blind I am, sir! Not that the pittance you get for missing parts can ever repay the loss, mind you. But it's somethin'. If you can get it, it's somethin', anyways."

I snorted. "I'm off to Orissa to set one of them paymasters straight. And I got just enough in my purse to get me there and back. With maybe a drink or two to calm my nerves. So that innkeep better pour me a straight one. Be-cause I'll be thinkin' about paymasters and missin' pensions when I look at that drink. And I swear I won't be responsible if he cheats me!"

"Can't blame you, Sergeant," the farmer said. "Wish I could go along and see he gets it right." He chuckled. "And maybe see what happens if he don't."

He had a jug hooked to his belt and he lifted it off, uncorked it, and handed it to me. "Here's a trickle to wet your throat until you get there, Ser-geant," he said.

I grinned thanks and took a long, gurgling drink. Fire hit bottom and blasted back to the top of my skull.

"Whooee!" I said, my grin wider still. "My throat's not wet, it's on fire!"

The farmer laughed and I took another chug.

"That's cider fit for the king of demons himself," I said. "Haven't been bitten by its likes for many a long day."

"Everyone says I jug a good cider," he said.

"If they didn't," I said, "they'd be liars and they'd have to answer to me, sir. And I don't take disagreement lightly."

The farmer eyed me. He hesitated, then pushed past that hesitation. "You be careful in Orissa, Sergeant," he said. "Things ain't right, you know?"

"You mean because of that new batch of bastards they got runnin' the place?" I said.

Although there was no one around for miles, the farmer reflexively looked over his shoulder. Then he said, "Somethin' like that, Sergeant. Lis-ten, you best not talk that way in Orissa. Callin' the Powers That Be bastards and all."

I snorted, but ducked my head as if chastened. "I'll watch my big mouth, Granddad," I said. "Although I don't know what the world's comin' to when a soldier can't complain. That's our right, dammit!"

"Not with this crew it ain't," the farmer said. He sighed. "I keep out of their way. Hide the crops and animals when the tax boys come. Pay 'em for what they catch me with. And grin as big as I can when I do. 'Cause these folks are serious about their money.

"Heard they took some farmers out and hung 'em in the town squares so everybody'd get the point. Well, I got it right enough. Stay low. Pay what you have to and keep a buttoned lip."

"I won't run from a fight," I said. "That paymaster's gonna hear from me. Rope or no rope."

"Just don't call his bosses bastards when you do," the farmer pleaded. "And when you come back this way, I'd be pleased to buy you a drink and you can tell me all about it."

I touched my hand to my hat brim in salute. "Thank you for the warnin', Granddad," I said. "And thank you for the drink in my belly and the other you promised."

I started to hand the jug back. He waved it away. "Keep it," he said. "In case I miss your return. If I do, I won't have that promise on my conscience."

I thanked him again and bid him adieu.

I was in a hurry so I passed by the inn he'd mentioned and was glad for the company of the jug. I definitely needed it when I came upon the first patrol.

Thankfully, I saw them in time and was able to get ready. The patrol cantered around a bend so sharp that the road seemed to disappear into the river. My first warning was the fluttering blue and gold banner of the Lyre Bird. Then I heard the clatter of armor and thunder of horses, and the whole patrol came into view. I saw the man carrying the banner point in my direction and turn to shout over his shoulder.

The patrol quickened its pace and headed my way.

There were ten in all. Eight on horseback. Two on an open supply wagon crammed with the makings of a barricade. They were off to some crossroads, no doubt, to set up a guard post.

Behind the standard-bearer were the patrol leaders—a grizzled sergeant and a downy-cheeked Evocator.

I drew up as they approached, uncorked the jug and took a hefty swig. I weaved slightly in my saddle.

The sergeant barked a halt, then cantered forward with the Evocator to inspect me.

I fumbled a salute, weaving dangerously wide.

"Evenin', Sergeant," I said. "I'm a sergeant myself, you know. So it's pleased I am to make your acquaint—uh, acquaint—to meetcha." I burped and took another pull on the jug, which put me off balance and I had to wave my arms to get straight in the saddle again.

Then I pretended to notice the Evocator for the first time. I let my eyes widen and hiccuped in embarrassment. " 'Scuse me, Your Holiness," I said. "Didn't see ya right off." I touched my ruined eye. "What with me missin' glim and all."

The young Evocator had a milky complexion and mean, beady little eyes. He sneered as only the young and spoiled can sneer.

"Look at the jug she's got clutched to her breast," he said to the sergeant. "It's plain she's half blind . . . blind drunk, that is." He laughed. It was a high, braying sound.

The sergeant cringed as if he'd been forced to listen to that grating laughter until he could bear it no more.

"Her kind are a waste of the pensions we spend on them," the Evocator said.

He deigned to look at me. I burped, tried to sit up straight, and knocked my forehead trying to make a salute.

The Evocator made that whiny laugh again. The sergeant shuddered, then quickly painted a weak smile on his lips and nodded agreement.

"That's the way of her breed, Evocator Jhanns," he said, "as you've been pointin' out to us for nearly a month." The young wizard frowned and the sergeant moved quickly on. "For our enlightenment, of course, Evocator Jhanns. And the lads are all touched you think so much of us. Repeatin' that bit of enlightenment ever' chance you get. So's we don't forget."

The sergeant kicked his horse closer, barking, "What's your business, Sarn't?" But the bark was show. I could read sympathy in his weary old non-com's eyes.

"What he said," I replied. Nodding at the Evocator and hiccuping.

The sergeant looked puzzled. "Gettin' drunk, you mean?"

I shook my head hard, nearly losing my balance in the process. My horse blew a long shuddering blast and shifted to help me recover. The old mare was grumpy at my sudden change in behavior.

"No, the other thing," I said. " 'Bout pensions and all. And a soldier gettin' her fair share."

Evocator Jhanns laughed that awful laugh. "Try to make sense out of that, Sergeant," he chortled.

I sat up straighter, drunken dignity offended. "It'sss ssssimple 'nough," I said. "I'm bein' cheated. Outta me rightful pension. Gonna see the paymaster in Orissa get it shhh . . . shhh . . . shhhtraightened out!"

Jhanns snickered. "Drunken fool," he said. He turned serious. "It makes you see what a terrible burden our leaders carry. Director Kato and the Goddess Novari are the most generous of rulers. And people like this drunken soldier are the first to take advantage of such generosity."

"You've said that before as well, Evocator Jhanns," the sergeant said. "And those words are as wise now, sir, as they was the first time you said 'em."

Jhanns' boyish face beamed pleasure at this. But I saw some of the troopers roll their eyes and hide grins, enjoying their sergeant's hidden insult.

"What about *her*, Evocator Jhanns?" the sergeant said. "Shall I let her pass? She may be drunk, but there's no harm in her."

The Evocator shrugged and started to turn his horse away. "I suppose you're right, Sergeant," he said. "Until we get some stricter vagrancy laws, I fear we're stuck putting up with such riffraff on the Goddess Novari's highways."

I hid my relief. It was short-lived, for the Evocator hesitated and turned back. I felt a warning prickle of magic and knew he was considering sniffing about my person and belongings for sorcerous contraband.

"Perhaps I should, uh," he was muttering, "investigate first . . ."

I quickly made the contents of my saddlebags and pack seem like the vomit-soiled clothing of a committed drunk. I felt him probe, hit the spell of disgust, and quickly withdraw.

Evocator Jhanns' face had the look of a man who'd stuck his hand in a privy. He glared at me. I met the glare with a wide grin of "Who me?" innocence. Then I belched and he turned away, snapping, "Let her pass, Sergeant!"

The sergeant pulled a dirty sheaf of passes from the bulging pocket inside his tunic. He peeled one off and handed it to me.

"This'll get you where you're goin', Sarn't," he said in a low voice. "And good luck to ya!"

He motioned down the road to Orissa. "Better get a move on, sister," he said. "Afore his freakin' holiness changes his mind."

I belched my thanks, took a good hard pull on the jug, and kicked the mare forward.

And off I went, weaving and drinking and roaring my old first mate's favorite bawdy song.

> "They sailed upon a boozy sea, my lads
> At the Tavern by the Glade.
> They danced and sang till the kettles rang
> Then diddled all the maids.
> And diddled all the maids . . ."

* * *

Over the next few days I traded that pass for several others as I made my way to the city. The once free highways of my homeland were now guarded at every major crossroads. At each point, you had to prove your purpose and present the pass that made it legal for you to travel into the area. That was stamped, and you were handed another to be examined at the next checkpoint. So the sergeant's gesture of sympathy proved of much more value than I had originally thought.

Most of the checkpoint warders gave me only a perfunctory glance, impatient as I told them my drunken woes, bitterly cursing that bastard of a paymaster in Orissa. Some were not so easy. But with a bit of magic to aid my angry pensioner's act, I always finally passed muster and was waved on.

The closer I came to Orissa, the more disheartening the surroundings.

In its whole history, Orissa had never known the heel of an oppressor. Our enemies had come close to overwhelming us before, but we'd always managed to turn the tide.

This time we'd not only lost, but the defeat had come from within. The scars of the civil war that had been fought were everywhere. Ruined villages. Fields and forests destroyed in battle. And the flag of the Lyre Bird flying from every official staff.

The most depressing thing of all was what the civil war had done to my people. Orissans are normally a warm and open people, noted for generosity to strangers. But now everyone scurried about, shoulders hunched in fear and suspicion in their every look. All conversation was guarded.

From the greedy eyes and twitching ears of all the spies I saw at the markets and inns, a set of locked lips was a prudent policy. As proof I saw the corpses of men and women hanging from gibbets in public squares. Most appalling of all were the gangs of chained laborers working under the lash of Novari's soldiers. Under Novari and Kato, loss of freedom was the most minor of all penalties for disobedience, and from the number of prisoners I saw, laws could be broken with tragic ease.

It seemed that not only had my family been wiped out, but the contribution the Anteros prized above all others—the end of slavery as an institution in Orissa—had been expunged as well.

I heard no news of the fighting at Galana. It was a subject not even a village fool would raise. Especially to a stranger. So I had no idea whether the rumors I'd heard from Mother Hana were true. Had Quatervals' soldiers and the remnants of the Maranon Guard really crumbled before Kato and Novari's forces? Had Emilie been seized and killed? Or was she still alive? And was the fight still raging? Palmeras, I recalled from Amalric's journal, was not only a powerful Evocator but as canny as they come. For all I knew, he'd erected a sorcerous shield that'd kept Novari at bay.

It was impossible to learn the answers to those questions in the countryside.

They'd have to wait until I reached Orissa.

All the entrances were heavily guarded as I entered the city on market day, hidden by the crowds of farmers and villagers who flood into Orissa three times a week. I'd cached my horse and most of my belongings outside town so I was afoot and therefore even less noticeable.

It was a warm and sunny day, but the sky was a dirty gray from the fetid mist rising off the river. It stank of garbage and overburdened sewers, a condition no decent Orissan would tolerate in normal times. To soil the river would be the greatest of sacrileges. The streets were also filled with litter and pools of filth, yet another sign that the new government wasn't doing well. Ragpickers and junk dealers and pigmen had traditionally been licensed by the city to keep it clean. Filthy streets meant that even this simple, efficient arrangement had broken down.

The crowd was oddly subdued and spilled through the gates with heads down and conversation at a minimum. I quickly saw why when we passed between two enormous statues set on either side of the main market road.

One was the heroic mailed figure of a tall muscular man posing with a standard in one hand and raised sword in the other. The standard carried the banner of the Lyre Bird. Carved on the base of the statue were these words: KATO—DEFENDER OF THE GODDESS NOVARI.

The other statue was of Novari herself. She was seated, stone face absorbed and gentle, fingers poised to stroke a glorious lyre.

My heart drummed against my ribs as I walked beneath her statue.

I tensed as a sniffing spell wafted over the crowd. It was emanating from Novari's statue, snuffling all around us for signs of threatening magic. I'd cast a shield so strong no one could penetrate it, but I was still nervous, waiting for one of the hovering soldiers to suddenly shout an accusation and rush me. The moment passed and I breathed a sigh of relief. My spell had worked. I was well-prepared for Novari this time.

To be certain, I'd have to be careful with my sorcery. I couldn't be too obvious. But I'd have my full powers at my command at all times. I had a masking spell surrounding me that would hide all but the most blatant and most powerful acts of magic from Novari.

I stuck with the main throng heading for the central market. Even the animals were silent as we passed under the shadow of the Palace of the Evocators. Not a chicken clucked or a donkey brayed. Though it was broad daylight, the palace seemed dark and forbidding. The windows glowed and the air stank of ozone. I tilted my head, peering at it with my ethereye. The palace had a red cast to it. Ghostly shapes swirled about, some moaning, some laughing. I concentrated and could hear lyre strings very faintly. And beneath that was a low rumbling sound, like a great fire raging many leagues away.

I pulled back to normalcy, letting the smells and sounds of the crowd root me in the natural world. But in that short time I'd gotten a definite sense that something was up. Novari was just as powerful as ever. Perhaps even more so. But I had the feeling her attention was elsewhere.

The city seethed with conspiracy and resentment. Many shops and homes had been gutted by the recent civil war. People had a gnawed, hungry look about them. I saw children standing alone in alleys, naked and crying for no apparent reason. I saw soldiers beating an old man. The crowd swirled around them without comment, but the looks they gave the soldiers smoldered with hatred. Scaffolding had been erected in the main square before the market. Bodies hung in chains from the scaffolding, ghastly reminders of what would happen to any who disobeyed the new rulers.

We all hurried by the corpses and entered the Great Central Market.

Here, as we still shivered from those awful displays, things were more normal. The sights and sounds and smells of Orissa's grand bazaar soon pushed away the feeling of dread. The atmosphere was charged with excitement—perhaps even more so than usual, for it had a hysterical edge of relief to it.

Hawkers cried out from their stalls as I passed:

"Pies! Fresh meat pies! Taters and beef and good gravy, too!"

"Honey! Sweetorange honey! Right outter the hive!"

"Pears, try me pears, dearie? Six fer a copper!"

The last came from an old crone, and I paused at her stall to get a juicy bit of fruit to clear the sour taste from my mouth. She had them on ice, and I picked a nice fat one to crunch into. I paid her a copper, waved away the change, and strolled on, looking as casual and innocent as could be, munching the pear.

I'd altered my pose slightly for the city. I was still the ex-sergeant, sorely wounded and badly treated by the pension board. But now I pretended my claims had been partly satisfied. I'd bathed, put on better clothing, and given the wooden bowl that covered my stump a good polish. My purse was fat with coin and I put out the aura of a person determined to have a good time after being so long and so unfairly denied.

I studied the crowd carefully, picking through fat-faced farmers and wide-eyed village lads and maids for a suitable target. I was soon rewarded.

I saw a barrow boy and his mate bump into a drunken bumpkin with their handcart. Fruit spilled on the ground, as did the bumpkin, and the barrow boy apologized profusely for his clumsiness. He helped the drunk up,

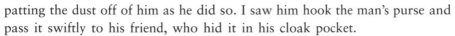

patting the dust off of him as he did so. I saw him hook the man's purse and pass it swiftly to his friend, who hid it in his cloak pocket.

It was all done so skillfully that no one noticed, particularly the bumpkin, who was hoisted onto his feet and sent on his way with a final friendly pat on the back. That motion, combined with a brush against the bumpkin's side, carried away his kerchief.

It was heartening to see that at least some of Orissa's traditions hadn't been ended by Novari and her latest man toy. The thieves were still thick as the flies in old Pisidia. I'd been depending mightily on the ability of Orissa's criminal class to survive even Novari's onslaught. I had no idea who among my brother's friends or comrades still lived. I was betting heavily that at least one of them had been canny enough to slip the Lyre Bird's net. And that man had once called these villains brother. I didn't know where I might find him. But I knew where I might look and who I might ask.

I followed the barrow boys as they wended their way through the market, fleecing four others in less than half an hour. Framing the far end of the central market were the familiar tenements that marked Cheapside, where thieving families have thrived since the dawn of Orissa. During my days as a young soldier on the prowl, I'd frequented the area, carousing with my mates, and it'd cost me much to become wise to their ways.

It was in Cheapside, I prayed, that those costly lessons in the gaming dens would finally pay off. I'd need all the low knowledge I could command, plus magic as well, to bend the villains of Cheapside to my will. The closer I came, the rougher the streets became. The stalls were heaped with all manner of goods, household items, mostly. And of fine quality. I knew they were contraband from regular nightly forays into wealthy neighborhoods. Good citizens rubbed elbows with crooks here, eager to benefit from someone else's loss. Spielers harangued from the edges, calling the names of notorious grogshops, brothels, and gambling dens.

The barrow boys headed straight for a table where ten or twelve bumpkins were gathered about a lanky dinksman. The dinksman was shuffling three nutshells, or dinks, and urging his enthralled audience to guess which one hid the pea. The fruit-cart lads stopped near the table and had whispered conversation with a flashily dressed rogue who'd been watching the dinksman's action. Barrow boys are the eyes and ears of Orissa's underworld princes. They haul fruit and produce and other goods from place to place, working their own little bits of larceny and spying on all concerned at the same time.

The flashy rogue listened intently to what they had to say, then nodded, slipped them a coin, and sent them on their way. I let them go and pushed up to the dinksman's table, bumping into Flashy Clothes as I did so to make sure I had his attention. He glared at me and brushed himself off, full of self-importance.

Good, I thought. You're just the fellow I'm looking for. Flashy Clothes would be the first rung on the ladder that I hoped would lead me to the men who ruled these thieves.

"Lemme at those dinks, boys," I roared as I bellied up to the table. "I gotta new silver piece says I find that pea straight off."

I belched into the dinksman's face so he got a good whiff of the spirits on my breath. I rattled my purse at him. "Sarn't Rali's the name, friend," I shouted. "And dink's me game."

The dinksman hesitated. He'd been working another mark and was reluctant to switch in mid-pitch. I slapped a silver coin on the table to get his attention. "Spread 'em out, my friend," I said. "Let's see them dinks."

His eyes glittered at the coin. I gave my purse another shake. He heard the rattle and his grin spread to his cropped thief's ear. "And my pleasure it'll be, Sarn't," he said, voice greasy with false respect. "I'd purely love to see yer take me money. Feel like it's me duty, don't yer know? Bein' as how yer wuz wounded servin' dear ol' Orissa."

He put his villain's hand over his heart and all the bumpkins applauded his generous words.

"Run them dinks," I said. " 'N' we'll see if the gods're smilin' on dear ol' Sarn't Rali."

He did his show. Displaying the three hollow nut halves on the table. Flourishing the hard green pea between finger and thumb. Running his dinksman's patter: "Inter the first bed she does go. Now it's inter the second 'cause the first is cold. Then she goes dossin' the third lad cause the second was slow. But his sausage's soft so it's back to ol' stiff 'n' cold."

The pea was rolled from shell to shell. I didn't bother trying to keep track. I could see the pea quite plain with my ethereye. Besides, he'd let me win the first round so I'd get a good taste.

Soon as he stopped I roared, "There she be!" I slapped my hand on the center dink. "Waitin' fer me like the good pea she is!"

The dinksman lifted the shell to reveal the pea and smote his head as if he were as surprised as the rest of us. "She got me good, boys," he shouted to the crowd. They crowed with delight at my good fortune. "Try her again, sister," the dinksman said. "Yer may only have one lamp, Sarn't, but it's worth two of yer normal civilian-type peepers."

I laughed, swept my winnings into a pile, then trickled a few more silver coins on top of that. "Te-Date's smilin' on me today, friend," I chortled. "Made that bastard paymaster choke up what he owed me." I hefted my fat purse for all to see. "She was at low tide till two hours ago," I announced to all. "But she's at high tide now. Four years wortha back pay they was cheatin' me of, boys. Four damned years!"

I pounded on the table. "How about we go for eight?" I said. "Show me that pea!"

The dinksman praised my good fortune to the skies, shifting the pea back and forth between the shells as he did so. He went slowly, though. Clumsily. As if he were trying to make certain I'd guess the right one when he stopped. My ethereye saw him palm the pea on the last shuffling round. His actions, however, made it seem like the center shell hid it once again.

"Go get it, Sarn't," he bellowed when he stopped. "Take my money. Get that pretty pea."

I slapped my hand down on the center dink. "Here she is," I shouted. "Hidin' in the same bed."

The dinksman's face was already turning to sorrow at my loss as he reached to turn over the center dink. I knew he'd slip it under the third shell while I reacted in shock. But when he turned up the dink, there was the pea, staring at him. The onlookers roared in pleasure. I saw the dinksman tighten the fist he thought he had the real pea hidden in. More shock registered as he realized it was gone. He gleeped at the exposed pea on the table, wondering how he could have made such a slip-up.

"Lookee that, boys!" I cried out to my new friends. "Sarn't Rali's luck's still holdin'. Let's do her again, whatcha say?"

The bumpkins were all for it. But the dinksman, still trying to figure out where he'd gone wrong, was reluctant. He was shying away from the table. I saw Flashy Clothes move closer, watching the action, then giving the dinksman a nod to go ahead when the bumpkins grew surly at his reluctance. I hit the pea four more times before I emptied his purse. Each time the size of the pot and the size of the crowd grew larger.

Finally the dinksman threw up his hands. "Wiped out, I am, boys," he said. He tried to grin with good humor but looked more like a smiling snake. "But I'll be sayin' prayers of thanks to the gods tonight, lads. Might a lost me money, but I lost it to a worthy cause." He clapped me on the back. "Good fer you, Sarn't! You're a game one, and that's a fact."

The crowd started to melt away and the dinksman handed me a jug. "Don't mind if I do, sir," I said, taking a long drink.

"Wantcha t' meet a friend of mine," he said, motioning to Flashy Clothes, who showed all his teeth when he smiled.

I smiled back and he came close. Smooth and deadly: one hand out to touch palms in greeting, the other close to his side, where I had no doubt he kept a sharp weapon. As we touched hands I sensed him looking me up and down, taking note of my infirmities but paying even closer attention to the quality of my weapons. He was eager for the contents of my purse, but wary of the well-worn look of my sword and sidearms.

"The name's Legg," he said, friendly but businesslike. "I'm a sportin' man myself, Sarn't Rali," he said. "Dinks ain't my game, though. Takes more guts'n I got to hunt that pea. And my congratulations to yer, Sarn't, for your nerve. It was a pleasure to see."

I drained the jug and tossed it back to the dinksman. I grinned, drunk and happy. "Never tried to beat the dinks before," I said. "Nothin' to do with skill. Just dumb soldier's luck. Which I been short of in the past." I thumped the wooden bowl guarding my stump by way of illustration.

"I happen to know a small but honest 'stablishment just down the way," Legg said, knocking a bit of lint off his gaudy cloak. "Dice and cards is what they got. Clean bones and straight cards, too."

I hesitated as if tempted. Then I shook my head. "I'm shy of strange grogshops, Legg," I said, solemn-faced but weaving slightly. "They got a way of skinnin' a poor soldier when she's alone. And without a friend to watch her back."

"Then you got a friend in me, Sarn't Rali," he said, clapping me on the back. "Tell you what. Your luck's ridin' high. Maybe me 'n' me pal, here, could ride with yer a ways."

I peered at him, suspicious. "Whatcha got in mind?"

"Whyn't I explain it over a splash of grog?" he said. He nodded at a small open-air grogshop just across from us. "If yer don't like the cut of my offer, why, no harm done. And yer'll get some nice free cheer in yer belly to go along with the good luck yer've had."

I accepted and we all repaired to the grogshop. Four or five drinks later we were the best comrades; Legg, the dinksman, and me. I told them my tale. How I'd come up all the way from the delta region to collect the pension I'd been cheated out of. How that bastard of a paymaster had finally relented and paid me my due after demanding and receiving a fat slice of it as his own reward. They commiserated with me. Worried with me that the sum I'd collected wouldn't last long and I'd soon be poor again. Then we conspired together to assure me of a gentler retirement.

We'd each put up equal shares. The stake they could afford, by odd co-incidence, matched exactly what was in my purse—which they'd expertly es-timated in a series of quick, greedy glances at the pouch dangling from my belt. I'd hold all the stakes—that's how much they trusted me, they said. And we'd all go to the gaming house in Cheapside. It seemed it was such an hon-est place that a lucky person like myself was sure to walk away with fortune enough for all of us.

I agreed. And off I went with my new friends, their purses hanging from my belt and their arms draped over my shoulders in an elaborate show of friendship. Whenever I tarried, I noticed, their arms tightened, making certain I didn't try to bolt with their money.

The "small but honest 'stablishment" proved to be a gambling hell of the lowest sort. It was set in a warren of dark narrow alleyways once known as "Murder's Row" because it was such an ideal place to cut a throat and dump a stripped corpse.

A battered sign marked the entrance, a rickety set of stairs leading to a cellar beneath an ancient tenement. The sign had peeling letters that read: THE BOAR'S BREATH. The name was apt, for that's exactly what the dimly lit place smelled like when the door opened to receive us. It had a low ceiling, with greasy smoke from the cooking fire curling up and around the timbers. Lizards swarmed through the smoke, hunting bugs, which there seemed to be enough of to keep their hides swollen. Despite the smell and appearance, it seemed to be a favorite spot for thieves. There were all sorts of rat-eyed villains gathered at the tables, drinking and bragging about their latest exploits. I found it mildly amusing that with my eyepatch and stubbed arm I hardly looked out of place. One end of the broad cellar was taken up by card and dice pits, and men and women were jammed elbows to arses above those pits, shouting the participants on.

"That's where the action be," I said to Legg and the dinksman.

Legg nodded. "Yer a sharp one for certain, Sarn't," he said. "Now whyn't yer two go see what's up while I get us a little sumpin' to drink and say hello to my friends."

The dinksman nudged me toward the gambling pits while Legg tarried behind to whisper in the ear of a squat muscular villain who was dripping with mismatched jewelry of every variety. He had four or five earrings on each ear, two through his nose, one dangling from a cheek, a dozen or more heavy gold and silver chains hung from his neck, and his short fingers were crusted with rings. He nodded and smiled at me as Legg whispered into his ear and I saw two gold teeth with diamonds embedded in them winking from his mouth.

The dinksman tugged me forward, and we pushed our way through the crowd of thieves. It was like stumbling on a crow's treasure hole. Half of Orissa's wealth seemed to be on display on the backs of the men and women gathered in the cellar. And the other half was in danger from all the conspirators gathered at tables, plotting new adventures. Beauties of both sexes held court in scanty finery that had their scar-faced and crop-eared swains swooning. Hard-faced thugs huddled at the tables in deep conversation. Drunken barrow boys danced to the tune of raucous music coming from a trio of sweating musicians. And everyone was shouting and pounding on the tables, demanding more drink from the scurrying servers.

We paused to study the action at one of the card pits where they were playing Evocators and Demons. There was a big pot on the table, and a dozen rogues and ladies were going at it hot and heavy, slapping their cards down in turn and roaring out their challenge.

"Demon King blasts the Dragon!"

"Dream Catcher nets the Demon King!"

"War Evocator seizes all!"

Around the table they went, slapping down elaborately painted cards of ever-increasing power. The dealer passed the first two times they came to him but stayed in the play by upping the house's stakes, which had to be matched or beaten by each succeeding player. I knew that on the third turn, however, the dealer'd have to make his move, which meant the house would have to double the size of any pot in play. Then the action would become ferocious indeed.

I whispered the liar's spell and snooped the dealer's hole card. It was a mere Market Witch, vulnerable to all but the most common peasant and farmer cards. Then I saw him move slightly, feet shifting under the table, hand coming back to scratch a knuckle. A flickering finger, and the Market Witch was exchanged for the all powerful Harlequin, a hole card guaranteed to capture any pot. It was an expert rendition of the card faker's twist: card kept trapped between knee and table; slip the knee back when you require the card and switch one for the other. With no one the wiser.

I shook my head at Legg. "Don't feel lucky at cards, friend," I said. "Whyn't we give the dice a go?"

Just then the dealer called out: "Harlequin fools them all! House takes the pot!" His announcement was accompanied by loud groans from the losers. When the dinksman heard that, he looked most disappointed at my refusal. But he quickly recovered, saying I ought to go with my feelings, and he led me to the dice pits.

Legg joined us at the center pit where the largest crowd was gathered to watch the shooters shake the bones and bounce them off the point wall. He was accompanied by the squat man I'd seen him talking to.

"Sarn't Rali," he said. "Like yer to meet an old dear mate of mine and owner of this here fine 'stablishment."

The squat man grinned, exposing his golden teeth. "Fiorox's my handle, Sarn't Rali," he said. "Owned this place near on to ten years now. Military's al'ays been welcome, I'm proud to say. Can't do enough for those who wear the uniform of our proud city."

I breathed boozy fumes on him as we touched palms in greeting and slurred my words as I expressed pleasure in meeting him. He smiled wider, exposing a broad tongue with a naked woman tattooed on it.

Fiorox would be my second target.

He said, "Legg's braggin' that you and the Dink are gonna challenge the house," he said.

Legg snickered. "All in good sport, of course," he said. "I pride meself on me sportsmanship."

"Of course, of course," Fiorox said, laughing back. The dinksman joined the laughter. And pretty soon all four of us were chuckling, although it was plain that the only joke being made was entirely on me.

"What's the limit?" I asked Fiorox.

"What's your pleasure?"

"My pleasure," I said, "is to take all you got!"

And, oh, how they all laughed at that.

Four hours later I was the only one of us still laughing. Most of the room was gathered at my pit, cheering me on and marveling at the great pile of gold heaped in my stakes box. Fiorox, the owner, was grim; he cast evil looks at an equally glum Legg, while the dinksman whispered reassurances in his ear.

I'd just made a measuring toss, and the dicewoman, a long-nailed trollop in a dress that exposed her rouged breasts, handed me back the bones.

"Six!" she declared. "Five sticks and a spot." She rattled off my choices loud enough for all to hear. "Any combination's even money. Hard way's double. High mark bones is triple. What's yer pleasure?"

I ignored the advice shouted from the crowd, and paused to consider. I made a drunken show of it, taking a long pull on my constantly replenished tumbler of strong but indeterminate spirits. "Lesh go the hard way," I said. "Five sticks 'n' a spot. On a high point wall toss. Nothin' lesser'll do."

That drew some gasps and gapes from the crowd. I was betting I'd make six the hardest way possible—five slashes on the sticks die and one dot on the spot die. Not only that, but I'd bounce the boneset off the highest mark on the point wall. To add to the drama of the moment I made a broad sweeping gesture at my stakes box, nearly falling over in the process.

"All of it!" I declared. "Alla friggin' it!"

The crowd screamed in pleasure at my daring. They called out news of my bet to those too far away to see or hear. The dicewoman frowned, then looked up at Fiorox. He hesitated. Legg whispered to him and he finally nodded agreement. But then he said, "House calls change a bones."

My rogue friends crowed disapproval. All knew the fix was in and that the house would pass me a pair of treated dice. Some even cried out warnings to me.

I waved at them, pretending I didn't hear. "Lesh go!" I cried, sweeping up the new bones the dicewoman handed me. At a glance I saw the telltale overly long face on the spot die and noted the waxy sheen on the stick die. I grinned. "Looksh good 'nough t' do the job," I said, rolling them up in my fist.

I bounced the fixed dice off the highest mark on the point wall, shouting, "Gimme a six, sweethearts—the hard way!"

In my mind I guided the dice in their fall, coaxing a five from one and a single spot from the other. They hit, I felt the long die tumble off the mark I set, and I gritted my teeth and forced it back. The dice came to a rest. All was silent as the crowd considered the impossible. Five slash marks on one die. A single spot on the other. The dicewoman gaped at me.

Then someone called out from the crowd with a voice full of awe: "A six, by the gods, a six! Five sticks 'n' a spot to boot!"

And the whole gambling hall went wild. I saw Fiorox whispering furiously at Legg and the dinksman. They shook their heads violently, declaring their innocence. I knew they'd be assuring him that *I* was the one that was to be skinned. Not the proud owner of the Boar's Breath.

I stuffed my winnings into my pack and hoisted it over my shoulder. I made like a clown and pretended to stagger under the weight of it to the delight of all the well-wishers—and to the mortification of the bejeweled Fiorox, whose gold it'd been.

"Tired a dice," I announced. "Goin' home, now! Go to sleep."

There were groans of disappointment. Fiorox's face was purple with anger. Legg and the dinksman leaped into the pit beside me. "You can't quit now, Sarn't," Legg pleaded.

"Why the frig not?" I said. "We're rich 'nough, ain't we? Split it whitcha soon's we get outta here."

Legg clasped me about the shoulder and gave me a squeeze as if he were my wise old uncle. "But think of the streak yer on, sister," he admonished me. "Yer can't quit now or it'll be a—a—a insult t' the gods, it'll be. That's what!"

Fiorox was in a murderous mood and I saw several of his thugs joining him as he fixed his bloodshot eyes on Legg and the dinksman.

Then, to my companion's immense relief I said, quite loudly, "Wouldn't wanna pissorf the gods." I raised my stubbed arm, displaying the stump bowl. "Done it afore, by damned. Paid me back good, they did."

Fiorox and his thugs paused. I knew what was going on. Legg and the dinksman had steered me to the Boar's Breath for a good shearing. The arrangement would be that they'd get a nice percentage from the house for bringing me in. But to Fiorox it now looked like my companions might have conspired with *me* to rob *him*. Fiorox would've probably done us all then. Had his thugs cut our throats, lift our purses, and be done with us. But the crowd of my new rogue friends was too enthralled with me for him to chance it. They'd rip the place apart.

I made as if I were turning back to take up the dice again, then, to my companions' alarm, I turned back and started out of the pit.

"Pissorf, or not," I announced, "old Rali's through with tossin' dice. Got them bones rattlin' in my head somethin' fierce."

I clambered out of the pit to the cheers of the crowd and advanced on Fiorox, my worried friends close at my heels.

He forced a broad smile. Crowd or not, he was desperate to get his money back. "Friggin' fantastic," he said. "Never seen such a run." He gave my arm a comradely squeeze. "Butcha gotta give me a chance to win some of my money back."

"It'd be rude not to, Sarn't," the dinksman advised.

"Wouldn't be right not t' give such a fine gentleman as Fiorox one more go," Legg agreed.

I belched, saying, "Tol' you, I'm tired a dice."

"Then how 'bout some cards, my friend?" Fiorox suggested. "Bet the deck's good 'n' hot for you."

I shook my head. "Don't like cards," I said. "Not me game. Nev'r has been."

Fiorox's thugs crowded so close I could feel the outlines of their daggers beneath their clothes.

"Oh, be a sport, Sarn't," Fiorox said. "I'll deal the cards meself. Make certain you get a fair shake." He was smiling, but there was death in his eyes. He took my arm and guided me toward one of the card pits.

"Oookayy," I said. Then I laughed and clapped him on the back. "Yer a good'un, yer are," I said. "Ya deserve 'nother go at me."

The whole house followed us to the center pit, which was emptied by Fiorox's thugs. Someone helped me sit at the table across from Fiorox. Someone else fetched me a fresh drink. I smelled the sharp odor of knockout drops rising from the tumbler.

I raised the tumbler to Fiorox in a drunken toast. "Here's to ya," I said. At the same time, I cast the spell I'd used all night to change the spirits to plain water, making the spell just a little stronger to eliminate the knockout drops. I downed the drink to loud huzzahs from the crowd, who'd been amazed as much by my capacity as my luck.

Then I dumped my winnings onto the table. "Yer such a good'un," I said to Fiorox, "I'll bet it all. Give ya the best chance I can."

Fiorox was stunned by my move. He eyed the big pile, almost all of which had originally been his money. I strongly doubted he had enough left in the house bank to match it. I saw him lift his head, eyes sweeping the crowd. A tall fellow with a look of weary royalty stood at the edge of the crowd. His rich clothes, imperious bearing, and the wide space granted by the surrounding crowd made his importance in Cheapside plain.

I buried a smile as I mentally scratched him down as my next mark. I was getting very close to my final goal.

The thug chieftain nodded at Fiorox. He was backing his play. A bearded thug, obviously in the regal fellow's employ, fetched a hefty purse. He upended it and the crowd gasped as a stream of rare gems poured out, glowing in the dim light.

Fiorox chortled and shoved a handful of gems into the center. "You're on, Sarn't," he said.

And he began to deal two hands of Evocators and Demons, the toughest, smartest, and most grueling gambling game in Orissa. In the highest circles of the decadent, not only had fortunes been lost, but in ancient times lords had gambled the freedom of their entire families on the turn of a card, condemning third and fourth cousins to slavery.

I grinned drunkenly, picking up my cards one by one. I adjusted my patch and got a good peek at Fiorox's hand with the ethereye. My host was a skillful cheat, and although my cards were worthy, his were better thanks to his shifty shuffling and bottom dealing. I concentrated, reached into nothingness, and changed my cards for a set that would beat his if skillfully played. I called on all my old talents as a barracks cardsharp and tipped the action toward my trap with every card I slapped down. I finessed him into a classic coven switch. I played the Market Witch and he gleefully banged that with his Acolyte card. But I closed the jaws of my trap by slapping down a Spell Trove, increasing the Witch's power and blocking Fiorox's action.

Then I allowed the game to seesaw for several hours. Sometimes Fiorox was ahead. But mostly I kept the lead, drinking all that was given me, letting my eyes fall to half-mast as if I could barely keep them open. Fiorox grew angrier and angrier. Shouting for new cards with every deal. Screaming at his people for no apparent reason. Although he and I both knew that the cards I was playing weren't the same as the hands he'd dealt me, he couldn't figure out how I was doing it. And he kept waiting for me to collapse from the loaded drinks I was being fed. Which was another puzzler for poor Fiorox, who'd spent a lifetime dosing drunks and rolling them. But I had him pinned by greed and fear of his backer as he was forced to shove gem after dazzling gem forward, only to lose again. And each time I gambled all my winnings, giving him constant hope that he could recover his money and his pride.

The important rogue had joined us. He stood behind Fiorox, flanked by the bearded man and another thug. Each time Fiorox lost another hand and his jewels became my property, he'd grimace and tap Fiorox lightly on the shoulder. And with each tap Fiorox became paler. More frightened. More determined to win it all back because now the stakes included his own well-being.

Then the key moment finally came. I waited until there was nothing left for Fiorox and his backer to bet. The center of the table was covered with coins and gems. Fiorox had set me up for the kill. He'd dealt me a weak hand. I'd surprised him by playing it as badly as possible. For the first time the cards he'd planted were being turned up like they were supposed to. He became confident, whispering to the regal rogue that this time he had me. The rogue gave him his head. I knew why, because just to make certain, Fiorox had set up the twist. He had a Harlequin card trapped between his knee and the table, waiting for the switch.

After conferring with the regal rogue he let the play pass twice, effectively doubling the house's risk.

Once again I'd relied on the Market Witch and Spell Trove to block him. I had one card left, a mere Goosegirl. Which he knew since he'd made certain that's what I got. Thanks to my ethereye, *I* knew he was holding the same card, which made us even in the play. But in Evocators and Demons evens is winners for the house. Fiorox thought he was safe. All he had to do was switch his Goosegirl for the Harlequin and I was done.

We both slapped our last cards on the table, facedown. I looked him in the eye, grinning as I turned my card over. He laughed victoriously, turning his. And without looking at either card he reached for the pot.

"Not sssso fasst, my frien'," I slurred. I shoved my card forward. "Gots a Harlequin, I does," I announced. "An' Harlequin makes the Witch with the Trove a Chief Evocator."

"You're drunk," he snarled. "All's ya got is a Goosegirl." He pointed at my card. "See? A friggin' Goosegirl."

Then he gawped. Instead of a Goosegirl I was showing a Harlequin. His jaw dropped farther when he looked at his own card and saw the milky-faced maid driving her geese to market.

"Friggin' Goosegirl's right," I chortled. "But yer the one holdin' her!"

There was a near riot in the Boar's Breath that night. The crowd went insane at my victory. My winnings were collected and put in my bag and I was lofted on their shoulders and carried to the bar. I was everyone's hero and it was Sarn't this and Sarn't that and "lemme buy yer anot'er drink, Sarn't, 'cause we ain't ever seen cards played like that!"

I laughed and drank with good cheer and dipped deep into my bags to haul out fistsful of money to shower on them and show what a generous sort I was. Soon I was hurling coins at people with every toss, and I made those with increasing frequency. At the same time I worked a round bundle loose from the bottom and slipped it into my cloak pocket.

Then the moment I'd expected came, and when I raised my glass, a shocking silence greeted my latest loud toast.

I peered about and saw the reason for the silence.

A half a dozen killers loomed near the entrance. The regal rogue was at their head. The crowd stared at them. Some licked their lips in fear. Coming from these villains, it was a sure sign that the killers were well-known. The regal rogue and his men stood there, silent, singling people out with their eyes and staring at them, flat, deadly. The crowd began to disperse. They moved slowly at first, with loud excuses about the lateness of the hour or a sudden feeling of sickness. The drizzle of departures became a trickle and then a flood.

And then the Boar's Breath was empty. Fiorox shut the doors and padlocked them. Legg and the dinksman were on either side of me, leaning against the bar.

Fiorox whispered to the regal rogue, who nodded. Then he advanced, followed closely by his killers. Legg and the dinksman stepped away from me, holding up their hands, protesting their innocence.

"We never set our lamps on her in our lives, Eriz, honest we ain't," the dinksman said to the royal rogue.

"Don't know what kinda game she's up to, Eriz," Legg whined. "But she's a sly bitch, she is. Fooled me good. 'N' I ain't easy to fool."

Eriz ignored them and stopped in front of me. "Who are you?" he demanded. "And who's backin' your play?"

He leaned close, nose about an inch from mine. His breath was rotten teeth scented with mint.

"You got time fer maybe two breaths before you answer, soldier," he snarled. "Or I'll cut your other eye out myself."

"Wouldn't want that," I said. "Hard enough to get around with only one glim, you know."

I reached for my cloak. Eriz tensed and his killers came forward.

"Hold on," I said, raising my good hand. "I got what you're lookin' for in my cloak pocket. Here. See for yourself."

I spread my arms wide. Eriz hesitated, then plunged his hand into my pocket. His fingers found the bundle and took it out. He stared at the raggedy bundle. Then looked up at me, sneering.

"What's this? Your dinner?"

"Unwrap it," I urged.

He did. Slowly. Cautiously. Peeling away the layer of white rags. The others inched closer, some even standing on tiptoes so they could look.

The last bit of cloth came away, revealing my golden hand—the magical material glittering even in this dim light.

"What in the hells—" Eriz began.

And I barked, "Hand! Take him!"

Eriz jolted back but was too late. My golden hand shot up, fingers gripping him by the throat. The men all cried out in surprise as he was lifted from the floor, gurgling as my etherfingers squeezed tighter.

"Get back," I roared, "or I'll kill him."

I made the fingers loosen enough for Eriz to squall for obedience. Then I tightened them again until he was kicking the air violently, squealing for breath.

"Do what she says, boys," Fiorox said.

They all stepped back.

"Now, drop your weapons," I commanded.

There was a clatter as they all obeyed.

I mentally made my etherhand float downward until Eriz's toes were just scraping the floor. He made quite a clown out of himself as he struggled to take up his weight.

I went to him, slipping out my dirk. I pared a small curl of wood from my stump bowl.

"I'm looking for a man," I said, sliding up into my normal speech. "I want your boys to find him for me and bring him here."

I touched the dagger point against Eriz's privates and he squawked and wriggled.

"Littler than I thought," I said.

I pressed harder and Eriz jolted as if he'd been burned.

"Have him here within the hour," I said. "Or it'll be littler still."

CHAPTER SIXTEEN

THE KING OF THIEVES

They argued with me, to my great relief. Fiorox and the others became alarmed when I named the man I sought and said he'd never agree to come. It was only then that I knew for certain he still existed. I let them whine, caused Eriz to entertain us with a bit more squealing and only a little blood for urgency's sake. And sent them on their way.

When they were gone and we had the place to ourselves, I released Eriz. He crouched on the floor, gasping and massaging his throat. He watched with amazement as I removed the wooden bowl and put my etherhand back on, covering it with a high-cuffed black leather glove.

Then I thumped the bar, giving it a good whack with my etherhand to make the dirt and Eriz jump.

"Get me a proper drink," I ordered. "I've been swilling nothing but water all night and I'm parched."

Eriz scurried to do my bidding. I drank, clutching the cup with my etherhand. I sighed, relaxing as the rough brandy made a warm bed of happy posies in my belly. It'd been days since I'd felt whole.

And I settled back to wait.

He arrived within the hour.

To my amazement, a company of what had to be the richest and coldest-eyed villains in Cheapside swept out of the night and into the Boar's Breath.

They paused at the entrance to make sure Eriz and I were the only ones present. The tallest rogue whispered to someone behind him, then stepped aside with an elaborate show of respect to let that someone pass.

I looked, saw nothing, and let my gaze drop farther. And then farther still, until I found the top of a tall hat.

Beneath that hat was Pip!

Although we'd never met, I recognized him immediately from the description in my brother's book.

But when I saw him, the first thing I thought was, I knew he was short, but not *that* short! Measuring from his brow to the tops of his high-heeled boots, he came to less than five feet.

The thought dissolved instantly when Pip stamped his staff and squared his narrow shoulders until they stretched the material of his fur-trimmed cape of royal green. He had a long narrow face, small eyes, and a twitching, pointy, mouselike nose. He held himself like royalty in miniature.

Which was only right. For to my immense surprise, Pip was now a king.

Cheapside's King of Thieves.

"Whatcher mean callin' me out, sister?" he growled in haughty tones. "Make her good an' make her quick or yer'll be usin' yer windpipes fer a yammer!"

I straightened, shedding the last of my disguise.

"You've done well, Pip," I said, nodding at his staff, which bore the emerald-eyed cat's skull of the King of Thieves. "Although I'm surprised at the path you've taken."

Pip quivered at that unexpected thrust. He came closer, waving his men back. He looked at me closely, puzzling.

"Do I knows yer, sister?" he asked.

"We've never met," I said. "But I suspect you know *of* me. Just as I know of you. You were in Amalric Antero's service for many years, were you not?"

Pip's beady little eyes turned fierce, his grip tightening on his cat's skull staff.

"Yer'll not speak that name to the likes a me, sister," he growled. "Amalric Antero was the best man what ever lived. I'll not have his name thrown about by some drunk old soldier!"

"I have more right to speak his name than any other, Pip," I said. "That's why I've come to you. You were one of Amalric's most trusted men. You scouted for him in his last expedition to find the real Far Kingdoms. You were among those who returned to Orissa with his final words to the world. You were well-rewarded for that service to the Anteros, I imagine. Although no amount could ever repay you for the risks you took."

I paused and let my eye sweep him up and down, taking in the full effect of this little man who'd risen to command Orissa's underworld.

"But by the gods that plague us," I finally said in unabashed awe, "I never expected you'd use that reward for this.

"Pip. King of Thieves!

"My poor brother must be laughing himself into a second grave!"

Pip jumped. "Bruvver?" he cried, gaping. "Did yer say 'bruvver'?"

"That I did, Pip," I said with a smile. Then I let my voice rise so all could hear. "I'm Rali Antero. And I've come to ask the King of Thieves to help me save Orissa."

The room went silent. The only sound was the clatter of Pip's cat's skull staff as it fell to the floor.

The Antero name is loved by some, hated by some, *feared* by some, but respected by all. To men and women like Pip, it also has the ring of true magic, good magic. It didn't stretch his superstitious and romantic soul one stitch to hear an Antero'd come back from the dead to ask him to go on yet one more grand expedition.

Pip had stood shoulder-to-shoulder with Amalric and Janela Greycloak in far Tyrenia. This little man had fought the Demon King with them. In histories it's always the generals and leaders who get the glory. The lowly soldier or brave civilian is ignored, although they are as key to the events as any of the grand folk who lead them. And perhaps even more important. Because, you see, *they* are the key that turns that lock.

Pip might have been born a Cheapside thief, but he was as great a hero as any son or daughter of Orissa.

And, as it turned out, he'd been waiting and praying for just such a moment as when I stood before him and announced I was Rali Antero come to ask him to join the fight.

There'd been some back and forth, of course. Some sharp questions and thoughtful answers. In the end Pip believed because he wanted to.

He dropped to his knees, weeping and clutching my hand.

"By the lice what gnaws Te-Date's beard," he bawled, "yer Rali Antero herself!"

His head instantly rotated and he fixed his streaming eyes on his men. "And I'll eat the nose off any face what say's she ain't!"

The men all shifted nervously, saying, "Sure, Pip, sure. Whatever yer say she is, that's what she be."

His head rotated back, instantly shifting from king to loyal subject. His eyes were fervent as he swore: "I'll foller yer, Lady Antero, just like I follered yer dear bruvver. Swear on any friggin' god yer want. Trot 'em out and Pip'll say his piece."

I attended to a tear or two of my own, then hoisted him up. "Rule number one," I said. "No kneeling."

Pip laughed, growing easier. "An' what's rule number two, Lady Antero?"

"Drop the 'Lady' business. I never liked it. Never will like it."

Pip nodded, grinning. "How about 'Cap'n'?" he asked. "You was a cap'n once, weren't ya? Commander of the Maranon Guard."

"I like that," I said. "Captain Antero it is, then."

And by the gods it felt good to hear that name again. It was like pulling on an old dress uniform and discovering to your extreme pleasure that it fit perfectly. With perhaps just a little squinting in the mirror.

Pip nodded, swept up his cat's skull staff, and turned to his men. "Yer there—Bugsboy! And yer—Treyfingers! Get us a rattler. A good'un, mind yer. Wi' curtains. Like a whore's rocker. So's the peeries won't spy us."

The two men—one with a face that looked like it'd been used for dirk practice, the other with a three-fingered claw of a hand—bobbed and chorused, "Sure, Pip! Right off, Pip!" And away they went to do his bidding.

For those of you who might be bewildered by thieftalk, I'll translate. Pip had ordered Bugsboy, the man with the bitten face, and Treyfingers, the one with two missing digits, to fetch us a carriage. A "rattler." He wanted a rather nice one, but was insisting it had curtains we could draw so the "peeries"—Novari's and Kato's spies—wouldn't see who was inside. Since harlots frequently ply their trade from exactly that sort of carriage, Pip'd suggested they get a "whore's rocker." Which is a "rattler," but with smoother springs, one would hope. And the "whore's rocker" would be easily found at this hour and come readily equipped with curtains and comfort.

All this in a short burst of a few pinched words. This was royalty in action, by the gods. Even if it did wield a thief's staff.

Pip would prove to be all I'd prayed for and more.

Pip made his thieves' palace in the sewers.

From its beginnings Orissa was always a fussy city with finicky ways, as clean in our habits as cats—always preening in the sunlight and burying our scat as deeply and as secretly as we could. The first sewers were built ages ago. As the city grew, so did the many layers of sewers. Most have been long abandoned and forgotten. Except by the denizens of Cheapside.

As a native of Orissa, I knew a little of this. But when I actually entered the criminal underworld with Pip, I was stunned to realize just how *under* that underworld was.

The old sewers make an intricate webbed maze beneath our city. There are hundreds of great old clay pipes and tunnels and chambers that lead everywhere. In some places, I learned, the sides of the pipe or tunnel might've collapsed, but there was always a way to get around that barrier if you took another route.

If you happen to be reading this journal while nodding on the pot, be warned. What I'm going to say next might make you jump and soil yourself. For the purposes of thievery, you see, there is no better pathway to your valuables than through the sewers of Orissa. Because the gate, so to speak, is beneath you. During my time in Cheapside with Pip, I learned that there are special gangs of thieves, called ratboys, who use the privy to gain entry to the homes of rich and middling rich. So with this in mind, and if you fit that financial description, it'd be wise to pay close attention to any scurrying noises you hear coming from the soil pit. It could be some of Pip's best ratboys.

We didn't go directly to his lair. We changed carriages several times, going only a little real distance each time but by a roundabout way, along alleys and streets that snaked and back-switched through Cheapside. The whole time, Pip's crew scattered out in front and behind us, going like swift ghosts. Shutters banged shut all around us so those inside could plainly show they hadn't witnessed what had passed beneath their windows. Such was the fear and awe of the King of Thieves.

The final leg of our journey took us deep into the bowels of a tenement. A wall swung away and we descended a flight of stairs to a broad tunnel brightly lit by firebeads hanging from hooks embedded in the stone. Two litter chairs were waiting below with four strong ruffians to carry them. We mounted the chairs and, with a snarled order from Pip, off we went, charging along at an alarming pace.

Soon we came to an enormous chamber of stone. The stone was covered with a thick pelt of carpets and tapestries and pillows of incredible design and value. The chamber itself was stuffed with all kinds of exotic articles and furniture. There were chairs and couches and tables carved into the shapes of fantastic animals. All were inlaid with fabulous designs and decorated with ivory and thin sheets of rare metals and light dustings of glittering gemstones. Some tabletops were mounded with knots of necklaces and strands of pearls intertwined with expensive cutlery and other valuable household items.

Pip led me into the chamber and through a dazzling garden of thievery. Statues were draped with stolen finery, burst-open trunks spilled silk and fur, kegs of looted incense and perfumed oil sweetened the air.

We came to a raised platform covered with a double layer of the thickest pillows. Pip stopped and looked around the chamber. Then he smiled, waving at the mind-numbing surroundings. "Nice place, huh, Cap'n?"

"For a pirate," I said.

Pip chuckled, rubbing his hands together. "Sorter what I had in mind, Cap'n," he said. "Saw some pirates, I did, in the Eastern Sea. Sorry lot. Disappointin', if'n yer want the straight truth. I thought they'd be . . ." He waved, vague. "I don't know, grander, somehow."

He shrugged, then nodded at the chamber filled with treasure looted from the trading ships and great mansions of Orissa.

"Thought I'd make a proper pirate's place," he said. "Like in the books, you know?"

I did and I was oddly touched as we sank down on the soft pillows. Pip sighed as he lowered himself and took great care adjusting the pillows beneath him.

"Sat on hard things all me life, Cap'n," he said. "Especially goin' to Tyrenia. I set me poor bum on so many rocks it begun to think it was a rock itself. Desert ain't bad—there's sand, yer know. Hate the woods. Too many snakes, which ain't healthy for a good honest gods-fearin' arse like Pip's."

I laughed. Pip shared my view of life. Take care of your feet and your arse, and the rest of you is likely to arrive safely and with a majority of its pieces.

" 'Twas inna critical moment," he explained, "that I promised me arse comfort fer life if it didn't get whacked off and leave me." He slapped one of the pillows. "This is me arse's reward, Cap'n," he said. "Fer bein' such a good mate."

As I was chortling over that, he motioned, and a ruffian wench with snapping black eyes and swirling skirts sauntered out balancing a wide tray. She laid it out between us.

"Got some good grog like yer asked, Pip," she said, indicating a large crystal goblet of delicate wine. "And some eats." She smiled at me and shrugged. "Didn't know what yer liked, lady," she said. "So's I thought what the hells, try 'em all."

She pointed out more than a dozen covered dishes of the rarest kind. When she lifted the covers, there were all sorts of things to tempt the hungry. Steamed oysters and fine cheeses and hams and deviled meats.

"Oh, I think it'll do just fine, thank you," I said.

The wench blushed and curtsied. She turned to Pip and put a hand on her hip.

"Some king a thieves you are," she said. "Don't even tell me yer gots somebody comin' to dinner, much less a quality somebody."

"Here, now," Pip said. "Mind yer manners. Give yer old da a kiss and get on about yer business."

He fished a large necklace from his sleeve as he said this, dangling it in front of her. The wench yelped delight, scooped up the necklace, gave him a peck on the cheek, and scurried off.

"Is that your daughter?" I asked.

Pip coughed. "Oh no, Cap'n, she wouldn't be anythin' like that. Young, she is. Call's me da outter deep affection. But we ain't related—if yer don't count cousins too close. She's sorter one a my wives."

I goggled at his description. "Sort of?" I said. "Wives?"

Pip hesitated, then said, "My situation's kinder complicated, Cap'n Antero. As King of Thieves, I got all kindsa responserbilities. Different guilds of cutthroats to look after. From the raggediest beggar to the flashiest Gentleman of the Pad.

"It gets, like I said, complicated. Gotter smooth things over sometimes. Especially when the families go at it. So I get married a lot. And sorter married a lot more. So I got sorta wives and wife wives, with some in betwixt lasses I ain't quite sure how they fit in. But I ain't sayin' anythin', long as they mind their manners in bed."

Pip looked up at me, serious. "A soft, quiet bed's an important thing, Cap'n Antero," he said.

"Like the pillows?" I asked.

Pip smiled, pleased that I understood. "Exactly like the pillows, Cap'n," he said. "Exactly."

At that moment something passed between us. An important bond was sealed over what on the surface seemed a very trivial matter.

Trivial, except to Pip.

So I told him my tale, leaving nothing out but keeping it brief. And I told him of my mission.

When I was done, Pip rubbed his hands together and said, "I'm sorry for what happened, Cap'n. And that ain't worth a pea on a dinksman's second pass. But I'll tell yer somethin' that is, Cap'n Antero. Put a spark, it will, in yer remainin' glim."

He leaned close, narrow face twitching like a mouse.

"Yer Emilie's alive, Cap'n Antero," he announced.

At my glad reaction, he grinned hugely and puffed himself up proudly.

"Not only that," he went on, "but she's in the care of yer own Maranon Guard. And they're all still with Quatervals and Lord Palmeras, fightin' the good fight at the siege of Galana."

I clutched his arm. "Are you certain?" I asked, fearing it'd prove to be nothing but a rumor. "How can you know for sure?"

"No one could be certainer, Cap'n Antero," he said. "Fer ain't it Pip himself who's the glims and ears of his mates in Galana?

"And ain't it Pip who sneaks in the arms and supplies so's they can keep fightin'? Supplies me rogues lift from 'neath the very noses of those arsewipes Novari and Kato.

"And ain't it Pip who fights the war right here in Orissa ever' day? Whack 'em a good'un ever' chance me rogues get. Don't let 'em rest, is Pip's motto. Hit 'em ever' time they shuts their glims."

He pointed to a large ornate hourglass that had to be straight off some old merchant prince's mantel.

"Mark it, Cap'n," he said. "See where the sand lies. In 'bout an hour, yer'll see old Pip's more'n just a flappin' yammer."

"I'm the one with the flappin' yammer," I said. "My mouth's flapping wide open with amazement.

"First I learn that my dear little niece still lives. And as long as she does, we have hope to stop Novari.

"Then it's revealed that the fighting spirit of Orissa lives on, as well. I'd truly despaired when I saw all the glum citizens in the streets. They acted whipped, beaten. Not like Orissans."

"Don't be too hard on 'em, Cap'n," Pip said. "Some deserves it. Some don't. It's the ones that don't what helps me devil Novari and Kato. Yer'd be surprised what kinda chances they takes. And who's takin' them chances."

"I'll take your word for it," I said. "But I swear this. If I live, the greedy men and women who let Novari seduce them will pay a high price.

"Orissa was given a gift not even the gods knew existed. That gift was from my brother and Janela Greycloak. Wisely used and freely shared, it meant no one needed to ever suffer again.

"Not only didn't they heed my brother, but they let my family be wiped out to achieve their own shallow dreams."

"Aye, Cap'n," Pip said grimly. "There be a high blood price some'un's gotter pay."

"But I'll have to be careful," I said, "that my anger doesn't cloud my view."

I glanced at the hourglass. Only a few minutes' worth of sand had fallen.

"Maybe you'd better tell me what's been happening, Pip," I said. "It's been a long jump to reach this ship, and if I'm going to take the helm, I'll need to know the course."

Pip thought a moment, then nodded. He drank some wine. To clear his pipes, he said. And then he began.

* * *

"Me and Otavi was the last outter Tyrenia," he said. "Yer bruvver give us the last bit of his journal and says, 'See it gets home boys. I'm countin' on yer.'

"So me and Otavi lit out fer Orissa, guardin' them pages like they was scribbled by the gods. And maybe they was, considerin' what's in 'em. It weren't an easy stroll down Market Street, yer know. Lots of villains took a shine to our hides. And some hungry critters mistook us fer their dinner from time to time. But we got home, okay. And that's the main thing.

"We was big heroes, of course. Hells, if a roach woulda gone to the Kingdoms of the Night with Lord Antero and come back unsquished, he'd a been a hero.

"We hands over the journal to Hermias, just like yer bruvver asked. With Lord Antero gone, yer nephew was head of the family, yer know. On account a Cligus bein' such a disserpointment to yer bruvver and all."

Pip touched an eye, smearing away a tear. "It was hard to kin tha' such a traitorous bastard was born to Lord Antero. 'Twas almos' as heavy a blow to all a us in his crew as 'twas fer him. Yer bruvver was a fine man and the gods oughter be 'shamed of theirselves fer what they done when they stuck him with Cligus fer a son.

"But yer bruvver picked well when he got his own choices. Hermias Antero was more of a son to him than Cligus ever was. And he was the best feller yer coulda asked fer to run the family business.

"Anyways, we give Hermias the journal. And he thanked us kindly and stuffed our packs with gold enough to make a hundred men rich. And he saw to it we got proper honors fer the part he said we played in history."

Pip shook his head and grinned. "Ever since I can 'member, me dear old muvver said I was born fer high places. I figgered it was a scaffold she meant. Seein' as me family's been right rogues since Te-Date was a pup.

"But when I hitched up with yer bruvver, I knew old Pip was meant fer better things. When I got to Tyrenia and saw things no man or woman's ever seen afore, I got a glim of what better was.

"And then we kicked the demons' arses and put the world straight again. Now, that's history!"

He thumped his chest. "And Pip's in it!

"So I come home a hero, like I said. And it turned out bein' a hero means I gots lots more responserbilities than other folks. It's up to old Pip to see that what's right stays right. And what's wrong is bashed in the yammer."

Pip paused to oil his throat some more, then continued.

"But old Pip didn't know that when he got back. First thing happened was that yer bruvver was mourned by all. Whole city was at the funeral for him and Janela. Strange, it was. On account of because there weren't no bodies, you know. But it was right grand, just the same. Not only Orissans came, but folks from all over. Kings and queens and princes was there. Stood next to old grannies and granddas what used to be slaves, afore yer bruvver freed them. All payin' their respects.

"After that was done, and done proper, yer nephew, Hermias, got a big celebration together. Said Amalric Antero and Janela Greycloak wanted us all to be glad fer them. That they'd gone on to a grander place, where'd they be happy. And maybe even was watchin' us just then and hopin' we'd have a good time. So we had that good time. Feasted almos' a month.

"After that, ever'thin' was fine fer a while. Lord Palmeras got together with King Solaris' wizards, and word was they was gonna put the whole world right with the stuff yer bruvver and Lady Greycloak discovered. Some kinda unified law, or other. Don't know much about it, but it sounded fine by me. Especially when things started gettin' better.

"Some of it was 'cause we'd licked King Ba'land. Weren't no demons around to devil us. But most was from the stuff comin' from the Evocators' workshops. New cures fer plagues. New ways to keep the weather sweet. New things to make life better fer the workin' man and woman. Yeah. Fer a time it sure looked like there was nothin' but bright days ahead.

"But then this Novari woman come along and hooked up with Kato. And the whole thing went busto. Flatter'n a rolled drunk's purse." He snapped his fingers. "Just that quick, it was. Just that quick.

"All a us rogues what went to Tyrenia with Lord Antero got set up pretty. So's we was probably caught squattin' on our sore bums. Life was pretty good, see? I hadda nice place here in Cheapside. Big manse, it was. Bought another fer me muvver and pa. Got a whole street a tenements fer me family.

"The others did sorta the same thing. Otavi got him a nice big farm. Quatervals got together with Cap'n Kele and was buyin' a fleet of merchant ships. Plannin' all kinds'a adventures, from what I heard. And the rest done the same, or similar. Livin' the good life and thinkin' we had reason to deserve it."

Pip snorted. "Buncha fools, we were. Never seen dumber marks. Wide open to the slick boys, we were. Like bumpkins with fat purses on an innercent stroll in Cheapside on a foggy night.

"I ain't a political sort by nature, Cap'n. So this Kato bastard didn't catch my attention right off. He was a Magistrate, see. He was an Evocator first, but then got his arse elected somehow.

"In fact, afore he was a Magistrate he was one of the Evocators what backed Cligus when he turned on yer bruvver. Don't know how he hung on to his office when it all came out about what Cligus had done. With the help, mind you, of rogues like Kato.

"He was in disgrace, that's fer sure. But there's more rogues in the homes of the rich than all a Cheapside, and that's the friggin' truth, Cap'n Antero. That's the friggin' truth."

Pip supplied us both with more wine. "Real graspers, some of them rich boys are. And they grasped real hard at Kato. Then the new magic stuff started comin' from the Evocators and they got good and pissorfed, they did. Because Lord Palmeras and yer nephew, Hermias, made sure ordinary folks got just as much as anybody else. Just like Lord Antero said to do.

"But Kato and his rogues wanted to control it. Said Palmeras was conspirin' with the Anteros to bust up the old families. Put the masses in charge. The riffraff. With them on top. Controllin' the whole thing.

"Most Orissans saw through it. Laughed at 'em, in fact. But those rich old rogues weren't laughin'. Not one chuckle, Cap'n. Yer can take old Pip's word fer that. They was noddin' and lookin' at all them riches bein' handed out to one and all and grindin' their teeth.

"Then Kato went off on some kinda made-up holy quest. Raised a fleet, he did. With money from those rich old rogues. Acted like he was Lord Amalric Antero himself, goin' on a great Findin'.

"Didn't take him far, as it turned out. Stopped at some island off a Lycanth. Said he had a vision there. Said he got the truth. And when he come back, he paid to put on a big show. At the Amphitheater. Whole city was there. Includin' Palmeras and the Evocators.

"Kato makes this big speech about his vision. Said he had proof Cligus was right all along. That Amalric Antero had conspired with the demons to cause all the troubles we'd had. Said he'd made a pact with King Ba'land himself. And that Cligus had tried to stop them and died bein' a big hero.

"We were all rattlin' our noggins at that nonsense. But then there was this music. Lyre music, it turned out. And this big damned bird appears outter nowhere. Settles next to Kato. Then we all jump, 'cause there's a lightnin' flash and the bird turns into this woman."

Pip's eyes glowed. "Never seen such a woman. Fry yer curlies, she would, just lookin' at her. And she had this lyre she was playin'. Wonderful music. Evil, too. Turned yer mind inter busted yolk.

"We all kinda gaped at her, women and men alike. And she played the lyre and sang this song about the demons and the Anteros. And how they'd been plottin' through all a history to sell our souls to the demons. Which was why the Anteros were so rich. And why so many of 'em had done such grand things. Which weren't grand at all, but a lie.

"But even with that spell music she was playin', the story didn't sit well with ordinary folks. Lost their noggins, they did. Started shoutin' stuff. Throwin' stuff. Yer don't insult the Anteros to Orissans, yer know. At least yer didn't then.

"Now this made her madder'n a coin clipper who comes up copper when he thought it was gold. She made her voice loud as thunder. Said Orissa was doomed if we didn't change our ways. And that she, Novari, was gonna turn her back on us and leave us to the mercy of them devil Anteros.

"Then, poof! She disappears. And Kato's in a fit, stalks outter there like a throat slitter just found out his cutter's dim.

"We all laughed, but whilst we was laughin' we weren't glimmin' to what was goin' on. Like all the rich old knaves that walked out with him. And some generals, too. Couple a Evocators, even. Regular rogues' gallery starin' us in the mush. And all old mates of Cligus. Old mates who got cut off at the knees when Cligus fell.

"But we didn't notice. And shame on us. Next thing we know, Kato's ridin' high again. Havin' all kinds a private meetin's with important types. Blackhearted types. Story made the rounds there was sex magic orgies goin' on. With that Novari woman the center of the orgies. I didn't pay it any mind, to tell the truth. Wished I had, Cap'n. Wished I had."

Pip stared out at the chamber, reflecting. Little mouse nose twitching, twitching.

Then he said, "Sex magic or no, that Novari is a schemer. She and Kato must a burnt a river of oil stayin' up nights conspirin'. Must a spent another river of gold passin' out bribes and makin' the stickers soft, if you know what old Pip means.

"One day I wakes up and Kato's been elected Chief Magistrate."

He looked at me. "It was the other Magistrates that went and did it," he said. "It's the Magistrates that vote fer things like that in Orissa. Not the citizens. Guess you Anteros didn't think of that. Here yer went and set folks free. But yer didn't think to give 'em the power to hold it. Trusted in the old families, yer did. Higher princerbles, and such, of the noble class."

I flushed. Pip was right.

He grimaced, sorry he'd had to say it. "Kato invites Palmeras and the top Evocators over to congratulate him. Like the new Chief Magistrate always does. Except, this time there was soldiers waitin'. Soldiers in Kato's pay. Wearin' patches with the Lyre Bird symbol on 'em. That's how ready Kato and Novari was. Same time, other soldiers were marchin' on the Palace of the Evocators.

"Went after Hermias, too. He was livin' at yer brother's villa, and a troop of cavalry was sent to bring him in.

"Whole thing would a ended there, 'cept Hermias got tipped. Rode out with Quatervals to stop Palmeras and got there just in time. Big friggin' fight commenced. But there was too many.

"Hermias and Palmeras just got out with their skins. Along with some of the other Evocators. Still wouldn't a made it, 'cept for the Maranon Guard.

"They got the word about what was happenin' and joined up with Hermias and the others just outside of Orissa. And it was a good thing, too, 'cause the soldiers were on 'em.

"The whole group fought their way to Galana with Novari blastin' away with her sorcery and Kato's troops choppin' at their heels. But they made it, they did. And turned and fought so hard that Kato was thrown back. Heard Novari was hurt by somethin' Palmeras did. But it must a not been that bad, 'cause the bitch got better by and by.

"Lot of the fellers in the army didn't go along with Kato. They snuck off to Galana. For a time things weren't goin' well for Kato, although he was still holdin' the Harlequin. Just bidin' his time, it turned out, until Novari got better.

"We knew she was back when the plagues started hittin'. Lot of people died. Then the insects came. Sky was black with them. Just at harvest time. Lot of people didn't eat.

"Then the talk against the Anteros got really hot. Blamin' 'em for the plagues and insects. Sayin' only Novari could save us. Sayin' all the Anteros had to die. The talk was from ferrety villains workin' for Kato. But after a while it started takin' hold and spreadin'. Then peeries started in. Spyin' on folks and tippin' Kato's rogues when the talk didn't favor them. Things started happenin' to people. Lot of trips to the river haulin' kin out.

"But some folks dug in, 'stead of foldin'. Raggedy armies popped up in the countryside. Under old Otavi, it turns out. Somebody'd told him what was up and tipped where some arms was to be had, and he roused up all the farmers to join with Hermias.

"Fought all the way to the gates of Orissa, they did. The sky was on fire night after night.

"Saw the Lyre Bird herself up there, soarin' across the moon, shootin' down lightnin' and dodgin' bolts thrown back at her.

"Then somethin' happened. Don't know what. Don't know how. But somebody got close to Hermias. Knifed in the back, it's said. Went after the whole command. Otavi was killed the same way. Went after Palmeras, too. But he got away.

"Whole thing collapsed after that. Quatervals had to retreat. Lost a lot of men and women. But he got 'em all back to Galana.

"Heart went outter everybody. Just got down and slunk like worms. And that's when they started killin' Anteros. It was an awful time. Didn't seem like a day passed without we didn't hear news of some poor Antero bein' murdered in her bed.

"But the Antero Novari seemed to want most was Emilie, yer little niece. And Hermias' darlin' daughter. Scoured the countryside fer her. Burned whole villages tryin' to track her down. Almos' got her more'n once. But ever' time she'd sniff little Emilie out, somethin' would happen to warn us. 'N' we'd get her away to safety.

"It took some doin', but we finally got her to Cap'n Kele—who died gettin' Emilie up the river to Galana. And yer know the rest."

"Actually, I don't," I said. "There's many mysteries to be explained. Such as your part in this, Pip. Who tipped Hermias and the Maranon Guard? Who saved Emilie and got her to Kele?"

Pip actually blushed. He ducked his head and mumbled, "It was me, Cap'n."

"I thought so," I said. "It appears Orissa owes more than it can ever re-pay to Cheapside and the King of Thieves."

Pip shrugged. "Didn't want the job," he said. "Had 'nough stashed to last me whole life. But it was the only way I could think of fightin' Kato and Novari.

"The rogues think well of old Pip," he said. "Got family ties, too, that made it a natural. It was easy, to tell the truth, Cap'n. I was even a bigger hero in Cheapside than I was in the rest of the city. Bein' a local lad, and all. So I had a whisper here and a whisper there and I twisted some arms and busted some heads and before yer knew it, was runnin' the whole thing."

He chortled. "It didn't hurt," he said, "that there's nothin' a villain hates more than a hard-fisted crew like this. Hurts business for good honest thieves, it does, when you thumps on regular citizens. They holds onto their purses tighter. Don't trust folks like they usta. Serspicious of ever'body."

Then he stopped and pointed at the hourglass. It was a few grains past the mark he'd set.

"Yer'll soon get a taste of what we been doin' here, Cap'n Antero," he said.

Then from far off I heard a heavy crump. The chamber shuddered around us. Dust showered, then all was still.

Pip grinned evilly. "Me lads just got one of the barracks," he said. "With luck maybe fifty or so of the Lyre Bird soldiers just kissed their arses farewell."

"An explosion?" I marveled. "So large. And without sorcery, it seems. At least I didn't sense any."

"Nothin' sorcerous about it, Cap'n Antero," Pip chortled. "Plain old horseshit and tar oil. Got the idea from Otavi. Bein' a farmer and all, he knowed that sort of thing. Get the horseshit good and dry, he said. Crumbly. Lots of that stuff layin' around the stables of Orissa. Then soak it good with tar oil and pack it real tight in some barrels. More barrels, bigger the hole in the ground."

He scratched his head. "I ferget how many we used this time," he said. "But it oughter make a big enough hole to give 'em pause."

He winked at me. "Only sorry we couldn't get Novari standin' over it when it went off. Send her someplace else to do her goddessin'."

"I saw the statues of her," I said dryly. "When did she become a goddess?"

"They done it right off," Pip said. "Kato got her declared a goddess. Swore in the troops. Sacrificed a herd a cattle and sealed off the other temples, like fer Te-Date and Maranonia and such.

"She's buildin' a new temple fer herself," Pip said. "Just laid the foundation." He stared at me a moment. "She's buildin' it out by yer bruvver's villa. Livin' there, she is. Until the temple's built."

My stomach roiled, thinking of Novari residing in Amalric's home. Strolling in the garden. Doing whatever she liked with my mother's shrine.

Pip patted me. "We'll get her outter there, Cap'n Antero," he soothed. "Now that yer with us, I knows we can do it."

He drew back and sipped his wine. "Anyways, that's the kinder thing us Cheapside villains have been up to. We hit 'em ever' chance we gets.

"Outside a town we got all the country villains with us. With a lot of honest folk bandin' with them. We used them to shuffle little Emilie about and get her to safety.

"But the biggest help they give us is gettin' weapons and supplies to Galana. We robs barracks and stores here and then smuggle 'em out to the country stiffs. They hide stuff in farm wagons, in their clothes—up their arses, even. And they've dared the Lyre Bird's snoopers and Kato's soldiers ever' hour of ever' day since this whole friggin' thing started."

His eyes suddenly shot up to the hourglass again. "What's this?" he said. "There was supposed to be another one go off right after the first.

"Somethin' must a gone wrong. Two barracks was supposed to be hit tonight."

Pip cursed and smacked his palm with a fist. "Must a been the horseshit," he growled. "I was serspicious of its quality, Cap'n. Not crumbly enough, I told the lads."

He sighed. "It's the details that getcha in this job, Cap'n. If yer don't take care of the horseshit, it won't take care of yer."

He said it so earnestly that I had to bury a burst of laughter, covering with a loud clearing of my throat and saying my father'd said similar things about merchanting, although without the barnyard reference.

Then I said, "Pip, I don't think we have much time. The Goddess Maranonia gave me until the first snowfall. I remember her words like it was yesterday, instead of nearly a year ago. 'When next the snow falls in Orissa,' she said, 'the child Emilie will reach the first level of her powers.' And she said Novari was determined to prevent this."

Pip's eyes narrowed. "First snow can't be more'n a month off," he said.

"It could be even sooner," I pointed out, "if winter comes early this year. Regardless, considering what we're up against, we've almost no time. I feared it was impossible when I set out for Orissa hundreds of days and thousands of leagues ago. I'm pointing my doubts out to you so you'll completely understand our situation. Our chances are poor, to say the least.

"When I fought the Lyre Bird before, I was confronting a primitive force with little knowledge and only the raw power of her hatred to drive her. Now she has the knowledge of the Evocators' workshops at her command.

"The only reason she hasn't succeeded so far is that Palmeras and the few Evocators who escaped with him also have that knowledge. They are using it to block her. But how much longer can they hold out?"

"If yer don't mind me sayin' so, Cap'n," Pip broke in, "yer on'y lookin' at this from one side. If we're runnin' outta time, so's Novari. Like yer said, first snowfall ain't far off. That means Novari's got as little time to bust the siege as we got to stop her."

I clapped him on the shoulder. "I can see why your knavish friends made you king, Pip," I said. "That's exactly right. And it cheered me just to hear you say it."

Pip brushed aside the praise. "Novari's gotter know the same things we know," he said. "And if old Pip was in her skin, I'd be makin' a big push soon. I'd be throwin' ever' thing I had into that siege at Galana."

"She's probably already started," I said. "I've sniffed around, and Novari's attention definitely seems elsewhere. There's all kinds of spells and magical traps set all over Orissa and the countryside on the way up here from the Delta. Not only was I able to avoid them easily, but I had the feeling that if I slipped a little, made a mistake, it might go unnoticed for a time."

"Which means she's concertratin' on Galana," Pip said.

"Exactly."

"What do we do then?" he asked.

"What does any self-respecting thief do," I asked, "when he sees a rich man's house left unguarded?"

"Why, he gets up to all the knavery he can, Cap'n," Pip said.

"That's what I had in mind, Pip," I said.

Pip laughed. "Yer couldn't a found a better villain fer the job, Cap'n Antero," he said.

"I didn't know that when I set out to find you, Pip."

I looked around the chamber at the dazzling treasures he'd stuffed it with to make it seem like a pirate's den.

And I said, "But I do now."

CHAPTER SEVENTEEN

THE WARRIORS OF CHEAPSIDE

The day after our meeting, Pip gathered his top lieutenants together to launch the first part of our campaign against Novari and Director Kato.

"Afore old Pip starts yammerin'," he began, "I wanna know if any of yer squints think Cap'n Antero here ain't what I says she is. Which is Rali Antero come back from the dead to stick the Lyre Bird's gizzard." He glared around at the assembled group.

It was a bizarre gathering. There was Queenie, head of the Thugs' Guild, a big muscular tub of a woman dressed in rich furs and sporting a gem-encrusted tiara. And Garla, the tall, handsome chief of the Beggars' Guild. Pearl, the tawny seductress who headed the Harlots' Guild. Palmer and Lammer, the baroness and baron of the Pickpockets. And Tink, ratboy leader, smaller even than Pip but powerful in presence—since he'd doused himself with perfumes and oils to hide the scent of his specialty, which clung to him no matter how often he bathed. There were others, just as colorful, but those are the ones I remember the most. Probably because they were the ones Pip first pointed out as they assembled and their names stuck more firmly in my mind.

It was a gathering of Cheapside's most dangerous men and women, but as deadly as this group appeared, they all turned away from Pip's steady glare. He didn't let up and the silence grew uncomfortable.

Finally Queenie cleared her throat. "What'd we do, Pip," she asked, "to make ya think we don't believe ya? She's whatever ya say she is, Pip. Rali Antero, if ya like. Lookin' not a day older'n thirty-six, thirty-seven. Even though she's been gone more'n fifty years. And was that age then, accordin' to all the tales we've heard since we were just wee dabs."

"Aha!" Pip roared. "So yers don't believe me!"

Queenie raised a meaty hand in protest. "I didn't say that, Pip."

"Might as well've," Pip growled. "Now, lissen to me. All a yers. Spit it out. Whatcha believe and whatcha don't. Old Pip'll set yer square."

More silence. The group obviously was too frightened of Pip to say what they plainly thought, which was that he was crazier than a chimney bird.

I came forward, raising my golden hand, making it glow like a beacon—emanating power enough to make their hackles rise. I smiled to lessen their fear.

"Forgive me for what I am about to do, my friends," I said. "But I don't have time for doubts, tricks, or quarrels. You must be with me to the end, no matter where that end lies."

I chanted:

> "Draw the veil,
> Part the curtain,
> See what's lying tale,
> And what is certain."

I sliced the air with my etherhand, and it was like a great window swept open. A frigid wind blasted through and the knaves all jumped and cried out in alarm.

Spread out before them was a wasteland of ice and swirling snow. Perched on the black rocky coast and washed by frozen seas was my citadel of ice, a hunched half globe so white it burnt the eye.

"My home," I said.

The rogues shifted and muttered.

I gestured again and the view changed. We were looking inside the citadel now. There were weapons racks set in the great hall. There was the empty wooden cradle where my silver ship once perched.

And set in a wide alcove was the tomb with the lid of ice as clear as glass.

Inside was the sleeping auburn-haired Salimar. My heart wrenched when I saw her, and I felt ashamed for bringing these strangers into our bower. She stirred, and I thought I heard her whisper my name. I wanted to answer but it was too far. And only a vision.

I gestured at Salimar. "My queen," I said. "And the woman I love above all others."

I heard the knaves murmur in wonder and sympathy.

Then Salimar stirred in her tomb. Her lips moved and she called out, quite faint, "Rali, dear. Please. I'm cold. So cold."

And she stretched out her arms.

I could bear it no longer. I pawed at the air and the vision collapsed.

Queenie, leader of the Thugs' Guild, sniffled and wiped her eyes. The others seemed equally affected.

Only Garla, Master of the Beggars' Guild, seemed unmoved. He had a knowing smirk on his handsome lips.

Pip must have noticed it, too. "Whatcher problem, Garla?" he snarled. "Yer think what yer saw was just caused by gas from bad eats?"

Garla shook his head. "Not at all, Pip," he said in surprisingly cultured tones. "I was only admiring the display. I consider myself a master at tugging heartstrings. But that"—he looked at me, sardonic grin growing wider— "was truly the work of genius. I wept a tear myself and I don't mind saying so, Lady Antero."

"She don't like bein' called 'Lady,' " Pip snapped. "It's Cap'n Antero."

Garla dipped his head in a slight bow to me. "Captain, is it?" he said. "How . . . *equal* of you."

Pip started to get angry but I waved him down. "Speak your mind," I said. "No one will harm you."

Garla shrugged. "Oh, I believe you, Captain Rali Antero. Who could deny what they just saw? Coupled, most importantly, with Pip's claim. Which I never doubted from the beginning. No, I'm a strong supporter of the King of Thieves. Who, after all, has seen enough and done enough for a dozen lifetimes, and is definitely no one's fool. You're Captain Antero, all right. Miracle though it may seem."

"Then why the sneer, my friend?" I asked. "Why the hostility toward me?"

"Not to you in particular, Captain Antero," he said. "But what you represent." He made an elegant gesture of disdain. "All the lords and ladies who were so quick to desert their fellow Orissans to keep their comforts and win a greater share besides."

He indicated the rest of the group. "We're all thieves here. We make no pretense we're anything else. But how is it that it's Orissan castoffs who stand for her now, when all else have bowed down or fled?"

"I can't answer that," I said. "And I must admit it amazed me."

"What will happen, Captain Antero," Garla continued, "if we win this fight? Who will rule when this lot is gone? The noble families again? A different group, perhaps, but of similar breeding, mind you."

"What do you want to happen?" I asked.

Garla raised an eyebrow, surprised. Then he nodded and said, "Why, if I were given the choice, the new leaders would be common folk with uncommon experience and strength." He gestured at Pip. "The King of Thieves would be one such man."

"If that's what you want," I said, "work to accomplish it when this fight is done. I have no future in Orissa after this. Make your own. Just make it fair for all, and you'll have no quarrel from me."

"That was honestly spoken, Captain Antero," Garla said. "And I'm your man. On *your* say so now. Not just Pip's."

He looked around at the others. "Do we all agree?" he asked.

The ragged chorus of agreement was quite loud.

In the days that followed, Orissa was struck by the greatest wave of knavery in its history. No lord, lady, or merchant baron could walk a public street with purse or person intact. These were the true knaves, as Garla pointed out. And we punished them severely.

We pilfered their carriages, looted their shops, and when they retreated into their homes, Pip sent his ratboys through the privy entrances and held them hostage while we stole all their worldly goods, carrying the loot away in their own carriages.

The assault was so furious and unprecedented that the nobles and merchants descended on Kato, gnashing their teeth. They demanded that soldiers be deployed, according to our spies. And Director Kato was hard-pressed to explain why he didn't have those soldiers to spare. This was a particularly sore point with the rich families who'd betrayed Orissa's citizens. The expense for keeping the populace down and maintaining the siege at Galana was entirely theirs. They chafed first at the high cost, and second that even with that too dear a cost, they weren't getting their money's worth if they weren't safe in their own homes. Kato promised to do something, but was so vague, our spies said, that the nobles went away grumbling and dissatisfied.

But harassing those rich traitors, satisfying though it might have been, was not my sole purpose. Not by half it wasn't.

What Kato lacked in troops, Novari made up for with an elaborate web of spies. They noted every suspicious act or word, endangering every plan Pip had worked out. I had to tangle that spy network into knots if any plan was to succeed.

The series of raids on the rich was a good start on the job. The peeries were pulled from their normal spidery tasks and hurled into the breach to stem the criminal assault.

At the same time, we created our own network of spies. The beggars and barrow boys and purse cutters were our key to the streets. The jewel thieves and ratboys were our snoops in the enemy's homes. And as the tension among the rich mounted, it spewed out in their vices. The harlots and gamesmen kept us busy listening to their reports from the dark side.

Those initial gains came as much from the new breed of sorcery as from the fervor of Pip's rogues.

I created spells for the pickpockets to make their game easier. Usually they worked in teams: a woman such as Palmer, who looked like a great-eyed innocent waif, and a man such as Lammer, who was fleet of foot. I gave the women charms that would make them seem even more appealing, innocently alluring. And I gave the men amulets that would cloud their victim's mind with greater confusion.

"All I do is gives 'em a bump," Palmer said to me, giggling. "I falls to the street wi' me best maidenly shriek. But makin' sure, yer knows, that I flashes more'n a maiden oughter. An' when they help me up, I makes sure they gets a good grab of me tit."

She winked at me. "It's a fact," she said, "that men got less brains'n women. Let 'em get a holt of a tit and they lose half of that."

Lammer groaned in mock protest. He'd heard this before.

"If I didn't get his purse when I bumped him," Palmer went on, ignoring him, "I gets it fer sure then. What with that spell you give us, they melts in their toes, they do. Dust me off. Feel me up. Try to buy me a little grog to make up fer the accident."

"Whilst she's plyin' her womanly wiles," Lammer broke in, "I rubs the amulet you give us. Say the verse, which I don't understand, but it works so good, who cares? 'N' they go goggle-glimmed 'n' almost ferget their names. Palmer hikes me the purse 'n' I'm off lickety-split wi' no one the wiser."

Palmer slipped a small hand inside her bodice, which was cut just low enough to weaken her prey but high enough to retain her waif-maiden pose. She drew out two sheets of folded paper.

"Someone'll be missin' these real bad about now," she said as she handed them over. "Got 'em off a squint not two hours ago. Bumped into him wi'out really lookin' at his face first. Careless of me, but tha' spell you give me's made things so easy, I'm formin' bad habits." She snorted in disgust with herself. She had a reputation to maintain.

"Anywise, I got his purse like I always do, and the squint's got his glims down me dress an' his hands are comin' up the other way, dustin' me off. Soon as I saw who he was, I got away 'mos' as quick as Lammer."

"It was Calin, it was," Lammer broke in. "Chief peery of the Central Market. Makes him the biggest peery in Orissa. Had those inky bits in his purse."

I hastened to open the papers. These were the documents of the Central Market's master spy.

The first was a list of names in a small cribbed hand. There were numbers beside the names: money amounts.

"That's a list of all a the peeries in Central Market," Palmer said, teeth glittering. " 'N' their pay. That's what old Calin was doin'. Handing out their money and collectin' the news."

"From the fat purse we took off a him," Lammer said, "he didn't get too far today."

I opened the next. It was in an official hand and bore the seal of the Lyre Bird. The document swore that the holder was in the employ of the Goddess Novari and was not to be detained from her business in any way.

"Tha's a pass for the peeries," Palmer said. "Show it to a soldier 'n' they let 'em go."

"Now *that* was a good day's work," I said. "And you can be sure just the right person will get each one."

I gave the list of names to Queenie. And within two days all the spies in the Central Market were gone. Her thugs did such a clean job of it, there wasn't a speck of blood or blurted cry to alarm anyone. Vanishing without a trace.

The second item I used in a duplication spell, creating scores of documents for Pip to hand out to his men and women. And by and by our own peeries were passing through the enemy's defenses like whey through cheesecloth.

I also made potions for the harlots, which they used to spice the wine they gave their marks to put them at ease. The potion made them randy as goats and babbling fools glad to burble secrets into the harlot's perfumed ears. It almost made them permanent customers: They became impotent except in the arms of their favorite whore.

"We've got every whore's rocker in Cheapside bouncin' on its springs all night long," the beauteous Pearl said one day as she poured a sack of jewels and coins into an already overflowing oak chest.

She shook the pouch to loosen a few small stubborn gems. Her lush body jiggled under the sheer wrap, a sensuous reminder of why she was Mistress of her guild.

"Got all this from jus' one panter," she said. "Las' one of the night, thank the gods." She groaned and rubbed her back. "Bumped me till near dawn 'n' was beggin' for more when I threw him outter the carriage.

"The panter said he loves on'y me and give me this." She indicated the pouch, then laughed. "Threw it back in his face and cursed him for bein' so tight-fisted wi' the woman he loves. But with that potion in him, he was whoreified through and through. Begged me to take it back and said he'd bring twice that tonight to make up for it."

Then she sat, crossing her fine, long legs. "But I got more'n that panter's balls in my fist wi' that potion," she said. "He's one a Director Kato's diplomats. Likes to brag on how important he is whilst he's bumpin' my poor arse into the carriage seat. He told me a lot last night about the latest doin's wi' King Solaris."

I jolted in my seat. "The King of Tyrenia?"

"That's what the panter said," Pearl replied. "Seems old Solaris is gettin' real irate about what's goin' on here. Although from what the panter said, Solaris don't know the half of it. All he knows is Kato and Novari are keepin' all the stuff your brother and Janela Greycloak discovered to themselves.

"Solaris says Orissa is violatin' the agreement he made with Amalric Antero. Which was that Orissa would share ever'thin' with all the kingdoms in this part of the world, whilst he did the same where he is. From what the panter said, Solaris is gettin' suspicious that Kato and Novari are makin' some kind a grab. That they'll take over ever'body near Orissa. Then maybe be so swell-noggined they'd try Tyrenia on for size."

I turned to Pip, who was listening to all this closely. "That's not only a possibility," I said, "but I have no doubt this is ultimately Novari's plan. She'll want the whole thing. Not just half of it."

Pip smiled. "I likes what I hears, I does," he said. "Maybe we'll gets some help from King Solaris. He's got a good honest heart, 'n' he won't like what's been done. Especially to you Anteros."

"He's too far away, Pip," I gently reminded him. "It'd take him more than a year to march and sail any kind of force from the Kingdoms of the Night to Orissa. And it'll not only be too late for us, but probably for him. The Lyre Bird will be so powerful by then that he won't have a chance no matter how many soldiers he brings with him."

Pip sighed. "That's true enough," he said. "But it makes old Pip feel better just the same. I'd a been sore diserappointed if King Solaris turned his back on us wi'out even tryin'."

I felt the same way. And although help from afar was impossible, I was comforted by the knowledge that my brother's friend was thinking of us.

I bolstered the wave of knavery with a series of fires aimed at the places the wealthy frequented, such as the fine costume and gem shops near the riverfront and the bathhouses and perfumeries near the Evocators' Palace. I used Queenie's thugs for this, supplying them with little balls of ordinary cotton wrapped about not so ordinary embers. All they had to do was put the cotton ball in a likely spot, find a hiding place—no more than twenty feet away, which was the tricky part—and chant a little spell I'd made them all memorize. The magical ember would burst into a ball of flame which would burn for hours no matter how much water or sand was thrown at it.

Some days they hit so many targets the whole city was filled with columns of smoke and the sound of soldiers fighting the fires.

While all this was going on, I kept waiting for Novari to show herself. If she did and by some wild chance I could get close to her, I might gamble all and strike at her openly.

But she must have sensed something was awry because she even failed to appear at the annual End of Harvest festival. It was a very odd thing for the self-proclaimed new Goddess of Orissa to miss.

It was just as well for her sake that she did, because Pip and I made that festival a bonus day for larceny and violence. We struck all over the city, setting fires, raiding homes, and generally creating a brief reign of terror in the wealthy neighborhoods. Kato was forced to cancel the ceremonies at the Amphitheater and rush soldiers into the neighborhoods. But by then we'd long disappeared into the warrens of the sewers.

Several times I cast spells to seek her. I sent my spirit out in different forms to try to slip up on her unaware. Although her spoor was all about, I couldn't find her through the many layers of confusion she'd piled up to protect herself from just such a search. Each layer contained an alarm spell, which I got past easily enough. But it would've taken weeks to make it through the whole thing—and there was no assurance that in the end she'd actually be there. For the time being I gave up.

I did learn something from the attempts. The confusion shield was not Novari's work alone. I'd sniffed the spoor of at least a score of Evocators who must have worked on it with her. I thought it was interesting that she'd tie up so many wizards she could've used against Palmeras for such a comparatively small purpose.

It made me think of all the other sorcery being used. All the shields and spells and spell sniffers required to keep Orissa under her thumb. All the Evocators required to guard the highways and waterways from smugglers of sorcerous contraband.

It seemed to me that the Lyre Bird's magical forces had been badly stretched even before I arrived. And I was pleased to know that since that time, I'd made her stretch her powers as tight as a sail in a gale-force wind.

Very good. I had her going at breakneck speed.

Now I needed to change her course. I had in mind a nice set of reefs.

* * *

Finally the day came when I could no longer delay pushing forward with the second and most important part of my plan.

I asked Pip to gather his lieutenants, and once they were settled in his chamber—which was crammed even deeper with looted treasures—I rose to speak.

I praised them for their efforts, taking care to address each woman or man and point up a particularly fine deed they'd done. And then when they were all full of good feeling, I said:

"We've hit Novari and Kato hard, there's no doubt about it. And as you all know, this is just the beginning of the arse-kicking we've got planned for them."

This produced loud cheers and many minutes of boasting about deeds yet to be accomplished. The thieves' cant was so thick I could barely decipher it, and what I could was so crude it makes me hesitate to translate further.

When I thought they'd gone on long enough, I raised my golden hand and there was a hush.

"Unfortunately," I said, "I can't stay here with you and see it out."

There were shocked stares all around.

"I have to get to Galana," I said. "I have to help them break the siege. Otherwise, none of this will work."

"All a us knew this time was comin', Cap'n Antero," Pip said. "We jus' didn't know it'd come so soon. Like today, so soon."

"There's something else," I said. "I need you to come with me, Pip."

His first reaction was a grin the size of a giant's warship. He glanced around at his comrades, fairly lighting the chamber with his smile. I knew what he was thinking. He'd be on the road again, seeing whatever was to be seen. Free of all burdens except the immediate journey. Ah, Pip. He had the wanderlust as much as any Antero.

Then he frowned as the full implications sunk in. "But Cap'n," he said, "old Pip can't leave his squints. He's got his responserbilities to think of. As King of Thieves."

"I'll need the king of knaves more than anything else, Pip," I said. "Sorcery and knavery. We make a good pair. Come with me for a while. Get me to Galana. We'll see which way the stick floats. And then you can return to lead the final fight in Orissa."

No one said a word or even raised a questioning eyebrow as Pip considered long and hard.

Then he turned to Garla. "Will yer run things till I get back?" he asked.

The handsome beggar gave a slight bow. "It'd be an honor, Pip," he said. "And don't worry. I'll play straight with everyone. See they get their fair share of the loot and glory."

"Yer better," Pip growled, "or yer'll answer to old Pip."

Then he looked around at the others. "Any objects?" he snarled. "If so, speak now. Or shut yer friggin' yammer fer ever more."

There were none.

"Well, Cap'n Antero," Pip said, "looks like yer got yerself a travelin' mate."

Before we left I asked Garla to help me prepare for the journey. I needed a new disguise. My pose as a pensioned Guardswoman would be useless in the war zone surrounding Galana. If anything, it'd make Kato's and Novari's forces even more suspicious, considering that their main opponents included the Maranon Guard and that the siege itself was centered at a former retreat for old Guardswomen.

I was in the market, and my mind was on the small details of our planning, so I wasn't paying much attention to anyone I passed.

As I turned onto the main street leading into Cheapside, a strange apparition dragged itself out of an alley mouth. It was an old legless man with a wooden plate fastened to his trunk, and he was dragging himself along on his fists, which were protected by thick fingerless gloves. He wore soldier's rags that barely covered horrible seeping wounds on his body. His face was a nightmare of boils and livid scars.

He humped over to me, cackling like an old hen over a fat bug. He stopped, barring my way, and fixed me with a piteous look.

"Give us a copper, Sarn't," he said. "Help a poor brother in need." And he held up a beggar's bowl.

A wave of guilt washed over me. Here I'd been posing as a needy veteran, forgetting that many of my brothers and sisters in arms were true unfortunates. They had no famous name. No one who cared if they lived or died. To most citizens they were a burden they begrudged.

I fished out a handful of coins, with much more silver than copper among them.

"Here yer go, mate," I said, dumping the coins into the bowl. "Have a good drunk on old Sarn't Rali."

The beggar swirled the coins around in the bowl and it made a merry sound. He peered up at me with rheumy eyes. "It's a joy to see, dear Captain," he said, "that your deeds are as generous as your words."

Then he uncurled himself from the platform, standing taller and taller on two fine legs and making a sweeping motion with his hand, peeling away tortured skin and purulent horrors.

And standing before me was the handsome Master of the Beggars' Guild.

"Garla!" I exclaimed.

He bowed low, doffing a wig of dirty gray locks as if it were a fine hat. "One and the same, dear Captain," he said. "One and the same."

I laughed to be played such a trick. I'd known quite well how the Beggars' Guild operated, had seen them in action many times during the past days in all sorts of pitiful costumes. And even if I hadn't known, I had magical powers to see through that kind of artifice. But I'd still been taken in. The impulse to haul out all those coins had been irresistible.

"That was your first lesson in disguise, dear Captain," Garla said. "Now shall we adjourn to my quarters and continue?" He offered the crook of his arm like a noble swain, and his smile was as smooth and charming as Janos Greycloak's.

I laughed again and slapped his arm away. "Don't waste your talents with women on me, Garla," I said. "I'm not so inclined. Flattered, to be sure, that I've drawn the interest of such a handsome fellow. But fellows, handsome or not, are not Rali Antero's drink of preference."

"Why I *knew* that, Captain," Garla said, most sincere. He offered his arm again. "But can't a gentleman still be a gentleman to a lady?"

He took me by such surprise that I giggled like a schoolgirl. Then I bobbed a mock curtsy. A pretty clumsy one, to be sure. I had only a dim memory of such things.

I took his arm, saying, "Lead on, kind sir." Then, "And I hope you have a friggin' drink wherever it is you're taking me."

Garla had more than drink in the underground chambers where the beggars of Orissa reign. There was much light and merry music and laughing and dancing people everywhere. Squealing children raced through the crowd, making the ancient stone chambers seem like a country fair. Everyone was dressed in the brightest costumes, which were festooned with colorful ribbons and scarves and strings of jangling bells.

It was a feast day for the beggars, and they'd all shed their cloaks of misery to celebrate. I made sober notice that among them were many true cripples and unfortunates, so not all presented a false front. These people, though, seemed as cheerful as the rest. And all were made to feel a part of the festivities.

Garla, who'd stripped off the rest of his rags and exchanged them for a soft silk robe, called them all together to meet me. Like any good leader, he was taking advantage of my visit to bolster his people's morale.

They all seemed pleased to see Rali Antero in the flesh and applauded my brief remarks as if every word were a gem.

I tarried a little longer, drinking with them and listening to the music of the strangest group of musicians I'd ever seen. They had the usual assortment of instruments—pipes and drums and bells and lutes. But each musician had an animal accompanying him. While the piper played, a hooded snake lifted from a basket. The drummer had a dancing dog. The others seemed to favor monkeys, which chittered and pranced and leaped about, performing all sorts of comic antics. We were being entertained, it seemed, by the animal charmers of Orissa. And I couldn't remember when I'd had such a good time and heard such joyous music.

Finally we retired to Garla's chambers. They were smaller than Pip's and sparsely decorated, but with such masculine good taste I was reminded of my father's private rooms, where all was burnished wood and soft leather. It had the same comfortable smell and I felt immediately at ease.

I sank into a deep leather chair and accepted a cup of light wine.

"I have to ask you this," I said. "So forgive my curiosity."

Garla raised a hand before I could go on. "You want to know," he said, "how such a fellow as me could turn up in such company."

"To be blunt," I said, "it's obvious you didn't end up with such manners by aping the nobility. They come too natural to you."

Garla chortled. The sound was rich and deep. "There's not much of a mystery to it," he said. "I'm one of those bastard sons of bastard sons whose fathers were bastards by breeding and strayed into the beds of servant wenches.

"The only difference between me and the others is I saw my father worry at his innards like a dog. He was tormented because he was unfairly denied the company of polite society. Drink put him in the streets. And I begged the price of it for him until he died."

Garla shrugged eloquently. "So I found my proper place in life fairly quickly." He raised his crystal cup. "And prospered."

"That explains much," I said.

"If you mean my attitude toward the nobility, whom I despise," he said, "then you are right on the mark. And I see no hypocrisy in it. I don't want what they have. I only want what they refuse others. Which is the respect every common man and woman deserves."

"How *high-minded* of you," I murmured. Using exactly the same tone and smile Garla'd used when he'd said something similar to me.

Garla laughed. "Now, that was a wounding blow, dear Captain," he said. "And a well-deserved one at that."

"Shall we call it *equal*, then?" I laughed.

Garla winced. "I'm twice wounded now, Captain," he said. "And I resign from the field."

We finished our drinks in good cheer and then Garla took me into a small room with a large wardrobe filling most of it. A mirrored dressing table took what was left. It was covered with as many strange pots and vials and jars as a wizard's bench.

Garla studied me critically. "What sort of beggar shall we make you, dear Captain?" he mused. "There's a beggar in all of us, you know.

"Some beg charity, some patience, some beg the gods, some the devils, and some beg your pardon when they cut your throat."

"There's mercy," I said. "You left that off your begging list."

"Oh no, dear Captain," he replied. "If you think there's mercy in this world, you are sadly misinformed."

While I enjoyed that remark he continued studying me. "What we have to discover," he said, "is exactly what kind of beggar's heart beats in the breast of Rali Antero."

I tried to think of different things but came up blank.

Then Garla suddenly snapped his fingers. "I've got it!" he said.

He hunched over, lifting a shoulder so it covered part of his face. His other hand snaked out, fingers crooked like claws. And he said in a high, quavering crone's voice, "Tell yer fortune, Cap'n? Copper fer yer dreams."

"A market witch?" I said, aghast.

Garla dropped the role and straightened up. "What better disguise could there be?" he said. "You can travel where you like. From market to market. Begging coin to tell lies people want to hear. It also seems fitting. An Evocator disguised as a market witch."

"Your attitude is bleeding through again, my friend," I warned.

Garla snickered. "I have to admit the very idea gives me much pleasure," he said. "But truthfully, what better disguise?"

"Fine," I said. "A witch it is, then."

Garla nodded and started digging through the wardrobe, looking for proper witchy rags.

"At least you're not a beggar with a monkey," he said. "You can take comfort in that."

"Actually," I said, "I was thinking of asking you for one."

"A monkey?" he said. "Whatever for? They're dirty little beasts always getting into mischief."

"Then you won't mind very much," I said, "if the monkey you give me comes to some harm."

Garla barked laughter. "Mind?" he said. "I worked with a monkey when I was boy. I hated the thing. Whenever it did something wrong, instead of punishing the animal, my master whipped me."

He shuddered at the memory. "I'll give you a monkey," he said. "And good riddance to it. You can send it into the hells for all I care."

"I'm afraid that's where the poor thing is bound," I said. "Or something quite close to it."

Garla didn't answer. He was unstoppering a wide-mouthed jar. He spilled what looked like little black dots on the table. He picked one up on the end of a finger and turned to me, saying: "Now, hold still. I want to show you how to apply a wart."

The night before I left for Galana, I retired to a dark little room. I'd sent for my horse and the rest of my supplies, some of which I'd used to prepare the spell. There was a pentagram inscribed on the floor with red chalk. In the center was a square chalked in green.

I placed a rickety cage on the square. In it was a small, frightened monkey with large sorrowful eyes and sharp teeth. It chittered hysterically and gnashed at my fingers as I set the cage down.

"I'm sorry, little brother," I said. "I'll do my best to see you come to no harm."

My promise produced an even more hysterical burst of chittering and gnashing. It leaped about the cage like a mad little thing.

I knew how he felt. I'd had similar promises from an all-powerful creature, and look what it had gotten me.

I fed him some orange slices, which seemed to calm him. But the whole time he ate he stared at me with those huge eyes.

I tried to ignore them as I sprinkled the cage with oils and incense.

The monkey stared at me as I chanted:

> "Clever little beast
> With clever little teeth
> And clever little hands.
> No knot can defy you,
> No sorcery can tie you.
> Unbind!
> That is your command!"

Cold flames bloomed up around the cage and the monkey shrieked in fear. I hardened my heart and thrust out my etherhand, stabbing a golden finger at the cage.

"Unbind!" I shouted.

There was a final squeak and the cage jumped as if struck by wind.

The monkey was gone.

I used my ethereye to spy him out in the realm I'd sent him to. I peeped this way and that and then saw his small figure scampering across rolling black clouds. He disappeared into a boiling cloud bank. By the squeal of pure pleasure I heard, I knew he'd found what I'd sent him for: Novari's many-layered spell of confusion.

I heard him chittering as he found the first knot that held the first sorcerous alarm. The chittering became more excited as he dug at it. Clever little teeth helping clever little hands untie first one, then another.

The task would take him many days, perhaps many weeks. In theory the protective spell I'd cloaked him in would keep Novari numbed to what was happening.

And when next I returned to this place, I prayed I'd find the monkey well and the way clear.

Pip and I left the next morning, mingling with the crowd coming into the city. As they poured in, we inched our way against the flow. No one seemed to notice that we were gradually going in the opposite direction.

I'd hitched a little dray to the old mare to carry our belongings, and I'd piled limp old vegetables on top of our baggage to add to our look of innocent poverty.

Pip and I walked at the horse's head, whispering encouragement and apologizing for the indignity of the dray. She was a riding horse, a war-horse, and didn't like dragging anything behind her, except, perhaps, an enemy's body caught in her harness.

Pip wore raggedy breeches and a canvas shirt with a wide belt. I wore a dirty black-hooded cloak that covered me from head to toe. Long gray strands of hair escaped the hood, and my nose poked out, made into a crooked beak by artfully placed clay. On its tip was a big wart with a few hairs glued onto it for effect. I gripped a sturdy walking stick in my etherhand, which was painted corpse-gray, with overly long fingernails glued in place.

When we reached the gate where the crowd was thickest and the guards the most overworked, we reversed our course and acted like we were entering rather than leaving.

A big guard loomed up. Suspicious eyes bored into both of us.

I cackled at him and snatched at his hand. "Tell yer fortune, dearie?" I quavered at him. "Give a poor granny a copper to glim yer palm?"

The guard snatched his hand back. "Keep yer hands off'n me," he growled. "Dirty old witch."

"Here, now," Pip said. "Tha's no way to talk to me poor muvver."

"I'll talk anyways I likes t' anyones I likes," the guard snarled. "Especially to rubbish like yer two."

I snatched at his hand again. "Half a copper, then, dearie," I quavered. "Tell yer if yer sweetheart's pissin' in strange pots fer half a copper."

This was too much for the guard's brutish feelings. He shouted for us to begone and barred us from the city.

"And don't ever try and come this way again," he shouted as we hurried off, me hobbling as fast as I could. "I'll break yer heads if you do!"

I looked back and saw him shaking his fist at us, framed in the arch of the big main gate. Behind him was the Palace of the Evocators, windows glowing in the new light.

I saw a rich carriage roll up to the gate, footmen clubbing the crowd back to make a path. The guards all bowed and scraped as the carriage swept through without delay.

"It's always been like that, hasn't it, Pip?" I said. "Even in the old days. Before Novari and Kato."

"That it has, Cap'n," Pip said. "Rich man prizes his special treatment maybe even more'n his gold. Likes t' see the poor man at his feet. Likes t' see the poor woman on her back. Makes him feel bigger, somehow. Maybe even bigger'n death."

"Garla's right," I said. "Things need to change. But first we have to set this current lot straight."

And off we went to Galana, heroes bold. A crooked old market witch and her doltish son.

I was a fortune-teller who couldn't read her own palm and see the future. I didn't know if I'd win or fail—or if I won, what was in store for Orissa. The rich do not easily share their wealth. The powerful, their power.

I had one consolation, though.

Before I left the city, I went on an orgy of spell-casting. For two days I churned out magical weapons and spells and potions and amulets of every variety a thief could dream of.

I made enough for them to continue the fight after I left. And I made more after that, just in case, filling several large chambers.

And it sits there still. Enough to last for many years of knavery.

It was my way of making things just a little bit more . . . equal.

THE ROAD TO GALANA

We struck east for several leagues, then north on the Great Harvest Road that meanders through the belly of Orissa's finest farmlands and vineyards. It was the longest route to Galana, but for most of the distance it would keep us away from the river, where the heaviest patrols would be. The Harvest Road was also one of several key routes Pip's smugglers used to get crucial supplies to the defenders of Galana. There were rebel supporters spread out along it, although thinly, who could help us along the way.

We spent our first night with one such family. They were servants at a crossroads inn that catered to rich landowners traveling from their Orissan mansions to inspect their farms. We slept in one of the inn's stables on fresh fragrant hay meant for their high-bred horses. We supped on delicacies—scraps from their table. And we shared a fine wine that'd been stolen from the room of a lord who'd been on a drunk for days and would never miss it.

We were disturbed once during the night when the ample-waisted barwoman crept up to our loft to warn us that some men were coming.

"They're friends," she whispered, "so's ya needn't fear. They'll be in 'n' outta here quick. 'N' ya'll soon be puffin' at the rafters ag'in."

We watched from our loft as men in dark cloaks and dimmed lanterns entered the stable. Horses were moved, hay pushed aside, and floorboards lifted. Hidden below were spears and swords and boxes of arrowheads. They quickly gathered the booty up and hauled it away, returning everything to normal when they were done.

One of the men raised a fist to us in a silent salute, then they were gone.

Pip said the weapons would be divided up and taken to local farms where they'd await transport to Galana. "Come outter an armory in Orissa on'y yestiddy," he told me. "Seems on'y fittin' ter use this place fer our first hidey-hole. Kato's darlin's are sleepin' upstairs, whilst we scheme on 'em down in the stables."

We didn't always have such commodious accommodations on our journey. Most of the time we slept rough in a field or wood. Once, we were quartered over a sty. The corn-husk mattresses were comfortable enough, but the smells and sounds of the pigs did not make for pleasant dreams. And when I awoke, the smell was so awful that for a moment I thought I was in long-ago Pisidia, when the flies and fumes from the great tanneries still poisoned the air.

We plodded along the road for many a day. At first there was much traffic—wagons and herdsmen and barefooted lads and maids driving flocks of geese or milk cows to market. They tied their footwear with string and carried it draped about their necks so it wouldn't be ruined by the rough dusty road. And if there was a fair in progress at one of the large villages, the young people would all stop outside to put on their shoes and their best go-to-market clothing.

I got a lot of unintended practice being a market witch with those young people.

"Will he be true, Granny?" a blushing maid might ask, pressing a copper into my hand.

"Does she love me?" a shambling farm lad would plead, shuffling from foot to foot or digging his toes into the dust.

I'd mutter and spit and scratch around the false wart on my nose as I considered, studying their palm and weighing the answer with much cronish concern. The palm studying was only for effect, for with my ethereye I could see such things quite clear in the aura that hovers about us all.

In my answers, however, I was mindful of Garla's instructions.

"No one wants the truth if the news is bad, Captain Antero," he'd said. "Please them with a lying present and let the future work itself out the best it can."

Pip had similar advice. "Talk sweet," he said, " 'n' no one'll note we passed. Talk hard 'n' ever' one'll mark us. Tell all a their friends and family 'bout the witch tha' glimmed dark days ahead. 'Sides, whatsomever you say, bein' young, they'll ignore yer advice 'n' jump whichever way their private parts lead 'em."

Wizards don't mind lies, but they do have pride in their reputations, even if that reputation is going about in disguise. So although I took their advice, I couldn't help but hedge my responses.

If the answer to both of those all-too-typical questions about true love, faithfully kept, was yes, I'd make a big show in my delivery.

"Aye, yer a lucky one, dearie," I'd say, sniffling and blubbering as if my old crone's heart had been touched from being in the presence of so much youthful romance. "Yer'll have nothin' but love from that one. An' yer can mark this granny's word on that. 'N' if yer keep yer bed willin' an' never let a harsh word rest between yer ov'rnight, that love'll be true fer the rest of yer life."

I'd had similar advice from grannies in my wild youth, and it still seemed sound enough. If not, it was harmless.

If the answer was no, I'd make less of a fuss. And I'd hedge. "Oh, I see love there, dearie, I do. 'N' it's faithful enough, I reckon. Only mind tha' it's yer heart I'm seein'. Not yer intended's. Yer'd have to bring 'em by fer me to be certain."

This satisfied most. And for those it didn't, Pip and I would be long gone before they brought their false lover around for a second casting.

But the questions weren't always so easy to skirt, and sometimes the necessary lies were too bitter for my tongue.

One day about halfway through our journey we tarried at a fair. We were waiting to meet a supporter whom Pip said would know what difficulties we'd face along the road just ahead.

The man never turned up, and along about dusk Pip was packing our things in the dray to leave when a stocky farm woman of some forty summers approached. She had a tall skinny lad gripped tightly by the hand and was dragging him along like a stubborn yearling horse.

She shoved him in front of me, saying, "I want'cher to put my young Natt straight, Granny." And she slapped two silver pieces onto the dray's gate with such force that it startled the horse.

I twisted my face and scratched my nose and hawked and spit in the dust. I'd slipped thoroughly into my role as a market witch by then—and was even beginning to enjoy it.

"Put him straight abou' what, dearie?" I cackled.

The woman gave me a look like I was the most ignorant mortal the world has known. "About soldierin', is what!" she snapped. "War and soldierin' and gettin' tucked inta his grave afore his time. Me and me dear husban'—may he be restin' easy with the gods, bless his soul—fed him 'n' clothed him 'n' raised him to be a good boy 'n' mind his manners."

She pointed at the silver coins.

"I wants a special casting, Granny," she said. "And I know such a thing is dear. Can't get it fer a copper, yer can't. But I'm willin' to pay whatever it takes to keep this lad home."

"Muvver, please!" young Natt protested. "I'm growed now. A man. You gotta let me be."

She swatted his arm and he yelped. "Sure, I'll let ya be! Soon's ya come to yas senses, I will." She swatted him again, producing another howl. "Ya may be the death of yas old muvver first. But I'd rather be dead 'n' cold than see a son of mine throw his life away!"

And then she burst into tears, shaking and bawling like an old cow past bearing age who's just lost her last calf to the wolves.

Young Natt squirmed in embarrassment. He tried putting a hand on his mother's shoulder, but she shook it off, crying all the harder.

Pip strolled over, quite casual like. "What's up, lad?" he asked. "What'cha do to make yer muvver cry so?"

"Nothin' but what's natural," young Natt said, stubborn jaw thrust forward. "Director Kato and the Goddess Novari are askin' the help of all a lads of Orissa."

He pointed north. "They needs more soldiers to fight the rebels at Galana," he said. "Offerin' a good bonus, too. One gold piece fer ever' volunteer."

Young Natt turned to his mother. "A gold piece, muvver!" he exclaimed. "Think a all yas can do wi' so much money!"

But she only wailed more.

The lad sighed and addressed Pip and me. "Time's been hard since me favver died," he said. "Hearth's so old it's all choked up. Smoke's somethin' fierce. Hadda sell off too much land. Now we can't grow 'nough to feed ourselfs. Much less buy seed fer next year. But that gold piece they're offerin' will set things right. I'm young. Can't farm. But I can soldier. And that's what they wants."

"Yer must admire Kato 'n' Novari somethin' fierce," Pip said, "to break yer muvver's heart like this."

Young Natt shrugged. "Don't know much about 'em," he said. "What's the difference?"

"There's people dyin' at Galana on the other side," Pip said, "tha' must think there's a difference. A mos' remarkable difference, from what Pip hears."

Young Natt glared at Pip. "Ya wouldn't be one a *them*, wouldja?" he asked accusingly. "Or maybe a symperthizer."

"Only person I'm symperthizin' with jus' now," Pip said, "is yer poor muvver. Cryin' her eyes out fer fear of losin' one a her sons."

"My *only* son!" the woman bawled. "Ain't gotta daughter, either. 'N' the gods know I would'na be grievin' like this if I'd a been blessed with a daughter."

"Muvver, please!" young Natt protested again. "Not in front a ever'body. Yer embarrassin' me!"

I picked up the two silver coins. "Lotta shine to this money, dearie," I said to his mother, "fer a poor widder woman."

"It's all I got," she said, sniffling and drying her eyes. "We was savin' it fer really bad times. Which finally come when my young Natt, here, gets it in his thick skull that he's gonna go fight some villains' war.

"I tells ya, I'd sell this fat old body a mine at the local brothel if it'd stop him. If anybody could stomach me, that is."

"Ya can't know somethin's gonna happen to me, muvver," young Natt said. "I'll be fine. You'll see. There's lots of other lads fightin'. It'll be some a them what gets it, not your young Natt who loves ya."

Naturally all this produced was another tearful gale.

So I cackled my best witchy cackle, flipped the coins to Pip and clutched at young Natt's hand.

"Give us a peek then, dearie," I croaked. "See if there's graves ahead or babes ahead fer the likes a young Natt."

He tried to pull back but I dug my long nails into his palm, trapping him.

"Don't fret, laddie child," I said. "Granny won't hurt'cha. Sweet little thing like you. Make a girl's heart melt like honey, Granny bets you do."

He struggled more, but his mother swatted the back of his head. "Stay still," she commanded. "Let her look. See what'll happen if ya goes soldierin' over yas poor muvver's wishes."

"What if she don't see nuffin'?" Natt asked, suddenly sharp. "Will yas let me go?"

The woman hesitated. She looked at me, and while she looked Pip slipped the silver pieces into her apron pocket. She wouldn't find them there until she got home.

Finally she said, "Will yas give us the truth, Granny? Will yas at least promise me that? If yas don't have the Second Sight, will yas tell me now? Keep the money, gods love yas. Jus' tell me true. Can yas do it, Granny? Can yas really see Natt's future?"

I felt a tear well in my own eye. I coughed and spit into the dust.

"Granny can see, dearie," I assured her. "She can see quite clear." I pulled aside my hood, showing my eyepatch. "She's got Second Sight. And Third Sight as well . . ."

I spread young Natt's palm open and chanted:

> "One eye t' see outward.
> One t' see inward.
> And one t' see all around and around.
> I can see Natt's birth—
> Still tied t' his muvver.
> See the cord cut—
> Knife t' his favver.
> Bury it deep.
> So the ghosts can't find it.
> Whippoorwill.
> And the crickets call.
> Will Natt live?
> Or will Natt fall?"

The vision descended on me like the Dark Seeker's cloak. It was night and there was fire on the hilltops. I was astride a horse shouting my battle cry and charging through a wall of enemy pikes. Men and women were screaming and dying all around me, and I was wounded and I hurt and I flailed about with my sword, turning pain into strength. Faces jumped up and I cut them down. Hands grabbed for my legs and I slashed them away. Then the pike line wavered and broke and I shouted in victory as my horse plunged through. Charging for those fiery hilltops where Quatervals waited.

Someone jumped up in front of me, jabbing with a long pike. The moment froze and I could see him clear. He was tall and so painfully thin that his rusted breastplate would barely stay on.

It was young Natt with a thin black streak for a mustache and there was fear in his eyes and he was bawling for his "muvver" but he kept coming with that pike—sure he'd die if he didn't kill me first. I tried to rein in, tried to stop the course of my blade, but then the moment unstuck and my horse was rushing forward, my sword was cutting down, and there was a bump and a wail and then I heard young Natt screaming his last as my horse ran over him.

The vision passed as suddenly and violently as it came and I was gasping in clean air without the taint of death and battle. I was still clutching young Natt's hands and his mother was saying, "Go on, Granny. Tell us what'cha see."

I dropped the lad's hand, breathing in deeply to get my weather anchor set. When I recovered I said, "Don't go, young Natt. Don't go."

His mother clapped her hands and cried out in joy.

But Natt wasn't satisfied. "What didja see, Granny?"

"I saw yer die, Natt," I said. "I saw yer die at Galana."

I started to turn away but he grabbed my sleeve.

"I don't believe it," he said. "Yas're makin' it up. Jus' t' please me muvver."

"She promised the truth, young Natt," his mother said. "'N' that's what we gots. Now, yas gave me yas promise. So let's go home now, where yas belong."

"I still say she was lyin'," Natt shouted. He pointed at both of us, voice loud and accusing. "They're rebels," he said. "Can't be any other reason."

Pip came up to the lad quick, pinching the flesh on the back of his arm to make him mind.

"Watch what'cher sayin', son," he said. "Yer's don't want ter get innercent folks hurt."

"She said I was gonna die," young Natt said, tones full of youthful outrage.

"Only if yer go to Galana, dearie," I said. "On'y then. Go home'n yer'll be safe from harm."

"I oughter tell the guard," young Natt said. "Report yas fer discouragin' lads from helpin' Novari's cause."

"Yas'll do nothin' of the kind," his mother said, taking him from Pip and pulling him back down the road. "Yas'll stay with me like yas promised. So come along now, young Natt, and leave these nice people alone."

Soon as they were out of sight we threw the rest of our things in the dray and took off as fast as we could.

An hour or so later we thought we were safe and slowed our pace.

"Might a been a good time fer a little lie, Cap'n," Pip observed, dry. "Lad's sure t' tell. Jus' like he's sure t' go t' Galana. No matter what his muvver says."

And I said, "I saw him die there, Pip."

"I'm sorry for him, then," Pip said.

My answer came out hoarse, as a lump suddenly formed in my throat. "But it's *me* who's going to kill him."

Pip was silent. He looked at me, then up the Great Harvest Road where Galana and our destiny waited. "Well, Cap'n," he said at last. "If I see him there, I'll kill him first and take the sin. And damn the lad fer makin' me do it."

Then we heard horses behind us. We got off the road in a hurry. I cast a spell to hide us, and no sooner had I done so when a dozen troops flying the Lyre Bird's standard rumbled into sight. It was a hunting party, moving fast. And we both had no doubt they were hunting a market witch who had told one truth too many.

After they'd passed, Pip said dryly, "I ain't no witch, Cap'n. But right now, old Pip fears fer young Natt's future. 'N' playin' the snitch ain't a real good start on it."

The late fall warm spell bid us farewell the following day. The skies became troubled, showers were frequent, and there was the beginning of a nip to the air.

But what was a "nip" for me was something much more for Pip.

He shrugged into a sheepskin coat, hugging it close as we plodded along, doing our best to avoid the big mud puddles forming on the road.

"Never liked the cold, Cap'n," he said. "If this was the old days, I'd a been whinin' t' yer brother about bonus pay t' compenserate me fer me sufferin'."

"Don't try it on me, Pip," I said, draping a wool scarf about my neck as my only consolation to the change in weather. "I *know* what cold is. This isn't cold. This is summer where I come from. Now is when we plow the ice and plant the 'bergs."

"Yer gotter hard heart, Cap'n," he said. "Makin' jokes at poor old Pip's expense. But facts be facts. It's colder'n a wizard's pizzle, 'n' there's no denyin' it." He pointed to a low bank of black clouds blowing in from the north. " 'N' it looks like it's gonna get worse, by 'n' by."

I studied the clouds, wondering if they were a harbinger of an early winter. Despite my teasing comments, I was worried this might be the first winter storm Maranonia had warned was my deadline. Then a bright orange light burst out of the clouds, followed by an eerie sound that seemed like many wailing voices. The black clouds rolled along the ground toward us.

"That's no storm, Pip," I said grimly.

The first tendrils reached us, filling our lungs with a bitter acrid stench. It choked us, searing our throats and making us weep. The horse reared in its traces, nearly knocking the dray over. We fought for breath and struggled with the horse at the same time. The wails were now horrific screams, and the stench was that of burning flesh. Then the wind shifted, blowing the clouds away. We dragged in shuddering breaths, patting the horse and trying to choke out soothing words.

The strange cloud bank had vanished, but so had the sun. The skies were leaden, with an odd glaring cast to them that made the green countryside seem suddenly menacing. The wailing sound was gone, but there was an insistent thrumming in the air. Like a fire in an overheated hearth. Even Pip, who had no magical senses, knew it was war's ghastly shadow show we were witnessing.

"We'd best hasten, Cap'n," he said. "Folks are dyin' at Galana."

From that point onward the signs of the long siege were plain. Villages and farms were abandoned. Grazing land was empty. Fields and orchards were stripped of all produce, forests leveled for campfires—all to supply Kato and Novari's soldiers as they hammered at the gates of Galana.

The sky itself was a mirror of that distant fight. Strange lights and fearsome shadows did a deadly dance in the heavens by day. And at night the moon and stars were captive witnesses to the sorcerous battle raging between the Lyre Bird's Evocators and Palmeras.

Demons on demon steeds grappled with many-headed monsters. Fire-spitting lizards locked with giant armored warriors. And packs of jackal-visaged men hunted the night skies, filling the air with their blood-chilling howls.

I cast spells to make us seem unimportant to any of Novari's wizard warriors, but the scale of the battle was so large that we felt as insignificant in the flesh as I made our spirits appear.

We ran into a few patrols, but they were so busy scavenging for food and fuel that they took little notice of us.

Pip used an old horse thief's trick to make our old mare appear diseased, which discouraged any who might see her as dinner on the hoof. And we appeared so poor that even the greediest soldier didn't think to shake us down for rations.

Once, a patrol tried to take the dray from us to break up for firewood. But I spit and cursed and threatened to turn their pricks into mop strings. At the same time I sent a real spell to shrivel their balls with a warning chill. They hastened away, not daring to turn their heads as I howled a stream of invectives.

The closer we came to Galana, the worse all appeared. The whole landscape became a smoking ruin, and the skies were a molten caldron of battle spells.

A day out of Galana we took another road, which made a wide loop around the settlement. It intersected with the river at a small port village a few leagues above the fighting. Our intention was to strike south from there, coming in from a direction where we hoped there was more chance of meeting friend than foe.

There was nothing left of the little port but charred posts and broken pavement.

Instead of taking the road out of town to Galana, Pip made a detour to the river. The docks had been broken up, leaving only a few jagged piles poking up out of the water. The only boats to be seen were stove-in scows too waterlogged to be burned.

We let the mare drink and stood on the bank in silence, staring at the dark currents rolling by. A feeling of immense sorrow came over me. I could hear voices, very faint and far away but at the same time seeming close, nibbling at the edges.

"This be where Kele died, Cap'n," Pip said, low.

There was a knot in my throat. I coughed, trying to clear it.

"She put Emilie down just below Galana," Pip said. "Then, whilst some other brave souls carried the child off, she retreated up the river. Fightin' all the way. Drawin' the villains wi' her."

He pointed at the small harbor and destroyed docks. "Caught old Kele there, they did," he said. He pointed at the ruined town. "They'd already taken and burnt the port, so they had her pinned 'tween the river 'n' the land. A fight commenced. Most fierce it was.

"Kele 'n' all the rest were killed in it. But they took lots of villains wi' them, Cap'n. Kele made 'em pay most dear, she did. Most dear, indeed."

He turned away. "Sorry, Cap'n," he said. "Jus' wanted t' pay me respects t' an old comrade in arms. She'd do the same fer me."

That night, we came to the hills that guard Galana's back. The whole sky was aglow with the fighting. Thunder boomed beyond the hills, and the higher we climbed, the more distinct became the shouted battle cries and clashing weapons.

Then the heavens opened up and rain poured down, turning the road into a river of mud. We struggled for what seemed like an eternity, stopping constantly to lift the dray out of the mud or to help the horse over a difficult section.

Finally we came to the top of the hill. We paused beneath the shelter of high-piled boulders and looked down at the valley below. Lightning crashed and balls of sorcerous fire exploded overhead, illuminating the scene.

Just beneath us, crouched in the hard-driving rain, was Galana itself. In the intermittent light I could make out sharpened timbers and guard towers where a fortress wall had been thrown up. I could see the barracks that'd once been home to my warrior sisters who'd grown too old to fight. A crash of lightning showed me the spire of the small temple to Maranonia, where the goddess had first appeared to me. I saw the glowing mouths of caves along a low hillside where our comrades had dug in.

Pip gripped my arm to get my attention, and as I looked, the gates of the fortress swung open and scores of defenders swarmed out. I could hear their screams of defiance above the roar of battle and see their spear points glittering like forged teeth as they charged a mass of soldiers.

The two lines met, crashing together like waves on an opposite course. My blood raced as I saw the enemy line bow under the weight of the furious assault. Off to the sides I saw reinforcement columns of enemy troops slog through the mud to stop the breach.

Pip squeezed my arm tighter. "Those sons a poxed whores ain't gonner make it in time, Cap'n," he chortled. "Novari's lads are gonner get their arses kicked tonight."

Then we heard music. Lyre music. It began with a sharp single note that cut through battle and storm. Then it was a shower of notes. And the shower became a torrent. And that torrent became a river of fierce music, wrenching all senses with its force.

The rain suddenly stopped, but the clouds churned about, scudding and bumping across the sky. Lightning cracked out when they touched, jagged spears that were hurled downward to blast among the battling troops.

Enemy and friend alike were lifted up and hurled aside by the lightning strokes. I could hear nothing but the lyre music underscored by the crashing bolts.

The violence of it drove us back from the hilltop. It doubled us over and we spewed our guts onto the stones. I forced myself up, groaning under the sorcerous weight. I raised my etherhand and gritted out a shielding spell.

The weight lifted and the hammering ceased and I could breathe easily again. I helped Pip up, but he paid me no mind and ran back to the edge to see what was happening. I shifted the shield to keep him under it and shouted for him not to stray too far. I could only protect so much ground without giving my presence away.

I went to Pip and stood with him to watch the carnage below. The lightning had stopped and I could see the troops regrouping. The enemy reinforcements rushed in just then, and our own troops were falling back to the gates of Galana.

I saw the defenders charge out to play rearguard while the main force withdrew through the gates. But the enemy's crush, driven harder by the Lyre Bird's mad song, was overwhelming the retreat. In a moment all would be lost and the enemy would break through the line and into Galana itself.

Suddenly, out of the gates burst packs of immense dogs with teeth as long as cave lizards. They had huge spiked collars with fire shooting off those spikes, and they plunged into the advancing enemy line and savaged it. The troops scrambled back to escape the slavering dogs, but the lyre music shrilled and they soon rallied and fought back. The dogs were overwhelmed by a series of concentrated and well-organized attacks.

And then the enemy turned to finish the job. But it was too late and the gates were crashing closed.

They charged, hoping to break through while the bars were being rammed into place. Galana's defenders were ready, pouring hot oil and molten metal into their ranks. They fell back, dragging their wounded with them.

Then the music stopped.

And the battle was over.

We watched the enemy troops march off the field, thick columns of troops and equipment dispersing into the hills ringing Galana.

And we saw Galana's defenders come out to get their own wounded and dead.

The clouds blew away, letting bright moonlight puddle through. I saw a glowing form swoop across the sky, riding the underbelly of the fleeing black cloud banks and heading toward Orissa. My ethereye caught the great flaming aura surrounding the flying figure. I saw the wide wings and the graceful tail.

"It's her, Pip," I said. "The Lyre Bird." I gritted my teeth in fury. "If she were only closer. By the gods, I'd be a fool to show myself. But I'd trade my other hand for a chance at her."

"Go easy, Cap'n," Pip said. "Yer said yerself she's got two hundred or more Evocators behind her. Yer'd never stand a chance."

He patted me on the shoulder, soothing. "If'n it was one on one, I'd say be a fool. But yer'd be fightin' two hundred and one, Cap'n. 'N' them's worse odds'n any dice game in Cheapside."

I slumped down on a boulder—so hard it bruised a haunch.

"We'll go down and see Quatervals 'n' Palmeras in the mornin', Cap'n," Pip said. "See what's what." He started making a cold camp. "Don't want t' surprise our mates just now," he said. "They're likely t' be edgy. Might not be able to separate friend from foe that quick like."

"They're in worse shape than I thought," I said.

"They made a good 'nough showin' fer themselves," Pip said.

"That had all the marks of a desperation attack," I said. "They were trying to catch the other side by surprise and didn't have the muscle or the magic for it. Those dogs were a good trick, but it was only a trick. Palmeras thought fast. Unfortunately, he doesn't have Novari's resources. Or her huge stable of Evocators to help him. I could feel the difference. And it was large, believe me. Very large."

"Yer'll soon be there, Cap'n," Pip pointed out. "They'll have yer powers to draw on, won't they?"

"It might not be enough, Pip," I said. "I can tilt the odds. If I'm lucky I might even get a small edge. But it's going to take more than luck to win this."

"Yer could be right, Cap'n," Pip said. "Howsomev'r, in all me long years, I never once turned my back on luck. She's got old Pip this far, she has."

He tapped his head. " 'Course it don't hurt t' use yer noggin. 'Cause smart luck's more certain than dumb luck, as me dear old granny used t' say."

I slept only a few hours that night but I slept deeply, and when dawn broke I awoke refreshed and ready to face whatever might come.

I found a small pool of clear cold water. I used a cream that Garla had given me to wipe away the paint and market witch's makeup. I scrubbed my skin until it was pink, then unpacked the costume I'd been saving since I left Salimar's side so many months ago.

It was the ceremonial uniform of the Maranon Guardswoman: gleaming boots, white tunic, polished harness bearing sword and dagger, a golden cloak, and a wide gold band about my head. I wore the spear and torch earrings to honor the goddess, although in my heart I didn't believe she deserved it.

Pip caught his breath when he saw me.

With my golden hand and rakish eyepatch, it seems I made a sight strange enough to jolt even the King of Thieves.

"Yer look like the avengin' angel of the goddess herself," he said.

"I suppose that's what I am, Pip," I said.

Then I clapped him on the back to put him at ease.

"But if I start to spit and scratch my nose like a market witch," I said, "give me a pinch. We avenging angels have to keep up appearances, you know."

Pip used a smuggler's hand mirror to signal Galana. A rapid exchange of light bursts ensued. They were surprised that the King of Thieves himself was present. A party was sent to fetch us. There were two fine horses for us to ride—Pip'd said he was accompanied by an even more important visitor than himself. But I felt sorry for the old mare who'd put up with the indignity of hauling that dray for so long.

She'd had a long, honorable career on the battlefields, and I felt mean for insulting her dignity. So I cleaned her up, put on the good saddle and bridle I'd hidden in the dray, and mounted her.

She tossed her head and stepped high as we came down the hill. Snorting and proud and dismissive of the lesser four-footed creatures who plodded along with us.

We were led on a complicated route, full of switchbacks and stream crossings, using every bit of cover available. Finally we were at the gates of Galana and they were swinging open.

Four people led the crowd that greeted us.

One was a tall, rangy soldier with a dark beard flecked with gray. His face was tanned and lined from many years in the elements. He had the rank tabs of a general.

There was no mistaking that he was Quatervals.

The second person was as tall as the first but so slender that he seemed larger. His face was long with a jutting black beard. He had yellow eyes and wore the robes and crown of the Chief Evocator.

He could be no one but Palmeras.

The third—wearing tabs declaring her Captain of the Maranon Guard—towered over even those two tall men. She was nearly seven feet high, with an hourglass figure that carried her armor with ease. She had light brown hair and fair skin and I saw with a shock that she resembled Polillo. Slightly smaller, hair just a little lighter, but they could have been sisters.

I gaped at her, wondering who she could be.

Then my eyes went down.

For clutching the woman's hand was a small child, made to appear almost like a doll standing next to the giantess.

As soon as I saw her I forgot the others, staring in wonder at the lovely little figure, formed so delicately it seemed only an artist could have made her.

She had porcelain skin framed by dark red hair, and she had eyes the color of sun-kissed seas.

Amalric's eyes. Amalric's hair.

I felt a magical touch like a butterfly's kiss. I smelled flowers and innocence and coltish curiosity as tender little fingers explored my aura.

I dismounted and the child let go the warrior woman's hand and came toward me.

We looked at each other, one marveling at the other.

Then I knelt down. "Hello, Emilie," I said. "I've come a long way to see you."

The child's eyes widened as if in sudden recognition. She smiled, lighting up the whole world with that smile. And she turned to the others, saying, "Don't you know her? It's Aunt Rali, everyone!

"My aunt Rali!"

CHAPTER NINETEEN

EMILIE

I won't gush about the moment. I won't grind that grain in Emotion's mills. I won't stain these pages with tears in remembrance of that glad greeting. Or tell you that as soon as she came into my arms, I felt Emilie was the daughter I never had.

I am a soldier. And a soldier is easily moved to sentiment. I am a wizard. And a wizard is more vulnerable to sentiment's thrust than you know.

She was the child of a man I never met: my nephew Hermias. But she had the face of the first and only child I ever loved: my brother Amalric.

I embraced her. I murmured glad things in her ear. Yet I checked feeling's gates, because to unleash that flood might prevent me from performing my task.

She had the Power, by the gods! There was no denying the strength hiding in Emilie's frail body. I could feel its sorcerous pulse beating under my etherhand, see with my ethereye the shower of sparks it hurled off. We embraced in this world, touched magical fingers in the next. And I could sense the fear in her. There was also a bursting sense of curiosity that would soon carry her past that fear. But in these times and in this place I knew she'd be sadly disappointed by what she would find.

For I had no choice but to make Emilie the first recruit in my war against Novari.

* * *

The next hours were too complicated to relate clearly. There was a muddy confusion of too many people saying too many things.

Identities were sorted out. The child's blurted remarks were confirmed by Pip, double confirmed by Palmeras' sorcery. And there was a great deal of exclaimed wonderment and unintelligible babble about the miraculous return of Rali Antero.

After so long a siege, Galana was eager for an excuse to proclaim joy. They all poured out of the chambers they'd quarried into the hillside for quarters and supply rooms.

Scarce supplies of food and drink were spent in a celebration lasting into the night. Then bonfires were lit and music was played and dances were danced—all out in the open under the stars in defiance of the enemy, whose campfires winked on distant hills and were so numerous that I first thought they were a cloud of mysterious, low-hanging stars.

I felt better when Quatervals said the celebration was loud and joyous enough to curse our enemy with a sleepless night worrying how much spirit was left in an army the leaders said was near defeat.

The whole time, Emilie clutched my hand, letting go only when nature presented its rude features. Even then I had to accompany her to the latrine and stand outside until she was done.

When she grew sleepy I carried her to her quarters, which were at the end of a long, winding corridor cut deep into the hill. I carried her past women with steely hair and steely eyes and swords gripped in big-knuckled fists. Women who'd sworn to Maranonia and taken a private oath as well that Emilie would live to celebrate the seventh winter of her birth.

Emilie became quite alert when I tucked her in.

"I knew you were coming, Aunt Rali," she said. She shivered and pulled the quilt tight. "You were in a cold place. The lady showed me. She was very beautiful. But she scared me.

"She woke me up. And said I had to help her wake you up. And then she showed me."

"What did she show you, my dear?" I asked.

"First you were in a warm place," Emilie answered. "And you were happy. I saw you with someone. Someone special to you, I think."

The little girl scratched at the quilt in embarrassment. "You kissed her . . . and stuff. And I felt you were happy. So happy I wanted to be with you.

"But then the beautiful lady said that wasn't really where you lived. That it was a dream. A very long dream.

"And then she showed me. A cold place. Ice everywhere. And a tomb. And you were inside it. Next to that woman I saw you being happy with."

"Her name is Salimar," I said. "And she's a queen."

Tears welled up in Emilie's eyes. "If she's a queen," she said, "she should've ordered the lady to stop."

She lowered her head. "I said it wasn't right to wake you up. You were so happy."

I patted her hand, careful to use my mortal one. "That's all right, Emilie," I said. "It wasn't your fault. Besides, I was the only one left who could help."

"Did you *see* me?" she asked, eyes as wide as the vistas only caravans witness. "Right after she woke me up that . . . *thing* . . . that . . . woman thing . . . tried to get me. There was fighting. People hurting. And getting deaded. And other . . . I don't know . . . stuff, is all. Bad stuff. Like dreams that are real and can hurt."

Her troubled little face suddenly brightened. "I wasn't afraid very long," she said.

She waved a hand and I felt a surge of power. "Sometimes I can make things go away that I don't like. So I made them go away. The woman thing didn't like it. And that made me glad."

She frowned. "But I still had to wake you up. And make you leave that happy place."

Emilie looked up at me with those clear sunny eyes. "Can I go there someday?"

I had to answer honestly. "I don't know, Emilie," I said. "But I don't think so. Not for a very long time, anyway."

"I miss my mother," she said calmly. A fact being noted, not a complaint. "Was she there?"

"No, my dear," I said. "She's probably with *my* mother. They have a special place for mothers, you know."

Emilie shook her head. "Just *some* mothers," she said. "I know where your mother is. She came once. Palmeras said she was a ghost. But I don't think so. Ghosts are unhappy. I see them all the time. Your mother wasn't unhappy. Just worried.

"She came after the beautiful woman made me wake you up. She said not to be afraid. That my aunt Rali was coming. And that your name—Rali—meant hope. Hope for everyone. But especially for me, because I was named after her. Emilie. That's your mother's name, isn't it? Emilie?"

"Yes it is, dear," I said. "And do you know who she was? Besides my mother, I mean?"

"No. Tell me, please."

So I told her the old familiar story. The one I'd told Amalric with many embellishments over the years. She'd died when he was but a babe—like little Emilie's own mother. And so the tale needed much repeating to make her real to such a small lonely boy.

I told her about the village of my mother's birth. The place the panther girl saved, although she'd been spurned by the very people she later helped. I told her about the wise and beautiful woman who was patient with my young fury and guided it to sounder ground. She'd helped me become a woman of note amongst a people who gave our sex small value. I didn't mention the other, all too adult, yearnings she helped me to recognize as normal—if anything human can ever achieve that state. Emilie was too young, I thought, to stray into the boggy realm of love and sex.

But little Emilie said, "You're thinking about . . . goyshy stuff. Like when I saw you kissing . . . Salimar. You don't have to talk about it. That's okay. Even if it's kind of crazy."

She made a face. "Kissing's okay. I guess. And gooshy's okay. I guess. Derlina says I'll know all about it when the time's right. And maybe I'll love a boy best. And maybe I'll love a girl best. But Derlina says that either way it's all a big waste of time. And that any time I think about it, I should practice with my sword. Because that's the only friend I've really got. And I guess she should know, 'cause Derlina's the best soldier there is. Captain of the Maranon Guard."

Captain Derlina, I gathered, was the giant woman I'd seen who'd resembled Polillo.

Emilie curled a lip. "I don't think about gooshy stuff very much," she said. "So I'm not very good with a sword."

She touched my etherhand and I felt a surge of energy jolt through.

"But sometimes I'm good at other stuff," she said. "Sometimes I can make bad things taste good. Like when the rations get old and rotten. I make everybody happy when I do that. And sometimes I can make good things bad. Like when Derlina drinks too much and gets crazy. I make her stop. Make the drink taste like"—and she wrinkled her nose—"a deaded fish.

"I can do other things. But just sometimes. I can make the sun feel cold a little bit." She sighed. "It's hard. But I can do it if I want to. I make a shadow. And it's cold. Then I make the shadow go away. And it's warm."

She shrugged. "It's boring," she said. "But it makes Palmeras happy. He's my teacher. So it's good to make him happy."

She yawned, the day's events finally catching up to her.

"Did you really beat the Archons?" she asked.

I said I had.

"And you beat that . . . woman thing, too. Once before. Didn't you?"

"Yes," I said. "I did. Her name is Novari. You should know that."

Emilie yawned deeper. "Oh, I know her name. I just hate to say it. I think it gives her . . . power . . . when I say it. So I don't very much.

"Sometimes she looks like a woman. Sometimes like a big bird. And she plays that music. Everybody says it's wonderful music. But I think it's ugly. And someday when she's playing it, I'll reach right out and I'll break all of her strings. And then people won't think she's so great anymore."

Then her eyes closed and she mumbled about this and mumbled about that. And before long the mumbles became a breeze fluttering through her bee-stung lips. And the scent of her breath was innocent milk.

Before I withdrew she whispered out of her child's dream, "I'm sorry I woke you up, Aunt Rali."

Derlina was waiting for me outside Emilie's chamber. She sniffed and knuckled a tear from her eye.

"Couldn't help but look in, Captain," she said, voice hoarse.

"Call me Rali," I said.

She bobbed her big head. "Rali, then. Anyway, I peeked in and saw you and little Emilie. And the poor little motherless, fatherless thing looked so happy to see her aunt Rali that I just about broke down."

She dabbed at another tear with a knuckle. There was a sound in the hallway and she swung her head fast. It was only a guard shuffling by, so she turned back. Then she looked a little shamefaced.

"I'd take it as a favor from one sister to another," she said, "if you sort of forgot to mention my weepy spell."

She flashed a dazzling smile. "Recruits call me Hard-hearted Derlina behind my back," she said. "And I wouldn't want to spoil my reputation."

"Your reputation is safe with me," I said. "I've long experience with a person you remind me of very much."

We started along the corridor. Derlina was escorting me to a late meeting with Galana's leaders.

"I thought I heard you say something regarding that when we met," she said, brow furrowed. "Polillo, you said. And I said no, I'm Derlina. You're thinking of the one they made statues of. My great-aunt Polillo. Some people say we look alike." Her frown deepened. "Usually recruits trying to get on my good side, I suspect."

"You not only look like Polillo," I replied. "But you sound like Polillo. Right down to the hard surface and soft center."

Her smile blazed anew. "Do I now?" she roared, and slapped me on the back with a blow that could've felled an ox team, except she remembered her strength and pulled back just in time.

"Sorry," she said. "Do I really look like my great-aunt Polillo?"

"Almost exactly," I said. "And no one would know better than me. Polillo and I practically grew up together, you know. Signed up with the Guard on the same day."

"Along with Corais," Derlina said, nodding. "It was Rali, Polillo, and Corais. The greatest three in the greatest class in the history of the Maranon Guard."

She laughed. The same rich earthy laugh Polillo had. I shivered. It was uncanny.

"You've been a hard lot to live up to," she said. "Don't know how many women have been cursed as laggards by countless drill sergeants who said how dare they insult the Maranon Guard with their maggoty presence. Taking up space where the three greatest warriors in history—Rali, Polillo, and Corais—once stood."

I snickered. "In our day," I said, "we were called the three worst to ever have blackened the Guard's name. And I must admit that in our green years we broke more heads in Cheapside grogshops than we did on the battle-field."

"I've heard that, too," she said, laughing low. "In some of those very same grogshops. Some of them carry your names. And there's friezes on the walls of your famous battles. And grogstains on the floor the management swears were made by rows you all had right on those very premises."

"I swear it wasn't me who broke that cask of wine," I said. "It was Polillo. On some Guardsman's head, if I recall. Made the mistake of mooing at her, mocking her cleavage, you know. She was very sensitive about that."

"I heard she smothered him," Derlina said. To illustrate, she embraced the air with her long shapely arms and squeezed them in against her own ample chest. "Like this. Smothered him against her tits."

"Maybe it was another fellow she hit on the head," I said. "There were so many they all run together sometimes."

She smiled, but faintly. Her thoughts were moving onward. I could read her clear features as easily as if they were my old friend's. And those features were troubled.

"I'm not one to sing a gloomy song, Rali," she said. "But we're in a fix here. And it's as plain as a rock, by the gods."

Derlina gripped two mighty fists together as if throttling an invisible enemy.

"You're going to have to grab us by the neck, dammit." Then she shook that invisible enemy like a rat. "And you're going to have to shake us up. Get some sense in us. Attach some ovaries to our wombs, by the gods. Or balls for those poor things that need them."

"I take it, Derlina," I said, "that you think your comrades in arms have a little less spirit than you'd care to see."

"Not by a quarter," she said, missing my dry tone. "Not by a half."

She smote her forehead with such force that I feared for her safety. Then she smote it again just as hard and I knew she'd survived.

"Take last night, for example," Derlina said.

"I *saw* last night," I said.

She stopped in her tracks and put her hands on her bell-shaped hips. "Good!" she snapped. "I'm glad you did! Now you know what I mean."

Another clout on the brow. "By all those in the heavens who squat like decent folks, did you ever see such a sight?

"Sure, that Novari bitch blasted us with some sorcery! So what? She was killing her own soldiers, too. We could have had 'em, dammit! All we had to do was pick ourselves up and fight! We'd have made a lot of poxed whores weep if we had. Mourning all those black-hearted sons we sent to the hells where they belong."

She started walking again, at a quicker, angrier pace. I had to hurry to keep up.

"If I'd have been there," Derlina growled, "things would've been different. But Palmeras and Quatervals ganged up and voted me down. They said it was because it was foolish to risk the Guard commander on such a thing. It was just a probe, they said. To test the enemy's strength. Well, I didn't need any ridiculous probe. Let's just do it, dammit! Let's just go out and clear those hills!"

I didn't answer. The path she was on was clearly wrong. And during the brief silence I could see her rethinking her words and coming to the same conclusion. We were so vastly outnumbered that such tactics, although brave, would bring swift and certain disaster.

She heaved a sigh. "Don't pay any attention to that, Rali," she said. "I was just . . . you know . . ."

"Lifting the lid off the pot," I suggested. "And letting go the steam."

Derlina grimaced. "Yes. Like that."

Then she shook her head. "Still," she said. "Still. We have to do something. And my guts tell me it'll all come down to do or die. One big toss of the dice. And shit on the gods that made us!"

Again I didn't answer. Although this time I thought she was right.

She led me into a vaulted room so large it had to be natural, for it would've taken years for a mortal hand to carve out. It was lit by a bright blue light that filled every hollow, erasing all shadows. Half the room was

filled with all kinds of strange and marvelous machines, all crackling with
sorcery.

Some were towering and bulky with moving belts and whirring gears
and glowing windows that looked into magical furnaces. Some were small
and delicately formed: glass webs with fiery droplets running up and down
the strands; a crystal tube that emitted purple puffs of smoky incense.

Strolling among them were a few sleepy-eyed Evocators, much-patched
robes swishing as they moved about making small adjustments: whispering
spells, pinching out herbs, or twisting knobs and wheels. And the machines
whirred or hissed, depending on their natures, without stop, casting so many
enchantments that it made me dizzy watching the mad whirl with my
ethereye.

Beyond the machines was a broad floor with a railed pit in its center.
The pit glowed eerily. And I could see three familiar figures moving along the
rail on the far side.

We headed for the pit, weaving our way through the aisles of wondrous
machines. I vaguely recognized the principles involved. Some were even patterned after the machine the Archon had used to nearly destroy Orissa. I'd
brought back its design, and from the looks at the marvels around me, our
Evocators had since taken the knowledge so far that I could only see dim
outlines of the original.

A few I didn't understand at all, and guessed—accurately, as it turned
out—that they were based on the new Unity Principles discovered by my
brother and the Greycloaks.

As we neared the pit, lightning flashed within. A moment later I heard
thunder, but the sound didn't come from the pit. It resounded behind me,
back from where we'd come. The thunder was from outside the cavern. Yet
the lightning had struck within the pit.

I hurried to the rail and looked inside the pit.

Below was a simulacrum of the Galana battlefield and the surrounding
region. It was like looking into a tide pool. The surface of that pool was the
night sky with a big knot of storm clouds on one side. Wavering beneath it
was a perfect duplicate, in miniature, of Galana and beyond, from the glowing cave mouths that led into the heart of our encampment to the winking
campfires of our enemy on distant hills. I could even see the small shadowy
figures of guards move about.

I caught the flash of a spear of lightning in the corner of my eye. It
crashed out of the angry cloud knot. The bolt struck near the front gate of
our fortress. Once again there was no sound of thunder within the pit. And
once again, after a breath's delay, I could hear the thunder boom outside the

cavern—which was evidence enough that the storm I saw gathering in the simulacrum was in reality gathering above my own head.

Scaffolding ran up the sides of the pit so that Evocators could walk along wherever they wished. In normal times, I guessed, they'd cast spells to sweeten the weather, enhance the growth of crops, and perhaps even control the wilder ragings of our river. My brother had seen such simulacrums in Irayas and Tyrenia.

I'd seen something similar the Archon had made. It was part of his doom machine. He'd used it to create a false Orissa to trap me. But his imperfect knowledge of our city made an imperfect duplicate, which in the end was his undoing.

After I'd gotten over my amazement, I started studying the details of that magical globe turned inside out. There was no one attending the simulacrum, and it spun slowly and without interruption on its invisible axis. I saw that the view shifted automatically, sometimes showing our fortress in closer detail, sometimes the terrain beyond the barricade. Once it turned so it favored the hill where Pip and I had crouched the night before watching the battle. Past the hill was the dark snaky outline of the roadway leading back to the ruined port.

The image tugged at me, and I felt my sorcerous muscles stir, then flex, cracking awakening joints.

As an experiment I directed my ethereye at the roadway. Instantly the simulacrum image froze. Then it slowly tilted, bringing the image I sought into easier view. I pointed down the roadway with my etherhand, willing the port to come to me. The image rushed up so fast I nearly ducked to avoid the impact. Then it steadied and I could make out quite clearly the harbor ruins where Kele had fought her final ship battle.

I heard voices behind me. I'd become so absorbed with my experiment I hadn't noticed Derlina depart my side. Now she'd returned with the others, who'd probably been standing there for long minutes wondering if the great Rali Antero had gone saggy in the topsails after all these years.

I turned to apologize. Instead I found four people goggling at me like I was an odd genius. Pip was scratching his head, and Derlina was staring wide-eyed, while Quatervals and Palmeras were exchanging astonished looks.

The Chief Evocator spoke first. "How did you do that, Rali?"

"Do what?" I asked.

Quatervals broke in. "Make the simulacrum move about?"

"I'm sorry," I said. "Isn't it allowed? Did I do something wrong?"

"Allowed?" Palmeras rumbled, yellow wizard's eyes boiling with what I hoped was amusement. "My dear Antero," he said, "what you accomplished was previously impossible. So how could we think to disallow it?"

"It usually takes Palmeras and half a dozen Evocators all working together to do the same," Quatervals said. "And they're most of the day doing it."

"And then you come along, my friend," the Evocator said, "and make the simulacrum dance to your merry tune, commanding this view and that without apparent effort."

"I don't know how I did it," I said. "It just came to me that I could. It seemed harmless enough, so I gave it a try. And it worked. But I don't think it'll work in every case."

I pointed into the pit with my etherhand. The simulacrum had returned to its previous view of Galana and the enemy campfires on the distant hills. It was those campfires that I was indicating.

"I know without even trying," I said, "that I can't bring up a closer view of the enemy so we could spy on their activities. Novari has that well blocked."

I concentrated, then a spark arced off the tip of my etherhand. It raced toward the enemy's encampment. But just before it struck there was a small flash and the spark was gone.

"There's her shield in place," I said. "And it's strong. Very strong. I can't get past it."

Palmeras sighed and stroked his jutting beard. "For a moment I had hope," he said, "that you could accomplish alone what we all couldn't do together."

I instinctively bristled at this, then calmed myself. "Excuse me, my friend," I said. "I'm your guest and don't wish to be rude. But I have to set your comments straight.

"This hero business is vastly overrated. No man or woman who was unfortunate enough to bear that mantle would disagree. Their deeds were not theirs alone, but of many acting in concert. It's a jest of the gods that one person's efforts should be singled out and those of braver people ignored."

I swept my hand around the cavern, taking in the wondrous machines and pit.

"As incredible as this sorcery seems," I said, "I know without asking that it's nothing compared to what Novari must have arrayed against you. She's got hundreds more machines, and Evocators to man them hour after hour. And she's got her man toy, Director Kato, with armies far greater than ours, poised outside these gates.

"Yet you have stayed the Lyre Bird's hand for many long months. No matter how hard she's struck, you've managed not only to recover, but to deal death blows of your own in return. And that, my wise friend," I said, "is a credit to every woman, man, and yes, even child who fights within the gates of Galana.

"All I can offer is a fresh mind and fresh strength to the problem. But in the end, whatever it is that must be done, we'll have to act together. And not one individual, but all who fight with us will be heroes."

Palmeras had been listening intently. I was glad to see he took no offense, but was nodding at my remarks. Quatervals and Pip were grinning. As certified men of courage, they knew very well what I meant about "the hero business."

And once again I saw Derlina knuckle away a tear. "There's nothing like a little arse-kicking," she said later, "to make my heart glad."

Then I said, "Why don't I look things over tomorrow? And then we'll all sit down and see if we can come up with some eggs to hatch."

I'd soon have cause to regret that simile. For as it turned out, the egg I came up with required my own warm behind for hatching.

No other would do.

A furious rainstorm descended on us the following day. The deluge was so heavy that it brought a welcome respite from the fighting. Troops and equipment would founder in the mud or lose their way because of poor visibility. So the enemy remained on the hilltops while the defenders of Galana tended their weapons and wounds.

I toured the encampment, Derlina at my side, trying to get a feel for the strengths and weaknesses of Galana.

On the surface it was a depressing sight. There were less than two thousand souls dwelling in that place, arrayed against what Derlina said was an enemy force nearly five times that number.

Two hundred fifty of our soldiers were Maranon Guardswomen, many gray-haired and past their prime, such as those steely-eyed women who kept Emilie safe. There'd been fifteen hundred—the Guard's normal force—to begin with, not counting the pensioners. Once more in its remarkable history the Maranon Guard was poised on the edge of being wiped out—down to the last crone with strength enough to grip a knife.

The rest were a mixed but highly skilled lot of former Guardsmen, frontier scouts, and hill and desert fighters. When they'd made the great retreat to Galana, there'd been three thousand of them. Now there were less than seventeen hundred.

Derlina assured me Novari's forces had suffered much higher casualties. Easily three to one, she said.

"But Novari can order Kato to bring up more whenever she likes," I said. Remembering my encounter with Natt, I added, "They're paying a bonus of a gold piece for every lad who joins up. And that means not only does she have an inexhaustible supply of young blood to shed, but that it's our own we're killing. Wrongheaded though they may be, those soldiers are our fellow Orissans.

"Novari is like a demon with many heads. Each time you chop one off, it grows back, except with the face of your friend upon it."

And Derlina growled, "You just give me a chance to take a whack at her. When I take an axe to a head, it *stays* chopped off."

Her spirited reply was evidence of the bright side of Galana. Reduced in numbers though the defenders might be, I saw no sign there'd been a decline in their will to fight, if need be, until the last drop of blood was shed.

No hand was idle during that day of respite. The kitchens were bustling with cooks getting as many meals prepared in advance as they could. The armories rang with the sound of hammers on mail. The stables were all cleaned, the horses shod. Blades were sharpened, fresh arrows made, wagons and war machines made ready. Even the wounded repaired the clothing and harness of others.

In the magic shops, Palmeras and his Evocators tended their machines, grabbing spare moments to create new spells while maintaining the magical war against Novari's wizards. For that never ceased. It was a seesaw Otherworld battle of attacks and counters and counter-counters, with neither side ever giving an inch away.

There was other more human activity on that day of relative peace.

There were the usual skirmishes to test the other's defenses and resolve. And the storm proved to be a blessing for the smugglers who supplied us. It turned out there were great caches of needed things in the outlying regions. And the storm was a chance to dig them up and carry them the last few leagues without fear of being spotted by enemy patrols. Pip went out early with one such group and returned quite worried.

He found me by the simulacrum watching Palmeras and his Evocators at work.

"Somethin's up, Cap'n," he said. "The squints what just come in said all the roads are crawlin' with wagons and workmen and soldiers to guard 'em. Had t' go a day outter their way t' get by all the patrols, they did."

I looked down at the simulacrum, puzzling at the distant hills where the enemy was camped. They were partly obscured by the heavy rain, but I could see the glow of many lights winking through. And the lights were moving.

"The squints said all a Orissa's full of scared talk about Novari. She's holed up at the villa and won't come out. Got all the Evocators there workin' on somethin'. Buildin' somethin'. A big somethin'. They put it together, piece by piece. Then take it apart 'n' start all over again.

"Word is they're almost done. The squints I talked t' called it a 'Vicious Thingie.' Gotter be vicious, right, if Novari's makin' it? Anyways, they said they thought some of that contraption was not only completed, but'd been loaded on wagons. Which was the wagons they saw. Goin' up into yon hills."

He pointed at the winking lights on the simulacrum.

"Somewheres up there," he said, "is where she'll be puttin' whatever it is she's buildin'. That's old Pip's guess."

I mused over his comments. "Seems like a little scouting is in order."

Pip frowned. "Yer not thinkin' about takin' a look in person, are yer, Cap'n?"

I sighed. "Don't see a way around it."

Pip opposed the notion. So did the others when they found out.

"You could wander the hills for hours," Quatervals said. "Days, even. And not find what you're looking for. Hells, Captain Antero, we don't even know what it is. Or even if it exists for certain."

"I think we have to assume it does exist," I said. "And it won't be all that impossible. Besides physical signs, there'll be a magical heart. A center.

"If it weren't for Novari's shield, we could locate it on the simulacrum and cast spells to spy out the details. If I can slip under the shield and get in close, I'll have free use of my powers to do all the investigating that we need."

Palmeras fumed. "You're just like your brother," he said. "Pretty speeches are the curse of the Anteros. You lectured us quite high-mindedly last night about the false myth of heroes. How great things are accomplished by the spirit of many, not the few.

"Then at the very next opportunity, off you go alone to take on the minions of our enemy. Which is the very same thing Amalric would have done, and I kick myself for being taken in by your little drama."

I grinned at him. "Who said anything about doing it alone?" I indicated Quatervals, Derlina, and Pip. "I'll require a few cutthroats to keep my own neck whole," I said. Then I pointed at him. "And I'll need the canniest Evocator in all Orissa to guard our backs."

Instantly all became smiles.

Strange, isn't it, how quickly their opposition vanished soon as they knew their lives would be at stake as well?

But such were the heroes of Galana.

"Flattery will get you everywhere with me, my dear Antero," Palmeras said. "As your brother often opined."

* * *

The Evocators in charge of such things said the weather would clear slightly after nightfall. They said they could stabilize it like that for a time—a few hours, perhaps—until Novari's wizards caught the scent of the spell and blocked it. Palmeras said he'd make certain the skies remained heavily overcast to help hide us when we slithered up to the enemy lines.

"That's when I'll cast the first diversionary spell," he said. "It should get you through in fine health. You won't be able to signal me when you need to return, so we'd better set a time right now. Then I can cast the second spell to get you home safely."

He thought a moment. "It comes down to guesses," he said, "even in this age of miracles. The weather ought to stay with us for about three hours. That's our best guess on this side. What's yours, my dear Antero? How long will you need?"

I looked at the others. Shrugs all around. "Make it three hours," I said. "That's guess enough to live by."

It was decided that the most reliable method of keeping track of the hours was to make Galana the clock. Flares would be set off moments before Palmeras cast his diversionary spell. That'd mark the first hour. Other flares would follow an hour apart. When we spotted the last flare, we'd know our time was up. We were supposed to drop whatever we were doing and rush back to the front lines as fast as we could. Palmeras' second casting would be made soon after the last flare was lit.

When that happened we'd best be in place, or it'd be most difficult to get through.

After we'd discussed the plan in depth and got ourselves ready, I stole a few moments for a promised visit with Emilie.

She was excited to see me and said she had a wonderful surprise.

"You have to come right away, Aunt Rali," she said, grabbing me by the hand and pulling. "Oh, do say you'll come. Please!"

I knew I should rest, but her smile was so sunny, how could I do anything except agree?

She led me outside, trailed by two large pensioners who were her ever-present guards. They were both former sergeants with scars enough for five careers. Their names were Torpol and Weene. They were big shy women with fierce features and eyes that became tender when they gazed on Emilie.

The rain had stopped briefly and the child ran ahead, dancing about in the puddles, happy to be free and in the open. She had on little boots to protect her feet and a blue-hooded cloak that she could grip in her hands and flap like a bird.

"She's what we're fightin' for, Captain," Torpol said, a smile creasing her rough face.

"Use'ter be Orissa," Weene added. "Took my oath to defend her when I was but a lass. Then they took away Orissa. So it's Emilie we fights for now."

"What she stands for, we mean," Torpol broke in. "The last Antero. If she falls, Orissa will never rise again, they say. And I, for one, believe it."

I didn't point out that Emilie was the last Antero but one. I was there, after all: Rali Antero in the flesh. But I don't think anyone at Galana really knew what to make of me. Was I a ghost or was I mortal? To tell the truth, I wasn't certain myself.

Nor am I any more certain now as I write this.

Emilie took us through the woodlot that surrounded the temple. From the easy way the two guards walked, I could tell it was a path they frequently trod. The air was heavy with moisture and smelled of fall's tired growth. When we came to the temple, the two women fell back to guard the entrance while Emilie and I continued on.

Memory flooded back when I stepped inside. The temple was the same simple little stone building I'd visited fifty years before.

I walked past the familiar offering box near the entrance and crossed the stone pavement toward the altar and the tall statue of the Goddess Maranonia. Above her was the patterned window in the high ceiling. When I'd last been there, a bright summer sun had streamed through. Now the light was cold and faint, making the statue somehow seem remote to us, as if the goddess' attentions were distant from the plight of her loyal subjects.

The same frescoes heralding the triumphs of the Maranon Guard graced the walls, including my own battle against the Archon. When I'd seen that fresco last, it'd been freshly painted. Now it was as faded and old as the others.

Emilie guided me to the raised pool near the altar. "First we need some water," she explained. "Special water. For the surprise."

She took a cup from her cloak pocket and dipped it into the pool. When the cup broke the surface, it released a faint cloud of perfume. She lifted the cup, and droplets glittering like small diamonds ran down the sides and fell back into the pool, hissing as if they were hot sparks, then vanishing as if they'd been quenched.

"It was already magical," Emilie said, indicating the pool. "But just a little bit."

She held up two fingers spread slightly apart to show the dimensions of a "little bit."

"So I kind of played around and made it more magical. And you know what?"

"What?"

"It was a good thing I did," she said solemnly. "The way it turned out, I needed a whole lot of magical water."

A most precise little girl, she spread her arms wide to demonstrate. "A whole, whole lot!"

Then she took me behind the statue of the goddess, and there, frail and naked under the cold light leaking in from above, was a little tree in a little pot.

Coming to about my waist, the tree was gray, with half a dozen graceful limbs no bigger than my smallest finger. Only a single silvery leaf clung to the tree. It was overly large, but delicately shaped, with fine veins tracing a lacy pattern across its surface.

"Isn't it wonderful, Aunt Rali?" Emilie cried. Then she ran to the tree and fell on her knees.

She poured the water into the pot, chanting:

> "I took a look
> In a book
> And there I saw a tree.
> And the tree lived here
> And the tree lived there.
> Wriggly, wriggly everywhere.
> Come and see
> Emilie's tree
> And you shall be
> Free like me.
> Wriggly, wriggly, Emilie."

The water came out of the cup as a glowing stream. The quantity seemed vast for such a little vessel, flowing on and on as she chanted, swirling about the base of the tree, overflowing the pot and spilling out onto the stone floor.

When she finished her chant, she stopped pouring and put the cup down carefully. Then she clapped her hands together, shouting: *Emilie says!*

The little tree shimmered, and the silver of the single leaf shone brighter. I could feel sorcerous energy stir from far away. The tree's roots were drawing on that Otherworld power, and I could actually sense woody life swell and grow stronger.

"The beautiful tree was in Uncle Amalric's book," Emilie said. "I didn't really read it. I can read a little. But Uncle Amalric uses pretty hard words sometimes. So I got other people to read it to me. All about their adventures looking for the real Far Kingdoms. My favorite part was when they got to the magic tree. With the silver leaves."

She pointed at the pot. "So I made one." She grimaced. "It's kind of small. And it doesn't grow so good in this light. But with the magic water to help, I got it to make a leaf."

Emilie touched the leaf and it moved under her fingers, seeming to rub against them like a kitten.

"Maybe you can use the leaf to win the war, Aunt Rali," she said, solemn as a temple priestess. "That's my surprise. I hope it works. I've been watering and making spells and working hard for ever so long."

I became kind of moist-eyed at that. To think of a child less that seven worrying about such terrible things. And plotting day after day to find a means to save her elders. But I didn't see how a leaf from even the most magical tree could help.

I said, "It's lovely, Emilie. And I'm proud you were able to do such a thing. I don't think Palmeras could snatch a tree out of a book and grow it. I certainly couldn't."

"It isn't *out* of the book," Emilie protested. "That just gave me the idea. I imagined the tree. I imagined a forest where they grew, but they were too big for me to bring back. So I took a seed. And grew it."

Her story was astonishing. She was only a child, but moving in and out of worlds with the ease of the most learned Evocator.

"The leaf isn't ready yet," she said. "It needs to grow some more. I think it'll fall off when it snows. Then it'll be ready."

"How do you know?" I asked.

She shrugged. "I just do. And you know what? I think it's going to snow on my birthday this year. So that's when the leaf will fall off and be ready. Isn't that a wonderful present, Aunt Rali?"

"Hold on a moment, child," I said. "Your poor aunt Rali's head is coming apart. First you show me a bewitched pool. Then a conjured tree. And now you're predicting the weather. Give an old soldier a chance to catch up!"

I sat beside the pot and pulled her into my lap. She snuggled close.

Then she said, "Are you ready yet?"

"I'm ready," I said. "Now tell me about the snow. It's important."

"What do you want to know?" Emilie asked, playing with her fingers.

"Can you really tell when it's going to snow?"

She frowned, thinking. Then shook her head. "Not exactly. But soon. Can't you feel it? It's out there." She pointed south. "Way, way far away."

And then we pushed into the Otherworlds together until we came to what I can only describe as a cold brittle place.

"There it is, Aunt Rali," I heard the child's voice whisper. "There's the snow."

I could smell it. Taste its metallic edge. Hear the bully winds blow just beyond.

"Let's go home, Emilie," I said.

I felt her stir in my arms and suddenly we were back in the temple.

"Thank you for showing me the snow, Emilie," I said. "I couldn't have found it on my own."

Emilie shrugged, unimpressed with her own powers. "That's okay," she said. "It was easy."

"The snowstorm doesn't seem many weeks away," I said.

"I told you," Emilie replied. "The first snow of winter. Just in time for my birthday.

"I'll be stronger then. That's what the pretty lady said, anyway. But I don't know. I'm kind of little, Aunt Rali. I don't think I can get that strong all at once, do you?"

"I can't answer that, dear," I said. "We'll just have to wait and see."

"Even if I'm not," she said, "you can use the leaf. Just like Janela and Uncle Amalric. Because soon as it snows, that leaf's going to be ready. And it'll fall off and I'll make up this—this—great big spell. And then the war will be all over. And maybe the pretty lady will let my mother and father come back and live with me again."

I looked up at the statue of the goddess. Her back was to me. And I thought, How like you. Turn around, O Great Goddess. Whom we all worship like fools. Turn around and answer the child. You explain why her mother and father can't come back. You explain why every member of her family has been slain. And while you're at it, maybe you can explain it to me.

Thankfully, Emilie became restless and squirmed out of my lap. She went over to the potted tree.

"I can make it snow without a storm, Aunt Rali," she said. "Do you want to see?"

I nodded, and she wriggled her fingers above the tree, piping: *"Emilie says!"*

Suddenly flakes of snow fluttered from beneath her hand and drifted down on the tree.

Emilie giggled, wriggling her fingers harder, making more snow fall. Some fell on the leaf, causing it to shake and jingle like the market bells on a horse-drawn sleigh. The flakes didn't melt but fell to the floor quite whole. I swept them up with my mortal hand and they crumbled like dust.

I started to blow the snow dust into Emilie's grinning face, then stopped.

"Could you make a little more of this, Emilie?" I asked. I pointed to the cup. "Enough to fill that?"

"Are you going to make a spell, Aunt Rali?" she asked.

"Yes, dear," I said. "And I'll need some *Emiliesays* dust to make it."

She laughed at that and wriggled her fingers to make more snow, chanting *Emiliesays* over and over again.

And later, when Quatervals led the scouting party out of the gates, I had the cup and her kiss to arm me against what lay ahead.

The rain had been replaced by a heavy mist that swirled around us like a watery cloak as we moved across the muddy swamp of the battleground. The mud and mist made it difficult going. There were sodden timbers of wrecked war machines to trip us up and stab us with pike-length splinters of wood. Abandoned fighting pits and trenches were invisible pools of muck to trap us and suck us down. In one place corpses floated out of their graves, rotted arms outstretched to embrace us.

Quatervals took the lead, displaying his vaunted talents as a scout by steering us past all danger. We must've looked like a giant centipede as we scuttled across the muck, weaving this way and that, blindly following Quatervals' signals. Sometimes he'd pause, tapping my hand to wait. I'd tap Pip, who in turn would signal Derlina. And we'd all stop as if we were a single creature. When whatever danger had existed passed by, Quatervals would tap and move forward, and off we'd go again.

We traveled like that for a time, then we came on the firmer ground of trampled grass. I felt greater weight on my legs and knew we were moving up an incline. Then the mist lightened and I could see the piled logs and boulders of a barricade. Beyond that was enemy territory.

One of our patrols was waiting for us there. It'd been their job to find and clear any ambushes that might've been set up. Now that we'd arrived at the jumpoff point, they'd hurry back and report to Palmeras so the flare clock could be started and the first diversion launched.

Hasty hand signals were flashed. No one had been seen behind us. No enemy patrols were immediately ahead.

Then they pressed our palms to wish us luck and hurried back to Galana.

While we waited, I crept up on the barricade and peered up the hillside with my ethereye. I saw the shimmer of Novari's first shield and searched along its edges for a flaw. The shield was meant both to block any magical attack and to give the alarm if anyone broke through. But it had to protect so much ground that I knew it'd make an imperfect fit. There'd be small hollows and dips big enough for us to get under.

I found a possible spot not too far distant. I jabbed a golden finger at that point, held it steady, then slipped a sniffer through. Knowing Novari, I did so quite cautiously. I snaked the tendril about, probing for the alarm net. I felt a familiar tingle as I touched the first strand and snatched the tendril back.

Nothing happened. My touch had been too light to trigger the alarm.

I took courage and probed about again, locating the strand. I felt out from there, nerves popping as I found a second and a third and then so many that my spiritself was a continuous buzz of discovery. No matter where I probed, I found an alarm strand. And in no place was there space enough to slip through. Pride kept me going, but I finally gave up and flopped over on my back to rest. I cleared my mind and settled into a soldier's cold comfort. It was someone else's job now.

It was Palmeras' turn.

The first flare went off, a hot burst of sorcerous fire that shot up from the valley and hovered over us for long moments, spitting sparks into the night.

We all rose to our feet. My comrades looked at me, waiting for the signal. I shook my head and held out a finger, telling them to wait. I pointed up, then forward, meaning we'd go with the diversion.

Just then I heard a great horn blare from above. We looked up. Above Galana we saw the moon glowing dimly through the haze. The horn blew again and the moon seemed to burn hotter and then a wide fiery road rolled out across the sky, sweeping the mist aside, plowing it into big boiling hills and banks.

We heard the drum of giant hooves and armor rattling like thunder. A spectral cavalry burst forth, Palmeras at the lead, and charged along the Otherworld highway. They were huge ghostly figures, formed of mist and magic. Their armor and weapons shone like the Gods Hearth itself. Their bellowed war cries slammed against the enemy hillsides like the Gods Hearth hammer.

Palmeras' roar sounded above all the others and he waved his sword, crying out for his enemy to come meet him.

My heart leaped at his cry and I thought then that nothing could beat us. But no sooner had that thought formed then I heard the twang of a lyre string, sounding the alarm. Then there was a whole stream of golden harp notes forming around the enemy encampment. Out of that stream boiled a second spectral cavalry. Black armor and golden swords and mailed horses with spiked hooves. Emblazoned on their shields was the symbol of the Lyre Bird.

A huge wizard in armor of silver and black led the charge. His great beard and streaming hair were tied up in flaming ribbons and he made an awesome sight as he rushed to meet Palmeras' challenge, screaming:

"For Novari!"

And his wizard warriors roared back:

"For Novari!"

Pip tugged my sleeve and whispered in my ear: "That be Kato, Cap'n."

Then the two ghostly armies clashed, horses rearing and screaming, wizard warriors flailing about with their swords.

As the ghostly battle raged above us, I leaped off the barricade and raced up the hill, the others at my heels. I led them to the large hollow beneath the first shield. I stopped there, indicated how to go, then slithered through. Twenty paces beyond, my senses brought up short at the second shield—more like an immense magical close-woven fishnet. I wasn't worried about setting off an alarm now. Palmeras had covered that. However, any rent I made would have to be immediately repaired. Otherwise the gap would be noticed as soon as the diversion ended. I carefully picked the magical fence apart, making space enough for the largest of us—Derlina. After we'd gone through, I quickly put everything back the way it was. And I powdered the area with *Emiliedust* to eliminate my spoor.

Derlina took us to the top of the first hill. Any opposition we met at this point would have to be overwhelmed immediately. She had her axe up and chin set, long legs eating the distance at a furious rate. I pitied any mere mortal who got in her way.

Just before we reached the top, the thunder and lightning of the battle stopped. The abrupt silence that followed was so sudden that the sound of my running boot heels seemed shockingly loud.

Then we were at the top, crouching among low boulders, catching our breath and getting our bearings. All of us, I noticed, sneaked peeks overhead. Marveling at the empty sky. Wondering if we'd only imagined Palmeras' grand diversion.

Then the second flare lit the sky, to remind us how real this was. We had two hours to go.

The haze Palmeras had promised was closing, and I had little time to study our surroundings before we were blinded. Beyond our perch was a dark rolling landscape dotted with hundreds of campfires.

Novari was erecting her secret weapon somewhere in that wide wing of hills. I had no doubt that's what she was doing. After seeing all the sorcerous machines in Galana, it was a logical conclusion. I knew Novari's preference for such machines. I'd slaved in her mines to feed one.

As I looked out at the hills and myriad fires, the problem looked enormous. Where could it be? Which way should we search first?

Then the mist enveloped us and all vanished from view.

I got out Emilie's cup of magical dust and, shaking it like a baker shak-

ing flour, coiled the white powder along the ground in the shape of a snake.
I made the head a bit broader than the body.

Then I unwrapped the silver splinter I'd kept from my ship. I kissed it,
whispered an apology, and pierced the snake's head to make an eye.

I held my golden etherhand over the snake head and chanted:

> "Fang and venom.
> Venom and song.
> The Lyre Bird sings
> And the serpent stings
> But serpent and bird are one.
> Sister find your nest.
> Brother find your mate.
> Fang and venom.
> Venom and song."

The *Emiliedust* snake stirred on the ground, white powdery scales sparkling all along its sides. Then the silver eye glowed into life and I heard
Derlina gasp as the sparkling head suddenly lifted up. It weaved back and
forth, inches above the ground, its single eye probing the mist, its glittering
ethertongue flickering to taste the air.

Then it caught Novari's scent and froze, tongue flicking in and out.
Slowly it rose higher, still facing the same direction, coming up until one-
third of its glowing white body was off the ground.

"Get ready," I warned the others.

"Too friggin' right!" came Pip's blurted whisper.

As if his blurt were a signal, the ethersnake shot forward, slithering
through an astonished Pip's legs and disappearing around a boulder.

"Let's go," I hissed, and we all hurried after the small hunter.

It took me a few minutes to get some control over the snake, making it
move slowly enough so we could maintain a safe pace or stop and hide if we
encountered the enemy. At any other time it might've been an amusing chase.
The glittering little creature would pause on mental command, then turn and
impatiently bob its head up and down at me, flicking out that silvery tongue
in protest at the delay. Much like Emilie herself, I suspected, when she got
caught up in play.

The scent of the Lyre Bird's nest drew the ethersnake along misty trails
that wound past hills and crept through gullies. The deeper we went into the
enemy's stronghold, the more times we had to dive for cover—flattening ourselves on the ground as soldiers wandered past, calling greetings to some and
cursing others under their breaths. Then a breeze stirred the air, clearing the

mist, and it became easier to follow the spectral hunter. But it also became easier to be discovered, so our progress remained painfully slow.

Finally we came to a low hill, wide and round as a dome. A road heavily rutted by cartwheels intersected with the hill and climbed its face to the top. At the base was a ramshackle tent camp. Men moved about the tents and campfires. Some wore uniforms and carried weapons. Some wore rugged workman's costumes with heavy boots and belts to carry hammers and hand axes. All were groaning and stretching and cracking joints as if they'd just ended many hours of hard work. A few oxcarts loaded with materials were being driven up the hill, and I could hear the thud of hammers and the screech of worked metal echoing from the top.

The ethersnake had gone very still, staring at the hilltop with its silver eye. Only its tongue moved, flickering eagerly as it tasted Novari's spoor.

The place we sought was on top of that hill.

I got out the cup and slipped up to the snake. It turned its head, eye glittering, tongue flicking, as if it were saying, "See there? That wasn't so hard?" Then it sagged down, weary, and collapsed into dust.

I swept the dust up and returned it to the cup. I wrapped the silver splinter that'd been its eye in a scrap of silk and slipped it into my boot.

We hid in a water channel just off the road and studied the work camp and hill for a long time, looking for a way up. Quatervals and Derlina slipped off in opposite directions to examine the ground while Pip and I waited, silent and cold.

They returned together. Smiles and hand signals were exchanged. There was a ravine, they said, on the opposite side. It cut right to the top and would cover our movements all the way.

As we prepared to move out, the sky lit up over Galana. Another flare. Time was getting short.

We kept to the water channel all the way around the hill. The ravine dumped into it and we had to wade through rushing, knee-deep water for the first leg. Then the water became a smaller but still swiftly moving stream running down the ravine's center. We kept to the sides and mostly stayed dry. Except for knuckles and knees skinned on the rocks, the going became easier. Then the ravine flattened and the stream became a slower trickle, and then stream and ravine both disappeared and we were climbing a short cliff face, moving quickly with Quatervals at the lead, showing us the many handholds in its weather-pocked surface.

Light and sound battered us when we cleared the top. The light seemed to come from a thousand torches and firebeads, and our ears rang with the racket of heavy construction.

We were all momentarily dazed and a second too slow finding cover.

Just as I hit the ground I heard a soldier bark alarm. A heavy weight struck me between the shoulders, knocking out my breath. But I forced myself up, reaching blindly with my golden hand. I grabbed cloth, but it was torn away and I stumbled around to find the enemy. I saw Quatervals grappling with a soldier with a ripped cloak.

There was a loud crack as the man's neck snapped and he sagged, dead.

Another soldier loomed up behind Quatervals, but a small shadow launched itself from a boulder. It was Pip, knife in hand, soaring like a deadly bird. He caught the soldier about the head and carried them both to the ground. His knife flashed and the soldier went still.

Then I heard running footsteps and turned to see another soldier racing away from us, heading for the lights and sound.

Derlina bounded over Pip and his victim, drawing her axe. She paused, hauled back—her form practice-field perfect—and hurled the axe after the fleeing soldier.

It struck him in the back and he went down, the axe sticking up from his spine.

And then it was over and we were all panting and trembling with after-battle shock. To our amazement, the entire violent incident had gone unnoticed.

Relieved, but wondering if we'd just used up all our luck, we gathered up the three bodies and dumped them over the cliff. Then we found dice and money on the ground. The soldiers had obviously been relaxing with a little private game when we'd stumbled into them.

Pip threw the dice over the cliff with the bodies. "Wouldn't wish them unlucky bones on me own worst enemy," he said later.

Then we crept toward the brightest lights and loudest sounds, making very sure we didn't come on another group of such unfortunates.

The last flare floated up over Galana just as we were moving into the shelter of a large supply tent.

It'd taken us too long.

Time was up.

I looked at my friends. Derlina shook her head, a firm no. Quatervals hesitated, then agreed. Pip pumped his hand up and down, signaling, "Let's keep going!"

And so we ignored the flare and our hammering hearts and slipped around the side of the tent, keeping well within its deep shadow.

Light glared out at us from across open ground.

And there, towering over a swarm of workmen and knots of guards, was Novari's secret weapon in the making.

It was a huge lyre sitting on a wide, stone base. Scaffolding was flung up on both sides of the metal structure. Men were working on all the levels, using pulleys to haul up pieces from the wagons below, hammering them into place or filing and cutting to make the fit easier. Forges had been set up on each level, and smithies in aprons toiled at their bellows.

I could see the sprocket holes where the strings would fit when it was done. I wondered what song Novari would play on such giant cables. And I wondered how she would play it.

Then the breeze quickened and somewhere far off lightning flashed and thunder rumbled.

I suddenly knew the answer.

I signaled to the others.

And we turned and raced back the way we had come.

THE LYRE BIRD SINGS

The return was bloodless and quick.

Palmeras made a second spectral attack and once again locked with Kato and his magical horde. We raced home with the battle raging overhead, encountering no one on the way. The gates were in sight when the diversion ended, and when we trotted through, a ragged chorus of cheers greeted our arrival.

Emilie broke away from her guards and leaped into my arms, covering me with kisses and tears.

"I was so afraid, Aunt Rali," she said. "I thought Novari might catch you. And—And—she'd have gotten everyone in my family. Everybody'd be deaded, then. And I'd have no one left."

I stroked her hair, saying, "There, there," and "everything will be all right, dear," and other such nonsense adults spew when they try to soothe a child.

She clutched me, saying, "There's going to be more, Aunt Rali! Isn't there?"

"Yes, Emilie dear," I said. "Novari's not done with us yet."

There was no time to rest. Torvol and Weene took Emilie away and I hastened to wash myself and change, hoping water and soap and a clean costume would help me fool the demons of weariness.

I sprinkled on a little perfume to fool them more, but instead the soft fragrance made me think of satin pillows and silken sheets. I thought of Salimar sleeping in our tomb, auburn hair all spread out and inviting. Sadness dripped slowly into a hollow place deep within me. I was not likely to touch that hair again. The realization brought a lump of self-pity to my throat.

I wept a little. Then dried my tears and erased their stain. As I did so, a plan began to form.

We met in Quatervals' sparse chambers. It was military neat—everything that might be quickly needed was close at hand, and everything that wouldn't was stored in a few big trunks that he'd put in the center and covered with a cloth to make a table. My friends, displaying various degrees of exhaustion, were slumped in camp chairs set about the table.

Palmeras was pale with fatigue, but his yellow wizard eyes glowed with satisfaction at the successful diversions. Derlina's long legs were sprawled out before her and she was clutching a cup of strong brandy to her chest. Quatervals was helping Pip dress a small wound he'd received in the fight with the unlucky soldiers.

I gratefully accepted a full brandy cup and sagged into a chair next to Palmeras.

I waved the cup at him in a tired toast. "The Lord Gamelan himself couldn't have staged better diversions," I said. "They must have given Kato an awful fright."

Palmeras nodded, pleased with himself—as he'd every right to be.

"Kato's pro'ly still scratchin' his noggin," Pip said, "tryin' to figger what it was all about."

"I can only pray," Palmeras said, "that Novari is his equal in confusion." He drank, then said, "They told me about the great lyre you saw. I don't know its purpose, but it's plain that we must destroy it at once."

"There isn't a chance of *that*," I said. "So put it from your mind. Just because a few of us got so close doesn't mean a force of any size could do the same. This lyre machine is too important to her. She'll be prepared for anything we can throw at her."

"So the machine, if that's what it is, shouldn't concern us, my dear Antero?" Palmeras said.

"Just the opposite," I said. "Once Novari gives that lyre life, I doubt if there's any force we can mount that will stand in her way."

I told them about the storm that'd caught me at Antero Bay more than fifty years before. How the Lyre Bird had used the natural force of that storm to crush all magical life, and the mortal force of the Ice Bear King's legions to crush all else.

"That's what she's planning to do now," I said. "But on an even grander scale."

I told them about the approaching winter storm—the first of the season—that Emilie had shown me.

"It's less than two weeks away," I said. "Novari will know that. And she'll be ready. I saw her workers rolling thick wires out of the wagons this very night. The lyre will be strung and ready by the time that storm hits.

"When the winds blow, Novari's great lyre will begin to play. And as the force of the storm increases, so will her spell."

I remembered the punishment I'd taken at Antero Bay, thanks to Novari. Without experiencing it, no Evocator, not even Palmeras, could imagine the intensity of the assault. And this time I knew it'd be worse.

"Soon as the storm ends," I said, "she'll command Kato to attack full-force. Although, there's likely to be so few of us left that it probably won't require much more than a mop-up operation.

"Her greatest concern will be Emilie. She'll want her alive. And unhurt."

Quatervals nodded. "Then Director Kato himself," he said, "will probably command that mission. Their soldiers are too raw to be trusted with anything but the most basic orders."

"Kill everything in sight, most likely," Derlina muttered. Then she said, "To hells with Novari! To hells with her blasted machine! To hells with all of them! Let's go fight, dammit! Fight her now before she has a chance to gain the ground."

"That's exactly what I intend," I said. "But I want you to know, before we start that in order to defeat the Lyre Bird . . .

" . . . first we have to lose."

It was a mad plan. A plan of last resort. No one agreed easily. And I don't think anyone ever really accepted it as the only way. But there was no time to think of anything else. Derlina, as expected, was the hardest to convince. In the end I had to use her own words against her.

"You told me yourself," I said, "that you knew in your guts that it would all come down to do-or-die. 'One big toss of the dice,' you said. 'And shit on the gods that made us!' "

Finally, it was agreed. There would be an all-out assault. Pip would rush back to Cheapside. He'd organize and command a general uprising. The uprising would be timed with attacks by us on Kato's troops surrounding Galana. We'd put everything we had into it.

Derlina ground her teeth. "And then we let the bitch win!"

"Yes," I said. "Then we let the bitch win. Like the dinksman lets his

Cheapside mark win the first few rounds. Until the mark's coaxed into risking all."

Derlina grimaced. "As long as you're certain," she said, "that Novari ends up playing the mark instead of us."

I told her I was quite certain.

The lie came to my tongue much too easily for comfort.

All know of the great deeds that followed.

All know of Pip's daring ride to Orissa, hurtling along the highway with a squad of Maranon Guardswomen, overcoming all who tried to stop them. It took them two days, pausing only to change horses at friendly stables and pass the word of the impending battle.

Once in Orissa, the King of Thieves roused his knaves, and the villains of Cheapside poured out of the sewers to confront the masters of Orissa.

All know how Queenie and the brutes of the Thugs' Guild went on a rampage of assassinations, killing key officers and city leaders.

And how Pearl and the whores of the Harlots' Guild helped them in that awful work, using their seductive wiles to spring doors that'd kept the assassins at bay.

The knaves fought furiously, sometimes in small surprise attacks out of alleys and sewer openings. And sometimes hand-to-hand. Force against force.

The pickpockets lost able leaders when Palmer and Lammer died in a skirmish at the Central Market.

Garla, the handsome chief of the Beggars' Guild, died in an assault on the Palace of Evocators.

These were just a few of the many villains who martyred themselves for Orissa.

And Pip! What a marvel he was. He seemed to be everyplace at once, weaving new strategies, plugging gaps when other leaders fell.

Finally his spark took hold, spreading from Cheapside into the populace itself. The citizens of Orissa at last were fighting back.

In the city, they took to the streets, attacking soldiers with the few arms they had. They added mightily to those stores, however, as they hurled themselves against the troops with wagon spokes and cobblestones and broken pavement.

At the same time, the whole countryside burst into flames as the villagers and farmers joined the battle. Slowly at first, but as our supporters stunned the enemy with the ferocity of their attacks, more and more people rushed in to swell their numbers.

Meanwhile, at Galana we kept Novari and Kato's largest forces pinned.

To quell the uprising they'd have to defeat us first.

Over and over again the gates of Galana swung open and we charged out to fight. We used every tactic to gain the slightest edge against the overwhelming numbers that faced us.

Derlina would lead what appeared to be a suicidal charge against the enemy lines. She and the Guardswomen would fight with berserk fury, driving so deeply into the enemy's mass there was no getting back. Then, when all would seem lost, Quatervals would pounce from the flanks, spearing in to meet her. They'd join, then make an orderly withdrawal, leaving the field strewn with enemy corpses.

Each time our own numbers grew fewer. Until only two-thirds of us stood.

I don't know what saddened me more. The sight of my dead comrades, or the bodies of the enemy in the field. All of whom, as I'd once told Palmeras, bore the faces of Orissans.

That point was driven home most sorely when I accompanied Derlina one night in a cavalry feint on the hilltop where the lyre machine stood. Quatervals had secured a nearby hill. The plan was to strike for the lyre machine, drawing as many enemy as possible into the fray, then to break contact and join Quatervals in a wide, looping assault on their flanks.

My purpose was twofold. First, I had to get Derlina past the alarms so we could get in as close as possible. Secondly, I was to assist Palmeras from the ground while he and the Evocators took on Kato and his wizard army.

As it turned out, the plans came to naught. Instead of surprising the enemy, we sprung his trap.

Suddenly arrows hailed onto us. There were shouts of alarm and pain. Something hot struck me in the side. I grunted, grabbing for it. And my hand came away slippery with blood from the glancing arrow wound. Then the men were swarming out of the darkness on all sides of us, screaming their war cries.

Derlina shouted orders and we charged for the center of their mass. It was the only way through. Beyond we could see the fires on the hilltops where Quatervals waited.

All that followed was exactly out of the vision I'd seen on the road to Galana, the vision in which my future tragically intersected with a village lad named Natt. Young Natt had betrayed us, but that betrayal certainly didn't warrant payment in blood. He was so young, his mother so frantic for his safety.

But that was the tale of most of the boys I faced that night.

My wounds, although not serious, hurt like the hells. There was a wall

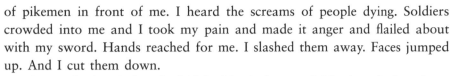

of pikemen in front of me. I heard the screams of people dying. Soldiers crowded into me and I took my pain and made it anger and flailed about with my sword. Hands reached for me. I slashed them away. Faces jumped up. And I cut them down.

But each time I thought it'd be Natt's face, and I hesitated—just for a breath. I nearly died several times because of that.

I spurred my old war-horse forward, and she whinnied and crashed into the pike line.

Then the pike line wavered and broke.

I shouted, glad to be free, as my horse plunged through.

Then the moment came that I'd dreaded.

A figure leaped in front of me, jabbing with his pike. My enemy's image froze and I could see him clear. He was tall and so painfully thin that his rusted breastplate would barely stay on.

It was Natt, with a black smear for a mustache. His eyes were wide and white and full of fear, and I heard him bawling for his "muvver."

Then the moment came unstuck and I shouted for him to make way.

But Natt kept coming—his pike digging for my guts—certain he was lost if he didn't kill me first.

I reined in, trying to stop the course of my horse. But she was off balance, swinging wide, carrying me toward Natt's pike tip.

Instinct flung my sword forward to strike him down. But at the last instant I willed my blade to turn and I struck him with the flat.

He went down, knocked cold.

And I charged on for the hills where Quatervals waited.

Derlina had seen the whole thing and later said I'd been a fool. She said I could have gotten myself killed for nothing. And after I told her the tale, she snorted and said it wasn't likely that young Natt would live much longer. That I'd only delayed the inevitable. Unless he deserted and fled to his dear "muvver's" side.

She was right.

But I slept a little easier that night.

In war you have to learn to treasure even the smallest of moral victories, or else you lose the part of you that makes you human.

Despite all the efforts and sacrifices and loss of life, it soon became apparent that the uprising had a hollow core. Novari was just too powerful. She and Kato were slowly grinding us down. And when the time came, they'd use the impending storm to finish us off.

But as I'd told Derlina, we had to lose to win.

Besides, I had plans of my own for that storm.

*　*　*

The last time Emilie and I visited the temple, there was frost on the ground and a sharp breeze in the air, and I could hear the strings of the great lyre stir in the enemy hills. She had on her little blue cloak, with the hood pulled up to keep out the cold.

There was a small gathering waiting when we arrived: Derlina, Palmeras, Quatervals, and a dozen other officers, noncoms, and Evocators.

We'd been greeted by a fiery dawn when we arose. The whole eastern sky had been ablaze, with huge black storm clouds boiling beneath sheets of red and hearthfire yellow. We hadn't needed sorcery to tell us the storm would be upon us in full fury by day's end. A ship's lad could've read the telltale signs while scraping pots over the side.

Everyone knew instantly what was to be done, and all of Galana went into motion, preparing to lash out for the final time.

We'd strike just before the storm hit.

The small group gathered at the temple was there to pray for the Goddess Maranonia's help.

Emilie stood beside me, clutching my hand, while Palmeras oversaw the sacrifice. She shuddered and turned her head away when he slew the lamb.

Palmeras cleansed the knife in the holy flame and approached Maranonia's idol. He threw up his hands to address the goddess for all of us.

"O Great Maranonia," he intoned. "Kind Maranonia. Loving Maranonia. We stand before you, obedient children, beseeching your tender care."

Palmeras' voice was rich and so full of deeply felt emotion that he stirred us all.

"Orissa has been led to the brink of disaster and ruination, O Sweet Goddess," he continued. "The chasm we face is wide and deep.

"Without your holy intervention, we are certain to plummet over that brink. And your glorious light will shine over us no more. Snuffed out by the evil Novari. The Lyre Bird. The foulest threat your beloved people have ever faced.

"Give us strength, O Goddess. Fill our hearts with your courage. Our limbs with your warrior's fire. Our souls with your exalted spirit.

"Bless us, O Great Goddess. Heed us in our prayers."

None of us expected much to happen. We'd make our plea and go on our way to confront our fates. If we prevailed, the goddess would be credited. If we didn't, the usual theological excuses would be made to preserve her dignity and sanctity.

Still, carried away by Palmeras' smooth rolling tones, I found myself waiting. Expecting that at any moment a beam of bright light would burst through the glass above and the statue would become the goddess herself.

And the glorious Maranonia would wave her torch and brandish her spear, and our enemies would be swept away without further ado.

I found myself gritting my teeth, thinking, Anytime you're ready, Goddess.

Then I heard little Emilie whisper, "She isn't coming, Aunt Rali."

And the moment passed.

Outside, I heard the rush of the quickening wind and the faint aria of lyre music.

Quatervals said it was time to go, and we made our farewells.

First I embraced Palmeras, wishing him wizard's luck in the fight that was about to commence. I could smell the incense on his Evocator's robes and it made me think of Gamelan and I nearly wept.

Quatervals gave me an awkward soldierly backpounding and said not to worry. We'd soon meet again, if only in the hells.

When Derlina approached, I braced for a crushing. But the giant warrior woman was most tender. She kissed my cheek and whispered, "Remember me to Polillo." And then she left.

The others filed past, hugging or pressing palms with me.

Finally only four of us remained: Emilie, myself, and the two old sergeants who guarded her.

The women wiped their eyes and drew their swords.

"You know what to do," I said. "We've practiced many times."

"Yer needn't fear, Captain," Torvol said.

Weene nodded, jawline hard. "We knows our duty, Captain."

"Wait here with Emilie, then," I said. "I'll be back in a moment."

I went outside to stand in the temple's leeway and face the gathering storm, bracing against the icy wind. It was cold enough to make my armor burn where it touched the skin. The sky swirled with black clouds swollen huge with snow. The lyre music was still faint, but the notes were more distinct as the wind grew stronger and plucked the giant strings.

Novari would soon come to direct the song.

I pushed into the Otherworlds, stretching as deep as I could. I found the edges of Novari's shield, searching along it until I came to a small rent in its magical substance. I listened closely, and far inside I could hear the little demon monkey busy at its work.

Chitter chit. Chitter chit.

Still picking away at Novari's defenses knot by knot. Piece by piece.

Chitter chit. Chitter chit.

I slipped a tendril through the opening. It was larger than I'd hoped, and my heart made a glad jump as I pushed through the hole deeper and deeper until I found the monkey. It was glad to see me, leaping about and chittering hysterically. I soothed it, renewed my promise to see it would come to no harm, then checked its progress more carefully.

My heart's glad leap became a dancing dervish when I realized how close the little monkey had come. The shield had nearly been gnawed and clawed through, and just beyond I could feel the faint but familiar buzz of Novari.

A sudden blast of wind and soaring lyre music forced me to break away.

At the same instant, the heavens opened up and Palmeras led his wizard cavalry out to do battle. I heard his challenge and Kato's shouted answer.

Beyond the woods the mortal battle commenced. The gates swung open to unleash Quatervals' and Derlina's final charge.

The first snowflakes fell, and I quickly shed my cloak and held it out-stretched in the wind's teeth until it was covered with fine white dust. Then I turned my back on the sounds of fighting and hurried into the temple.

I found Emilie crouched by her little tree with the single silvery leaf. It was hanging by just a thread now, quivering in the increasing cold.

"It's almost ready, Aunt Rali," she said, voice trembling.

Her eyes were wide and I saw fear there. But I also saw Antero bravery warring with the fear. I sat beside her, pushed back the little blue hood, and kissed her and stroked her curls for luck to help win that war.

When she was calm, I said, "Make it snow please, Emilie dear."

Emilie gave a little sigh and got up. She stood over the potted tree and wriggled her fingers like before. Once again snow drifted from her palm, touching the silvery leaf and transforming into glittering magical dust.

I caught the *Emiliedust* in a stone bowl, stirring it together with Novari's snowflakes, which I'd brushed off my cloak.

"That should be enough," I finally said.

I set the bowl on the floor and beckoned for her to sit in my lap. We cuddled for a time, each thinking her own thoughts.

"I hope Derlina will be all right," the child said after a while. Then quickly, as if they were present and she didn't want to insult them, she added, "And Palmeras and Quatervals, too." She waved a hand. "I hope they'll *all* be all right."

"They will, Emilie," I said. "With your help."

"I'm glad you don't think I'm too little, Aunt Rali," she said.

"Of course you aren't," I said. "I know you're a big enough girl to do everything exactly right."

She wriggled in my lap, delighted. She tried to make a fierce scowl. "I'll show that—that—that—Novari. Just you wait and see!"

"I know you will, darling," I said.

She was quiet for a time. Outside I could hear the lyre music growing louder. But beneath it I could hear the sounds of the raging battle.

Soon our forces would pretend to stumble and fall back in seeming disarray. Novari and Kato would be too eager to wait for the storm when they saw our weakness. They'd hit us with everything they had. The troops would panic. Quatervals and Derlina would struggle to keep order, but in the end they'd all flee, Palmeras and his Evocators included.

Abandoning us here in the temple.

"Do you think I'll be as good a soldier as you are when I get old, Aunt Rali?" Emilie asked.

I smiled. "Better," I said.

"And as beautiful?"

I patted her, thinking, Bless the child.

I answered, "Even more so."

She turned to stare at the silver leaf, dangling from the tree by its slender thread.

"It's almost my birthday," she announced. She pointed at the leaf. "Soon as that falls, I'll be seven winters old."

She counted on her fingers, "One, two, three, four, five, six . . . and seven." She held the fingers out. "And then I'll be *really* strong!"

Emilie flexed a tiny arm, straining her face as she tried to make a muscle.

Then her shoulders slumped. Another sigh. "But not as strong as Novari."

"She has more on her side," I said. "It isn't an even fight."

"But I'll keep getting stronger, won't I, Aunt Rali?"

"Every seven winters," I said. "Remember how we figured it out. When we cast the Evocator's bones."

Emilie nodded. "Sure I do," she said. "Every seven birthdays I'll get to a new level. And each time, I'll get stronger and stronger. Until I'm so strong I could cut off her toes with lightning." She clapped her hands. "Emilie says, off with her toes!

"And her toes would be offed."

Emilie giggled. "Then she'd fall over when she walked."

We both laughed.

Then we heard a sound like chimes. And we turned to see the silver leaf break free and flutter to the stone.

I caught it with my golden hand and held it up before Emilie's eyes.

"Congratulations, Emilie," I said. "It's official now. You're seven winters old."

Her eyes were full of innocent wonder. She reached out and took the leaf between quaking fingers.

The moment she touched it, I felt a surge of sorcerous power blast out of the Otherworlds.

Emilie cried out: "It hurts, Aunt Rali! Make it stop!"

Her whole body trembled and I held her tight. Fire overflowed her veins and flooded mine. Power and pain were one, wracking us both. I tried to absorb as much as I could.

But it was Emilie's power. And Emilie's pain. And she had to suffer the most.

Then the agony ended and she went limp and sobbing in my arms.

"Is it over, Aunt Rali?" she wept. "Is it over yet?"

"Just about, dear," I said.

I dried her eyes and turned her in my lap to face the bowl of *Emiliedust* floating in the melted snow from Novari's storm.

I heard sounds of fighting from close by, and then temple doors boomed shut and the bar was slammed into place.

"They're comin', Captain," Weene called.

Emilie sniffled her last sniffle and stood straight and tall as she could.

"I'll do it now," she said.

She dipped the leaf into the bowl and stirred the *Emiliedust*, chanting:

> "Little is little
> And big is big.
> Doesn't matter,
> Except to a pig.
> Rain can shine.
> But the sun can't get wet.
> Emilie's here, so don't you fret."

The bowl of liquid and glittering *Emiliedust* turned molten, silvery, thick like mercury.

She dipped some out with the leaf and spattered it about, chanting:

> "East is east,
> And so is west.
> World's upside down.
> 'Cause Emilie's best."

Then she drew herself up, spreading her little arms wide in unconscious parody of Palmeras, and shouted:

"EMILIESAYS . . . STOP!"

Outside, the wind ceased and the lyre music halted. I heard loud cries and the sounds of our soldiers' panicked retreat.

Then there came a pounding at the temple doors. And an imperious voice boomed: "Open for Director Kato!"

Emilie calmly handed me the silver leaf, which glowed with a hardened shellac of *Emiliedust*. I rolled it into a tube, slipped the metal splinter from my ship into the center, and gave it back. With elaborate care, Emilie placed the tube in the inside pocket of her blue cloak.

Then I kissed her. We clung for a moment.

The voice came again: "Surrender the child at once!"

I stepped away from her. Torvol and Wcenc came running up to stand at her side.

"Good-bye, Aunt Rali," Emilie said.

"Good-bye, Emilie," I answered.

Then she clapped her hands.

The sound was like a great blast of thunder, then her child's voice became that of a giant's as she shouted:

"EMILIESAYS, GO!"

And Novari's storm, pent up by Emilie's will, slammed its icy fist down on Galana.

All sound collapsed in its roar. All sensation bowed low under its weight. I felt the sear of Novari's magic wither the ethers around me.

Emilie and her guards became smoky, faint. She held out her hand to me. Her lips moved, but I heard nothing.

Then she waved.

I stabbed a finger at the smoky images, and she and the women vanished.

From somewhere far off I heard Novari's voice, calling, "Emilie . . . Emilie. Where are you Emilie?"

And from nearby I heard, "Here I am, Novari."

Novari's voice floated closer, buoyed up on waves of marvelous lyre music. "Emilie . . . Emilie . . ."

And I heard a child's voice plead, "I'm here, Novari. Please. I'm scared!"

Then the air stirred beside me, and I smelled a familiar perfume.

Novari's voice came just at my ear. "There you are, child! Come with me. Novari will make you safe."

The temple dissolved around me, and a great wind lifted me up and carried me away. I bobbed on fast currents, like an insect clinging to a stick. I collided with clouds, bouncing from bank to bank, then was grabbed by the wind current again and hurled farther along Novari's sorcerous river.

Suddenly the wind ceased and I was falling from a great distance, the ground slowly floating up at me.

Then I heard a hunting creature's glad cry and the shadow of the Lyre Bird fell over me. She caught me in her claws, like a hawk swoops up a fish. Powerful wings stopped my swift descent. Then the wings flapped once, twice, and all dissolved again.

And I found myself standing in Amalric's garden.

The sun was bright, the flowers were blooming, and the fountain played sweet music on my mother's shrine.

A beautiful woman stepped out from the shadows of the trees. She wore a gown of virginal white with long floaty sleeves and a veil as delicate as mist drifting behind her in the breeze.

The woman came toward me, seeming very tall.

"Hello, Emilie dear," Novari said in a voice as sweet as mountain springs.

"Hello," I piped, holding out my hand, which was very small. As small as my child's voice. Then I let that voice quaver. "You won't hurt me, will you?"

"Of course not, Emilie dear," Novari said, taking my hand in hers. "I'd never dream of hurting a pretty little girl like you."

"Really?" I said, tears welling up in my eyes. "You swear?"

"I don't have to swear, dear," the Lyre Bird said. "I'm Novari. The Lyre Bird.

"And the first thing you should know about me, is that . . . I can never tell a lie."

EMILIE'S REVENGE

N ovari peered down at me, a sweet smile playing across her perfect
features.

On the outside I was Emilie, delicate as a meadow flower. I had
Emilie's innocent eyes. Her pearly milk teeth. Her child's translucent skin.
But inside I was Rali Antero. With a false hand and single eye and cauter-
ized soul.

But the Lyre Bird saw only Emilie when she said, "I've been waiting to
meet you for *such* a long time, dear."

She posed before me, white gown dazzling in the sun. She had a tiara
of daisies woven through her golden hair, and daisy bracelets encircled her
slender wrists. Her sun-kissed skin was misted with the delicate aroma of
lemony musk.

But I remembered the seductress and saw how the gown flowed about
her lush figure, caressing every soft hill and hollow. I remembered her attempt at sorcerous seduction. Hot hands and lips bruising my body while I
waited for my chance to kill her.

And here I was with Novari once again.

Waiting.

I looked about with childlike curiosity. Moments before I'd been in the
center of a winter storm, but here in the villa of my birth, magic had ban-
ished all of winter's cares.

The garden was springtime warm and the flowers were nodding under a happy sun. Insects clung to their blossoms, sipping the nectar inside. Songbirds flitted among the trees, while an old gray cat crouched under mint leaves waiting to pounce. It had one eye, I noted, like my Rali self.

Then Novari said sharply: "Well, Emilie. What do you have to say for yourself?"

I ducked my head, pulling the blue-hooded cloak closer as if I were suddenly cold. "Was I very bad?" I asked.

Novari put a hand on a round hip and gave me a scolding look. "Well, you *did* interfere with my storm."

"I put it back the way it was," I piped in defense.

"But *really*, dear," she said, "you spoiled the whole thing." She waved in the vague direction of Galana. "Because of you, the storm ended too soon. It only lasted a few hours, instead of days. I wish you hadn't interfered, Emilie. It was quite naughty of you."

"People were getting deaded," I said. "That's why I inter—whatever you said I did."

"I suppose that's understandable," Novari said, features softening. "You do have such a delicate nature. I have to make allowances for that. And those . . . people . . . *were* your friends, after all."

"Are they all deaded, anyway?" I said, lower lip trembling.

"No, my sweet," Novari said. "They aren't all . . . deaded. Your friends are alive. But I can't say much for their future. My troops are hunting them now."

"Why don't you just let them go?" I asked. "I'll tell them not to be bad anymore."

"Oh, I can't do that, sweetness," Novari said. "I'd like to please you. But I can't. Even if I wanted to, I can't. Especially now that they've gone and killed Kato, poor man."

"Kato's deaded?" I gawked. "How?"

Novari shrugged. "I think one of your friends cut his head off. With an axe. A big woman, I was told."

I had to force myself not to smile.

"I don't really mind that much, sweetheart," Novari said. "Kato was no friend of mine. He thought otherwise. But men think all *kinds* of things. And their notions of friendship with a woman begin and end with their loins.

"But Kato *was* useful, I'll give him that. He was Director of Orissa, after all. Although there's plenty of candidates to take his place, I can't let poor Kato's death go unpunished."

Then she smiled, teasing. "But I'll tell you what," she said.

"What?"

"I promise you that when they catch your friends, I won't permit torture. It will be a quick death. Painless as I can make it." She clapped her hands delightedly, as if she'd just offered me the greatest gift. "See? Doesn't that make you feel better already?

"Can we be friends now?"

I frowned, as if considering. Then I smiled and said, "I'm hungry."

Novari burst out laughing. "What a delightful child," she said. "I just know that we're going to get along very well indeed."

Then she said, "Come, Emilie," and held out her hand.

I stared at her, hesitating, as if weighing a difficult decision.

"I don't bite little girls, Emilie," she said.

I gave a nervous giggle. Then, acting reassured, I took her hand and skipped along the path beside her. She led me to the familiar garden bench where I'd last supped with Amalric and Omerye more than fifty years before.

There were little trays of delicacies waiting, sweets and tarts and finger cakes. There were sweating pitchers of cold milk and fruit juices. Fresh fruit and cheese and small, covered pots of sherbets sitting on a bed of ice.

I scooted onto the bench near a sticky pile of sweets. I made certain I stayed in character, choosing a frosted date with the greatest of care. Then I nibbled on it delicately, brushing away any sugar crumbs from my cloak as fastidious as little Emilie ever was.

"This is good," I said.

"Why don't you take your cloak off, Emilie?" Novari suggested. "It must be awfully hot under there."

My Rali self chortled: You have no idea, woman. But my Emilie self pulled the cloak closer. I patted it like it was an old friend, feeling the lump in the inside pocket—the pocket where the silver leaf and splinter were rolled up tight.

"That's all right," I said. "I get cold easy." And then I said, dignified as I imagined a small child could be, "I do hope I am not being rude."

Novari laughed. "Such a little princess," she said. "So proper. So sensitive and sweet. I love you, Emilie. I really do."

And I thought: You always were too quick, Novari. You really rush a girl, don't you?

But in Emilie's high voice I said, "Why are you deading everyone, Novari?"

The Lyre Bird's smooth brow furrowed into a lovely frown of great concern. "You've been listening to my enemies too much," she said. "I'm not . . . killing everyone. Only those who deserve it. And even then only when it becomes necessary."

My face suddenly pinched up and tears spilled out. "You deaded my father!" I accused.

"And I'm so sorry that I did, sweetness," Novari said, tears of sympathy welling in her own eyes. "I felt very cruel to hurt you so. But I didn't do it because I wanted to be mean. Novari isn't mean. She doesn't hurt things for pleasure. She hates to hurt people. But sometimes they make her hurt them.

"And that makes her mad. Really, really mad."

Lower lip trembling, I said, "Were you mad at my father? Is that why you deaded him? And all the other Anteros. Were you mad at them, too?"

"I suppose I was, Emilie dear," she said. "I told you I can only speak the truth. Which means I sometimes have to admit things to myself that make me feel quite uncomfortable."

She sighed. "Such sorrow truth brings," she said. "It's a heavy burden. You have no idea."

"Why were you mad at them?" I asked. "What did they do to you?"

"I don't want to say bad things about your family, dearest," Novari said. "But the truth is one of them tried to kill me long ago. Her name was Rali Antero. Your aunt, I believe."

I nodded. "I've heard stories about Aunt Rali," I said. "She was a great warrior. And Evocator."

"That's the very same Rali Antero," Novari said with a bitter smile. "A hero to all." She added quietly, "Even to me."

"Why did she try to deaded you?" I asked. "Were you mean to her? Were you mean to my aunt Rali?"

I was amazed when I heard Novari sob. I looked up and saw her struggling to answer. Sudden tears running down her cheeks.

"Mean to her?" she said. "Why, I offered her everything. I loved her, Emilie. She was the strongest and the most beautiful woman I have ever met. Rali was so sure of herself. Completely confident. Even when I had her locked in the dungeon."

Novari shrugged. "That was because of a little mistake I made. And I don't blame her for being angry about the mistake." She waved, vague. "People were killed. Things like that. But I tried to atone for it.

"I wanted to make her my queen. My equal." She hesitated. "Well, almost equal. But close enough. And all I asked was that she share her power with me. The power of the Anteros."

"If you were being so nice," I asked, "why did my aunt Rali say no?"

The tears vanished and Novari became angry. "Because she was a fool," she snarled. "A fool! How could she spurn *me*—the Lyre Bird? I have suffered all the sorrows that women everywhere have suffered. Who could understand Rali's pain more than me? How could she turn her back on my own womanly pain? I am the embodiment of all such suffering. She knew that. I told her everything, Emilie. Everything! So she had no excuse."

She leaned closer, her perfume swirling all around me. "I am the creation of hundreds and hundreds of young girls just like you, Emilie. Girls who were degraded and tortured for the pleasure of evil men." She tapped her breast. "They're all inside of me, Emilie. The souls of all those poor girls. And they weep all the time.

"You can't imagine what it's like to hear them crying. Always crying. They're crying now. But how can I let them out? And still be . . . the Lyre Bird?"

"So you deaded her," I said flatly. "You deaded my aunt Rali."

Novari calmed herself. Then she nodded. "Yes, I did, Emilie. I killed her. But she tried to kill me twice. The second time she almost succeeded."

She shrugged. "I don't die easily. I'm not even certain I *can* die. I suppose I'll find out someday."

"You can live *forever*?" I asked, voice full of childish awe.

"I think so," Novari said. "And that's what I'm offering you, Emilie. You can live forever, too. And someday, when you grow up beautiful and strong, you can be my queen."

"If I say no," I asked, "will you deaded me? Like you deaded Aunt Rali?"

My question jolted her. She stared at me for a long time. Then she laughed, trying to make light of it, saying, "What a question for a pretty child to ask."

She rose and slipped onto the bench beside me. "You're such a dear, Emilie." Her eyes were wet. "So intelligent and perceptive."

She hugged me, and I pressed my face against the softness of her bosom. Her fingers touched my hair in an absent caress.

But when she answered, I noticed she tried to slip around my question.

"We'll have lots of time to talk about things, sweetness," she said. "You're upset now. Worried about your friends. I don't expect you to be convinced all at once.

"And we'll have all kinds of fun. I'll show you some magical games you can play. And there'll be lots of clothes and toys and presents. More than any little girl could ever dream of." Novari had never known such childish delights, so there was a wistful edge to her tones.

"And people will have to do what you say, Emilie," she continued. "Because you'll be a real little princess. Novari's princess. And whatever Emilie commands, all will obey."

"Except you," I pointed out.

Novari laughed. "What a child!" she exclaimed. "Fired directly at the target."

She patted me. "We're going to get along just fine, sweetness," she said. "We'll have a wonderful time. You're going to love every minute of it."

"What if I don't?" I asked.

"Don't what, my sweet?"

"Love every minute of it?"

Novari paused, then said in a low voice, "Then I'll have to do without you, child. Like I had to do without your aunt Rali."

So there was my answer.

Circuitous as the route might have been, Novari had finally been forced to tell the truth.

Suddenly I hugged her fiercely, saying, "I'll be a good girl. I promise I will." And I burst into tears.

Unlike Novari, I could lie.

She comforted me and made soothing noises. So I hugged her harder still, covering the sorcerous tendril I slipped out and sent sniffing into the Otherworlds. Searching for the little demon monkey I'd cast there . . .

And I heard him close by:

Chitter chit. Chitter chit.

He'd broken through the Lyre Bird's shield.

Chitter chit. Chitter chit.

I released him from the spell and he chittered wild joy and went scampering off into some monkey paradise.

Then I loosened my embrace and squirmed in Novari's lap as if I were suddenly restless.

She let me go, and I leaped off and skipped toward the fountain and my mother's shrine.

"Where are you going, child?" she called, getting up to follow.

"Over here," I said. Which is answer enough for any child.

I stopped at my mother's shrine. "I used to play in this garden all the time," I said as Novari came up, so light and graceful on her feet she seemed to float above the path.

"I suppose you would have," she said. "It was your home, after all. And now it'll be your home again. But with me. And you can play here all you like."

"I used to play with Amalric and Halab," I said. "They were my brothers."

Novari frowned. "How could you, Emilie? I don't know who Halab was, but Amalric Antero was your great-uncle. Not your brother."

I shrugged. "Maybe they were ghosts." I pointed at the shrine. "That's my mother's special place." I pointed out the fountain. "And that's her special fountain."

Novari grew impatient. "Come now. You know very well that shrine belongs to Emilie Antero, your great-grandmother. That's who you're named for. What game are you playing, child?"

"It's no game," I said. "It's the truth."

Then I frowned. "Or maybe another ghost," I said. "There's lots of Antero ghosts. Lots and lots of ghosts."

I turned away, taking the rolled-up leaf from my cloak pocket. I unrolled it, hiding the splinter in my palm. Then I dipped the silver leaf into the water.

It came up glittering and fresh as if it'd just fallen from the branch. Glowing drops splattered on the pavement.

I turned back to Novari, suddenly blushing and shy.

"What's that, Emilie?" Novari asked, indicating the sparkling leaf.

I said, shy as I could, "A present. For you."

Novari looked pleased. "What a treat," she said. "Your very first present to me." But she hesitated, fingers inches away from the leaf.

She examined it. "A silver leaf," she finally said. "How pretty. Where did you get it?"

"I grew it myself," I said proudly. "I worked ever so hard growing it. Because to get a leaf you have to grow a tree first. And I had to water the tree every day for weeks and weeks and weeks and weeks. And then a leaf got borned."

I held up a finger. "It's the only one."

I pushed the leaf toward her. "You can have it if you want." I shrugged, suddenly indifferent. "I can grow another any old time."

Her hand moved to the leaf.

I had the splinter hidden beneath it, and I gave a little push just as she touched—pricking her with the sharp point.

"Ouch," she said, snatching her hand back. She frowned at the speck of blood on her finger.

"I'm sorry," I said.

I held out the splinter. "This was in my pocket, too," I said. "It must've gotten stuck to the leaf."

"You should be more careful, Emilie," Novari said, a bit angry.

I felt my eyes fill with tears. "I didn't mean to spoil the present," I said, all atremble. "You won't get mad, will you?" A hysterical edge caught my voice. "You won't deaded me, will you? Just for a little mistake."

"Of course I won't, child," Novari said impatiently. "Here. Give me the leaf. I love the present. Thank you very much.

"And then I'll give you a present. And we'll be the best of friends."

"Forever and ever," I said.

"Yes, dear. Now, give me the leaf."

I gave it to her, fumbling as I did so she'd touch it with her wounded finger and her sorcerous blood would mingle with the magic of the silver leaf.

Novari howled as if she'd just plunged her hand into a vat of lye.

She leaped away, flailing the air, trying to let loose the leaf. But it had become molten, adhering and burning her with its sorcerous heat.

"Get away, get away," she screamed, shaking her hand furiously. Then she recovered wits enough for spell-casting and shouted, "Begone!"

The molten leaf vanished. But the skin on her hand was an angry red.

She stormed over to me, anger searing the air with a heat as intense as the burning leaf—and I smelled the sulfurous poison of the killing spell she was forming in her mind.

I pretended to cower, but I was reaching for my own magical weapons, senses finding and marking the weakness in her shield.

"What did you do, Emilie?" she screamed. "What did you do?"

The heavens were split by lightning.

And the voice of a giant child called out.

"EMILIE? YOU WANT EMILIE? WHERE, OH WHERE COULD SHE BE?"

There was a giggle and the skies shimmered with the child's amusement. And then she chanted:

> "Emilie here.
> Emilie there.
> Emilie, Emilie everywhere.
> Up and down.
> All around.
> Better look out for
> Emilie, Emilie, EmilieEmilie."

There was another blast of lightning and a great white cloud scudded into view.

The cloud had Emilie's face.

Novari stared at me, then the cloud. Her mouth opened wide. It was the first time I'd ever seen her features less than perfectly composed.

And then we heard:

"EMILIESAYS STOP!"

The sky seemed to crack. First a long jagged thread splintered the blue. Then other threads formed. Faster and faster.

And then they shattered, and pieces of blue sky and bright yellow sun fluttered down from bleak winter heavens.

A harsh wind swept through the garden. Flower heads froze to their stems. Insects fell to the ground. The water in the fountain popped and cracked, then froze in midair.

And the gray one-eyed cat squalled and ran for shelter.

Then, echoing from far off Galana, I could hear the strains of music coming from Novari's great lyre machine.

But it wasn't Novari playing.

A child's voice accompanied the music, singing a merry tune:

> "Emilie here.
> Emilie there.
> Emilie, Emilie everywhere.
> Up and down.
> All around.
> Better look out for
> Emilie, Emilie, EmilieEmilie."

It began to snow, light glittering flakes drifting down from the cloud and swirling all around us.

I took a step toward Novari, my heavy soldier's boots crunching the snow. Novari stared at me, features clotted with surprised disbelief.

I was tall and strong now. A mailed warrior woman with a pirate's patch, a single fierce eye, and a golden hand glowing with power. And in that hand I held a silver spear, the transformed splinter from my ship.

"Rali!" she exclaimed.

I saw emotions at war on her face. The surprise dissolved into anger and the anger became hate. And then hate was routed and a strange soft light played about her.

She said, soft and low and yes, even with a touch of love: "Rali . . ."

I'd thought of this moment many times. I'd seen the confrontation in countless dreams. And in rolling seas and billowy skies as I sailed from the ends of the world itself for this meeting.

There were a thousand things I wanted to say. *Had* said in those imaginary meetings. All were wounding. All were hateful.

But now when I finally did face her, the hate was gone.

It surprised me.

Then Novari nodded. An understanding passed between us. And she said again, flatly, "Rali."

I parted my lips as if to speak. A smile twitched at the edge of her lips, and she leaned slightly toward me to hear my first words.

But I didn't speak.

Instead I hurled the spear.

My etherhand gave the spear such force that its rush through the air was an explosion that wracked the ears.

Novari flung up her arm to strike it down. But I guided the spear with my ethereye, driving through her spell and striking deep into the wound in her shield.

I willed it to go deeper and deeper, piercing all the way through until it found the magical heart of her.

Novari was flung across the garden, clutching her breast and screaming in pain. She fell on the snow, staining it with her blood.

She screamed again and I was rushing forward—for against all belief the wound had not been mortal.

I grabbed for the spear haft, meaning to drive it all the way through and into the ground. But just as I touched it, Novari vanished and my hand closed on empty air as the spear clattered to the ground.

I whirled to find her, drawing my sword.

She was sagging against my mother's shrine, blood streaming down her white dress.

Novari saw me charging toward her and she cried out. And the cry became that of a wild creature of the skies, and I saw her transforming into the great golden Lyre Bird.

A magical claw ripped the sword from my grasp and flung it away. There was a blast of light and I rammed into a hard opaque surface.

Just beyond that invisible shield I could see golden wings arching from Novari's back.

Then there was an Otherworldly shrill as she tapped the ethers for still more power and it came rushing to her like a pent-up river that had been suddenly released.

I smashed at the shield with my golden hand, trying to get at her. I felt it give, then firm again.

In a moment it would be too late. And all would be lost.

And then I heard a child shout:

"EMILIE SAYS NO!"

It was like a thunderclap. The air was seared by the force of Emilie's spell. The snow melted and ran across the ground in little glowing creeks.

The creeks gathered into a single stream that flowed between my feet and under Novari's shield.

It touched my mother's shrine and light shimmered all along the stone's surface.

I smelled the scent of sandalwood, my mother's favorite perfume. Then I heard her ghostly voice whisper in my ear: "I'm here, Rali."

And I hammered once more on the shield.

It shattered under my golden hand and I stepped through, drawing my dagger.

The Lyre Bird—fully transformed now—rose from the ground, mighty wingbeats sounding like drums in a giant's village. There were long, jagged lightninglike spurs gripped in her claws, spitting sorcerous fire. And she swooped forward to attack.

I braced to meet it, my mother's ghost by my side.

Then all time seemed to stand still and a strange peace came over me. My mind was free and I knew I was ready to die. In that shadowy moment I thought of all the other Anteros who'd fought and died. Some nobly. Some not so nobly. But they were Anteros just the same. And I felt as one with them all. I thought of Emilie, who was the family's only hope for the future. If there was to be a future.

And my mother's ghost whispered, "Rali means hope."

And the wind sighed, "Rali means hope."

I heard other voices, ghostly voices. Antero voices. First Halab and Hermias. Then others, men and women and children, all calling my name.

And then I heard Amalric say, "Take our strength, Rali. Take our power.

"Strike, Rali! Strike!"

And so I did.

I felt as strong as the goddess herself. I stamped the earth and the earth split, and I reached for the power of the hells. Greycloak's laws became mine. All that makes weight and heat and light and the very storms that toss us became mine. To that I added Rali's law: the will to live. And I made it into a great molten ball and I hurled it at the onrushing Lyre Bird, shouting:

"EMILIESAYS!"

There was a wild shrill of bursting harp strings. And the bird plummeted to the ground.

As I ran to it, the bird was transforming into Novari. Beautiful Novari . . . taking form while music wept rivers of sorrow.

I stood over her as she breathed her last. She became quite still. Then her face relaxed into a look of great peace. And her lips parted.

And I heard a whisper: "Free . . ."

The whisper rose on a perfumed breath, and I stepped back in wonder as shimmery forms misted up from Novari's body. They rose to the cold skies, floating on musical streams made of lyre notes.

They were the ghosts of maidens, hundreds of them. Some just girls. Others young women. All so beautiful that the gods themselves must have marveled to see them.

And then they were gone and the music stopped.

All was silent. I felt suddenly very alone, and knew the ghosts had departed.

I looked down and there was only a gown of virginal white where Novari's body had been.

My strength drained away and I stumbled as I turned, looking about the garden. It was cold and the melted snow had already frozen into pebbled ice that reflected light like spectral jewels.

And I thought of Salimar, who waited far away, across icy seas and frozen lands where the earth ends and love begins.

I wept for joy.

But a few of the tears I shed had the taste of salty sorrow.

Sorrow for the tragic creature who was the Lyre Bird—and for the poor woman I'd known as Novari.

THE LAST
ANTERO

So there you have it.

The last testament of Rali Antero. And all the Anteros who came before.

Only one of us will remain: Emilie.

She came to me yesterday in my brother's study, the old one-eyed cat clasped firmly to her chest. It was draped across her arms like a limp, gray bath towel, its head nearly as low as its tail.

"Guess what, Aunt Rali?" she piped. "I'm going to fix Pirate."

The animal looked up at me with its single eye and gave a great sigh of infinite cat patience.

"What's wrong with her?" I asked. "Other than the eye, that is."

"That's what I'm going to fix," she said, hoisting Pirate onto my writing desk. The cat purred mightily as Emilie stroked it. "Her eye."

"I don't know if that's possible, dear," I said. I touched my eyepatch. "I think once an eye is gone, it's gone forever."

"Maybe so, Aunt Rali," Emilie replied. "But I thought I'd try."

With that she made a flourish, chanting, *"Emiliesays come Spider, come."*

There was a small glow in the air, and then a huge spider plopped down on my desk, fierce jaws clacking in fear. I jumped. And the cat hissed, arching its back and extending its claws.

"Stay, Pirate!" Emilie commanded. But the cat paid her no mind and started to scramble away.

Emilie grabbed for her, reflexively blurting, *"Emiliesays stay!"*

Pirate froze. So did the spider. And I was suddenly immobile, as if gripped by a huge hand.

Emilie quickly saw what she'd done. "I'm sorry, Aunt Rali," she said. "I meant Pirate stay, not *you* stay!" And she swiftly reversed the spell with an *"Emiliesays go!"*

A weight lifted and I was suddenly free again.

At the same time, Pirate bolted off the table, darting through the open door, and the spider leaped to the floor and quickly found a hiding place beneath my father's ancient leather couch.

Emilie stamped her foot in frustration. "Now I'll have to start all over again," she complained. "Get Pirate. Catch the spider." She extended her arms wide. "The whole thing!" Emilie gave a dramatic sigh. "I've been working *ever* so hard on this," she said.

I didn't ask her how she intended to use the spider to "fix" Pirate's missing eye. Whatever she had in mind, I'm sure it had a chance to work. Although the results might not be exactly what she expected.

Instead I said, as gently as I could, "I know you're trying to help, Emilie," I said. "But maybe you shouldn't this time. Maybe Pirate wouldn't like it as much as you think. She's been without that eye for a long time. She's probably used to things the way they are."

Emilie nibbled on a finger, thinking. Then she gave me a sad look. "Are you sure, Aunt Rali?" she asked. "Because if I could make Pirate better, maybe I could make you better, too."

I thought, So that's what this is all about. I gave her hug. "Thank you, Emilie dear," I said, feeling a tear mist my living eye.

Emilie grew sadder still. "That means you don't want me to do it, right?" she said.

I patted her red curls. "No, I don't," I said. "I'm like Pirate. I'm used to the way I am. And sometimes the world even looks a little better when you're seeing it through just one eye."

I pulled her up on my lap and kissed her.

"It was supposed to be a present," she said, a catch in her voice. "A going-away present."

My heart lurched. How did she know the time was drawing so near?

"I can feel the pretty lady waiting real close, Aunt Rali," she said, as if reading my thoughts. "She's going to take you away when you're done with that book, right?"

"That's what the goddess promised," I said, quite soft.

"Salimar misses you," Emilie said. She sniffled. "I can feel *that*, too. Even though she's far away. That's how much she loves you, Aunt Rali."

"And I her," I said.

"But you're not happy, are you, Aunt Rali? You want to go. But you want to stay at the same time." Her little arms clutched me. And she whispered, "You want to stay with *me*."

A knot rose in my throat. I choked it back. "I want to very badly, Emilie."

"You love us both," Emilie said. "But you can't be with us both."

I couldn't answer. Not without losing control. So I held her tighter. We hugged for a time and then Emilie drew back, her face quite firm and serious for such a small child.

"You can't stay here," she announced. "It'd really, *really* hurt Salimar. And she needs you, Aunt Rali. She needs you something awful. She could maybe even get . . . deaded." She put her hand on mine. "We don't want her deaded, do we?"

"But what about you, Emilie? I don't want to hurt you, either. Who will take care of you? Who will teach you all the things you need to know?"

She shrugged, casual. "There's lots of people," she said. "They've been taking care of me all along. And teaching me all sorts of things. Sometimes they teach me so much I want to shout for them to stop. And they all love me, Aunt Rali. Derlina. Palmeras. Quatervals. And *all* the women in the Guard."

She spread her arms wide, declaring, "*Everybody* loves Emilie!"

Whenever I think of Emilie, I'll remember most of all how she looked at that moment. Red hair gleaming in the light streaming through the window. Face glowing with happy confidence. Delicate arms uplifted like the wings of a butterfly ready to take flight.

Grandly announcing that, "*Everybody* loves Emilie!"

In that moment, she gave me the strength to steer the only proper course.

I've made all the arrangements for Emilie's future. She'll be raised by our friends, who will have the wealth that remains in my family's coffers to ensure she never wants for anything. Palmeras will tutor her in magic, guiding her blossoming talents. Derlina and Quatervals will teach her about life and how to arm oneself against the worst of it. And Pip will make her canny, teach her how to see around corners and into untrue hearts.

Emilie is a glorious child. The last gift of the Anteros to the people of Orissa.

She has tremendous powers that will only become greater, and she'll have to be treated gently as she grows. Like a god's child come to live among small savages and causing damage out of clumsiness or mischief rather than intended harm.

I have faith in Emilie. I know she'll eventually grow to be a woman of graceful power and beauty.

Whatever she becomes, however, all should remember that when "Emilie says," she *means* "Emiliesays!"

As for me—soon as I've penned the last lines of this journal I shall go find my niece and kiss her good-bye.

Then the Goddess Maranonia will carry me away to Salimar.

Once again we will live together in a crystal palace with jetting fountains and gardens of roses, all pink and red and yellow. We will have a life of laughing days and sweet sighing nights.

And by the gods, I will be loath to leave it!

My old scribe would have told me that at this point in the journal I should speak to Orissa's future. He'd want me to play seer like my brother.

I won't attempt it. Wise as he was, Amalric was too kind a man to see the future in anything but a glorious light. I have only one eye and it isn't kind, so I won't look into the hearts of those who dwell in this world that I will soon depart. I won't search for the blackness there and denounce them for sins past, present, and intended.

Make of the world what you want of it. It's not for me to judge.

But I will give you all a warning. As I said at the beginning, that was the final purpose of this journal.

Heed these words:

I leave behind a child most precious to me.

Do not harm her or you will know my wrath.

It matters not if you possess riches greater than all the kings time has known. Or legions by the thousands to command. Or wizards with the powers of the Archons themselves.

If Emilie is harmed in any way, I *shall* return.

And if I come again, I will come with fire to blast your palaces.

I will come with cold to freeze your larders.

I will come with vermin and plague and war.

And those who survive will curse your name across all history for awakening me.

This I so swear.

I, Captain Rali Emilie Antero.

Late of the Maranon Guard.

ABOUT THE AUTHOR

ALLAN COLE is a bestselling author, screenwriter, and former prize-winning newsman who brings a rich background in travel and personal experience to his imaginative work. Raised in Europe and the Far East, Cole attended thirty-two schools, visited or lived in as many countries, and from an early age made a point of observing everything very closely for future reference. He recalls hearing *The Tempest* for the first time as a child sitting on an ancient wall in Cyprus—the island Shakespeare had in mind when he wrote the play. Rejecting invitations to become a CIA operative like his father, Cole became an award-winning reporter and newspaper editor who dealt with everything from landmark murder cases to thieving government officials.

Since that time he's written fifteen novels, many of which have become international bestsellers, as well as numerous screen and television dramas. He currently lives on a ranch in Elephant Butte, New Mexico, with Kathryn, his strongest supporter, and "Squeak," the cat who rules writer elves. If you want to communicate with Allan directly, his E-mail address is 75130.2761@compuserve.com.